The Argentia Dasani Adventures

The Shadow Gate Trilogy
Lady Dasani's Debt
The Gathering
The Dragonfire Destiny

The Crown of the Revenant King

C. Justin Romano

The Guildmaster's Gauntlet

An Argentia Dasani Adventure

iUniverse LLC
Bloomington

THE GUILDMASTER'S GAUNTLET

iUniverse books may be ordered through booksellers or by contacting:

iUniverse
1663 Liberty Drive
Bloomington, IN 47403
www.iuniverse.com
1-800-Authors (1-800-288-4677)

ISBN: 978-1-4917-2442-2 (sc)
ISBN: 978-1-4917-2444-6 (hc)
ISBN: 978-1-4917-2443-9 (e)

Library of Congress Control Number: 2014902116

Printed in the United States of America.

iUniverse rev. date: 4/21/2014

For Maddy

Acknowledgements

With grateful appreciation to Amy McHargue, George Nedeff, Eddie Wright, and the iUniverse editorial and production teams for their exemplary work; and to my family and friends for their unwavering support and patience.

And now…

Part I

Opening Movements

1

Ewuel Truffalt looked up from his desk as the Westing House's door opened. The majordomo stared in amazement, snapped a thick ledger closed, and stepped quickly from his post to cross the inn's foyer. "Lady Dasani! I must object!"

Argentia Dasani watched the red-faced little man hustle toward her. *This ought to be good,* she thought. There was little doubt what Truffalt was objecting to.

Argentia attracted attention wherever she went—just as often for the weapons belted across her hips and the pack slung over her shoulder as for her looks. She was a shade less than six feet tall in her battered, sand-crusted leather boots, with an athlete's lean-muscled limbs and effortless grace to her movements. Her cardinal red hair was pulled back in a long braid, accentuating her high cheekbones, slim, straight nose, full lips, and eyes of a peculiar cobalt, like ice on the Sea of Sleet in a certain slant of light.

She was dressed in a pair of fitted, low-slung leopardskin pants, and a sleeveless black sheath that tied behind her neck and waist. Road clothes. She had just put to port in Argo this morning, after months in the Sudenlands helping her friend Skarangella Skarn save his sultanate. Her skin was tan from the southern sun. A silver carving of a dragon's tooth dangled at her throat.

Truffalt's eyes darted from Argentia to the over-groomed, over-coiffed, and over-perfumed guests passing by. Already people were pointing and whispering. It was beyond tolerance. "This is the Westing House, not some brothel! Have you no shame?"

"None." Argentia laughed, the bell-like sound ringing across the marble foyer. Grinning, she stretched her arms above her head and arched her bare back, her top rising to reveal her taut stomach and the twinkling silver-and-sapphire ring piercing her navel.

"Stop that! Stop it!" Truffalt demanded.

"Mmm— Sorry." Argentia lowered her arms and fixed cold blue eyes on the majordomo like a lioness regarding a jackal. "I must have left my manners in the brothel."

Truffalt realized what he had blurted, and that he had blurted it to a noblewoman of Argo—however scandalous she might be. "I will summon the porter for your bag," he said stiffly.

"Never mind the porter. I know the way."

"Wait, wait! At least take the servants' stairs," Truffalt begged. But Argentia was already walking away, and the majordomo saw to his unending horror that she was actually waving to the couple descending the grand staircase.

"Ah! Lady Dasani," Lord Horndrake called down. They met at the bottom of the steps, Argentia stooping to receive the old noble's embrace, kissing his wrinkled cheek.

"My Lord, that's a wonderful hat," she said, tipping her finger appreciatively at the tall, purple creation, shaped like an inverted corkscrew.

"Rather thought so myself," Horndrake said with a wink. He turned to his wife. "You remember Tanqueril Dasani's daughter, of course. The one who rescued me that night in the alley?"

"Certainly. Delighted to see you again," said Lady Horndrake, who was a good three decades younger than her husband.

"The same," Argentia replied.

"I trust you're keeping out of trouble, my dear?" Horndrake said.

Argentia laughed and patted her katana. "Nothing I can't handle."

Bidding the Horndrakes farewell, Argentia climbed to her suites on the Westing House's top floor. She'd rented one for herself and one for her butler Ikabod while she renovated her manor, before some local trouble had launched her on the unexpected trip to help Skarn. She smiled as she imagined the surprise on Ikabod's face when he came to the door—only there was no answer when she knocked. Of course, Ikabod could not have known she would return today, but she felt strangely disappointed. *Oh stop it*, she chided herself. *What did you think; he spent the whole time just sitting here waiting for you? Go get changed. Maybe by then he'll be back.*

Argentia crossed to her own suite. Found the key in her coin purse. Amazingly, throughout all her adventures, it had not been lost. The room was cool and dark. She dropped her pack beside the door and touched the lightstone, already thinking of the shower that awaited her.

Something on the table caught her eye. *What the hell is that?*

It was a small carving of a skull with a folded parchment set between its teeth. *Weird....* Argentia picked the skull up and studied it. It had a peculiar, acrid aroma that she couldn't quite place. Frowning, she pried the skull's jaws open, pulled the parchment free, and set the skull back on the table.

The paper was a piece of Westing House stationery. There was a stack of identical leaves in a box on the table, along with a quill, a bottle of ink, and a blotter. Above a seal that looked disturbingly like a splotch of dried blood was written:

> *To the Lady Dasani,*
> *In Confidence*

The scrawl wholly unfamiliar, but it sent a shiver of dread through Argentia nonetheless. She broke the seal. Read the note:

> *We have taken the butler.*
> *Come and get him.*
> *Come and play.*
> *In Telarban.*
> *At Vloth's.*

Ikabod— Argentia could almost hear the twins' mocking laughter as she crumpled the parchment in her fist and flung it down. "God *damn* you!"

On the table, the skull's eye sockets were glowing.

What— Memories tumbled into place: the roar of the explosion, the burning manor, the acrid stench of smoke-filled air.

Argentia spun. Took two steps clear of the table. Dove for the bath chamber.

The skull detonated behind her.

2

The four Watchmen shouldn't have been there at all. Three lieutenants and a wizard, their days of walking patrol through Argo had ended years ago. Or so they'd thought.

That had changed with thunderbolt swiftness this morning. They had been hauled before the Magistrates and accused of abetting their former captain's escape from the city. There was no proof, but they had been seen talking to Tierciel Thorne at the docks shortly before he vanished. Given their refusal to testify as to the nature of that conversation—and since they were, in fact, guilty as charged—they could have counted themselves lucky to have escaped with a month of foot patrol.

Not all of them saw it that way.

"Fools," Tiboren Gyre muttered, chomping on his pipe's stem. Tib was short and slim, with the swarthy looks of a Cyprytalyr and the short temper those islanders were famous for. He was particularly bitter about the patrol sentence.

"Who? The Magistrates, or us?" said Kest Eregrin. Kest was a tall, bespectacled Nhapian, almond eyed, brown skinned, black haired, and calm as a cherry blossom falling to earth. He had been Thorne's second in command, and was the nominal leader of the group now.

"Them," Tib said."

Kest shrugged. "Maybe."

"Maybe? Care to explain how they're not fools?"

"Do you think they'd have let us learn about the warrant without considering that we might have warned Thorne?"

"So what are you saying? They wanted us to help him escape? That they engineered this?"

Kest shrugged again. "Some of them, maybe. Thorne had a lot of enemies among the Magistrates. People who feared he was angling for their seat. But he had a lot of friends, too—and Gringoir's enough of a fox to pull something like that off."

"Then why punish us?"

"This is hardly much of a punishment," said Guntyr, his bass voice rumbling up from behind Tib and Kest.

"Speak for yourself," Tib retorted. Guntyr was a barbarian, with the size, strength, and constitution of a cave bear. "You could probably walk back to Nord from here without getting tired. I hate walking."

"Finally we agree on something," said Augustus Falkyn. It was meant to add some levity, since Tib and the halfling famously disagreed on almost everything, but Tib wasn't biting.

"I warned all of you that no good would come of helping Thorne," he said.

"Yet you agreed to help him," Kest reminded him. "I trust you haven't forgotten why?"

Tib hadn't forgotten. None of them had. The whole damnable situation was the rotten fruit of Thorne's foolhardy decision to attempt to capture a pair of murderous twins with only another lieutenant, Vendimar Stelglim, as backup. Vendi had died and the twins had escaped from the city. Thorne had been dismissed from the Watch.

The Magistrates, pressured to deliver results by Argo's Noble Council, had declared the case closed based on circumstantial evidence: two bodies found in the Undercity, one of which had clearly been the work of the real killers. 'A quarrel among villains ending in a double murder,' the Magistrates ruled, tying up the matter with a bow, turning their backs on the truth and sending Thorne on a vigilante rampage through Argo's nights to learn the twins' identities.

Suspicion of Thorne's role in the death of the informant Kemelix had led to the warrant, and to his lieutenants' decision to warn him of the impending arrest. That warning had given Thorne a small but critical window to make good on his own escape to pursue Vendi's murderers. In retrospect, maybe it hadn't been such a good career move, but Thorne had been their Captain, and Vendi their comrade. They all felt guilty about her death.

On their way to confront Thorne at the docks, the lieutenants had argued about whether to arrest him, warn him, or go with him. They decided that the time had come for their paths to break. Their duty lay with Argo and the Watch, his with revenge. Thorne had understood—after all, he had instilled much of that sense of duty in them himself—and he had set them a last task.

"Find the traitor," he said. "Before Kemelix died, he spoke of a traitor in the Watch."

If true, that explained why the killers had been always a step ahead of Thorne and his lieutenants, and why seventeen people besides Vendi had died during their months-long reign of blood and fear. The lieutenants had given their word that they would find the traitor. How they were going to do that—especially while consigned to foot patrol—was something they hadn't wrestled with yet.

"Were these damned shirts always this scratchy?" Tib said, fidgeting with his starchy collar. The uniform was another point of contention with him. Working in the Undercity, where a uniform was the fastest way to make people shut their doors and windows against you, he hadn't worn one in years.

"They're not scratchy, they're clean," Augustus said. "That's what you're not used to."

"The Undercity's a dirty place," Tib said. "And I still think you should have to wear a uniform too."

"Watch wizards don't have uniforms," the halfling replied. "Just the crest." He patted the sigul of the Watch—a shield with a golden eye in the center—on the breast of the traditional blue robes of his Order.

"Yeah, right. More like they don't make uniforms in child sizes," Tib sneered.

"Careful," Guntyr said, placing a huge hand on Tib's shoulder. The Norden was almost a foot taller than Tib and twice as broad from shoulder to shoulder. "Among men, you are accounted as short. Should I start calling you a runt?"

"That's it, jump to the poor halfling's defense," Tib said, pulling free of Guntyr's grasp. "Everybody gang up on Tib."

"Take it easy," Kest said as they rounded the corner opposite the Westing House. He knew the source of Tib's ire wasn't Augustus or Guntyr but the outcome of the whole situation with Thorne. "Nobody likes this, but we got ourselves into it. Considering what the consequences could have been, I think—"

A roar and a blast of fiery light sent them sprawling.

3

Tib sat up in the gutter. He clutched his forehead and winced, tasting blood. He'd bitten his tongue when he smacked his head on the curb. Spitting a red glob on the sidewalk, he looked up.

Part of the top floor of the Westing House was simply gone. Glass and pulverized stone from the windows and wall had hailed down to the street, and billowing smoke and licks of flame poured out of the ragged frame of the blast hole. People on the street were screaming and pointing in panic.

"We've got to get up there!" Kest shouted. So far, the damage seemed confined to that area, but it would surely spread quickly. People were already stampeding out of the grand old inn, adding to the chaos. One of them, a small, bug-eyed, red-faced little man in an impeccably neat Westing House uniform ran up to Kest. "You! Why aren't you doing anything to help?" the man shouted.

"Sir, we're trying—"

"Don't make excuses! Are you blind? The Westing House is on fire! Now do something!"

Guntyr stepped over and, with surprising gentleness, took the little man by the arm. "Get off!" the man exclaimed, turning. When he saw the imposing barbarian standing there, he was momentarily silenced.

"Calm down, sir," Guntyr said.

"Don't tell me to calm down! I'm Ewuel Truffalt. I'm the majordomo of the Westing House. Why are you wasting time down here when you should be doing something to put this fire out?"

"What I'm going to do is ask you to step over there with those other people, sir," the unflappable Guntyr said. "We're going to do our best to get this situation under control, but you aren't helping."

"Well you'd better do something or I'll see that you're removed from the Watch for incompetence," Truffalt sneered.

Guntyr pointed across the street. "Go," he said.

"What a jackass," Tib muttered when the majordomo had taken up a position in the front row of the ever-increasing crowd. "We ought to let this place burn down just to spite him."

"Yeah, well…." Kest turned to Augustus. "Can you put it out?"

"I can try."

The halfling waved his wand. Summoning the aether, he channeled the magic and levitated toward the fire while the others took control of the situation on the ground. Already he could hear the pealing of the alarum bells. It would only be minutes before help from the garrison arrived, but those minutes would be precious to anyone trapped in the inferno.

Augustus drew on the aether again, cocooning himself in a silver-blue shield, and flew into the smoke. Magic was everywhere in Acrevast, but only a select few—the magi—could touch and harness its vast power. The gift was rare among humans. Among halflings it was almost unheard of. Though normally proud of his abilities, right at this moment Augustus wasn't sure his exceptional talent was all that much of a blessing. Heat seared at him as he dropped into the burning room. He could feel it even through the protective glimmer of his shield, its furnace force staggering.

A stroke of his wand sent blasts of icy rain to douse the nearest flames. The fire roared at him: a hot, hungry elemental beast. Augustus fought it, but it drove him backwards. He was losing the battle.

Suddenly the temperature dropped around him. He felt a pull upon the aether that was not of his doing. Turned to see Bardian, a fellow Watch wizard, floating behind him, his stout body also shielded in shimmering blue aetherlight.

"Together," Bardian said, summoning a snow-struck wind. Augustus fed his sleet into the wind, which strengthened it tenfold. In minutes they had extinguished the last of the flames and blown the smoke out, leaving a rime over the desolation.

"Thanks," Augustus said, wiping his sweaty mop of brown curls off his forehead and glancing somewhat sheepishly at Bardian. "I thought I could handle it."

"You did well," Bardian said. "This was no ordinary fire."

They looked around. The once-decorous suite had been blasted into ruin. One wall was completely obliterated. Furniture was twisted and warped into scrap. Augustus saw a tremendous scorching where the heart of the fire had burned the deep-piled rug through to the wooden floor beneath. The door had been blown from its hinges out into the hallway.

Most of the wall leading into what might have been a bath chamber looked as if an angry giant had slammed through it. Dust choked the air beyond the gaping hole.

"Just like the warehouse," Augustus muttered. When they had been hunting Vendi's killers, a carriage taken into evidence had been destroyed in a similar explosion. The halfling had a disquieting moment where he wondered if the nightmare the murderous twins had visited on Argo was truly ended. *It's over*, he reminded himself. The twins were gone. Thorne was hunting them. It wasn't his problem anymore. Besides, there was enough to worry about here. "Do you think there were survivors?"

Bardian shook his head. "Not with a blast like this. No chance."

They searched anyway. Bardian conjured the aethereal wind again, sweeping the dust away. Debris was everywhere. The floor was sodden with wet char.

"Oh no," Augustus said, peering through the gash in the wall between rooms.

"What?" Bardian asked.

The halfling pointed. "Body."

4

Strange voices brought Argentia back to consciousness.

A group of men were talking about her and the amazing fact that she was alive—which, Argentia reflected, was pretty much the truth. Someone suggested they move her. Someone else countered that they should wait until she woke up. A third said to fetch a cleric from below. A fourth, who sounded like a child, volunteered to go.

I am *awake, and I don't need any cleric...* With that, Argentia came through the last of the haze and opened her eyes.

She was on her back in the tub. The tub had saved her life. It was sunken into the bath chamber floor and she had thrown herself into it just as the skull detonated. The brunt of the explosion passed above her, leaving her covered with debris and chalky powder that made her choke.

She coughed. The trio of Watchmen in the doorway turned quickly. Stared at her as if she were some revenant rising from its tomb. Argentia blew a strand of red hair out of her face. "Well—you going to help a lady up?"

Shaking off their surprise, Tib and Kest went to her assistance. "We've sent for a cleric. Can you move?" Kest asked as they climbed down into the tub, shoving rubble aside.

"Yeah. I'm all right." Argentia extended her hand. The two Watchmen pulled her slowly to her feet. "Thank you," she said. Her left shoulder was throbbing. The flesh was raw and red, but not bleeding. She rubbed it gently. It hurt. She rotated her arm. That hurt worse. A spear of pain. She winced.

The Watchmen gave Argentia some space. Plastered with dust from head to toe, she looked a wreck. *But a pretty wreck*, Tib thought. *Great body. Great outfit, too*, he added in his mental inventory. Then his Watchman's eye for details narrowed and he noticed the weapons belted across her hips. "You're lucky to be alive, Lady…"

"Dasani. Argentia Dasani."

Tib looked at Kest and Guntyr. Before his expulsion, Thorne had been greatly interested in finding Lady Dasani. She had been named as a witness to the slaughter of nine members of the Black Fang—a massacre that inaugurated the twins' bloody siege on Argo's streets. Thorne had been convinced that Argentia, whose house had been destroyed in an explosion just a month or so before the twins arrived, and who had a reputation for what Argo's other nobles termed 'aberrant behavior'—meaning she preferred a sword to a soiree—was somehow involved with the murders.

"Is there a problem?" Argentia asked, catching the exchange of glances between the lieutenants.

"That depends on how cooperative you're willing to be," Tib said.

"What do you mean?"

"You're under arrest."

5

"What?" Argentia exclaimed.

"You're under arrest." Tib repeated. "What part didn't you understand?"

"Everybody take it easy," Kest said, lifting his hands. "Tib, you maybe want to think about this for a minute?"

"I'm arresting her," Tib said. "You know why." He turned to Argentia. "Let's go. Got a cell in the dungeons waiting for you."

"I think not." Argentia's draw was lightning, the katana at Tib's throat before he could blink. "Back away," she ordered Kest and Guntyr.

Stunned and taken completely off their guard, the other lieutenants obeyed. Tib stared defiantly at Argentia. "In a rush to meet your friends?" he sneered.

So that's what this is about... The Watch thought she was leagued with Vloth's twins. "Are you crazy? They're assassins sent by Togril Vloth. They're the ones who did this." She gestured at the destroyed suite. "Look, I'd explain, but there's no time. My friend's in a lot of trouble and—"

"And ours is dead," Tib spat. "Vendimar Stelglim. Just a girl. Barely twenty. They butchered her."

"I'm sorry," Argentia said. Meant it. "But I'm still going. I have to—before it's too late for Ikabod as well."

"You will not get away," Guntyr said. Argentia spared him a glance. She'd traveled for a time with a barbarian. Kodius had been taller than this man, but the lieutenant was broader and more defined in his musculature, which bulged hugely beneath his uniform.

"We'll see. Lose the weapons," she commanded. "Cross handed. Nice and slow. Put them on the ground and then kick them away."

The lieutenants had no choice. One look at Argentia's posture with her blade and the memory of her draw, as fluid and precise as a mongoose

14

uncoiling, made it clear that the rumors about her being an accomplished swordswoman were grounded in fact. They did as she ordered.

"Good. Now get in the tub and lay down. You with the glasses first, then you, big boy. I don't want to hurt anyone, but believe me, I'm getting out of here."

"If you're innocent, this isn't helping," Kest said, making a last appeal to reason.

"In the tub," Argentia said. Kest climbed in and lay down. Guntyr followed, settling his massive weight onto Kest. Argentia used her katana to back Tib up until his heels were over the edge of the tub. He stared daggers at her.

"Bye," she said, flicking her katana up to tap him beneath the chin. Tib overbalanced and fell onto Guntyr.

Argentia sheathed her blade, dashed out of the room and into the hall, adrenaline pumping through her, dulling the shards of pain that shot through her shoulder with every gazelle-like stride. At the end of the hall was a corner. Around the corner, a stairwell.

Between Argentia and the corner were two Watchmen.

They looked at Argentia in surprise as she ran toward them. "Hey, what—"

"Stop her!" Tib shouted, bursting out of the ruined suite. "Grab her, damn it!"

Not good… Five against one in mortal combat and Argentia would lay the odds on herself every time. But she wasn't going to kill Watchmen if she could help it, which put the balance of a battle decidedly in their favor, especially in the confines of the hallway.

Then one of the Watchmen charged her—an amateurish mistake that gave Argentia all the edge she needed. She twirled aside, barely breaking stride as the Watchman dove for her, his arms closing on empty air.

The second Watchman held his ground. He was fat: a human barricade. He set his legs apart, his arms out wide, a mace in each meaty hand. "Halt!" he bellowed.

Grinning, Argentia ran right at him.

"Halt!" the fat Watchman shouted again. Argentia showed no signs of stopping. "Come on, then," he growled, bracing for the impact. He would crush her. This would be the easiest capture of his career.

The impact never came.

At the last instant, Argentia threw herself into a hard slide. The wooden floor, polished daily by the Westing House staff, was as smooth as a frozen lake. Argentia shot feet-first between the guard's splayed legs. She bounced up, her shoulder screaming after the jarring impact, skidded around the corner, took the stairs three at a time. Tib's cries to "Stop her!" echoed in her wake.

Guntyr straight-armed the fat Watchman aside as if he was a chasecrow. The lieutenants raced down the stairs after Argentia. On the landing of the floor below, Kest grabbed Tib, pulling him up short. "Wait," he said. "Listen." They heard no noises on the steps below them.

Tib yanked open the landing door. The hallway was empty. "Son of a bitch! Where'd she go?"

"And why did she run?" Guntyr asked.

"Isn't it obvious?" Tib said.

"No," Guntyr rumbled. "Maybe if you'd given her a chance to explain instead of threatening her with the dungeons, we would know whether what she said about those twins coming from Togril Vloth was true or not."

"So what, it's my fault she ran?" Tib challenged, jabbing his finger into Guntyr's massive chest. The Norden could have broken the skinny little lieutenant in half, but Tib knew Guntyr was as slow to anger as he was terrifying when so roused. "That's horseshit! She's guilty and you know it!"

"That's enough, both of you," Kest snapped. "Tib, the Magistrates closed Vendi's case, remember? We all know that the real killers got away, but that's in Thorne's hands now. We made that decision this morning."

"So what do you want to do, just let her go?" Tib demanded.

"No—and stop shouting. We do have to find her. We need to know what happened here—who tried to kill her, and why. She's a citizen of Argo, and our job is to protect the citizens. If her answer has any bearing on what happened to Vendi…then we'll deal with it. For now we just need to find her."

"What happened?" Augustus asked. He was coming up the stairs with the cleric he had brought to attend Argentia. "We could hear you shouting three floors down. Where is she?"

"Gone," Tib muttered.

6

Argentia crouched in the darkness.

She had left the stairs one floor below her suite, taken a dumbwaiter from the hallway down to the serving level of the Westing House, and snuck down another floor into the cellar, escaping the Watch, at least for the moment. She was sure the lieutenants were searching for her. They had her story all wrong. Worse, they didn't seem interested in hearing the right version, even if she had time to tell it.

I've got to get out of here... Argentia had left danger behind her in Argo when she sailed south to help Skarn. Ikabod had paid the price for it. She had feared something like this would happen, had even tried to warn the butler—all for naught. The twins had still taken him, striking at her through the one person in the world she held dearest. God only knew how long they'd had him, and how much longer they would keep him alive.

And unharmed. He'd better be unharmed...

Argentia clamped down on her guilt and anger. Those things would fuel her when she needed them. Right now she needed a little patience. Things had spun well beyond her control. It was time to reel them in again.

She wondered how the Watch had ever come to associate her with Vloth's twins in the first place. *Of all the lousy luck that this bunch would end up here today—*

Enough! Think, Gen. Think... She shut away the increasing pain in her shoulder and concentrated on her immediate problem: escaping.

The Reaver... Her ship was at the dock. The First Mate, Dorn, would be on board, but her crew was on shore leave. Without them, there was no way to sail the schooner. She wondered if the Watch knew she had her own ship in port. If they did, they would seize it. Perhaps they already had. *God damn it! I've got to get word to Dorn—but how?*

She needed an oculyr. There was one in her pack. Should she risk going all the way back up to her suite? *No. It probably got blown to Hell with the rest of the room, anyway. There must be one at the ledger desk, though—*

She heard a noise, and then dim light appeared at the far end of the cellar.

Mikael Greystone peered into the unending pitch of the Westing House's cellar. In one hand he held his sword, in the other a moonstone. The gem drank the light from the stairwell behind him and radiated it out again, but not nearly far enough to illuminate the cavernous dark before him.

Mikael paused, looking around. He took a deep breath and went a few steps further, heart pounding, palm sweaty on the hilt of his sword. He was only a year out of the Cadetery. This task—to hunt out a criminal responsible for destroying the upper floor of the Westing House—was something entirely different from the mostly quiet foot patrols that had filled his time since graduation.

The cellar was a colossal mess. A central aisle divided the space roughly in half. Dozens of walkways branched from this main artery into stacks of cobweb-covered clutter. The stacks appeared to be mostly furniture, some broken, some still in good repair. Crates and boxes were intermingled with these relics of the inn's decor. Everything was stacked taller than Mikael stood, making moving through the cellar akin to moving at night through a hedge-maze.

Worse, there didn't seem to be any organization. There might have been some type of system once, years ago, but the Westing House was very old. It had accumulated massive amounts of furniture and furnishings. These had been consigned to the cellar as wear, seasons, and fashion dictated, and any semblance of order beyond the central walkway had long since vanished. The tributary walkways were narrow and twisting as paths in a forest. Mikael was loath to go down any of them. The air was close and musty with the scents of old wood: smells that reminded him of the cellar in his childhood home, a place he had always secretly feared.

That fear resurfaced now, playing games with his imagination, making the shadowy shapes seem to lurch and reach. He wiped sweat from his brow, telling himself he was being ridiculous, that there were no monsters in the cellar of the Westing—

The thing with red eyes came out of the dark.

It skittered low, bursting towards Mikael, who almost screamed as he jumped backwards. The rat, just as frightened, veered sharply and darted beneath an ancient armoire. Gasping, Mikael glanced around and steadied himself. The cellar was his lot, and he would search it, rats or not.

Mikael moved carefully down the makeshift spaces between discarded bureaus and broken beds. He discovered the paths intersected with other paths deeper in the stacks. Sooner or later they always came out to the main passage, but Mikael could not shake the nagging worry that he might be lost in the cellar forever. More pervasive was the fear that the stacks themselves might not be safe. The narrow paths were hard to navigate without bumping and jostling the piles. What if one toppled as he passed, crushing him?

Despite these horrible imaginings, Mikael concluded his search without incident. Though he'd heard an occasional noise from within the junk—and froze, his heart leaping in his chest each time he did—he saw no more rats, nor any sign of Lady Dasani.

Standing in the central aisle, wondering how anyone could find anything in this supposed storage area, he sheathed his blade and pulled a small stone from his belt pouch. "Lieutenant Eregrin?" he said.

Kest's voice came back through the auralith. "Go ahead."

"Greystone here, sir. The cellar is clear."

"Seal it off and guard the door in case she tries to get down there."

"Yes, sir."

Mikael replaced the auralith in his pouch. His moonstone was already weakening. Anxious to get out before it failed altogether, he turned for the door.

Something hard struck him on the back of the head and all the lights went out.

Argentia knelt beside the fallen Watchman. "Sorry, kid," she whispered, dropping the chair leg she'd used as a club. She checked his neck for a pulse. He was alive but unconscious—just the way she wanted him.

Working swiftly, Argentia stripped the Watchman of his uniform and pulled it on over her clothes. By now she could barely raise her injured arm. Maneuvering it into the Watchman's coat was possibly the most painful thing she'd ever done. *Gonna have to get that fixed...*

She looked at herself by the moonstone's little light. She was tall enough that the coat and pants weren't a bad fit. The cloak would help further the illusion. She fastened it about her shoulders, wound her braid up into the tall, plumed helmet, and buckled on her sword-belt.

Her disguise completed, Argentia dug into the Watchman's bag. If he was carrying the usual equipment, he would have an oculyr in addition to the auralith, which was only good for communication with stones enchanted with the same spell. She smiled when her hand closed over the small sphere.

"Seek," she said, using the typical word for awakening an oculyr's magic. The smoke within the crystal began to swirl. "*Reef Reaver*," she said.

The smoke cleared, revealing an image of a neatly kept ship cabin. Her First Mate was seated at a small table. "Cap'n?" he said.

"Dorn. Listen fast." Argentia said.

The last of evening hung dim over the street.

Watchmen who were not part of the detail searching the Westing House had secured the area, but a good crowd was still gathered, with everyone telling their version of what had happened to anyone else who would listen.

Argentia came out of the Westing House through the main doors. She nodded briefly to the two Watchmen stationed there as she passed. They saw the uniform and not much more. Didn't stop her.

Good so far…. Argentia had invaded many a supposedly secure place in her days of bounty hunting. She knew the secret to any good disguise was not in the clothing as much as the attitude. To play a part, one had to become that part.

At the bottom of the steps, she saw the three lieutenants from her suite clustered off to her right, taking statements. *No problem….*

Argentia turned left. Crossed the street, not hurrying, not loafing: a member of the city's guard with some important business to be about. She kept her eyes ahead, as if the crowd wasn't there at all. Once she was clear of the onlookers and out of the vicinity, she would be—

"There she is! Her! This is all her fault!"

7

Argentia turned as Ewuel Truffalt lunged out of the crowd. Her disguise had not fooled the sharp-eyed and vengeful majordomo. "Get away from me," she warned, trying to move past without causing a scene.

Truffalt blocked her way. "This is all your fault, you bitch! You did this! You destroyed the Westing House!" His face flushed with righteous anger as he pointed wildly at her, spittle flying with his words. "But at least you'll go to the dungeons, where you belong. Guards! Guards!"

"See a cleric for that," Argentia said.

"What?" Truffalt stopped, confused. "A cleric? I don't need—"

Argentia drove her knee squarely into Truffalt's groin. "Now you do."

The majordomo squealed in agony and toppled onto the marble street. People in the crowd nearby grew suddenly quiet. Argentia quickly stepped around the writhing Truffalt, but it was too late.

The commotion had caught Kest's attention. He looked over just in time to see a Watchman strike someone from the crowd. *That's just great. What else could possibly go wrong today?* "Come on," he said, motioning for Tib and Guntyr to follow. Augustus had gone back into the Westing House to try his hand at divining Lady Dasani with magic.

The injured man—Kest saw it was the disagreeable majordomo—was still down in the street. The Watchman was walking away. "You there. Stop," Kest called.

The Watchman didn't stop. He ran.

"Unbelievable," Kest said.

Then the fleeing Watchman's helmet toppled off, revealing a braid of blazing red hair.

"Aeton's bolts!" Tib shouted. "It's her!"

Argentia raced away. The lieutenants had been slow to react, but a glance over her shoulder showed them already in pursuit. With every step sending bolts of pain through her shoulder, she could not outrun them for long. *Maybe I won't have to....*

She saw a wobbling light as she approached the intersection ahead: a carriage, its night lantern bobbing on the end of its pole. It was heading towards the docks.

Grinning, Argentia put on a burst of speed. She leaped up behind the passing carriage, catching hold with her good hand, clinging to the back of the frame as it rattled and rolled away from the astonished lieutenants.

"God damn it! She's getting away again!" Tib shouted.

Guntyr was already out in the street, standing in the path of another carriage. "Stop!" the Norden bellowed.

The carriage driver jerked on the reins, clattering the horses to a hard halt a few feet short of Guntyr. The Norden never flinched. "We need your carriage," he said. It was not a request.

Tib climbed onto the driving board before the man could protest. "See that carriage with the woman on the back? Follow it."

"I don't—"

"Just do it or I'll throw you in the dungeons for impeding justice. Now drive!"

The man driving the carriage was convinced. Kest and Guntyr hopped up on the running boards and they were off after Lady Dasani.

Up ahead, Argentia's carriage took a turn. Now they were heading away from the docks. Cursing, she bailed off the back, staggering as her boots hit the marble street but keeping her feet. She started to run, hoping the Watch would follow the carriage.

A corner lantern caught her in its yellow light. Kest spotted her. "There she goes! Toward the docks!"

"Then we've got her. The docks are a dead end," Tib gloated.

"No." Kest cursed his stupidity. "She's got a ship." It should have been obvious. Almost all Argo's nobles had private ships. "We should have thought of it before. Sent men ahead to secure the docks."

"Damn it!" Tib glared at the driver. "Hurry the hell up!"

8

The wind was in Argentia's face as she ran. She didn't hear the carriage coming. Didn't realize it was there until she happened to glance behind and saw it almost on top of her. *These guys don't quit...* Argentia veered away from the horses. The driver, hardly adept at chasing people down, failed to adjust and shot past her. Two of the lieutenants jumped from the running boards and took up the chase on foot.

Argentia dodged among the benches set up on the docks so people could wait for arriving passengers or simply enjoy the view of the harbor, angling for the *Reef Reaver's* berth. A pair of guards from the Dockmaster's station, alerted by a cry from one of the lieutenants, ran to intercept her. Reaching for the hasp of her Watch cloak, she yanked it free and balled the cloak up as she ran.

The dock guards were closing from the right. The lieutenants were behind her. The *Reef Reaver* was ahead on her left. She saw the crew moving about on deck. Dorn had rounded them up and gotten them all back on board. "Weigh anchor!" she shouted. "Weigh anchor! Pull the plank! Go! Go!"

The dock guards had the angle on Argentia, cutting off her path to the *Reaver*. As the first man grabbed for her, Argentia snapped her arm out, casting the cloak into his face. The guard stumbled in surprise, lost his balance, and went down. His flailing leg tripped his partner and sent him sprawling.

Argentia leaped over the tangle of thrashing limbs but she wasn't clear yet. Kest, a good runner himself, surged past the fallen guards and almost had her from behind. Argentia sensed him at the last moment and jigged away from his grasping fingers. Desperation gave her the strength to sprint. She opened the gap between her and the lieutenants like a lioness in full flight from poachers. Closed on the *Reaver's* berth.

A volley of arrows sailed over her head: cover fire from her sailors. "No—don't!" Argentia shouted. Behind her, she heard one of the lieutenants yell, "Down!"

Then she was out of land.

Her crew had followed orders and drawn in the boarding plank. The *Reaver* shuddered as the propulsion stones on the hull's lateral lines fired, bursts of aether driving the schooner away from her berth.

Argentia leaped from the edge of the dock, long legs kicking as if she would run on the air, good arm stretching up. She sailed over the water. Slammed into the side of the *Reaver*, falling short of the railing she'd been aiming for but catching the ladder that the sailors used to board from the lowering boats. She hung there for a moment, her boots scrabbling until they found purchase on the lower rungs. Gritting her teeth, she started climbing the ladder—awkward work with her bad arm.

Before she reached the top, Dorn was there. The First Mate was a big, solid, blunt-featured man with close-cropped steely hair and an air of military discipline. He leaned down, caught Argentia's hand, and hauled her over the rail. "Welcome aboard, Cap'n."

Argentia grinned. "Thanks."

On the dock, the lieutenants were standing up again, unharmed but helpless to stop the *Reaver* as it moved into the harbor, the cloth of its black sails catching the night wind that blew incessantly over the shores of Teranor.

"Told the men not to hit anyone," Dorn said. Argentia nodded. She should have figured a former Watchman would understand the men on the dock were just doing their duty. "Unless it was necessary," he added.

Argentia arched a brow. "Good call," she said. She figured she was in enough trouble with Argo's Watch without adding a body count to the list. "Thanks for getting everybody here."

"Aye, Cap'n. You all right?" Dorn asked.

Argentia was bent forward, her hands on her knees, fighting a wave of pain and nausea. As the adrenaline of the chase wore off, she became aware that her legs were trembling, her mouth was full of copper, her heart pounding hard above a vicious stitch in her side. The shoulder she'd injured in the explosion was on fire, and she was pretty sure she'd done something bad to her other arm when she caught the ladder.

But I made it… She blew a perpetually stray strand of hair out of her eyes and straightened up. "I'm fine."

"Good deal, then."

One of the sailors walked up to them. "Cap'n, beggin' your pardon, but Helmsman Canini sent me."

"The rocks," Dorn said, nodding.

Somewhere in the dark ahead of them was Argo's seawall, its mouth barely wide enough for two ships to pass abreast. Though magic could have easily made the wall visible, the rocks were left unillumed to help protect the harbor in the event of a siege. Unless the moon shone bright upon the foaming spray of broken waves, the wall remained invisible and deadly in the dark. It had foundered so many ships trying to navigate the harbor's tricky currents that it was forbidden for any ship to sail into or out of the port after sundown.

"I'll take care of the rocks," Argentia said. She headed for the helm and stood beside Canini, the *Reaver's* grizzled Cyprytalyr helmsman. She would have taken over the steering herself, but her arm would not allow it. "Do exactly as I say."

Argentia knew the trick to getting past the seawall at night. Her father had taught her when she was a child, before Fortune had torn them apart. The rocks could not be seen, but they could be heard, Tanqueril Dasani had said, and his voice was loud in his daughter's mind as she focused hard, marking the crashing of the breakers against the dark stone. *We're too far to port....*

She snapped a correction to Canini. The *Reaver* swung to the right. Plowed ahead. Argentia kept listening, hearing the balance of waves breaking to either side. *Got it....* "Hold this line."

The *Reef Reaver*, running left-of-center but well out of danger, passed through the breach and out into the White Sea. The crew cheered. Argentia clapped Canini on the shoulder. "Well done."

Behind them, the lights of Argo glowed against the black. Argentia stared at them for a long moment before heading to her cabin. She had left the city many times, but never before as a fugitive.

She wondered if she would ever see her home again.

9

Magistrate Krung had a problem. Its name was Tierciel Thorne.

Krung was the traitor Thorne's lieutenants sought, although the Magistrate would not have called himself such a foolish thing. He had no cause to be traitor to. He did not believe in ideological right and wrong. He had no interest in justice or injustice. His only concern was profit.

Krung had been born into the Watch. The son of a corrupt lieutenant, he had learned the game quickly. He had huge ambition and a spider's patience. His father had been content to extend favors to certain influential individuals or turn a blind eye to certain offenses in exchange for well-loaded purses. Such petty pursuits were not for Krung. If he was going to risk the Headsman's axe, he was going to risk it for obscene profit.

He began by making himself unimpeachable. He mercilessly pursued Argo's criminals, sending thieves and murderers by the dozens to the dungeons. His accomplishments allowed him to rise quickly through the ranks of the Watch. Once a Magistrate, his made his reputation as an iron-fisted defender of justice, meting out the harshest punishments within the bounds of the law, never giving ear to any talk of leniency or mercy.

He was honored, feared, and mentioned in the small circle of men likely to succeed Head Magistrate Gringoir.

His position secure beyond suspicion, Krung played his hand. He made himself a carefully concealed minister of information to the most powerful of Argo's criminals: men more than willing to pay to learn when the Watch was planning its raids.

And pay they did. Handsomely.

Krung had used a single contact—a thief named Kemelix, who was his half-brother (there were many skeletons hanging in the dark closets of Krung's family)—to farm out his intelligence. The invisible web of his influence grew to cover the entire city, and his fortune grew with it.

Now everything Krung had worked for so many winters to build was in jeopardy. If the other Magistrates learned his secret, he would not merely be stripped of his rank, he would be executed for treason to the city.

All because of Tierciel Thorne.

Thorne, relentless in his pursuit of justice even after the hunt for the killers of Vendimar Stelglim had officially been dropped, had tracked down Kemelix. He had killed him, but apparently not before the thief had talked, giving Thorne enough information to lead him out of Argo in pursuit of Stelglim's murderers.

The question that was driving Krung nearly mad was: what else had Kemelix told Thorne? Did Thorne know, for example, that Krung had been the one feeding the killers from Togril Vloth's guild the information that kept them a step ahead of the Watch?

If Thorne did know, and had he been given time, he would have dealt with the matter personally. Krung knew the man well enough to be sure of that. Forced to flee Argo ahead of the warrant for his arrest, however, and faced with the possibility that he would not survive his encounter with Stelglim's killers even if he caught them, Thorne would never leave such a matter as a traitor in his beloved Watch open behind him.

So who had the self-righteous bastard told? His former lieutenants were the likeliest choice. They were out there even now, serving their time on foot patrol as a punishment for their role in helping Thorne escape. Who knew what their plans were? Or even if they were the ones Thorne had told. If he had indeed told anyone. Assuming he had something to tell.

It was maddening. So many questions. So many dark possibilities. Only Thorne knew the answers.

It could not remain so. Thorne had to die for Krung to be safe again. But first he had to talk so Krung could be certain no one else needed to die to preserve his secret.

Before Krung could move to ensure both these things happened, something else had happened: something not even Krung could have anticipated. Argo's Noble Council, at the instigation of Lord Stelglim, who hated Thorne for his role in his daughter's death, demanded the Crown's Unicorn Cavalry garrisoned in the city ride Throne down and bring him back to stand trial for Kemelix's murder.

Technically the Council had no control over the Unicorns, who answered to the Crown through Lord Paladin Grefaulk. But the cavalry commander in Argo was a family friend of the Stelglims, so he followed up with the Magistrates, who confirmed there was indeed a warrant for

Thorne's arrest. Since Thorne was officially a criminal loose on the Crown's roads, and the roads were the jurisdiction of the Unicorns, the commander had no problem giving the order to bring Thorne in.

That order was very dangerous to Krung. If Thorne returned to face trial, who knew what he might say? Even if he was discredited and convicted and executed, there would be whispers. Krung would never be secure again.

The Magistrate opened the bottom drawer of his desk. Beneath a buckler and a hand crossbow loaded with a poisonous dart was a flask. Krung drew it out and slugged down a swallow of liquor. The bitter drink matched the bitter irony of the last few days. Krung brokered information, yet by the time he'd learned of Kemelix's death, Thorne had been beyond his reach.

He would not remain beyond it for long. In a few minutes, Krung would leave the garrison to make a rendezvous he had hastily arranged. That he was going himself was a sharp reminder that Kemelix's death had created a quandary for him beyond the problem of Thorne. He would have to find someone else he could trust to be his eyes and mouth on the streets.

There was no time for that tonight, however. Tonight the risk would be his. That was the only way. Grimacing, Krung took a second, longer pull of liquor.

"That venom will speed you to the grave, Magistrate," said the black-clad form that slipped with barely a rustle from behind the heavy window draperies.

10

Krung fumbled the flask, nearly spilling it. "You!"

Gideon-gil bowed mockingly.

Krung was a large man, stout and solid, but he could not contain a tremble as he stared at the slight figure before him. "How the hell did you get in here?" he blustered, trying to regain some composure. The elf had put him completely off balance—not a situation Krung was accustomed to. But then, did anyone ever deal with Gideon-gil on even footing?

"Many are my ways, Magistrate," Gideon-gil said. He was short and wiry. His jet-black hair was tied back, accentuating the alabaster, angular features of his elven heritage. One of his pointed ears boasted a single diamond stud. A silver ring glinted on one black-gloved finger.

The elf stood perfectly still. His arms were folded. His pale jade eyes were full of the quiet self-possession of one who knows he is the true and peerless master of his craft.

Gideon-gil's craft was death.

The infamous assassin was the only certain method Krung knew of eliminating Thorne. He might have trusted Vloth's twins to do the job if Thorne finally caught them, but paranoia ran too deeply in his veins. He could not leave it to chance, and with Gideon-gil, there was no chance. Once the elf set upon a mark, death was sure as if the Harvester itself drew the victim within the sweep of its scythe.

"So, Magistrate, to what do I owe the honor of this invitation?" the assassin asked. His tone was light, almost mocking.

"That bastard Lasher!" Krung exploded. "I told him to keep my name a secret." Aric Lasher, Argo's most powerful Guildmaster, was one of the few men who knew how to reach Gideon-gil. When Krung called in a favor, Lasher arranged for the magistrate to meet the assassin at midnight in East

Wharf—a rendezvous that Krung had planned to attend in disguise. "I'll see his guild destroyed for this treachery!"

"I would advise against that course, Magistrate," Gideon-gil replied. "Unless you wish your own name to be the next one handed to me. You placed Lasher in an unenviable position. It is not every day a Magistrate, even a viciously corrupt one like you, solicits my blades. Had Lasher let me walk into a trap, imagine his fate when I survived."

"There's no trap," Krung insisted. "I told the fool that."

"Lasher could hardly trust your word, could he, Magistrate? Neither could I. Thus, I took the liberty of rearranging the details of this little meeting. If you truly have a proposition, I suggest now would be the opportune time to deliver it."

The threat implicit in Gideon-gil's words was not lost on Krung. "Thorne," he said. "I need you to find Tierciel Thorne."

"I believe there are enough people looking for the erstwhile Captain already."

"That's the problem," Krung said. "I need you to find him first."

"Indeed? Why?"

"He may have information that could compromise me," Krung said. He told the elf what he feared Thorne knew.

"That could compromise you straight to the gallows, Magistrate," Gideon-gil said, smirking.

Krung's face reddened. He slammed his fist on the desk. "Do you think I don't know that? Don't toy with me, elf. Will you take the job or not?"

"Perhaps. We have not discussed my fee. My talents do not come cheaply."

Gideon-gil named his price. Krung took another swallow from his flask. "That will take time to arrange, even for me."

"Then I suggest you work swiftly. I will expect payment in full upon my return."

Krung nodded. "What about the pursuit? They leave at dawn. You have to get to Thorne before them. Get him to talk. Learn all Kemelix told him of me, and if there are others who know."

"He will talk," Gideon-gil said. He was quite skilled at making people talk. "You have, of course, considered that he may know nothing? What would you have me do with him then?"

Krung did not hesitate. "Kill the sanctimonious bastard anyway."

Gideon-gil almost smiled. Humans—so predictable, so governed by their emotions. They were weak and foolish, and Gideon-gil had no use for the weak or the foolish. Such creatures were better dead, he reasoned—so he killed them.

He had been doing so for centuries, either at his own whim or at the behest of those select men he permitted to employ him, and he had begun to grow bored with his success. Though he continued to sell his services, what he was truly seeking was a challenge.

He doubted Tierciel Thorne would qualify, but one never knew. The kill would be simplicity, but the hunt and the questioning might provide some amusement. More interesting was the fact that Magistrate Krung would almost certainly try to betray him when the job was done. He could read that in the man's eyes.

"Very well," the elf said. "I will collect my fee when next we meet." He started for the door.

"Wait!" Krung almost shouted. "You can't just walk out of here!"

"I can walk where I wish, Magistrate." Gideon-gil turned and stared at Krung. His jade eyes seemed to bore into the man's soul, chilling it. Then the elf's form glimmered—growing, widening, changing.

"God—" Krung gasped, his blocky jaw gaping in amazement.

"Hardly," Gideon-gil said. Then he opened the door to Krung's chamber, walked past the Watchmen on duty at their desks, and out into the night.

11

Mikael Greystone stowed his lucky gryphon's claw in his pack. It was foolish of him to even keep such a thing, the young Watchman knew, but his little sister Ydalia had given it to him when he graduated from the Cadetery, and he was unwilling to leave it behind. If he'd had it with him at the Westing House, maybe he wouldn't have needed a change of Fortune in the first place.

By order of the Magistrates, Mikael was accompanying the Unicorns to track down Tierciel Thorne, the very man he had once hoped to serve his lieutenancy under. Until the death of Vendimar Stelglim, Thorne had seemed an unassailable rock of righteousness and order. A Magistrate's seat was all but guaranteed, and there were few who doubted that Thorne would one day be running all of Argo's Watch.

Now Mikael, one of many cadets who had passed through that school striving to emulate Thorne's model of disciplined justice, was tasked to bring the Captain back in chains. It was a bitter assignment, tempered only by the fact that Mikael was grateful to have any assignment at all. After the debacle in the Westing House's cellar—capped by the humiliation of having to go out to the street in nothing but his breeks—he had feared the Magistrates would expel him for his ineptitude.

Instead he had been given this duty. He suspected that Head Magistrate Gringoir, as wise a fox as had ever held that seat, was behind the decision. The hunt for Thorne would conveniently removed Mikael from Argo, sparing him more of the abuse he'd taken from his fellow Watchmen over the past three days.

Mikael was still coming to terms with being so easily bested—and by a woman, no less. He had to get past that shame. This was a good place to begin. Whatever their reasons, the Magistrates had given him a chance to prove himself again. Mikael did not mean to waste it.

A violent knocking startled him from his ruminations. He'd already been to his parents' house to say farewell. Who would have business with him at this hour of night?

Again the knocking, even more insistent this time.

Mikael went to the door. Opened it the width of the chain. "Magistrate Krung! Sir, this is a surprise. Is all well?"

"Most well," Krung said. "You ride out tomorrow?"

"Yes, sir. I'm just making my final preparations, sir."

"That is exactly what I wish to speak to you about. A matter has come up. It requires some delicacy in its handling."

"Of course, Magistrate. Come in, please." Mikael loosed the chain and stepped back. Krung always made him nervous. There was a tension about the man, as if he were coiled almost to snapping. Tonight, however, Mikael did not get that sense from the Magistrate. His burly form was the same, with its short, spiky white-blond hair and ochre eyes that bulged from the flushed block of his face, but he seemed more at ease than any other time Mikael had encountered him.

"May I offer you a drink, sir? I think I have a good bottle of Cyprytalyr red here somewhere. Or tea or caf?"

"Nothing." Krung looked around as Mikael closed the door behind him and slid the chain home. "You live alone?"

"Yes, sir." Three rooms in one of Argo's boarding houses were all he could afford, but he'd had his fill of dormitory life as a cadet.

"Good. Then I can speak freely. As I said, this is a matter of sensitivity. It involves, of course, the taking of Captain Thorne."

"Yes, sir. Have you told Sir Reth?" Orion Reth was the leader of the Unicorns assigned to capture Thorne.

"You are better suited than Sir Reth to help me resolve this problem."

"Thank you, sir." Mikael flushed with pride. Magistrate Krung had never shown any inclination to praise him in the past. "What can I do, sir?"

A black-bladed dagger plunged into Mikael's chest. "You can die."

12

Tierciel Thorne rode through the night.

He would have to stop soon, he knew. Were it up to his will alone, he would have gone all the way to Telarban without pause, but the horse needed rest. He had a month still to journey. If his horse died, it would take longer.

Still, he went on for another hour before reluctantly halting. He made his camp with no idea of what dangers lay behind him in Argo. His only thoughts as he ate his dried, spiced beef and brewed his bitter caf were on dangers that lay ahead, although he did not perceive them as dangers, merely obstacles between him and his purpose.

Thorne was a fanatic. Once Justice had been his goddess. Now She was in eclipse, and he turned his zealot's focus to a new star.

Thorne was going north for Vengeance.

Guilt drove him like a scourge. Determined to bring an end to a series of brutal murders that had plagued Argo, Thorne had finally tracked the killers to their lair. Instead of waiting for reinforcements from the garrison, he had used Vendimar Stelglim as bait to draw the killers out, never imagining the situation would slip beyond his control.

Never imagining the twins.

The cat-women had killed Vendi. They would have killed Thorne as well, but for the timely intervention of his other lieutenants.

Thorne touched the scar running across his right cheek from his nose to the curve of his jaw. The mark was not of the battle with the twins, but from earlier in the hunt, when the cat-women had blown up a warehouse at the Watch garrison to destroy evidence.

Vendi had saved Thorne that night. He had repaid that debt by asking her to take a fool's risk. A gambit that would have ended in disaster nine of ten times—and had ended in something far worse.

Yet she had done it, trusting him.

Vendi's death had cost Thorne so much more than a lieutenant. He had lost a girl of rare ideals and unflinching principles. A girl whose inner beauties had far outshone the plainness of her face. A girl who had loved him, and whom he might have loved in return, had there been time.

Instead, Vendi was gone. Thorne could not bring her back. Could not change what he had unwittingly wrought.

But he could avenge her.

He remembered Vendi's father at the funeral. Standing haggard in the pyre's light, where the scent of incense could not mask the fact that they were burning his daughter, the old man had condemned Thorne for living, and for failing for find Vendi's murderers.

Lord Stelglim's words had echoed in Thorne's heart for days. During his trial, in which he was convicted of recklessly endangering his lieutenant and expelled from the Watch, ending the righteous duty that had been the sole focus of his life since the murder of his wife and infant son fifteen years before, their knell sounded again and again, beckoning him to revenge.

He turned vigilante. Left a trail of broken bodies behind him, until at last he came to Kemelix. The thief had died before Thorne could extract all the information he needed from him, but he had told enough to set Thorne on his course for Telarban and the guildhouse of Togril Vloth.

That was where the twins had come from. That was where they would return.

That was where Thorne would find them and kill them.

His meager meal finished, he extinguished his campfire, saddled up, and rode north beneath the stars.

The next afternoon, he met the bandits.

A quartet of horsemen, they came riding hard out of a copse between the Toll Road and the Dimrithyl River, surrounding Thorne, crowding close, swords drawn, forcing him to halt.

Thorne's horse shied, whickering nervously. "Steady," Thorne whispered, patting its strong neck. His other hand was concealed beneath his cloak.

"Your coin or your hide," said the bandit leader, a tall, pale man with lank hair falling across one eye.

"No—my stick." Thorne threw back his cloak and smashed his steel baton across the leader's face, knocking the man from his horse.

Seizing the instant's surprise, Thorne wheeled his horse in the tight space, colliding with the bandits' mounts, his baton sweeping viciously, connecting with hands, arms, and heads, breaking bones with each blow.

Moments later, three bandits were down and finished for the fight. "Come." Thorne beckoned to the fourth. His black eyes gleamed with falcon cruelty.

"Like hell!" The bandit spun his horse around and fled.

Thorne let him go.

Once, and not so very long ago, he never would have done such a thing. Once Justice would have demanded he catch the man and drag him and his fellows to the dungeons of the nearest town, making the Toll Road that much safer for Teranor's merchants and travelers.

Now all he did was cast a disdainful glance at the three who writhed in the dirt and resume his ride toward Telarban and the twins.

Vengeance, Thorne was learning, was an even harsher taskmistress than Justice.

13

As Thorne rode north, the very twins he hunted cowered under a lash.

Blue aether crackled in the air as the Whipmaster brought his magically charged nine-tails snapping across the pretty, bare backs of Puma and Pantra, setting them yaowing in agony. The tails left no marks—Togril Vloth did not want the cat-women scarred or disfigured—but they imparted a jolt of energy that would not soon be forgotten.

The Whipmaster was a Nhapian, but his tan skin was mottled with port-wine discolorations, as if he had been badly scalded. Rather than conceal this condition, Salis Yip flaunted it, wearing only a skirt of studded leather and a pair of sandals. His bandy arms and chest were as cut with muscle as a smith's. His glossy hair, drawn up in a steel sheaf, stood atop his head like a black-fronded palm tree.

Like all Vloth's torturers, Yip delighted in his trade. He was particularly glad to have his sadistic way with the twins. He had stripped them of their clothes—he stripped all his victims, having long ago learned that the naked condition increased vulnerability—and whipped them with the same glee that he had shown when strangling stray kittens as a child.

"Very much love to kill Yip, heh pretties," he laughed, slashing the nine-tails against their buttocks, drawing screams. "Sa-so. Very much love to tear him and gash him, heh—but so sorry, pretties can't get free."

Puma and Pantra, their hands shackled above their heads, hissed and spit at Salis Yip. The Whipmaster had come into Vloth's service while they were in Argo. Though the twins had seen the torturer work on Lady Dasani's butler, they had paid him little mind. There were many servants, guards, and strange persons in the guild, but the twins had walked its halls with impunity—until they had crossed Vloth.

The cell door opened. A quartet of armored guardsmen entered. Togril Vloth hobbled in behind them, silk pants flowing about his trunklike legs, a silk robe belted about his tremendous girth, a diadem gleaming on his bald head.

Yip stopped in mid-strike and bowed. "Continue," Vloth said with an imperious wave of a bejeweled hand.

"Sa-so, Guildmaster."

Leaning on his walking stick, Vloth watched as Yip lashed the cat-women. The guildmaster regretted such punishment was necessary, but the twins had made it so. They were highly dangerous and had to be made to understand his control over them. Otherwise, they would persist in their willfulness and sooner or later become more of a nuisance than they were worth.

Until yesterday, Vloth had never been more pleased with any of the many acquisitions he had made in his long years of power—a career begun as an orphan on the streets of Khemr-kar and brought to fruition on the streets of Telarban—than he was with the twins. He had purchased Puma and Pantra at a mighty cost from Mouradian, a shadowmage who dwelt upon a secret island where he bred hybrids of animals and women. The twins were Mouradian's superlative creations. Tall, lithe, splendid, they were dark and light mirrors: Puma tawny and blonde, Pantra tawny and brunette. Physically, their inhumanity was betrayed only by their clawlike nails and the feline casts of their faces: pert noses, green cat's eyes, and small, sharp fangs hidden behind sensual red lips. In their mannerisms, however, they were purely cats: stealthy hunters and heartless killers.

And cunning, Vloth grudgingly allowed. How else could he describe the way in which they'd betrayed him?

Vloth had learned of the near disaster at the Westing House from Inger Solrand, the man he had dispatched to replace Orik Totenkampf as his agent in Argo. Puma and Pantra had made an end of Orik, who had been a failure anyway, and then they had embarked on their private little game with Argentia Dasani, leaving the explosive skull in her suite when they abducted her butler.

Dasani had not been killed, and she had escaped Argo by ship after leading the Watch on a chase through the city, but Inger did not know where she was bound.

Furious, Vloth had summoned the twins. "How dare you!" he thundered. "How dare you set such a trap! She was to be brought to me to suffer—not to be killed in some painless explosion!"

"We are sorry," Puma said.

"Yes, very sorry," Pantra echoed.

"We meant…"

"No harm…"

"And we knew…"

"She would survive."

But what they thought—for they could share their minds in the same way they shared their speech—was:

She should have died…

In the explosion—yes and then…

We could be done with this silly game…

This boring waiting game and find…

New prey…

New toys to play with…

Their posturing did not convince Vloth. A flare of light from one of his many magical rings stunned the cat-women, and they had been given over to the whips of Salis Yip.

The twins hated magic, which rendered all their physical superiority useless. They hated pain even more.

Yip gave them both in abundance.

"Enough," Vloth said, when at last the twins were hanging limp in their chains, barely conscious. "Let them loose."

Reluctantly, Yip lowered his nine-tails, scurried to the wall, and released the winch holding the twins aloft. Puma and Pantra crumpled to the cold stone and lay in a tangled sprawl. Yip snapped his crackling whip in the air above them as a warning, then bent quickly and unfastened their shackles.

"Go," Vloth commanded.

"Sa-so, Guildmaster." Yip bowed and exited the chamber, giggling under his breath.

The twins crawled weakly toward Vloth. "Forgive us," Puma whimpered.

"Yes, yes, forgive us," Pantra mewled.

"And please do not let…"

"The man whip us…"

"Lash us…"

"Hurt us…"

"Any more," they concluded in a plaintive chorus. Bending their heads, they began licking at the curled toes of Vloth's shoes.

The guildmaster felt his lust stir. "Bring them to my chambers," he instructed his guards.

Later.

The cat-women were twined languidly atop satin pillows. Weak from the magical whipping, they had submitted passively to Vloth's desires, letting him plunder their bodies while they made all the appropriately urgent moans and purrs.

When it was done, Vloth called them his "beauties," and left them. The twins, believing they had put on enough of a show of subservience to recover Vloth's favor, held each other amid the satin of the guildmaster's bed. But even as they commiserated, comforting with touches and kisses, the memory of their abuse was strong. Their punishment was over, but not forgotten.

Their green eyes flashed as they communicated in their odd telepathy, plotting.

They had been humiliated. They had been hurt.

They would have their revenge.

14

From the crow's nest, Argentia watched the city of Harrowgate appear beneath an overcast sky.

When she had first taken over command of the *Reef Reaver*—the black-sailed, black-hulled schooner was a gift from Skarangella Skarn— she had refused to be a captain in name only and took her share of all the duties on board the ship. Her actions had cemented the loyalty of a crew that already respected her from several previous voyages, but that was not the driving reason for her participation. She simply loved to sail; she had ever since she was a little girl. The vistas of the open sea, the feel of the ship surging beneath her, the exhilaration of the occasional storm, all enchanted her.

Keeping the lookout was her favorite duty. The crow's nest, poised almost a hundred feet above the decks, offered a place of perfect privacy. A place where she could be alone with her thoughts.

She had much to think on.

Argentia was sailing to Harrowgate because that was the fastest way to reach Duralyn. It was a six-week journey over land from Argo to the Crown City. It was a three-week voyage around the southeast tip of Teranor and up the coast to Harrowgate, but from there only an instant's aetherwalk to Duralyn.

If she could convince Colla to aid her.

She'll help. She has to. A life is at stake...

Ikabod's plight had forced Argentia to move obliquely. Had the jeopardy been hers alone, she might have taken the confrontation straight to Vloth. With Ikabod in danger, she wasn't taking any chances on rushing in blindly and perhaps getting both of them killed.

That was why she was bound for Duralyn. She needed help. She knew just where to get it.

Of course, nothing ever went easily for Argentia, and she could not make contact with Amethyst Pyth.

She had tried reaching the guildmistress by oculyr several times during the voyage. The crystal ball only revealed the very troubling image of an empty chamber. Argentia had been away from Duralyn for more than a year; what if something had happened to Amethyst? The secret world of Teranor's thieves' guilds was full of danger. What if Amethyst was no longer in power—or worse, dead?

Might as well try her one more time, she thought, as if to refute such possibilities.

Argentia swung out of the crow's nest and climbed down the rigging, reveling in the sweet, full range of painless motion that Wanpo, the ship's surgeon, had restored to her injured shoulder.

She crossed the rolling deck, nodding in passing to her sailors. In her cabin, she brought the oculyr to life, directing its magic once more toward the guild of the Golden Serpent. She despised having to ask for help even more than she despised being hurt, but hating her own infirmities was one thing; letting Ikabod die because of her pride was something she could never permit. So she would ask for help. If Amethyst couldn't help her, she would find some other way of learning what she needed to know.

The oculyr cleared. This time, Argentia was rewarded for her persistence with an image of Amethyst Pyth. The guildmistress had been vacationing at Vildenor, the Crown's retreat in the hills north of the city—a perk of her alliance with the Crown.

"I'll have a carriage waiting for you at the monastery," Amethyst said when Argentia explained what she needed. "And don't worry that pretty red head of yours. I'll take care of everything."

Harrowgate.

Argentia left the *Reef Reaver* at its berth. She told Dorn to have the men stay at the Mermaid's Tail, the brothel where she and her companions had first met Skarn and his crew. "Sure you don't need help?" Dorn asked.

Argentia shook her head. She appreciated the offer, but she wasn't risking any of the crew in a personal war with Togril Vloth. "I have to do this on my own."

"As you will. Fortune follow you, Cap'n." Dorn saluted her.

Argentia returned the salute, winked, and walked away. She had been to Harrowgate several times. While it was no slum like Shriv's Port, it hardly compared to the artesian gem of Argo. Still, she would have liked the chance to stop at some shops she favored or to take a room at the Mast & Nest and have a long bath, a good meal, and a warm bed. But all that would have to wait.

As she went up from the docks into the city proper, she kept a wary eye out for the Watch, uncertain whether report of her flight had passed to all the major cities in Teranor, or if she was still only wanted in Argo. If word had spread, it apparently had not reached Harrowgate and she arrived without incident at the huge sandstone cathedral that was her destination.

Though the rest of the city paled in Argentia's esteem, Coastlight Cathedral, at least, was worthy of Argo. Argentia gazed fondly at the spectacular architecture: towering spires, flying buttresses, lofty walls full of cornices, crouching gargoyles, and decorative rainspouts.

Within, Coastlight was even more splendid. The sanctuary was all vastness. Soaring arches swept into the vaults of the frescoed ceiling: panels depicting the creation of Acrevast, the casting down of Bhael-ur and the demons, and the instruction of the magi and clerics by the mysterious divae of Aelysium.

Beneath these brilliant paintings, a hundred rows of pews flanked an aisle marching to the marble of a raised altar and pulpit that glowed softly with veins of dwarven mithryl. Behind the altar a gilded sun, symbol of Aeton, thrust the innumerable spears of its rays high and wide, refracting the light of a thousand candles.

As Argentia stood in the tall doorway, breathing the incense that sanctified the air and letting the magnificence of the cathedral dwarf her for a moment, she was disappointed to see that several of the colored-glass windows had been draped with black cloth. *Wonder what happened?*

She went in, moving with a quiet reverence. A few worshippers were scattered in the pews, whispering orisons. She knew where she needed to go, but was reluctant to simply intrude. *Where in the hell is a priest when you need one?*

Off to the left, she heard voices descending a stairwell. She recognized one of them. It was not one she had expected to hear in this place.

"Ah-yes. That is easily obtained. I have many contacts in the quartz quarries of Janzikar. Many contacts. The rose quartz is most very precious, but they will have it for me."

I don't believe this… Argentia slipped back through the doorway and out of sight as the pair—a cleric and a gnome—approached and turned toward the transept, still conversing. Argentia let them pass, and then reached out and clamped her hand on the gnome's shoulder. "Hello, Nekim."

Nekim Babush turned in surprise. The gnome had relocated to Harrowgate after his misfortunes in Argo—misfortunes whose origins he traced to the foul day he'd agreed to bring in tiles for Lady Dasani's manor.

His eyes flew wide at the sight of Argentia. His jaw plunged. "Y-y-y—" he stammered, his leathery head flushing, huge ears twitching. "No!" He tore free of Argentia's grasp and fled as madly as if he'd come face to face with a fiend.

Argentia smirked as she watched Nekim catch his feet on the hem of his robe and go tumbling down the cathedral steps. *Hope that hurt…* She had no love for the double-dealing gnome.

"Now what was that about?" the cleric asked, looking from Nekim Babush, who had picked himself up and was running as fast as his little legs would carry him across the street and away, to Argentia.

"Let's just say that if you were considering trade with that worm, I just saved you a lot of money and aggravation," Argentia said.

"Nekim Babush comes very highly recommended," the cleric said. He was a man of middling winters, with a bushy mustache and light brown hair just beginning to show white. "He left a lucrative business importing tile in Argo to work in glass, which was always his first love, or so he told me."

"I know all about his business in Argo. Trust me, you're better off without him."

"It seems we are without him, at least for the moment."

"Keep it that way," Argentia suggested.

The cleric digested that advice silently for a moment, and then shrugged. "Well, Aeton will provide. My name is Maren. How might I assist you? That is, presuming you did not come simply to disrupt the repairs on our windows—for good or ill."

"Nope. I came to see your boss."

"Pardon, Lady—you mean the High Cleric?"

No, I mean Aeton Himself… "Yes. Is she in?"

"And who might I say is calling?"

"Argentia Dasani," said a woman's voice from behind them.

15

Argentia turned to see the High Cleric of Harrowgate walking towards them.

Colla was a few winters shy of Argentia's thirty. With her short mop of dark, curly hair, sweet smile, and winsome face, she looked very much more like a village maid than one of Teranor's most powerful clerics—until you saw her eyes, where the weight of responsibility and power lay heavy.

Colla's eyes were old.

Argentia had first met Colla in the village of Sharelywis. The cleric, who in fact had been a shepherdess both before and after taking to her ministry, had healed the huntress and the rest of her company after their escape from the undead monsters of Hollowdale. Colla had since been raised to her current position, and it was widely rumored that once old Midelwyn passed on to Aeton's eternal embrace, Colla would be elevated again, this time to High Cleric of Duralyn, Steward of Teranor.

Argentia wasn't certain how much Colla relished that position—or even the one she had now—but she believed the girl from Sharelywis would do her duty well. She had always liked Colla. There was something about her, some rustic simplicity she had never lost, which tempered her power and made her worthy of trust and faith.

"I'm sorry to barge in on you like this," Argentia said.

Colla made a dismissive gesture. "Nonsense. The doors of Coastlight are open to all." She studied Argentia carefully for a moment. "Tell me how I can help," she said.

Argentia launched into her tale. "I need to get to Duralyn. Fast," she concluded. "I need to use the gate."

The aethergate between Coastlight and the Monastery of the Grey Tree in Duralyn was a secret thing, one of a quartet designed to serve as a last escape for the Crown should Castle Aventar ever fall to siege. Argentia had used it to come between the cities in the chase for the Wheels of Avis-fe, but that had been with the Crown's permission. She was not certain she would be able to use it for her own purposes.

Her fears proved groundless. Colla said, "Of course. Come with me."

"Thank you," Argentia said.

"If you can save your butler's life, then surely our gate has served its purpose," Colla replied. Then she grinned impishly—an insouciant flash of the village girl. "Besides, if what I overheard you telling Maren is so, perhaps it is I who owe you thanks for steering us clear of Nekim Babush."

A stroke like lightning strobed the Gate Chamber in the Monastery of the Grey Tree.

Argentia tumbled out of the aether onto the hard stones and lay there shuddering. Teleporting—walking the aether, as the magi called it—was the worst: like stepping through a doorway into a tornado. Argentia felt as if her entire body had been ripped to shreds and rejoined in an instant many hundreds of leagues away—which was more or less what had happened.

The debilitating effects of aetherwalking were proportional to the distance traveled. A short aetherwalk might leave a person only slightly shaken, but a long teleport always took its toll. Argentia had heard that the number of times you traveled the aether was also a factor: the more familiar your body became with the aether, the easier it was to recover. Personally, she didn't care to find out.

Groaning, she sat up and rolled her neck back and forth to loosen a crick. It didn't help. Her head was pounding. Her stomach was a nauseous roil. She felt as bad as the time she'd entered a rotgut whisky drinking game in some no-name tavern in Byrtnoth. The game had gone all night and she had held her own, but paid for it the next day, when she was sicker than she'd ever been in her life.

"God damn it," Argentia muttered, struggling to her knees. She held her hand over her eyes, still flash-blind from the silver-streaking aether that had brought her from Harrowgate to Duralyn in less than a breath. Slowly, the world stopped spinning. The chamber came into focus.

Midelwyn himself stood beside the door.

Ooops...

"Go easy, child," the Steward of Teranor said, smiling. If he'd marked her blasphemy, he showed no sign.

"I'm all right." Argentia rose and staggered out of the circle of magical glyphs carved into the stone floor. She was on her feet, but not steady on them.

Midelwyn placed a gentle hand on her shoulder. Immediately Argentia felt the nausea wash from her, replaced by a reinvigoration of health and energy, as if a wind had blown within her, scouring the aftereffects of the teleport.

She exhaled a long breath and bowed gratefully to the cleric, who nodded his white head. Midelwyn was as old as Colla was young, but the benevolent strength they shared was the same. "When you are ready, I believe your escort awaits you on the street," he said.

"My thanks, Steward." Argentia checked her weapons. Everything had survived the aetherwalk. She wondered what might happen to something lost in the aether. Decided she didn't ever want to learn.

Argentia bid farewell to Midelwyn. A monk waiting outside the Gate Chamber led her through the silent monastery. "Aeton's Light guide you," the monk said, making a gesture of benediction as Argentia exited.

"And you."

Outside, the sky was bright and clear above the Crown City. Duralyn was larger than Argo, but the city's design, which consisted of a series of concentric rings around Castle Aventar, gave it a more intimate feeling, the walls of each ring making it seem as if Duralyn was really six separate cities in one. Because trade and commerce were confined to the outer rings, the interior of the city, where the monastery stood among the residences of the wealthiest nobles, was typically quiet and peaceful.

Argentia followed carefully groomed paths through a garden surrounded by a high stone wall. She passed beds of white lilies, a stone well, and the solitary, towering grey ash for which the monastery was named without really seeing any of them. She was anxious to meet with Amethyst. She wished she'd been able to contact the guildmistress sooner. She couldn't do anything about that, but now that she was finally in Duralyn she intended to learn what she needed to know and be on the road to Telarban by nightfall. *Sooner if I can...*

Argentia passed through the garden gate. She paused on the cobbled sidewalk, looking for Pyth's famous six-wheeled, six-horsed scarlet coach on the street.

Instead, there was a group of armed, armored knights.

Because it was home to the Crown, Duralyn didn't have a City Watch. The Guardian knights responsible for keeping Castle Aventar safe were also responsible for maintaining order in the city. The arrangement ensured a seamless chain of communication and command in the event of an attack, when a confusion of orders and duties between the Crown's forces and a municipal guard might lead to disaster.

The knights outside the monastery, however, were not wearing the blue-and-silver armor of the Guardians, but the black-and-gold colors of the Sentinels: the Crown's personal protectors.

What are they doing out of Aventar? Where's Amethyst? Did something happen to Solsta? Argentia had a bad feeling as one of the Sentinels stepped forward. The sun flashed on his polished armor and plumed helmet. "Lady Dasani?" His voice was gruff, his demeanor that of a man who brooked no nonsense.

"Who's asking?"

"Travien Lockwood, of Her Majesty's Sentinels."

"I'm Dasani. Is everything all right? Is the Crown—"

"I'm not here to answer questions," Lockwood interrupted. At his signal, the other Sentinels drew their swords and formed a circle around Argentia. "You're under arrest."

16

"Such nerve!" Solsta Ly'Ancoeur exclaimed.

From her seat atop a flight of polished black marble steps at the end of the long throne hall, the Crown of Teranor glared imperiously at Argentia, who stood at the base of those steps, flanked by her escort of Sentinels. Standing beside the throne was Ralak the Red, the Archamagus of Teranor, somber in his ruby robes.

The Crown rose. She was eleven years younger than Argentia. Her petite form, clad in a long, beautifully fitted gray skirt and emerald blouse whose collar and cuffs were embroidered with silver, stood two inches shy of five feet tall, but the magnitude of her person was regal. She could command a room with her gaze, silence crowds with her voice. Argentia had seen her do both.

But she had never seen her this angry.

"Such *nerve*," the Crown repeated, descending deliberately. Her dark eyes were stormy. The diadem upon her brow and the blaze of white in her tangled chestnut hair—the Mark of her rule—gleamed in the well-lit hall. Ralak looked on impassively, as if he did not know Argentia at all.

What the hell is going on here? I thought they were my friends…

When Lockwood had said he was arresting her, Argentia's impulse had been to fight free. She was no more use to Ikabod as a prisoner in Duralyn than she was as a prisoner in Argo. "Fair warning. You're not taking me to the dungeons," she'd said, drawing her katana.

"No," Lockwood said. "We're bringing you to the Crown. Do us all a favor and come quietly."

Argentia didn't really want to fight with the Sentinels, so she decided to take a chance. Even if word of her flight from Argo had reached all the way to the throne, surely Solsta would hear her out and take her side. Or so she'd believed.

Now she feared she'd made a grave mistake.

"Did you think you could sneak into our monastery, sneak into our city like some thief, and be off again without our knowing?" Solsta paused a few steps above Argentia. "Without even giving me the chance to say hello?"

Solsta's eyes went from wrath to sparkling mirth as the astonishment showed on Argentia's face. "Oh Gen! I have missed you!" Solsta swept down and embraced the huntress with all the fondness of a sister. "Forgive me," she begged. "I couldn't resist."

Argentia nodded. For one of the few times in her life, she was speechless.

"Kodius and Kirin are still wandering. They stopped in a few months ago, on their way west," Solsta said. The Crown, Ralak, Argentia, and Amethyst Pyth were seated at table, waiting for dinner and catching the huntress up on the doings of their other friends.

"Iz was last seen in Harrowgate. He booked passage on an eastbound merchant ship and seems to have vanished," Ralak added.

Argentia suspected Ralak knew exactly what had happened to Iz l'Aigle. She would bet her fleet it involved a certain silver-haired mermaid. "Have you—" She brought her question up short, but it was too late.

"Seen Artelo?" Solsta completed for her.

"I'm sorry," Argentia said, cursing herself.

"It's all right," Solsta replied with a wistful smile. Artelo Sterling, another of Argentia's companions, had been Solsta's lover before she inherited the throne. Political maneuverings had forced Solsta's betrothal to Kelvin Eleborne, and she and Artelo had been sundered. Now Kelvin was dead and Artelo was wedded to a shepherdess in a village not far from Duralyn.

To Argentia, who had watched Solsta mature in a cauldron of brutality—her parents assassinated, her husband murdered, her own life threatened, her crowndom besieged by political strife and an apocalypse of demons—Solsta's enduring the loss of her true love to another woman was the greatest testament to the Crown's strength.

After the demon Ter-at had killed Carfax, Argentia had been long in recovering. But death was irrevocable. To go on as Solsta had, with Artelo every day so near yet so utterly unreachable, showed courage in the face of Fortune at Her abject cruelest.

Solsta touched a small scar on her cheek—the remnant of an assassin's blade and the sole blemish on her otherwise flawless features. "No. He has not been to Aventar. Nor do I expect him, though I hear his daughter is doing quite well— Mirk, stop that!"

The meerkat, Solsta's magical pet and longstanding companion, jumped in alarm. He had been fencing olives with the small sword he carried. "Mirk is sorry," he said.

"Put your sword away at the table," Solsta chided. "You'd think I hadn't taught you better manners."

Argentia grinned. It was very much like old times. Things had changed, of course, but the camaraderie around the table remained. When you stood and bled together, those bonds were difficult to sunder. She was glad to be back, and gladder still she had such friends to turn to in her need.

Amethyst had gone to work on the problem of Togril Vloth immediately after hearing from Argentia. She had a man in Telarban, but Vloth controlled the city. Getting information on the weaknesses of his guildhouse was going to be difficult, and it was going to take time.

Argentia rebelled against the idea of having to wait idly for an answer. Ralak and Solsta, who also knew of Ikabod's plight, calmed her. "Be patient a while longer," the Archamagus said. "Let Mistress Pyth work. With her information, we can best determine how to save Ikabod."

"In the interim, anything you need will be at your disposal," Solsta said.

"How about a host of Unicorns and some siege weapons?" Argentia joked.

Solsta smiled, but shook her head. "The throne cannot be openly involved in such a matter—not even for one so dear to me as you. It would set an impossible precedent. I'm sorry."

Argentia nodded. "I know. This is personal, anyway."

"Mirk will help," the meerkat offered.

"No, little one," Argentia said, smiling.

"Mirk not help?"

"Nope. You have to stay here and keep Solsta safe."

"But Mirk would like another adventure."

"No more adventures," Solsta scolded, catching the meerkat and tickling him until he squeezed free and scampered off in feigned annoyance.

"How long?" Argentia asked Amethyst.

The guildmistress of the Golden Serpent was not much taller than the Crown, but with her wild, brassy hair and voluptuous body—some parts magically enhanced, it was rumored—and her penchant for six-inch heels she cut a figure that almost matched her outsized personality. Her face was round and rouged, her eyes green as Jengikutoian emeralds. Gold dripped from her wrists and throat, big gems sparked on her fingers.

"Hard to say, honey." Amethyst pursed her puffy lips. "It's the information on accessing the guild that's the problem. That will come at a high price, but it will come. Just give my people a little more time."

Argentia sighed. After pressing madly to escape Argo and reach Duralyn, it was hard to muster patience now. Yet that was what she would have to do, trusting Amethyst to come through and Fortune to take care of Ikabod a little longer.

Bitter as it was, she had to wait.

17

Thorne knew he was being followed.

He had first seen his pursuers' campfire when he was a week out of Argo. Every night, the distance between them had closed. Merchants or random travelers would not be mirroring his movements so exactly: riding long into the night, stopping for a few short hours respite, riding again before the dawn.

Thorne had hunted men long enough to know when he was the prey.

He endured the pursuit for a fortnight, hoping his instinct was wrong. He wanted no trouble, only to get to Telarban and avenge Vendi. With the brutal pace he was setting, he could beat his pursuers to the city, but there he would face the dual problems of assailing Vloth while keeping clear of his mysterious shadows.

So he decided to put the matter to rest.

Another reason also drove his decision. He could not keep from wondering if the party pursuing him might be Tib and his other lieutenants. It would be good to have the others with him. It would be right to have the others with him.

He did not let this worm of hope burrow deeply, however. The stone of his heart was hewn of stuff far too pragmatic for that. Rather, when he set camp early on that twenty-first night of his journey he fully expected his pursuers would not be his lieutenants. What they might be he would not guess—that also was not in his nature. But he would learn.

From the shadows beyond the light of his campfire, Thorne watched four cloaked forms approach his camp. They had dismounted and left their steeds a safe distance away. Keeping carefully clear of Thorne's horse, they made a stealthy creep toward his bedroll.

Thorne heard a curse as they discovered his ruse: a bedroll stuffed with his pack and cloak to give a semblance of human form. He almost smiled as he moved to take them. It had been so easy to gain the advantage.

Then the men turned about. The firelight glanced off their armor. Thorne froze in his tracks. These were no bandits, but knights—and a Watchman!

But not one of his Watchmen, Thorne realized in the moment before one of the knights bellowed, "Tierciel Thorne! Surrender in the name of the Crown!"

That voice belonged to Orion Reth. Thorne and Reth had a long and unfriendly history. Reth had been posted to Argo the same year Thorne had graduated from the Cadetery. Each was a rising star in his sphere. Since the knights and the Watchmen moved in some of the same circles, they had inevitably come into rivalry over a woman. Thorne had won the hand of Aielyn to wife, and those who knew Orion Reth said he had never forgiven Thorne for that—or for letting her die. Now, in a show of Fortune's perversity, it was Reth who was come to arrest Thorne on behalf of the Magistrates.

No matter, Thorne thought. These were servants of the Crown and the city of Argo, not brigands come to cut his throat in the night. They were to be dealt with honorably, whatever the outcome.

Thorne stepped into the firelight. "I would bid you good evening, but I doubt you wish me well."

"Thorne." Reth's voice drooled with anticipation. "We've come to take you back to Argo to stand trial for your crimes."

"I know why you have come, Orion," Thorne said quietly. "I will not be turned."

"Then you will die!" Reth rang his sword free from its scabbard. Thorne leaped back, his baton already coming up to meet Reth's charge.

Mikael Greystone struck Thorne from the side, shoving him away. "This is madness!" he shouted, facing off against Reth.

"Out of the way, boy," Orion Reth snarled.

Mikael stood his ground. "I won't let you do this! The Magistrates said to bring Captain Thorne back, not to kill him!"

"I said out of the way!" Reth growled, swinging his weapon viciously.

Mikael's sword appeared out of nowhere to make the parry. Reth drove the young Watchman back and out of the firelight.

The other two knights, determined to carry out their orders, closed on Thorne. "You were warned!" Thorne cried, hating what he had come to but knowing he had no choice.

There was a clash of steel. A slamming of bodies. The baton rose and fell, its blows punctuated by cries of pain.

Brutal moments later, Thorne stood above the two unconscious knights. And here was Mikael Greystone, walking towards him again. Blood dripped from his sword. "What have you done?" Thorne said.

"Nothing I regret, assuredly," the young Watchman replied. "Sir Reth's temper always was going to get him into trouble one day."

"Do not make me do this, Greystone," Thorne said, raising his baton as Mikael continued to advance. "Leave be. I will not be taken."

"We shall see."

Thorne didn't waste time on more words. He launched a furious barrage. Mikael blocked every stroke without the slightest effort and spun in to spike an elbow sharply against Thorne's jaw, stunning him. An instant later Thorne's baton was gone and a blow to his knee collapsed him to the ground. Growling, he surged upward.

Mikael's blade chopped down to meet him.

Darkness descended like death.

But it was not death.

When Thorne dragged himself up from unconsciousness, it was still night, though the fire had burned low. He forced himself awkwardly to his knees. His head hurt. His hands were bound behind him. There was no sign of the knights and his horse was gone, but Mikael Greystone was crouched nearby, watching him. "Where are the others?" Thorne asked.

"Dead," Mikael replied. "I weighed their bodies with stones and sank them in the Dimrithyl. It need not concern you. We have other matters to speak of."

Mikael's form began to glimmer. When the aurora faded, a black-clad elf crouched where the Watchman had been.

"Gideon-gil," Thorne breathed.

"Indeed," the elf replied, inclining his head briefly.

"Murderer!" Thorne struggled against his bonds, but the ropes were fast about his wrists. "What do you want?" he demanded.

Gideon-gil rummaged in his pack and drew forth a slim, silver flute. "Tell me, Captain, do you enjoy music?" the assassin asked.

Thorne glared at him.

"I thought as much. Perhaps this will...enlighten you." Raising the magical instrument to his thin lips, the elf began to play.

18

"He's dead! Dead and rottin', I tell'ee!" the hag with the broom exclaimed.

Tib forced himself not to recoil as Matron Edi thrust her face toward his. The crone reeked of stale tobacco and liquor and dusty age, so much so that even Tib, whose nose was dulled by the many winters worth of his own pipes, was offended.

"Tenants been complain' a week about the stench," Edi continued, brandishing her broom. "I ain't got no answer to my knockin', so today I finally took my key and went in—and he's dead!"

Standing on the stoop of her three-story house, the old woman did not seem so much horrified as salaciously pleased, which heightened Tib's disgust. He was about to say that what Edi's tenants smelled was just as likely her reek as any dead body, but Kest placed a restraining hand on his arm. Sighing, Tib said, "We're happy to take a look."

Edi smiled at the four Watchmen. The few teeth she possessed were as brown as a corpse's, save one green stump directly in the front of her mouth. Augustus flinched. The hideous grin reminded him of the smiles carved into the chasecrows in the village fields where he'd grown up when the pumpkin heads had rotted after the reap.

"If you'll kindly point us to the door?" Kest said.

The old woman tottered off down the hall ahead of the Watchmen. "I hate foot patrol," Tib muttered.

"And you remind us every day," Guntyr said.

For the past three weeks the Watchmen had dealt with domestic disputes, reports of lost pets, complaints from shopkeepers about the vagrants sleeping near their doors and frightening away customers, tavern-room brawls, and dozens of other problems that plagued Argo's streets on a daily and seemingly endless basis. More nights than not they went home physically and mentally spent.

Worst of all, they were no closer to solving the riddle of the traitor in the Watch.

"Only five more weeks," Augustus—ever the optimist—said, patting Tib on the back. The fallout from the disaster at the Westing House had ended with their reprimand and a second month on patrol. The Magistrates had made it abundantly clear that if they stepped out of line in that time, their jobs would be in severe jeopardy. None of them, not even Kest, thought that was part of deeper plan by Head Magistrate Gringoir.

"I don't think I can make it," Tib groaned.

They followed old Edi down a dark, narrow hallway. Yellow lamps guttered on walls with peeling paper long faded to the color of old bones. Tib sniffed. The cramped passage smelled of musty age and filth, but was there something else? Some under-smell that might indeed be decay? He shook his head. If it was anything at all it was probably a mouse or a rat that had died in one of the walls. Those things could stink like hell.

He had all but convinced himself and dismissed the old woman as yet another loon—there seemed to be an inordinate number of people in Argo who had nothing better to do but waste the Watch's time with imagined or exaggerated nonsense—when Edi opened the door at the end of the hall.

"Aeton's bolts!" Tib shoved his hand reflexively to his mouth as the cloying odor of putrefaction belched out of the chamber.

"Whose rooms are these?" Guntyr asked.

"Don'ee know? Boy named Greystone. One of yours," Edi said, rubbing at a wart on her sunken cheek.

The lieutenants exchanged sharp glances. Mikael Greystone had been sent with the Unicorns to collect Thorne. He hadn't even been in these rooms for the past three weeks.

"Wait here," Guntyr ordered Matron Edi.

The Watchmen went in. There were framed portraits of Mikael and his parents and sister on a table in the hallway. A few books on a set of warped wooden shelves. An empty pot that once had held a plant. Everything appeared in order, but the sickly sweet and gamy stench of rotting meat was stronger.

There were two doorways, one straight ahead, the other opening off to the left. Kest motioned to the nearer room and led them in.

"Ah— God..." Kest's voice trailed off into silent dismay.

Mikael Greystone was seated in a chair. He looked more peacefully asleep than dead, but the dagger in his chest dispelled that illusion.

Kest pulled the weapon free. Black handle, black blade. "Gideon-gil," he said, casting the assassin's trademark dagger to the floor.

"Why would Gideon-gil kill Mikael Greystone?" Tib asked. "That's—"

"See? See? Dead—like I told'ee!" Matron Edi shrilled from the doorway, making the lieutenants spin around in surprise.

"Get her out!" Kest barked. "Get her out of here now!"

Guntyr blocked the old woman's way, forcing her back into the hall despite her protests.

"I don't understand it," Tib continued, growing angry. "Why do this? What a goddamned waste."

"There's another problem," Kest said, calmer now that the shock of the discovery had settled. He took off his glasses, rubbing them on his vest. "A bigger problem."

"What?" Augustus asked.

Kest gestured at the corpse. "If Greystone's dead, who went after Thorne?"

Part II

City of Shadows

19

The early sun beat upon the courtyard of Castle Aventar, where Argentia was working with the stick and the cats.

Sweat sheened her body despite the fact that she was wearing only a black lace brassiere and beige linen pants. The muscles in her bare arms, shoulders, and stomach stood out in sculpted detail, gleaming tight and hard in the bright morning light.

Argentia had not formally trained in many years, instead counting on her skill and speed to see her through her battles. Those things had always been enough, but against the twins she'd been lacking and lucky to escape with her life.

The next time they met, things would be much different.

She didn't want revenge. Didn't give a damn about the cat-women, in truth. Ikabod was all that mattered. If she could get him free without confrontation, she would do it and deal with Vloth and the rest later. But she doubted that would happen. Vloth was expecting her. The twins would be waiting.

She would be ready.

She turned a half-circle, focusing on the stalking cats. The two pards from the Crown's menagerie circled her, just out of reach of the stick. They moved with easy grace, their pace smooth and steady, no hesitation or coiling to indicate an impending attack, just circling, circling—

There! A scrape of paw on stone as the cat behind her tamped down and leaped. Argentia spun and lashed her stick against the leather armor protecting the spotted cat. She continued spinning through the blow and the second pard's swiping attack narrowly missed her. The cats had been de-clawed, but Argentia had learned their big paws still hurt when they hit.

She dropped to a knee, thrusting the stick behind her. The tip jabbed against armor, catching the first cat coming in again. Up like lightning, Argentia turned hard and unleashed a flurry of blows. The cat went down.

"Coat—stay!" shouted Croftian. The Beastkeeper was watching the bout, restraining the cats if Argentia struck a blow that would have been mortal in true combat.

Coat stayed down.

Where's the other? Argentia whirled, but the cat had outflanked her. A paw slammed her arm, knocking her sideways and down. She rolled, lessening the impact. Lost the stick. The pard leaped to bury her.

Argentia twisted onto her back, reaching for another weapon as several hundred pounds of cat pinned her. Before the muzzled face could thrust down into her, she jabbed her arm around, stabbing a short wooden dagger into the great cat's armored throat.

"Spot—stay!"

The pard went limp atop Argentia. "Oomph! Hey, get off me." Argentia dropped her weapon and swatted at the pard, but Spot did not move until a laughing Croftian called for him.

Freed, Argentia came to her knees and wiped her brow.

"Are you hurt, Lady?" The Beastkeeper was a young knight, not more than twenty-five, but very good with the animals.

"No, I'm fine." Argentia rose, took a drink from a pitcher of water on a stone bench, and then dumped the rest over her head. *Ahhhh—much better...*

"Good rounds today, Lady," Croftian said, stripping the armor and masks off Spot and Coat. The two pards flopped lazily in the sun.

"Thanks. The cats are great," Argentia replied, toweling off her dripping body. She'd been training with the pards for the past week, trying to prepare for the feline style of the twins, whose tandem attacks had all the speed and cunning of hunting cats.

"Will you want them again tomorrow?"

"I don't think that will be necessary," Amethyst said, crossing the courtyard.

It's about time, Argentia thought. In the fortnight since her arrival, she had trained hard every morning, shopped obscenely every afternoon—often with Amethyst, once or twice with Solsta, which caused quite a stir among the merchants of Duralyn—and eaten well every night. She had thoroughly enjoyed the luxury of Aventar and the company of her friends, but none of that could disguise the fact that she was really just waiting.

Now it seemed that waiting was about to end.

Amethyst strode up, her high-heeled, shiny, leather boots clicking on the stones. She wore a rust-colored skirt with a fringed hem and a diaphanous, tiger-striped blouse that clung like a second skin to her swollen breasts. She caught Croftian staring at her and blew him a kiss that made the Beastkeeper flush and turn his gaze hastily aside.

Most people believed Amethyst enjoyed nothing more than watching men fawn to receive a smile, but Argentia knew that behind that flirtatious facade was a true and fiercely loyal heart.

"Well?" Argentia asked. She could sense the guildmistress had news.

"We need to go shopping," Amethyst said.

"I think we've shopped Duralyn out." This wasn't what Argentia wanted to hear.

"Not quite. You need a gown."

"A gown?"

"A gown," Amethyst repeated patiently.

"Why do I need a gown?"

"I just spoke to my man in Telarban. We're going to a gala."

20

Argentia whistled under her breath.

The courtyard of Briarstone, Lord Parcifel's hilltop estate, overlooked Crescent Lake and all the southwest quarter of Telarban. On this warm, late-summer's night, the view was impressive. Piled thunderheads sweeping up from the south threatened the horizon—this was not called the Storm Moon without reason—but stars still littered the dark above the water of the lake, and the whole city spread out below, windows and lanterns glowing gold.

Somewhere among those buildings was Togril Vloth's guildhouse.

Somewhere in Briarstone was the key to getting into the thief's lair.

Because a direct assault on Vloth's guildhouse was out of the question for fear Ikabod would be killed before Argentia reached him, stealth was needed. Amethyst's agent in Telarban, Bendrake Ironclaw, had learned that the only way to access the guild with any hope of secrecy was through the sewers.

Unfortunately, Vloth knew this; he had been robbed that way once before. Now all the entrances to the sewers in Telarban were guarded—save one.

Blakeny Parcifel was Telarban's wealthiest noble. Blakeny had inherited his fortune; how his great-great grandsire had built it was something more shadowy. Beneath the Parcifel's hilltop estate was a warren of tunnels, some leading directly to Crescent Lake, others to the sewers. Much of the wealth young Blakeny enjoyed came from the profit on goods and treasures smuggled into the city.

The Parcifels were no longer involved in such trafficking. Blakeny's father had put an end to it, sensing the thieves' guilds that had grown to power in Telarban were too unpredictable to risk making enemies of.

By then, there had been no need of smuggling anyway. Their legitimate enterprises were more than sufficient to sustain them.

But the tunnels remained.

As did the trapdoor in the wine vaults that accessed them.

As did the key—passed on from father to son as a token of Fortune—that opened the trapdoor.

Argentia's plan was simple. Ralak had teleported the huntress and Amethyst in from Duralyn that afternoon. Bendrake supplied forged invitations as well as a diagram of the estate and a map of the sewers below. Once inside, they would isolate Lord Parcifel. Argentia would distract him while Amethyst lifted the key, which the lord was reputed to carry always on his person. Amid the commotion of the revel, Argentia would slip to the wine vaults, and from there to the tunnels, the sewers, and Ikabod.

Thunder rumbled disconsolately in the distance. Argentia gave a last glance to the coming storm then turned to Amethyst. "Shall we?"

"Let's," Amethyst replied, catching Argentia by the arm. They crossed the courtyard together and merged with the crowd converging on Briarstone.

The house was aptly named. Its stone facade and the twin towers of its east and west wings were covered with elegant masses of climbing roses. Delicately crafted windows peered out from these brambles. Squat blue firs flanked a pair of wrought-iron gates. Beyond the gates, a portico of chiseled columns supported a stone roof where two peacocks paced, squawking irritably at the guests.

At the rear of the portico were five stone steps, covered with a black carpet to prevent anyone slipping, leading to Briarstone's main doors. A constant flow of murmured amazement filtered back from the people entering to those still waiting in the train. When they were almost to the head of the line, Argentia finally able to see the source of all the ado.

Beyond the wide-flung doors, the floor of Briarstone's foyer was a smooth, unbroken plane of glass. It caught and reflected the glow from crystal chandeliers hung at different heights beneath the soaring vault of the ceiling. The effect created was as if the guests were stepping onto a lake of light.

Three huge fountains—alabaster leviathans spouting turquoise water to fill pools ringed by walls of pink marble—stood like islands in this lake. Beyond the fountains, two curving staircases mounted to a balcony backed by a huge colored-glass fresco depicting the Parcifel peacock, its tail spread in chromatic glory.

Guests were everywhere. Some stood upon the stairs, caught in conversation as they ascended or descended. Others loitered in the foyer, marveling at the monumental colored-glass window, while others danced to music from a string septet playing in the corner. But most were moving about the fountains, where pretty serving girls dressed as mermaids reclined on the walls encircling the pools, proffering food and drink from gilded trays.

Argentia, who had been in the company of real sea-elves, almost laughed.

"Your invitations, ladies?" a porter said, drawing Argentia from her distraction. Her heart skipped. If their forgeries were discovered, the whole plan was undone.

She needn't have worried. The porters were much more interested in Amethyst's cleavage than in the falsified parchments she handed over—nor were the doormen the only ones guilty of such a trespass.

Amethyst wore a glittering sheath. Its black-and-gold diamond pattern was pebbled like snakeskin, its cut scooped low and tight across her breasts so that those creamy mounds swelled above the fabric like twin waves gathering to break. Matching sandals, impressively heeled, lifted her short frame several inches higher, making the muscles in her calves stand out like juts of rock. Brassy hair tumbled down her back in gorgonian coils, thick and perfumed and inviting. A golden serpent wound its way down her left arm. Her right was bare of any accessory that might impede her from snaring Lord Parcifel's key.

Argentia wore emerald: a sleeveless, backless lace confection that tied behind her neck, split down the front almost to her pierced navel, and was so teasingly sheer that it left little doubt about the lines and curves of her body. Black heels, black earrings, and a black pick in the red braid wound tightly atop her head completed the ensemble. The dragon's tooth token was a silver highlight.

It was by far the most revealing gown Argentia had ever worn, but that was all right. They had come to be noticed—and noticed they were.

Trills of laughter, currents of conversation slowed. Men and women both eyed the newcomers. Had two such beauties ever been seen together in Telarban before? And to enter so brazenly—unescorted, no less. Women sniffed and sneered, though the more secure among them acknowledged the pair with brief smiles or nods. Men suddenly found the foyer much more interesting in the area where Argentia and Amethyst were standing.

There were invitations to dance. Offers of drink and food. Amethyst accepted everything gaily, reveling in the attention and atmosphere.

Argentia, who normally loved such affairs just as much as Amethyst did, had a harder time. She rejected company out of hand, no matter how smooth the approach or how handsome the man. Suitors went away confused, some even a little angry. The fiery presentation and frigid demeanor were off-putting.

Argentia didn't notice or didn't care. Her mind was on Ikabod, her eye constantly roving, her hands fidgeting with her small black purse.

Finally Amethyst drew her aside.

"Where is he?" Argentia whispered fiercely. "I only have until midnight."

"Calmly," Amethyst clucked. "Midnight's two hours away. He'll come. Have a drink. Go dance. You need to relax."

"Don't tell me—"

Amethyst cut her off. "I will tell you, honey. I know you're worried about Ikabod, but the last thing we need is somebody causing a scene later because they're bitter you rejected them and drunk enough to say something about it."

Argentia sighed. Amethyst was right, and she knew it. She was letting her thoughts get too far ahead of her.

"You go on," Amethyst said. "I'll watch for our friend."

So Argentia went and caught the first man she saw that she remembered had approached her. "How about that dance?" she asked, putting on her most dazzling smile.

It worked like a charm.

Partner to partner, piece after piece, Argentia danced, and danced, and was still dancing when the gong sounded.

"Ladies and lords! Ladies and lords!" a butler in immaculate black livery announced as the crowd quieted. "I present Lord Parcifel."

Finally.... Argentia disengaged herself from her latest companion and turned with the rest of the revelers toward the balcony, where at last their elusive host appeared.

21

Lord Blakeny Parcifel was tall, trim, and gorgeous, with bright hazel eyes behind gold-rimmed glasses and thick blonde hair swept back from his face like the crest of a golden eagle. His clothes were elegant: a long black silk jacket over a stark white open-throated shirt (the key, Argentia noted, hung brightly around his neck, just above the broad slab of his chest) and fitted charcoal pants.

Turned twenty-two this very day, he looked the perfect young aristocrat, but he seemed ill at ease as he peered down from the balcony, blinking owlishly behind his glasses. One hand was hidden in the pocket of his coat, the other clenched the railing tightly. The crowd applauded him, but even before he spoke Argentia heard some snickering. It didn't take her long to figure out why.

"L-l-ladies and l-lords. Th-th-th-thank you f-for c-c-coming t-to m-my age r-rite," Blakeny stuttered. The snickers increased. "I am honored, and I h-h-hope you enjoy the h-h-h-hospi…hospitality…" He forced out this last word, gave a short bow, and retreated from the balcony amid applause that was only partially sincere.

At a quick signal from the severe-looking butler, the septet started playing again. Argentia looked around for Amethyst. *Where the hell is she?* The bells that kept the hour had not yet struck eleven. There was plenty of time—if they could get to Parcifel now.

A hand tapped Argentia's shoulder gently. She turned and saw a Watch uniform.

No! She flinched, ready to wheel and flee.

"Pardon, Lady," the strapping Watch Captain said. "I didn't mean to startle you." He flashed a smile full of square, white teeth and nodded towards the dance floor. "May I have the privilege?"

Argentia recovered quickly. "I'm sorry, but I'm afraid I'm going to stand this one out. My friend—"

"—has been looking *all over* for you!" Amethyst said, appearing beside them. "And of course I find you in the company of the most handsome man here. Captain, how delightful!" She extended her hand and the captain pressed it to his lips. "But you must forgive us," Amethyst continued. "We've an audience on the balcony that positively can't wait."

"I understand, ladies. The loss is mine." The captain bowed and withdrew.

"Thanks," Argentia said as Amethyst towed her along towards the steps. She felt unbalanced: her mind still on Ikabod and on the way she cringed guiltily every time she saw a Watchman. *Better get it together Gen, and fast. You're only going to get one try with Parcifel...* "Did you see the key?" she asked.

"I saw it. Bad luck there, but not the worst. It's on him. I can get it," Amethyst replied confidently.

But by the time they reached the balcony, there was no sign of Lord Parcifel. "Where the hell did he go?" Argentia muttered. "He was just here."

There were perhaps two-dozen people milling about, goblets in hand, chatting in groups of four or five. Parcifel was not among them, but there were corridors to the left and right of the colored-glass peacock; he could easily have gone down on of those.

Like that one, Argentia thought, spotting the butler coming out of the passage on the right. "Pardon me," she said, moving to meet him. "We're looking for Lord Parcifel."

"Lord Parcifel has retired for the evening."

"But we have to speak with him. It's very important. Please?"

"Lord Parcifel has retired," the butler repeated with an air of finality. "Now if you will excuse me, I have duties to attend." The butler marched away and down the steps.

"Retired, eh?" Amethyst echoed.

"Right. Let's go." Argentia glanced to make certain they were unobserved, and then led Amethyst quickly down the hallway. At its end, they peeked around the corner into a short corridor. Saw a doorway, the beginning of a flight of steps, and two guards.

God damn it... "He must be upstairs. Can you distract those two?"

"Please. Do you have to even ask?" Amethyst scoffed. She lifted her serpent-wound arm and perfumed herself with a cloud of mist from the ornament's open mouth. "Now, what are *you* going to be doing?"

"I'm going up to get that key."

"How?"

"I'll think of something."

"You're mad."

"I've heard. Can you give me half an hour?"

"I don't think that will be a problem."

They stepped out into the corridor, Amethyst leading. The guards saw them. "Excuse me, ladies. You're not supposed to be back here," one said, though from the way his eyes roved over Argentia and Amethyst, he didn't seem too put out by their intrusion.

"We have an audience with Lord Parcifel," Amethyst said. The men were tall but not particularly muscular or fit. They were wearing the livery of the Parcifel house, and unarmed. The guildmistress marked them as servants playing guards for the night, which would make this little trick that much easier.

"Lord Parcifel has retired for the evening. He's not to be disturbed."

"Oh…" Amethyst looked crushed. "There must be some mistake. He promised… But… I don't suppose *you'd* give me a tour of the manor?" She stepped closer, crooking a finger under each man's chin. Her eyes shone hypnotically. She ran her palms along the guards' cheeks, letting the magic of her perfume wash over them. Argentia could almost see their eyes glazing over. *What the hell is she doing to them?*

Whatever it was, it was working.

Amethyst stepped back and pulled open the nearest door. "Oooooh—a *bed*! Let's start our tour in here."

The men nodded eagerly. "What about her?" one asked, still in enough possession of his wits to notice Argentia. "She coming too?"

"Tut—never mind about her," Amethyst scolded, ushering the men into the room. "Half an hour," she mouthed to Argentia. Then she blew her a kiss and followed the guards into the chamber, closing the door behind her.

Argentia hesitated a moment, suddenly not sure if this was such a good idea. *She can handle herself. Go get the key….*

With a final glance around the empty corridor, Argentia started up the steps of Lord Parcifel's tower.

22

The door at the top of the tower was unlocked

Argentia pulled it open, pausing on the threshold. Within were books. Books on shelves that reached the ceiling. Books on ornate tables. Books stacked on the floor. The room smelled of parchment and leather: good smells. There was also a bed, a desk, and a chair where Blakeny Parcifel sat with a volume open beneath a lamp.

The lord of Briarstone raised his head at the creak of the door's hinges. "Who are y-y-you? I d-don't s-see v-vi-visitors!"

Argentia came in anyway, closing the door behind her. Parcifel looked as if he would shrink into one of the desk drawers if he could. His eyes darted every way, seeking escape that was not there.

Argentia lifted her hands as she approached him. "Easy, my Lord," she said. Bendrake Ironclaw had doubted Parcifel had any ties to Vloth; the noble likely did not even know what the key around his neck was for. That doubt was enough to keep Argentia from treating Parcifel as an enemy, but not enough for her to extend trust.

It was a quandary. She wouldn't assault him without provocation, she couldn't risk just asking for the key in case he was in Vloth's pocket, and to complicate matters further, she found herself pitying this unfortunate young man who had a house full of guests who mocked and scorned him for his infirmities yet were willing to take advantage of his hospitality.

But I need that key, damn it…

"What are you reading?" she asked, stalling for time.

"It's the Inquisition of Mag-magus F-Faestos," Blakeny said in his halting speech. "H-have y-you r-read it?"

Argentia smiled sadly. "No. I like to read, but I don't have much time. I'm frequently on the road. I'm Argentia Dasani, from Argo."

Blakeny took her proffered hand, hesitated a moment, then raised it briefly to his lips. When Argentia did not flinch, he seemed to relax a little more. "I n-noticed you from the b-balcony," he admitted, flushing a little."

"I'm flattered," Argentia said. For a moment the air between them was charged with attraction. Blakeny, unschooled in how to navigate those waters, retreated to safer shores.

"W-what are y-you d-doing up here, L-Lady? M-most w-women d-don't w-want to b-bother with m-me because of my s-st-utter. D-don't you w-wish to b-be w-with the other g-g-guests? I'm s-sure you'd have you ch-ch-choice of m-men who are b-better company than m-me."

"Actually, I find their company boring." Argentia laughed. Blakeny smiled: a flash of moonlight. Argentia wondered if he had any idea how ridiculously handsome he was. *And I'm not even that into blondes...* "So I came up to see if I could give you something for your age-rite. I hope you won't find it too forward a gift." She bent and took his head in her hands and kissed him.

Blakeny drew back in surprise.

"What's wrong?" Argentia asked.

"Are y-you one of th-those w-women?"

"One of what women?"

"The ones my m-m-mother w-warned me about. The ones after my f-f-ortune. She t-told me th-they w-were the o-only ones who w-would want m-m-me."

What a bitch. No wonder he's hiding up here... "I don't want your fortune. I have more money than I know what to do with. I promise, I'm not one of those women."

"Then wh-why are y-you d-doing th-this?"

She pressed a finger to his lips. "Do I need a reason?"

"N-no! It's j-just I...."

"I mean, if I've offended you, if you want me to leave—"

"No! I c-couldn't im-magine a f-f-finer p-present," Blakeny said.

"Flatterer." Kissing him again, Argentia pulled the ties on her gown. When she straightened up, it slid down her body like emerald rain. Her green thong followed it. Blakeny gawped at her dragonfly tattoo, as if waiting for it to fly right off her flesh.

Argentia smiled and extended her hand to him. When he rose, his bespectacled face wore the look of a frightened rabbit. "I've—"

"It's all right," Argentia said quietly. "Leave everything to me."

She led him to the bed.

Somewhere in the manor, a bell tolled eleven.

A breathless, exhausting half-hour later, Blakeny Parcifel was snoring soundly. Argentia, dressed again, plucked the key from the pile of his clothes and kissed the young noble gently on the forehead.

"Sleep well," she whispered, just a touch of guilt in her voice. It wasn't the first time she'd used her body as a means to an end, or her first one-night stand, but those were hardly habits, and even then the circumstances had never been quite like this.

What else was I supposed to do? Knock him over the head and just take the stupid key? She hoped Blakeny wouldn't think ill of her when he woke and she was long gone. Perhaps what she'd done had been crueler than simply knocking him over the head.

She shook such thoughts away. She'd done what she needed to do. She had the key that would help her save Ikabod. Now it was time to put it to use.

Argentia went quickly down from the tower chamber. As promised, Amethyst was waiting where she'd left her. Argentia held up the key and grinned triumphantly.

"What kept you?" Amethyst asked. Then she noticed Argentia's rumpled gown, the loose tendrils of hair falling over her forehead, and the flush creeping from her throat down between her breasts. "You didn't! You *are* mad! Where is he now?"

"Sleeping like a baby."

"That was your plan?"

"Not exactly—"

"What if he didn't fall asleep?"

"They all fall asleep."

Amethyst laughed. "True. Well—how was he?"

"Let's just say the local girls don't know what they're missing," Argentia leaned and whispered in Amethyst's ear.

"What?" the guildmistress exclaimed. "This I have to see."

Amethyst put a foot on the steps. Argentia caught her arm and pulled her back, "Will you just come on!" She started down the corridor. "Hey—what happened to those guards?"

"Oh, they're all tied up."

The foyer was still loud and full of guests when Argentia and Amethyst descended. They stood together against the wall near the hallway adjacent to the left-hand stairwell. According to Bendrake's map, the hallway accessed the kitchens and serving wing. Midnight was nigh. Thunder crashed over the music of the septet. Argentia didn't hear any rain, but she could tell the storm was very close now.

"Ready?" Amethyst asked quietly.

Argentia nodded. "You'll be all right?"

"Don't worry about me. I'll make enough of a fuss to get you clear of this crowd and I'll meet you back at Bendrake's." Amethyst's smile was so insolently confident it put to rest Argentia's pang of concern.

"By dawn at the latest," Argentia confirmed. "If we're not there by then, you get the hell out of this city and back to Duralyn."

"I will," Pyth lied. "But don't worry. You'll be there. Both of you." She popped up on her toes and kissed Argentia's cheek. "Fortune follow you."

With that, the guildmistress headed into the crowd. Moments later there was a feminine shriek, a noise of glass shattering, and Amethyst's outraged voice crying, "Look what you've done, you clumsy sow! You've ruined my dress!"

Argentia bit back a smile as all the attention folded in on the railing guildmistress, including a bunch of maids hurrying to attend the spilled wine and broken glass. *Okay, go....*

She ducked through the doorway into the serving corridor and was gone.

23

Corridor to corridor Argentia raced against midnight.

Fortune was with her. She saw no servants and soon had left the din of the foyer behind. A narrow stairwell brought her down into the cellars: chambers dank with the smells of sunless stone.

Following the route she'd memorized off Bendrake's map, she entered the wine vault. It was a massive, dimly lit, and cryptlike. Bottles by the dozens were laid to rest in dark wooden racks. Tuns were stacked two and three high in long rows. *Ralak would love to see this*, Argentia thought. The wizard was a great connoisseur.

A minute of searching and she found the trapdoor. It was artfully seamed into the stone floor, but Argentia had looked for such things in other places, and her eye was true.

The keyhole was a simple notch in an adjacent stone. At a glance, it looked to be no more than a deep chip. The key turned a hidden lock. The stone tilted up, revealing a shallow recess and an iron ring.

Argentia pulled on the ring, which was attached to a chain in the floor. Metal grated. The trapdoor tried to spring up, but failed. *Come on...* Argentia pulled again. Felt the grinding in the floor beneath her feet, where the mechanisms had warped with age and disuse. The trapdoor was stuck.

No. No... She pulled again, to no avail.

Heard the voices.

She yanked on the chain with all her strength, breaking two nails. The stubborn door remained jammed.

Cursing, Argentia kicked the panel shut and ducked amid the racks, withdrawing into the darkest corner, crouching low in the cobwebs, praying the voices belonged to servants and not guests who had snuck down for a tryst—and if it was servants, that they weren't coming to steal a break over a bottle of Briarstone's finest. If midnight struck while they were nearby, she was going to have a lot of explaining to do.

Again Fortune was with her. Two servants entered, loaded a tun onto a wheelbarrow, and departed.

Thank God... Argentia pulled off her heels, hurried back to the trapdoor, and jumped on the stone, trying to loosen the hold of many winters. Then she dragged on the chain again, pouring all her will into the effort. This stupid piece of rusted machinery would not defeat her.

Come on, damn you! Another pull, and a third—

The resistance broke, sending Argentia stumbling backwards. She caught her balance and punched the air triumphantly as the trapdoor rose with a gnashing, grating protest to reveal a ladder into unbroken darkness.

Argentia tossed the key into the entrance of the wine vault, where—she hoped—it eventually would be found and returned to Lord Parcifel. She fastened her heels on again, climbed partway down the ladder, grabbed a handle on the underside of the trapdoor, pulled it closed above her, and descended in the black.

When her sandals touched the ground, she opened her small purse. Blue light flooded forth, illuming the rough-cut stone and low ceiling of the tunnel that would take her to the sewers.

Crouching, Argentia shoved her arm elbow-deep into the purse—which was really an aethereal pocket cleverly disguised by Ralak—and pulled out her weapons, her pack, and a torch. She snapped the purse closed, lit the torch, and waited.

For a long minute, nothing happened. Then, just as her impatience was getting the best of her, Argentia's gown began to glimmer. In moments she was blazing more brightly than the torch, light shooting off her body as the emerald lace refashioned into a black halter and buckskins, and the heeled sandals became once more her trusty boots.

Midnight had come, breaking the enchantment that had transformed her traveling clothes into a replica of the gown she'd purchased for Lord Parcifel's gala before she'd realized there was no way to wear such an outfit and bring what she would need to rescue Ikabod.

The scintillating glow faded. Argentia glanced over her reborn attire. *Perfect. I owe you one, Ralak,* she thought as she strapped on her weapons. Somehow she was sure she'd have a chance to repay the Archamagus for his magical assistance: wizards were famous debt-collectors.

Argentia consulted the map of the sewers that Bendrake had provided, shouldered her pack, and started walking.

Just hold on a little longer, Ikabod. I'm coming...

24

Telarban in the teeth of the storm.

The wind whipped Crescent Lake into waves and howled through the empty streets and alleys of the city, driving rain that quickly flooded the cobbled ways. Thunder rolled. Lightning raked the roiling sky. Telarbanians shuttered their windows tightly against the woeful night, wishing the storm to end.

Thorne wished it to worsen.

Already the lanterns posted on many streets had blown out, leaving blocks of the city drenched in darkness. The more the rain and thunder fell, the more distracted the guards at Vloth's guildhouse would be—and the easier Thorne's assault.

He stepped back from the alley's mouth, rain pouring off his hood and cloak, and looked at those gathered behind him: Tiboren, Kest, Guntyr, and Augustus. Though he gave no sign, he was glad they were there. It closed the circle. They had been there when Vendi died. They would be there when she was avenged.

"It's time," he said.

"We're ready," Tib replied, spitting a bit of fingernail into a puddle. They weren't—he didn't know how anyone could be ready to lay siege to a guildhouse with no inkling of what waited within—but they were going anyway. *And we knew it. We knew when we left Argo that it would come to this...*

Standing there in the rotten chamber with the corpse of Mikael Greystone, it had taken only minutes for the lieutenants to piece together the plot.

Gideon-gil had murdered the Watchman and then—through some magic or another—assumed his guise and gone off in pursuit of Thorne.

"There are such spells," Augustus assured the skeptical Tib. "Very powerful, very rare, but I wouldn't put it past Gideon-gil to own such magic."

"Great," Tib muttered. The thought that the infamous elven assassin might have the capacity to appear in shapes other than his own was hardly reassuring. "But *why* is Gideon-gil after Thorne?"

"The traitor," Guntyr rumbled.

"Has to be," Kest said, replacing his glasses and running a hand through his spiky hair. "Someone doesn't want Thorne to come back. Someone who fears what Thorne knows."

"But Thorne doesn't know who the traitor is," Tib protested.

"We know that," Kest said. "But the traitor doesn't."

"What do we do?" Augustus asked. "There must be someone we can tell."

"No," Kest said, making the last connection. "The only ones we could tell would be the Magistrates, and we can't do that because one of them is the traitor."

The others stared at him.

"Think about it," Kest said. "We should have seen it weeks ago. Who else but a Magistrate would have access to enough information to keep those twins ahead of us for so long? And who but a Magistrate would have enough to lose to risk murdering Thorne to keep their secret?"

Tib nodded. "You're right. A lieutenant, even a captain, they'd be imprisoned or exiled, but a treasonous magistrate would be executed."

"So what do we do?" Augustus repeated.

"We go after Thorne," Guntyr said. "We have no choice. We cannot leave him with such danger at his back."

The Norden's words hung in the air like a curse.

"It's not that easy," Tib said. "We don't even know where he's gone."

"We do," Guntyr replied firmly. "Lady Dasani mentioned those twins were from Togril Vloth. Vloth's domain is Telarban. That is where Thorne is bound."

It made sense, but it didn't make their decision any easier. "You know this will mean the end for us here," Kest said quietly. "As Watchmen, at least. If we desert."

The others nodded, one after another. They had let Thorne go his own way to pursue the twins, believing themselves duty-bound to serve the city, not vengeance. Now things had changed. Thorne was in deadly peril from Gideon-gil. To do nothing was tantamount to sentencing Thorne to death.

None of them said they were going. None of them had to. "I can get us to Pont," Augustus said. "That's as far north as I've ever been, but it should still save us weeks of travel. We can get mounts there."

"Meet at my house at seven," Kest said. "That's enough time for everyone to settle their affairs, right?"

"What about Mikael?" Augustus pointed to the young Watchman's corpse.

"We dare not risk reporting this," Guntyr said.

"We can't just leave him," Augustus argued.

"Actually, maybe we can," Tib said. "At least for a night. Depends on whether you're actually any good with that magic you're always talking about."

"What do you mean?"

"I want you to have a little chat with Matron Edi on our way out. Make her forget we were ever here. Can you do that?"

"Can you lace your own boots?" the halfling replied.

"Good. Tomorrow she'll summon the Watch again and the body will be found, but we'll be long gone."

That evening, the four renegade Watchmen met at Kest's small home, where Augustus took them through the aether to Pont. Left behind, Guntyr's wife Bryget—tall and blonde and stoic—and Kest's wife Lyrissa—small and mousy and red-eyed from crying—wondered what danger their husbands were going into, and what would happen to them when they were expelled from the Watch on their return.

If they returned.

25

Riding hard out of Pont, the lieutenants caught up with Thorne on the Westway, about a week east of Telarban.

"Come to arrest me as well?" Thorne asked, facing them as they dismounted at his camp.

"No. To rescue you," Tib said.

Thorne smiled harshly. "From Gideon-gil, no doubt."

The lieutenants were stunned. Thorne told his tale: the murders of Orion Reth and the Unicorns, the revelation of Gideon-gil, and the assassin's strange flute.

"That music... It was like being trapped in a dream," Thorne said, shaking his head. Even now his memories of that brief time as Gideon-gil's prisoner were vague and twisted. "I spoke...of things— I don't know what. I had no power, no control. He questioned, I answered..." He trailed off, shaking his head again, clearly still frustrated by the violation of his mind. "Then I slept. When I woke, I was alone and unbound. I have seen no sign of the assassin since."

The lieutenants glanced at each other. Despite their haste, were it not for the strange and frightening mercy of Gideon-gil, they would have failed.

For his part, Thorne was little concerned with the assassin or the traitor who had sent him, though he agreed with his lieutenants that it was likely a Magistrate. Those things were to be dealt with after Telarban.

After the twins.

"What will you do now?" Thorne asked. He did not thank them for coming for him, nor did the lieutenants expect it: such was Thorne's way. What emotion he owned had mostly died with his wife and child, and the fragile thing that had survived that tragedy had perished with Vendi.

Again the lieutenants looked at each other. Telarban was only days away. Could they stand so close to vengeance for Vendi and turn again from the deed that in their hearts they knew they should have been about all along—especially when they were already derelict in their duty and had nothing to look for in Argo but the stripping of their rank and expulsion?

They could not.

So they set their course with Thorne's and entered Telarban as five travelers, their uniforms and official identities abandoned in Argo. The Gate Keeper directed them to lodge at an inn called the Black Gryphon. Once there, Thorne sent Tib, who had an infallible nose for the streets—even those he had never trod before—to learn where Vloth was lairing.

Telarban's mercantile district was divided into several interconnected squares. There were a few street vendors, but almost all trade was conducted in shops and stores. Tib, accustomed to the bazaar-like atmosphere of Argo's great Market Square, found the dreary, crowded streets of Telarban little to his liking. *And filthy. This place is worse than the Undercity,* he thought, realizing how much he'd always taken for granted the pristine white marble ways of Argo. *Probably only see them once more—for my sentence to exile,* he lamented. But he had made his choice. If exile was to be his fate, he would find a way to survive.

He turned a corner, fighting these grim thoughts. A crooked sign in shaky scrawl reading *THE MARKET* caught his attention. It hung over the door of an unassuming little produce shop. It was the type of place that looked as if it was barely scraping by, and might, therefore, escape the attention of a guildmaster's extortionist eye.

Tib opened the door. The Market smelled of overripe fruit and rotted vegetables. The proprietor was an old man named Nikreid, who was ninety but looked seventy and moved with what Tib thought was remarkable vigor and surety. His eye gleamed when Tib set a coin on the counter and said, "I need some information."

"Costly, in Telarban," Nikreid said. A second coin joined the first. The old man slid them into a pocket, then reached out and took Tib's arm. His hand was liver-spotted, but his grip was firm. "What would you know?"

"The location of Togril Vloth's guild."

"Costlier still, that." Nikreid glanced around, as if the mere mention of Vloth frightened him. He and Tib were alone amid the vegetables.

Tib placed a third coin on the counter. "Do you know it?"

"Might be that I do."

Old man Nikreid's directions had been worth their cost. By midnight, Thorne and his lieutenants were positioned in an alley across the street from Vloth's well-disguised guildhouse: a run-down, five-story shamble of bricks that, like so many buildings in Telarban, looked abandoned or condemned. They were waiting for the storm to reach its pitch.

Now that time had come.

"There will be bowmen, no doubt," Thorne said.

"The windows of the warehouses," Kest agreed, pointing to the two long, low building flanking Vloth's guild. His own bow was beneath his cloak. It would be little use in the initial moments of this attack.

"No matter. The rain and dark will cover us well enough if we are swift. Wizard, I want that door down well before we reach it."

Augustus nodded. His wand was out and ready. The magical glyphs warding the guildhouse door were strong enough that he could sense them from where he was standing. *I won't fail*, he told himself to bolster his confidence. *Not tonight...*

The others drew their weapons. Touched the blades against Thorne's baton.

"Remember Vendi," Thorne said. "No mercy."

They charged from their alley, splashing through the puddles. The storm covered them. It had already driven all the vagrants they had seen lounging about the warehouses earlier—guards in disguise, they were certain—indoors.

The way was clear.

The archers were at the windows, positioned to turn the alley between the warehouses into a killing floor. By the time they registered the five fast-moving forms in the storm, Augustus' wand was glowing white-hot.

"*Eloin-han!*" the halfling cried.

The lightning answered.

The night was broken with brightness as a jagged stroke boomed out of the torrid skies, following the thrust of the halfling's wand down the alley and obliterating the door to Vloth's guild.

Augustus' eyes went wide. He had summoned lightning before, but never from a storm like this. The power of the elements conjoined with the power of the aether had been devastating. The lintel and frame of Vloth's door were blazing, and the door itself had been blown to smoking shards.

The archers banged their windows open and fired, but wind and rain and haste defeated their aim. The five ran on, bursting through the flaming ruin of the door.

Confusion reigned within. The guards who had been stationed at the door lay in blasted heaps, dying or dead. Others were rushing toward the shattered entrance, uncertain whether the damage was from the storm or from an assault.

By the time they realized the five charging Argosians weren't men of the guild, it was too late.

26

This is ridiculous...

Argentia was in water past her knees. The storm had struck when—according to Bendrake's map—she was about halfway to Vloth's guild. The sewers had quickly begun to flood. The churning current was strong enough that if she fell she might be swept a good distance away, but Argentia went recklessly on. Now that she was so close to Ikabod, every moment she was delayed seemed to increase the butler's risk a hundredfold.

She tried not to think about it as she forged her way from tunnel to tunnel, sometimes in passages so wide she could not see the walls in the torchlight, other times in spaces so cramped she had to duck to keep below the slimy ceiling. The sewers were dark and deafening with the thunder of cataracts dumping down runoff from the streets of Telarban. They stank like nothing Argentia had ever encountered before: a foul miasma of rot and refuse stirred up by the deluge. It seemed to cling to her beyond any hope of washing off.

Floating debris, including various dead animals, clipped at her legs, trying to trip her up. She frequently had to throw herself against the algae-crusted walls to avoid particularly large crates or sacks of God-knew-what, and once even a bloat corpse.

Worst of all, however, was when she turned a corner and saw a pack of rats pouring by the dozens out of the holes in the walls, squealing as they tumbled and splashed into the dark water.

Revolted, Argentia hurried past, swiping with her torch at any red-eyed vermin that swam near. She hated rats.

After an hour's nightmarish navigation from the tunnel beneath Briarstone, light appeared ahead of Argentia, filtering from a grate in the ceiling of a shallow alcove. From what Bendrake had told her, the grate had originally been an escape route from the lower floors of Vloth's guild. Tonight, it would provide her entrance instead.

Argentia extinguished her torch and shoved it in her pack. Entering the alcove, she looked up through the grate into Vloth's guildhouse. She could see at an angle into a corridor, but there was no way to determine if there were guards. *Have to risk it...*

She mounted a short iron ladder bolted into the wall, slipped her fingers into the grate, and pushed. The iron grill was sealed tight, or simply too heavy for her to budge. *All right, we do this the loud way...*

Argentia dug a small Nhapian firestick out of her pack and poked it through a metal square so it lay across the grate. Striking a lucifer to the short wick, she dropped off the ladder and splashed around the corner.

Seconds later, a flash of light filled the alcove. There was a roaring blast of heat as the firestick detonated. Argentia heard things falling into the water.

Smoke wafted out into the sewer. When it had cleared, Argentia reentered the alcove and climbed the ladder again, peeking her head up through a gaping hole edged by twisted, smoking iron.

The corridor was empty.

Argentia boosted herself into the guildhouse. There were still no guards in sight, nor any sound of their approach, which made her very nervous. Even with the storm, there was no way the firestick's explosion should have gone unnoticed.

Trap. But how did he know I was coming tonight?

Vloth had expected her, of course—the whole point of abducting Ikabod had been to ensure Argentia would come for the butler and fall into whatever vengeance the guildmaster had plotted—but he couldn't have been prepared for her arrival tonight, or by the sewers. *Unless he got to Bendrake somehow. Or Amethyst...*

Argentia hoped her friend was all right. *Can't worry about her now. Can't worry about any of this...* She would just have to try to find Ikabod and get out, trusting her blade and her luck to see her past whatever Vloth had waiting for her.

She started searching. The corridor was lined on both sides with gilded vault doors that stood open to reveal a trove more massive than anything Argentia had seen since the horde of Dracovadarbon.

There was an entire vault that looked to be full of gold coin: stack after stack, each nearly as tall as Argentia, in rows a dozen deep or more. Another vault was devoted strictly to diamonds, and a third to emeralds.

Just the stones, no settings. Finished pieces of jewelry were collected in two other vaults.

It was an amazing, audacious display of wealth and power. Not only to have such vast treasures, but to be so confident that you were unassailable that you didn't even need to lock them away—Vloth's arrogance boggled Argentia's mind.

Unless it wasn't arrogance. Unless things weren't what they seemed. Just because Bendrake's man had made no mention of magical wards didn't mean there weren't such defenses in place.

Argentia had no intention of finding out whether her instinct was on the mark. She didn't need to enter any of the vaults to see that Ikabod wasn't in there. *Like it would be that easy…*

Argentia headed for the stairs. She'd been in Vloth's guildhouse before, but only on the upper floors, so she didn't know exactly what the other levels contained. She would have to search room by room, floor by floor until she found Ikabod or until Vloth's guards found her.

Speaking of which, no one had come to investigate the explosion yet. More convinced than ever that she was walking into a trap, Argentia started climbing.

Lamps in golden frames lit the stairwell. The rug carpeting the stone steps was a rare import from Nhapia. It would have been a meticulously cared for treasure in Argentia's home. Here it was used like a two-copper junk weaving to be trod on by filthy boots. For some ill-defined reason, Vloth's cavalier treatment of the rug made Argentia angrier than the wide-open vaults. She thought about the extra firesticks in her bag. *I ought to throw one into a vault. Blow all his stuff to Hell….* She smirked. *Maybe on the way out. But first…*

The level above was just as deserted as the vault floor. This was all so clearly a set-up, yet there was nothing Argentia could do but go on. She passed by several gruesome-looking torture chambers stocked with demonic instruments. At the end of that hallway was a grim, oaken door banded with iron: a dungeon door if she'd ever seen one. A ring of keys hung on a nail beside it. *How convenient*, Argentia thought blackly.

She opened the door. Torchlight glinted within, breaking the shadows. It was very quiet. "Ikabod?"

No answer.

Argentia went in. Unnoticed, a small glyphstone above the lintel flashed as she crossed the threshold.

There were a dozen cells, all on the left-hand side of the dungeon, which made things somewhat easier. Their doors were solid iron. Argentia went quickly down the line, banging on each one, calling Ikabod's name, praying to hear his voice.

No answer.

That didn't mean Ikabod wasn't here, though. He could be bound and gagged, or unconscious—unable to hear her or respond. She had to be sure before she moved on.

Returning to the first cell, Argentia fumbled with the key ring. There were twelve keys for twelve doors, but none of them were marked. Cursing, Argentia glanced around. The eerie silence in the dungeon was disturbed only by the crackle of the torches. Where were the guards? The twins?

Doesn't matter. Just hurry...

Argentia tried key after key, her nervousness increasing with each mismatch. *Come on, come on, damn it...*

The lock turned.

Argentia pulled the door open and grabbed a torch from its sconce, thrusting the light into the dark cell.

Empty.

Clenching her teeth, Argentia went to the next cell and repeated the process.

Empty again.

The pattern continued down the line. Argentia's hope faded a bit more with each empty cell. By the time she came to the tenth cell she was convinced they were all empty, but she tried anyway, her movements rote, her mind frantic. If Ikabod was being held in the upper levels, she was going to have to fight through Vloth's entire guild to get him. Even she had to admit the odds of success were grim.

The tenth cell was unoccupied. So was the eleventh. Argentia pushed the key into the lock of the twelfth and final door. Opened it. Raised the torch.

A human shape lay beneath a blanket on a long metal bench. Argentia caught her breath. "Ikabod?"

She entered the cell, her heart racing with dread. "Ikabod?"

Argentia pulled the blanket back.

Ikabod's blackened skull grinned at her from above the collar of his livery.

27

Argentia screamed and fell to her knees, the torch dropping from her senseless fingers. "No," she gasped. "No no no no..."

Ikabod was gone. The man who had been like a father to her was now this charred bag of bones, his flesh disintegrated by some fell fire. Not since Carfax had died in her arms had Argentia's heart broken like this. *Oh God—I tried. I tried. Oh Ikabod...* She slumped against the bench and sobbed.

"Look at this, crying like some tit-sucking little baby. Thought you were supposed to be some tough bitch," a voice mocked her.

Argentia twisted around. Vloth's guards were moving into the cell: two in the lead, two more in the doorway, six more behind them in the dungeon. All were clad in chitinous armor. All were armed with cudgels and maces.

Argentia rose, tears in her eyes, rage in her soul. She drew her katana with slow deliberation. Leveled it at the guards. "Dead," she said quietly.

She had been training for the twins. Vloth's guards, who would have been pressed to defeat Argentia at her worst, never stood a chance against her at her best. She cut through them like a reaping wind. Killed the first four before any of them could even raise a weapon against her. Then she was out of the cell, charging the remaining six, not even aware that she was screaming.

A guard rushed her from the left. She didn't even bother with the parry. Beat him with pure speed, spinning and slashing her katana into his neck. His helmeted head flew into Ikabod's cell. His body stumbled past her, driven aside by the force of the blow.

Argentia turned with her momentum, coming around to meet the guard trying to blindside her. She lashed her blade across, nearly cutting his armored head in half. The katana stuck and she lost an instant twisting it free, but it was no matter.

The four remaining guards were in full flight.

Argentia let them go. Lowering her dripping blade, she stood amid the carnage for a moment, gathering herself. Then she turned for the door.

Her initial fury was spent. Her vengeance for Ikabod was only beginning.

28

"Guildmaster—we're under attack!"

Togril Vloth was reclining on a chaise in a small chamber on the top floor of his guild. Compared to the opulent excess of the rest of his home, this room was sparsely furnished. Besides the lushly pillowed couch was a glass table with a crystal decanter of a fine old Rhynish, a gold plate piled with fat white Makharanian figs, and an oculyr seated in a silver stand. There were no windows, and thick burgundy curtains draped the walls save for one space where a full-length, gilt-framed mirror hung.

Vloth was sipping on his wine, but what he was truly savoring was the image in the oculyr of Argentia Dasani crumbling in sorrow beside the burned skeleton of her butler. It was a scene that would warm his memories for the rest of his life. Her despair was intoxicating. He had waited years to see her so reduced. How he wished the oculyr could be made to show the image time and again. He would never tire of watching it.

When the guard banged open the door, Vloth took another long, slow sip of wine before setting the crystal goblet down beside the figs. "I would not go so far as to call this an attack," he said when he finally deigned to look at the guard. He had already decided the man would be executed tomorrow for his histrionics. "Has Dasani been taken yet?"

The guard shook his armored head. "Guildmaster, it's not Dasani. It's men downstairs. They destroyed the door. They have a wizard!"

"What?" Vloth had known Argentia was coming and that she was coming through the sewers. He did not know how she had come into the city—none of his men in the Gate Guard had seen her—but the butler he owned at Lord Parcifel's estate had been quick to recognize her and report her presence. If she was at Parcifel's, it stood to reason she knew about the sewers. That was hardly a surprise. Though he hated her, Vloth had to admit Argentia was a resourceful foe. He had prepared for her arrival, and everything was proceeding according to his designs.

But now came this guard. For one of the few times in his long and prosperous career, Vloth felt the clench of blind panic. Who would dare attack him? *No one in Telarban...*

Hefting his bulk from the couch and hobbling as fast as he could with his walking stick—his left knee had been devastatingly injured in one of his early encounters with Argentia, and it would never fully recover—Vloth shoved past the guard and out into the hallway. Sounds of combat echoed up the stairs. "What are you standing here for, fool?" he snarled at the guard. "Get down there. Find Ravail. Send him to me."

"Yes, Guildmaster!" The guard ran off. Vloth limped back into the chamber.

A few minutes later, Ravail entered without knocking. "You have heard?" the head of the guild's guards asked calmly.

"Who are they?" Vloth demanded. "Are they with Dasani?"

Ravail shrugged the spiny shoulders of his insectoid armor. "They are five, I am told. Dasani is not among them."

"Whoever they are, I want them dead, Ravail. They must not be permitted to interfere."

"Understood. And Dasani?"

"Captured and brought to the audience chamber, as planned. *Unharmed*. I have waited a long time for this, Ravail. I do not wish my game spoiled."

Vloth let the threat hang in the air, and then turned and waved a ringed hand at the mirror on the wall. The glass glimmered until the golden frame seemed to be holding silver light. Vloth stepped up to the mirror, stepped into that light, and vanished in a flash.

The glow faded. The mirror was glass once more.

Alone in the chamber, Gideon-gil stared for a long moment at his armored reflection. Then he walked over and drove a mace into the mirror, shattering it. Vloth had left by a swift way. His return would be made by a slower route—if at all.

The assassin did not truly care what happened to the guildmaster. Vloth was just a means to a much more interesting end, but it was amusing to try him and see if there was mettle beneath that disgustingly obese frame, or merely malice.

Smiling coldly at the broken glass, Gideon-gil left the room, closing the door behind him. The sounds of the fighting were louder now. *They have reached the second floor,* he judged, though his keen hearing was somewhat impaired by the ridiculous headgear his disguise forced him to wear.

Gideon-gil had arrived in Telarban three days earlier.

He had come because he was curious.

The interrogation of Tierciel Thorne, like his capture, had gone all too easily. Magistrate Krung had worried needlessly. Thorne had no idea who the traitor was, and from what the elf could judge, scant inclination to learn. Even under the control of the flute, Thorne was obsessed with vengeance on the cat-women who had killed a girl named Vendi.

It was the cat-women that intrigued the assassin. Master killers, Thorne had called them. Fast, strong, cunning, and merciless.

A challenge? the elf wondered.

Several winters past, Gideon-gil had reached what he feared would likely be the pinnacle of his career when he assassinated the Crown, the Queen, and the Archamagus of Teranor at a swoop. Later, he had failed to kill the new Crown—his first failure in more centuries than he could remember—and then had been forced to save her life to preserve his own honor when he found her at the mercy of another killer's blade.

That was behind him now. He knew that he would have succeeded in his second attempt to kill the young Crown had the demi-goblin not interfered. That knowledge was enough. Gideon-gil had gone on his way, performing other tasks here and there, waiting for something worthy of his talents to pique his interest.

Now it had come.

He would see these twins Thorne spoke of. He would determine if they were indeed a challenge and—almost as interesting—if by virtue of their hybrid nature they were an improvement on mankind.

If they were, perhaps he would not kill them after all.

So the assassin left Thorne alive, knowing that there would be ample opportunity to complete his contract for Krung. Where the twins went, Thorne would follow, and there Gideon-gil would be waiting as well.

It was against Thorne that the elf intended to measure the cat-women. If they fell to Thorne, they would hardly have been worth Gideon-gil's time. He would make certain Thorne did not long outlive the twins, and he would seek his challenge elsewhere.

If the twins killed Thorne, the terms of the assassin's arrangement with Krung were satisfied quite nicely, and Gideon-gil would be free to deal with the cat-women as he chose before returning to Argo.

Infiltrating Vloth's guild had been child's play. There was only one problem: the twins were not there.

The elf was unperturbed. His plot was still viable. All that was required was a touch of patience.

Gideon-gil was nothing if not patient.

Leaving Vloth's mirror chamber, the assassin descended swiftly to the melee. Vloth's guards fought fiercely, but Gideon-gil sensed that Thorne and his companions—he was well aware of who the intruders were, though he had declined to share this information with Vloth, enjoying the guildmaster's confusion—would not be denied. They would win this fight and discover the twins were gone. Would they also discover where they had gone? Gideon-gil believed they would. When they did, they would pursue them.

What the assassin had not anticipated, however, was being left behind by Vloth tonight. Now, instead of continuing his subtle game by waiting with the guildmaster and the twins for Thorne to arrive, the elf was forced to find means of reaching the place where Vloth was on his own.

Easily remedied, Gideon-gil thought as he moved to join the battle.

It merely necessitated a change of disguise.

29

Up and up.

Argentia passed through the levels of Vloth's guild, following her strangely perfect memory for routes and ways she'd traveled in the past. She knew where Vloth's chambers were.

She knew where this would end.

As she mounted the steps she heard noises of battle echoing down the halls. Something else was afoot in Vloth's guild tonight: an attack or an insurrection. She paid it little heed. It had nothing to do with her—as long as she got to Vloth before whoever else was trying to.

Fury flowed through her like fire. Winters past, the blademaster Toskan had taught her that to fight with anger was to lose the contest before it was begun. Her experience had proved his words true time and again. Angry fighters made mistakes—ones they usually did not live to repent.

But on this night, anger was all Argentia had left. Vloth had robbed her of everything else.

So she embraced her anger. Fused it until it burned pure in her veins: a perfect white flame that drove her to destroy.

Before, all her focus had been on rescuing Ikabod. If Vloth and the twins had lived and she had escaped with Ikabod, she would have been satisfied. Doubtless the guildmaster would have continued hunting her, but she would have dealt with that on another day.

Now there would be no other day for Togril Vloth.

Up and up.

Thorne, Kest, and Tib battled their way through Vloth's troops. It was a running fight against guards rushing out of transecting corridors or charging down the steps.

Thorne led without slowing to do more than bludgeon whoever stood in his way. Tib wondered if Thorne knew they had become separated from Augustus and Guntyr on the last floor, or that he and Kest were still behind him. *Probably not,* the lieutenant thought as he ducked a mace and drove a dagger between plates of armor and into the guard's thigh. The man screamed and fell. Tib ran on, following Thorne and Kest down another hallway.

At the far end, a flight of stairs was littered with the bodies of three dead guards.

What happened here? Tib wondered. Had Guntyr and Augustus found some shortcut and gotten ahead of them?

Before he could ponder the strange scene further, crossbow shots rang at them and they were diving for cover as another group of Vloth's men charged.

Two huge eunuchs blocked the entrance to Vloth's audience chamber. They raised their crossbows when Argentia appeared at the top of the steps. "Surrender!" one of them shouted.

Argentia walked forward. She was spattered with blood. Her blue eyes were full of cold death.

The eunuchs glanced at each other. This was obviously the woman the guildmaster wanted. They had been given strict orders not to harm her, but there was a limit to their loyalty. They'd heard the cries of the dying down below. If they had to wound her to preserve their own lives, they would.

Argentia was ten paces away. The eunuchs took aim at her legs. Despite their ponderous size they were quite good marksmen and were confident they would not miss. "Last chance," the second eunuch said.

Argentia kept coming.

The eunuchs fired: the one on the left a fraction faster than the one on the right.

Without breaking stride, Argentia whipped her katana back and forth, deflecting both quarrels. "Your turn," she said. "Surrender—or die."

The eunuchs glanced at each other again and then fled for the stairs. Argentia ignored them. Crossing the last distance, she kicked the door to the audience chamber open.

Vloth reclined upon his chaise. His fat face betrayed no surprise at her entrance. "Lady Dasani." He smiled. "At last."

Argentia didn't wait. Her hand was a blur, flinging a dagger across the chamber. The blade tumbled toward Vloth. Stabbed into his forehead—

—and stuck into the upholstered back of the chaise.

Illusion! God damn it—I should have known... The guildmaster was using magic to project his image into the audience chamber while he was safely away from Argentia's attacks.

Vloth clapped his bejeweled hands, roaring laughter. "Oh, my dear. Would you kill me so quickly?"

"Quickly, slowly, whatever—as long as you die. Why don't you quit hiding and face me, you fat bastard? Too scared?"

Vloth scowled. "You are the one who should be scared, Lady Dasani. You were a fool to have ever crossed me. Now—finally—you begin to pay."

"There's nothing else you can do to me, pig," Argentia spat. She continued to move slowly to her left, away from the door, wary of what other tricks the guildmaster might have prepared for her. "You killed Ikabod already."

"Did I?" Vloth waved a ringed hand. The air beside the chaise glimmered as an aethereal window opened to reveal three figures.

Argentia's heart leapt. "Ikabod!"

The butler was kneeling with his head bowed. He was in chains, but he was alive. Behind him, the twins stood with their arms folded across their breasts.

"Your precious butler lives," Vloth said. "For how much longer is up to you."

Puma reached down and yanked Ikabod's head back. Argentia saw something awful had happened to his eye. Pantra's clawed hand flashed across the butler's face, drawing bloody furrows in his cheek. Ikabod screamed.

"Don't!" Argentia cried, stepping involuntarily towards the image of the twins. "You bitches!"

"Old blood..." Puma said.

"But still tasty," Pantra completed. She licked her cruel nails. Puma purred laughter.

"Come for your butler, Argentia Dasani," Vloth said. "Come to my Frost Palace and save him—if you can."

The image of Ikabod and the twins changed to that of a huge crystalline pyramid rising above a bleak white landscape.

"Be swift," the guildmaster said. "My kittens are bored already. I do not know how much longer I can keep them entertained. If you have not come in one moon's time, what you just saw will seem a mercy."

"I swear, if you touch him—"

"Then come!" Vloth pointed a fat, ringed finger at Argentia. "One moon, Dasani. My gauntlet has begun!"

30

Vloth's image flashed and vanished. Argentia did not even have time to lower her katana before a trio of men burst through the audience chamber's door. She recognized them immediately. *Great—what else can go wrong?*

"I *knew* I was right," Thorne said, pulling up short when he saw Argentia.

"No, but you're persistent, I'll give you that." Argentia spun her katana to the ready. "Don't even think about trying to stop me."

"Where are the twins?" Thorne demanded.

"Not here," Argentia said.

"Lying won't save them—or you. Tell me where they are." There was something wild and dangerous in Thorne's dark eyes.

"Are you deaf? They're not here. And I'm not lying about anything, so just get out of my way." Argentia started forward.

"Just a damn minute," Tib protested.

Vloth's guards rushed into the chamber.

Thorne and the lieutenants, nearer to the door, caught the brunt of the assault. The guards numbered nearly a score. Many of them bore wounds from earlier encounters with Argentia or the Argosians. They attacked in a last effort to protect a guildmaster they did not know had already departed his guild.

Argentia skirted wide of the fray, hoping to use the chaos to make a break to freedom. She had to find this pyramid where Ikabod was held. *One moon...*

Already time was short.

A guard spotted her and charged. "Don't kill the woman! Remember the Guildmaster's orders!" another guard shouted.

Argentia had no such restraints. She cut the first man down. Two more replaced him, swinging maces. She parried. Countered. Killed.

The Watchmen formed a fighting triangle, Thorne at the point. They held their own against the press of guards until Thorne bashed one enemy aside so viciously that he careened into Kest, taking him down.

The triangle was broken.

Two guards buried Tib. He covered up as the blows rained upon him. Thorne remained standing and fighting, but could not reach his fallen lieutenants.

They were nearly overwhelmed when Augustus appeared in the shattered doorway, wand blazing.

Bolts of aethereal energy wracked across the guards' steely armor like miniature forks of lightning. They fell, screaming and thrashing.

"About time," Tib shouted, staggering to his feet.

"If I'd known you were still conscious, I would have waited," Augustus snapped, unleashing his magic on a guard trying to sneak up on Thorne.

"Where's Guntyr?" Kest shouted,

"I don't know!" Augustus said. "We got separated."

An armored body flew past the door.

"I think he just caught up," Tib quipped as a second guard went tumbling past.

Moments later, Guntyr entered the chamber. "More behind me," the Norden panted. The lieutenants heard the reinforcements in the hallway, like a stampede of wild beasts upon the Plains of Aeyros.

"Wizard—get us out of here," Thorne ordered, dealing a backhanded blow of his baton that smashed a guard's jaw apart in a bloody spume.

Augustus conjured. An aethereal gate appeared.

Argentia made a snap decision. Wheeling, she vaulted a guard diving at her knees. Sprang after the Watchmen just as the magical portal sealed shut.

An instant later Argentia was in an alley, hunched and gasping after the teleport, getting soaked by warm rain.

Her mind was reeling as much as her body. She'd focused everything on tonight and had fully expected to meet the dawn with Ikabod safely beside her or to die trying to free him. *But I wasn't ready for this...*

Vloth was playing a game. *His gauntlet*, she thought bitterly, remembering the guildmaster's words.

With Ikabod's life still at stake, Argentia had no choice but to play along.

She straightened up. The alley was across the street from Vloth's guildhouse. What remained of the doorway was on fire. *So that's how they got in...*

The Watchmen were between Argentia and the mouth of the alley, staring at her by the light of the halfling's wand. Argentia didn't know what they intended, and she wasn't waiting to find out. Scabbarding her katana as a show of faith, she moved toward the Watchmen. "Thanks for the ride."

"Where do you think you're going?" Tib asked.

"None of your damn business," Argentia snapped, pushing past.

Guntyr, moving swiftly for so big a man, blocked her way. Tib caught her shoulder. "You've got some explaining to do."

Argentia pulled free of the smaller man. "I said—"

"Lady Dasani."

Thorne stepped squarely in front of Argentia, appraising her silently with his dark eyes. She returned the stare evenly, unblinking in the pouring rain.

Thorne slapped her across the face.

31

"Bastard! What the hell was that for!" Argentia touched her stinging cheek in shock.

"For Vendi."

"What—"

"Where are the twins?" Thorne pointed his steel baton at Argentia.

"Put that thing away!" Argentia shoved the weapon aside. She'd first met Thorne in the aftermath of the destruction of her estate, before Vloth's twins had descended on Argo and triggered the chain of events that had led them all inexorably to this night. He had been hostile to her then, and seemed little changed now.

"Tell me where they are," Thorne repeated.

"Why should I? You people have treated me like a criminal since I met you. Now you expect me to help you? Go to Hell."

"You ran from us," Tib accused.

"I told you, I had to rescue Ikabod."

"Yeah? So where is he?"

"Still a prisoner."

"How convenient."

"Whatever." Argentia sidestepped Thorne, who made no move to stop her, and stormed out of the alley.

Tib started after her. "Wait," Thorne said.

"But she— Don't tell me you believe her?"

"Tib, she was fighting Vloth's guards," Kest said.

"That wasn't staged," Augustus added. "She was *killing* them. I don't think she's been lying to us."

"That is what we are going to learn," Thorne said. "Perhaps there is some truth to her tale, perhaps none. All I am certain of is that she knows where the twins are, and she will tell me—one way or another."

"Then what are we waiting for?" Tib asked.

"We are giving her rope," Thorne said. "To see if she swings or hangs herself."

The Watchmen lingered until Argentia was almost out of sight. Then they followed her at a careful distance through the rain and the twisting streets of Telarban until she entered a nondescript building not too far from Vloth's guild.

They were moving toward the window to peer inside when they heard the click of crossbows behind them.

"Argentia?" Amethyst came out of a back room in Bendrake's quarters. She took one look at the rain-soaked, blood-spackled huntress and rushed to her side. "Oh Argentia— Honey, what happened? Where's Ikabod? Are you all right?"

Before Argentia could begin to reply, they heard shouting from outside. The door slammed open. Bendrake and his men herded in Thorne and the lieutenants.

"Well, isn't *this* a surprise," Argentia muttered. She glared at Thorne. "Here to slap me again?"

"You know why I am here," Thorne replied as coolly as if there were no crossbows pointed at him.

"What's this about?" Amethyst had changed out of her gown into snakeskin pants, heeled shoes, and a half-unbuttoned gold blouse that strained against her ample bust. The heady scent of her perfume bloomed in the air. Tib's eyes were lost in her cleavage. Even Kest and Augustus were staring. Thorne, cold to such seductions, kept his eyes on Argentia.

"We caught them sneaking around outside, Guildmistress," Bendrake said.

"Guildmistress?" Tib asked.

"Amethyst Pyth, Mistress of the Golden Serpent. At your service." Amethyst smiled at him and Tib's heart race a little.

"You've expanded beyond Duralyn, Mistress Pyth," Guntyr observed.

"Not really." Amethyst chuckled, giving the Norden an appreciative glance. Like Thorne, he seemed unaffected by her charms. "Just a token here, a token there. Vloth has similar arrangements in Duralyn. Bendrake's true job is to warn me should Vloth's eye ever turn seriously to my city."

"Enough chatter," Thorne interrupted. "Tell me where the twins are," he said to Argentia.

"How about I tell you that you've got the manners of a yeti?" Argentia retorted. They glared at each other again: two unflinching wills thrown into opposition.

"I take it these aren't friends of yours," Amethyst said. "What do you want to do with them?"

Argentia frowned through a moment of internal debate. "All right," she said, mostly to herself. Brushing a limp strand of wet hair out of her eyes, she sank down on a couch. "Let them go."

Bendrake looked at Amethyst. The guildmistress shrugged. "Do it."

"Have a seat," Argentia invited when the crossbows were lowered.

"Just tell me—" Thorne began.

Argentia cut him off. "You want to know what happened to the twins? Then shut up and listen."

Grudgingly, Thorne motioned for his lieutenants to sit, though he remained standing.

Stubborn ass... "Suit yourself," Argentia said. Then she spun her tale from the beginning, so they would understand. Told of her capture by Vloth after she tried to stop him from abducting girls for his harem. Of the magic collar he'd used to control her and of the battle in which Carfax had rescued her and Vloth had taken his crippling injury. She followed that with destruction of her manor, the twins' attack at the docks in Argo, her unplanned sojourn in Sormoria, returning to find the twins had taken Ikabod, and the explosion in the Westing House.

"The rest you pretty much know," she concluded, running rapidly through her entrance to the guild by the sewers, her ghastly discovery in the dungeon, and the illusory message Vloth had left behind to mock her and goad her on.

"Why'd Vloth order his guards to leave you unharmed?" Tib said. He'd been convinced of Argentia's guilt since she fled in Argo, and he was clinging to that conviction despite the fact that her tale, though full of wild chance, rang true when she spoke it.

"Don't you get it? Vloth *wants* me alive. He *wants* me to come after him so he can kill me himself—slowly and painfully, I'm sure. It's all a game of revenge to him. That's why he took Ikabod—to make me keep playing."

"What about the explosion at the Westing House? That looked like a pretty good attempt at killing you to me. Not a slow, painful one, either."

"I don't think that was Vloth. I think it was the twins. I doubt Vloth even knows about that. He was prepared for me tonight."

Surprisingly, Thorne nodded. Such a capricious act of destruction fit the murderous character of the cat-women, whose visit to Argo had left nearly a score of people dead. "Where are the twins now?" he asked, his voice quiet for the first time that night.

"Vloth moved Ikabod to some crystal pyramid. In Nord, I think. Somewhere with a lot of snow, anyway. The twins were with him. That's where they'll stay, at least for a moon."

"Why a moon?" Kest asked.

"If I'm not there in a moon, they'll kill Ikabod."

"Oh, honey." Amethyst put an arm around her. She knew how close Argentia was to Ikabod and shuddered to imagine what seeing the burned skeleton dressed in the butler's clothes had done to her.

"Do you know this pyramid?" Thorne asked Guntyr.

"No, but Nord is vast. Such a thing could exist there openly and still be hidden from the eyes of many."

Argentia rose. "So, now you know the truth," she said to the Watchmen. "Make of it what you will. I'm leaving."

"Where are you going?" Kest asked.

"Duralyn." Argentia paused. Took a chance. "If you want your revenge on Vloth and those twins, come with me."

32

Without waiting for an answer, Argentia left the room. Amethyst followed her out. Tib stared after both ladies. Dasani was beautiful, but Pyth— *What a woman...*

Augustus' voice drew him from his thoughts: "Well, what now?"

"I am going on," Thorne said flatly. "I have sworn it. Let Lady Dasani find her butler, if he still lives, and let her lead me to the twins."

"Then you trust her?" Tib asked.

Thorne smiled his cruel smile, his eyes like a falcon's. "I trust she will lead me to the twins. Whether her purpose is what she claims doesn't matter, as long as I find those two. The rest of you are freed of any bond. If you return to Argo now, I will think no less of you for it."

"I will continue," Guntyr said.

"And me," Augustus added.

"You think this Pyth is going?" Tib asked.

"Why?" the halfling asked.

Tib held his hands before his chest and grinned.

Augustus rolled his eyes and ran a hand through his mop of curls. "Oh that's a great motivation."

"It's the best," Tib laughed. Then, turning serious again, he said, "I'm in."

"Kest?" Thorne asked.

Kest took off his glasses and rubbed them on a dry part of his vest. *We came this far...* If he went back now, even for Lyrissa, his conscience would gall him. *Besides, I don't think there's much of a future for any of us back in Argo, unless it's in the dungeons...*

He replaced his glasses. "I'm with you, too."

"Then let's go," Argentia said when Thorne gave her his group's answer.

While the Watchmen had convened, Argentia had used Amethyst's oculyr to contact Ralak. She told him of her failure to rescue Ikabod and of Vloth's Frost Palace. "I need you to find it," she said. "Don't even waste time coming for me. I'll go to White Spire."

Because of the uncertainty surrounding her attack on the guild, Ralak had proposed the cathedral in Telarban as a second escape route. Like Coastlight in Harrowgate and Wavegard in Argo, White Spire also held a secret and powerful aethergate linked to the Monastery of the Grey Tree.

While the Archamagus set to work hunting out Vloth's pyramid, Argentia and Amethyst bid farewell to Bendrake and led the Watchmen through the rain to the teleport chamber in the cellar of the cathedral, where in a moment's magic they exchanged one city for another.

Midelwyn, up before the sun to meet the day in prayer, greeted them after the trauma of the aetherwalk wore off. "An escort will be sent for you later in the morning. Until then, rest."

Thorne stared hard at the old Steward. He had little tolerance for clerics since the night they had arrived too late to save his wife and son. "There is no time to rest."

"There is," Argentia said.

Thorne turned incredulously to her. "I would not have thought you so weak."

Argentia shook her head, closed her eyes, and leaned back against the wall. She was emotionally exhausted, but that was not why she agreed with Midelwyn. "We can't do anything until we learn the location of the pyramid," she said, fighting to keep the exasperation from her voice. Thorne was single-minded to the point of madness. "I've got a friend working on it, but it's going to take some time."

"What you will," Thorne said curtly. "I am not the one supposedly rushing to save a life."

Argentia's blue eyes snapped open. "I will save Ikabod," she promised. "And when I have, I won't forget you said that."

They retired to separate cells to rest, though none of them except Augustus actually slept. Breakfast was taken in the monastery's dining hall, an austere chamber of unclothed wooden tables and benches. While Tib battered Amethyst with incessant talk, Argentia and Thorne pointedly ignored each other.

It was after Ninth Bell when their escort finally arrived. Argentia wasn't surprised to see Sir Lockwood and his Sentinels waiting for them outside the monastery, but the Watchmen certainly were.

"Those are the Crown's guards," Kest said quietly, recognizing the distinctive armor from descriptions.

"The Crown?" Augustus whispered back.

Kest could only shrug. Lady Dasani had been surprising them since her escape from the Westing House. He had no reason to think she would stop now.

It was a relatively short walk from the monastery to Aventar, but that was time enough for the Watchmen, none of whom had ever been to Duralyn, to take in some of a city that rivaled their own in its beauty, if not in shining brightness, and a castle that surpassed Argo's most splendid architectures. Not even Thorne could keep his gaze from roving up the grey stone to towers soaring above the blue slate roofs. "Friends in high places, eh?" he said archly.

"At least I *have* friends," Argentia shot back.

The lieutenants exchanged glances. It was rare for them to see someone challenge Thorne. They wondered how long the truce between the headstrong huntress and the unyielding captain could possibly last.

They climbed the wide flight of steps that led from the courtyard of the Royal Ring up to the great bronze double doors of Aventar. The Guardians stationed there saluted Sir Lockwood and admitted the party to the castle. Lockwood led the group down a wide entrance corridor rich with hanging tapestries and accents of gold. Two more Sentinels drew open the towering doors to the throne hall.

My God, look at this place... Augustus had always thought the Court of the Magistrates in Argo, with its deep-sunken floor and tall Circle of Judgment, was imposing, but the throne hall of Aventar dwarfed that chamber into foolishness.

Seats for an audience of hundreds tiered the walls. Banners proclaiming the noble estates hung from the vaulted ceiling. The walk from the tremendous doors to the marble steps where the throne stood on high seemed to take forever; their footfalls echoed loudly in the huge space. As they drew closer, the Watchmen felt pressed upon by the gazes of the Sentinels posted on each step, halberds glinting readily, and even more by the regard of the Crown on her throne and the Archamagus standing behind her.

"Welcome to Aventar," Solsta said. To the surprise of the Watchmen, she rose and descended.

She's so short, Tib thought, taking care not to smirk.

Short or no, he saw that the Crown was also beautiful: not a brashly sexual invitation like Amethyst or the fire-and-ice dynamic of Argentia's flaming hair and blue eyes, but a petite study in softness. Her eyes were deep and dark. Her skin was smooth cream, finely boned, flawless save a single, tiny scar on her cheek. Her lips were small and expressive. She wore a long brown skirt, matching boots, and a blouse of rusty orange dusted with gold. Her hair—rich chestnut save the white forelock that was the Mark of her rule—was unbound and tumbled past her narrow shoulders.

She looked fragile as a child, but there was nothing helpless in her manner. Rather, she exuded command, richness, confidence, and strength. The lieutenants could all sense there was will in her: will even beyond what they had felt from Thorne, who had virtually defined that quality for them.

It was an impressive—almost frightening—juxtaposition.

Reaching the bottom of the steps, the Crown surprised the Watchmen again by embracing Argentia. "I'm glad you're safe," she said. "Ralak told me about Ikabod. Gen, I'm so sorry."

Argentia nodded. "I'll get him back." Catching the floral air of Solsta's perfume, she realized she was a sodden mess. Her damp clothes still bore the taint of Telarban's sewers. *Need a shower...*

More importantly, she needed information. "Did you find Vloth's pyramid?" she asked Ralak.

"I have and have not," the Archamagus replied, gliding down the steps in a rustle of red robes.

Argentia could almost feel Thorne tense at the cryptic response. She wondered what would happen if he tried to order the Archamagus around. *Maybe Ralak'll turn him into a toad...* The thought was nearly enough to make her smile.

"The pyramid cannot be discerned through any means of magic. It is shielded from the aether—a forbidden spell, and one that only the most powerful of magi can muster," Ralak said. "Does Vloth have a wizard?"

Argentia shook her head. "Not that I've seen."

"Interesting," Ralak stroked his short, dark point of beard. "At all events, I cannot tell you the whereabouts of this pyramid."

"Then why—" Thorne broke in, unable to contain himself.

The Archamagus raised a finger, silencing Thorne. "I said *I* cannot tell you."

"Then who?" Argentia asked, her own patience beginning to fray.

"Me."

The voice rang from the seats to the right of the steps. A squat figure none of them had noticed sitting there stood up.

"King Durn?" Argentia asked in amazement.

"Aye, e'ry inch Durn." The dwarf's long, ashy beard wagged against his silver coat as he tromped towards them. His coal black eyes swept over the company, fixing on Argentia. "Looks like th' dwarves o' Stromness are comin' t' yer aid again."

Interlude

Togril Vloth's Frost Palace was a promise fulfilled.

Growing up on the streets of Khemr-kar, Vloth had come to despise most things of the desert—the heat, the sand, the absence of water, the absence of beauty—but he could not despise the pyramids of Makhara. Those monumental constructions, visible from the walls and rooftops of the city, had seared themselves upon his young mind as symbols of power. He had sworn then that he would someday have his own.

Now he did.

The Frost Palace was a perfect crystalline imitation of Makhara's pyramids, built as far from the squalor of Khemr-kar as Vloth could conceive. The ice reaches of Nord were even emptier than the sandswept leagues of the Sudenland kingdom, but they were starkly beautiful, with glacial mountains and fields of pristine snow shining like blankets of diamonds beneath the pale ever-light of the northern vale.

Vloth's pyramid stood alone in this frozen vastness. The nearest barbarian settlement was ten days distant. The nearest town or city was south of the Gelidian Spur.

Vloth enjoyed the isolation. The Frost Palace was his retreat from the rigors of ruling his shadowy empire. Within its crystal geometries was an oasis of luxury and excess. The climate was controlled by magic, giving no hint of the harsh world outside. Culinary delicacies were imported from the reaches of Acrevast, so Vloth's table did not suffer. There were infinite other indulgences, including a hot spring and a harem of the Norden women that Vloth particularly favored.

But from the moment he arrived, lurching forth from the aether through another enchanted mirror, the guildmaster knew that this visit would offer little enjoyment.

Vloth was furious. The only instance he could conjure in his memory that even approached his present rage was when the Wheel of Avis-fe had been stolen from him.

This time it was his sense of security that had been stolen—a worse theft by far.

Communication by oculyr with his house in Telarban told him the grim aftermath of the assault. More than a score of his men had been killed, among them Ravail, and many more were wounded. One of the intruders was dead. The others had escaped, taking Lady Dasani with them.

Who were these others? Were they leagued with Dasani? Were they from some rival in another city making a play for power in Telarban? Were they his guildsmen turned traitor? Mad though that seemed, Vloth was all too aware that among thieves—even his thieves—treachery was the rule, not the exception.

Worse, he could not even get back to the guild to restore order. The gating mirror was broken—another mystery without an answer.

He had tried to contact Mouradian, but the wizard who had made the magic mirrors and placed the enchantments on the Frost Palace was not responding. Until he did, Vloth was trapped in his pyramid—unless he wanted to make the excruciatingly long overland journey back to Telarban.

If he did that, he would miss what he had come for to begin with.

Embittered, Vloth hobbled through his Frost Palace. The pyramid's interior was designed around open space. There were neither hallways nor stairs. Instead, a central crystal support pillar rose from the ground to the apex of the palace. From this trunk crystal ramps reached to the pyramid's various levels like the lines of a gargantuan spider's web. Soft bluish light emanated from the rough crystal walls, which had been crafted to imitate ice caverns, but Vloth did not find the ambiance to be soothing at all. His mind was too wrought by doubt.

Since leaving Khemr-kar to forge his future, one rule had governed Togril Vloth's existence: get power and keep it. For the first time in uncounted years, that mantra stood in danger. He needed answers. Until he had them, there would be no rest. Not truly. Even the thought of finally disposing of Argentia Dasani had soured. What had begun as a leisurely conquest had become a thing of haste and urgent need. A matter to be ended so he could address these other problems.

Still, one thing was certain: whether she was responsible or no, when she finally arrived at the Frost Palace, Argentia would suffer for Vloth's suffering.

While Vloth retired to his harem to seek solace among the Norden girls, Puma and Pantra stalked the ramps of the Frost Palace.

The twins hated the pyramid. Hated the cold and ice and snow that surrounded it forever and ever. Hated the boredom that this arctic wasteland forced upon them.

For one month—since Vloth had deceived them, feigning forgiveness and then exiling them to await Lady Dasani here—they had languished in this beautiful prison: predators without prey.

They played with the servants and guards (the Norden women were not soft and pliant, and did not please the twins) but they could not kill them or even hurt them too badly since that might anger Vloth, and it was important to their plans that Vloth no longer be angry with them, so there was ultimately no fulfillment in those dalliances.

Their single respite had been a great white bear that wandered past the pyramid one morning. They battled it long and gloriously, painting the snow crimson, but it died, as all that the twins hunted died, and no more of the animals had come.

Left to their boredom, the cat-women roamed the Frost Palace incessantly. Discovered its secrets. Plotted their revenge.

When Vloth arrived, the twins greeted him with shows of subservience, playing his perfect minions again. Though he was angry and distracted, their beguiling ways had their effect, and he had rewarded them with a brief part in his illusion.

It was exactly what the twins had hoped. They would continue in these fawning roles until they had killed Dasani. Only then, when they were fully in Vloth's favor once more, would they show their teeth, making their triumph over the fat fool all the sweeter.

In a moon, Puma thought, green eyes glinting.

Yes, a moon, Pantra answered, licking her lips.

Not long...

No, not long at all now.

Their yaowing laughter echoed through the crystal space like breaking glass.

Part III
Ice Reach

33

The company raced through the dark on iron rails.

Argentia had traveled in the dwarven mine carts during her quest for the final Wheel of Avis-fe. She loved the exhilaration of careening along the narrow path through close tunnels and across abyss-spanning bridges beneath the Gelidian Spur.

The cart was courtesy of King Durn, who had come to Aventar to seal a trade pact ending centuries of isolationism between Teranor and the dwarven holt of Stromness. The armies of the dwarf king and the Crown had fought together against the demons in the Battle of Hidden Vale, but it had been the bravery of Argentia and her friends that had won the dwarven aid in the first place.

Durn, who held Argentia in his esteem even though she was a human— and a woman to boot—had offered his assistance when he learned of her plight from Solsta and Ralak. The dwarves did not know exactly where Vloth's pyramid was, but there was a tribe of barbarians they traded with who had spoken of it.

"A great thing o' ice it be," Durn told Argentia and the Watchmen. "In Nord, beyond th' settlement o' th' Walros."

"Can we reach it in a moon?" Argentia asked.

"Aye, if ye've wings. But not wit them four-legged beasts ye favor. Not a chance in Hell."

"We have to try," Argentia said. Ikabod could not just be left to die. "Can you map me the fastest way to this tribe?"

"Who d' ye think yer talking to, girl?" Durn snorted. "Map ye th' way? I'll bloody do better'n that, or I'm no King o' Stromness."

"But you said—"

"Ye'd need wings, aye. Don't got no wings, so ye'll have t' settle fer th' Iron Way, like ye did afore. That'll get ye t' them big oafs in th' snow quick enough. I'll send someone wit ye t' act th' part o' liaison. Whether ye convince them barbarians t' take ye th' rest o' th' way or not's on yer head."

"Thank you!" Argentia hugged the dwarf king impulsively.

"Bah! Enough o' that," Durn gruffed, though he did not look entirely displeased.

"What can I do to repay this?" Argentia asked.

"Ye done enough. Weren't fer yer comin' t' see th' Ancient t' find them Wheels, I'd still be in me holt instead o' standin' here lookin' t' make Stromness a force o' trade among all th' kingdoms. Ye reminded me th' old ways ain't always th' best ways."

"I hope we both shall profit from your wisdom, my friend," Solsta said.

Durn nodded. "Aye—ye can be damn sure we'll be doin' that."

Solsta placed the five Watchmen in the capable hands of her butler Herwedge. Argentia was left to her own devices. She spent the next hours bathing the filth of the sewers off her body, and the rest of the day getting outfitted for her journey. That night, she dined with Solsta, Mirk, Ralak, and Amethyst.

The guildmistress would not be joining the rescue mission this time. Solsta needed her in Duralyn. "Besides, I hate the cold," Amethyst said. "I'd complain so much you'd wish you'd left me behind."

"I'm in your debt enough already," Argentia said, sipping on her caf. "You didn't have to help me at all, and you certainly didn't have to come to Telarban."

"You know I never miss a gala—even if you did have *much* more fun."

"I wouldn't call slogging through those sewers fun."

"Not the sewers."

"Oh—that. Well…"

"What?" Solsta asked.

"Nothing." Argentia scowled at Amethyst.

"No, tell them," Amethyst said provocatively.

"Yes, tell us," Solsta said, leaning eagerly forward.

"I don't really think it's a tale for mixed company," Argentia protested.

"Nonsense," Amethyst urged, enjoying the trouble she was causing. "It's like a faerie story. Lady Dasani and the Horse-Hung Heir."

"Amethyst!" Solsta gasped. Ralak burst out laughing. Argentia blushed until she was crimson.

"Mirk does not know what is funny," the meerkat complained.

Later, Argentia found herself alone on the parapet of Aventar's north tower. She hadn't been there since she'd scattered Carfax's ashes to the wind, but for some reason she had come tonight. It felt even lonelier than the last time. "Please," she whispered, her hand around the dragon's tooth token at her throat. "Don't let Ikabod die too."

Hush, Carfax's voice whispered in her mind. It said no more; perhaps there was no more it needed to say. Argentia knew she was being foolish. She had made her peace with her husband's death, but sometimes the bitterness, the unfairness of it all, would steal back upon her and she would ache.

From her thoughts of Carfax she returned to equally painful thoughts of Ikabod, wondering what torment he was languishing in. *I'll get you out*, she vowed. *If I have to chase you to the ends of Acrevast, I will, but I'll find you and I'll free you. I swear it…*

With a last look at the stars, as if to hold them to her promise, Argentia descended. The chamber below the tower's roof had belonged to Carfax, who had sojourned in Aventar when he was not making himself useful elsewhere. For a short, sweet time, Argentia had shared it with the ranger and she preferred to keep it despite Solsta's offer of any of the castle's many guest chambers.

But I really should clean this place up, she thought as she sat on the edge of the bed. Dust had taken over the room, covering Carfax's books, clothing, weapons, maps, and all the clutter of a man who spent most of his life traveling. It was a disarray that Argentia had always found at amusing odds with the ranger's personality.

An inspiration struck her as she glanced around. *I wonder…*

She searched. Fortune was with her. She discovered the elven *esp* she'd been hoping to find, and something else as well. Something wholly unexpected but even more useful. *I never knew he had two*, she thought, holding the silver handbow up in the lamplight.

A magical weapon forged by the cyclopes of the Skystones, the bow was barely bigger than her hand, with a crosspiece no wider than the hilt guard of her katana. It fired crescent-shaped bursts of aether similar to the bolts wizards could conjure from their wands and staffs. Argentia had seen Carfax blow holes the size of spear wounds in enemies with the little weapon, which required rest only after it had expended nearly a score of shots.

Can't hurt, she thought, tossing the handbow into a pile with her other gear.

The company met Griegvard Gynt in the courtyard at dawn.

The dwarf was a leathery stump with a long blonde beard and wild blonde hair that stuck out in every direction from beneath a battered iron helm, burying most of his face save his pale grey eyes and his stabbing dagger of a nose. A great axe that appeared to be taller than Griegvard himself was strapped across his back. He was sitting reluctantly astride a pony—dwarves hated and feared horses, and only rode ponies when they absolutely had to—and cracking his stony knuckles impatiently.

"Now that we're all bloody here, kin we get this carnival on th' road?" he groused at Argentia, who was the last of the group to arrive. The dwarf had been none too pleased with the early start.

Argentia, hardly a morning person on her best days, was none too pleased herself. She'd slept poorly, disturbed by dreams of death in the dragon's den. She was tired and sluggish. Her head hurt, and her packs felt unusually heavy as she slung them over the saddle horn and mounted up, but she retained her civility, not wanting to get the expedition off on the wrong foot. "My apologies, good dwarf," she said, rubbing the back of her neck. "I slept like a jackass."

"Hah! 'Pology accepted," Griegvard said, somewhat mollified. "Let's be goin'."

"Farewell," said Solsta, who had gathered with Ralak and Amethyst to see the company away. "Fortune follow you."

Argentia saluted her, and they were off to the realm of the Mountain King.

34

Onward through the dark.

Argentia glanced at Griegvard. From the grin visible between his wild moustache and beard, the dwarf was enjoying the ride just as much as Argentia was. In the back of the cart, Guntyr was the typical stoic Norden, and—though halflings were notoriously unadventurous types—Augustus seemed strangely unaffected by the travel.

The others were not doing so well.

Tib, whose propensity for talking incessantly reminded Argentia of her friend Iz, was blessedly silent. Beside him, Kest looked almost nauseous. Even Thorne, whose jaw remained set and his eyes focused on what was visible in the patch of light thrown by the cart's lantern, flinched as they rattled around tight curves or suddenly dipped in the almost absolute darkness.

Despite herself, Argentia couldn't help feeling a bit pleased at that. Thorne did not like her at all, and so far the feeling was mutual. Argentia was beginning to regret her decision in Telarban. *I should have gone on alone*, she thought, not for the first time. *Why did I even bother to try to help them?*

But she knew why.

Vloth's little game in the dungeon had angered Argentia. Ikabod remained her sole priority, but these men were bent on revenge. If that revenge destroyed Vloth and his twins while Argentia got Ikabod to safety, she would be more than happy to help them.

So she had invited them along, and on the journey from Duralyn to the East Gate of Stromness, she had tried to forget their heavy-handed treatment of her and make her peace with the group—even Thorne. They had essentially the same goal, and Argentia had led enough parties to know that the friction caused by mistrust was often fatal. The earlier those walls were broken down, the better.

If they'll give me a chance…

She did her best. After tending her horse at camp that first night, she joined the Watchmen, Griegvard, and Crostian, who was going as far as the dwarven gate to bring the mounts back to Duralyn, around the fire. She was wearing a variant of her usual traveling garb: pale gray leather pants tucked into her black boots and a short white halter that showed off the curves of her breasts and the glittering ring in her navel. Pulling a battered silver flask of clear liquor from her pack, she proffered it to Thorne. It was a trick she'd used countless times to get past the awkwardness most men felt about traveling with a woman. She'd thought about brewing the esp, but decided to save it for Nord, where they would likely need it.

Thorne stared at her briefly, rose, and walked away. Argentia frowned. Took a pull from the flask. "Anyone?" she asked.

"I'll drink wit ye, Lady," Griegvard said.

Argentia handed over the flask. "Enjoy—and don't call me Lady."

"Why not?" Tib asked, taking the bottle from the dwarf.

Argentia paused. Her response to the dwarf had been habit, born of winters trying to dissociate herself from her father and her name. That was behind her now. She had embraced her heritage and the truth of a man much more victim than villain, and she had avenged his death and the death of her mother—but her dislike of the title remained. "It's complicated," she said, smiling. After Thorne, Tib would be the hardest sell of this bunch. If she could win him over to her side, the others lieutenants, whom she sensed were already partly convinced she was trustworthy, would follow along.

"How so?" Tib passed the flask to Kest and lit his pipe. Sweet smoke curled through the fire light, merging with the dark.

"It was tough enough being a woman in my profession without being a noblewoman."

"Your profession?" Augustus asked, receiving the flask from Crostian and handing it on to Guntyr without drinking.

"No," the Norden said with a shake of his blonde-maned head.

"You're not drinking?" Tib asked with a smirk.

"Not tonight."

Guntyr was always reticent, but since the mention of Nord he'd been even more withdrawn. *Nervous about going home*, Augustus surmised. God knew he'd be nervous if he ever returned to the hills of his birth, but it must have been even worse for Guntyr. When a barbarian left Nord he was seldom, if ever, welcomed back.

"More fer me," Griegvard said, retrieving the flask.

"Go on," Kest said to Argentia. "Your profession?"

"Bounty hunter."

"You're a bounty hunter?" Tib laughed. "I've never heard—"

"Of a woman bounty hunter." Argentia rolled her eyes. "Yeah, I've only heard that one about a thousand times. Give me that flask." She snared the liquor from Griegvard, who was liable to finish the whole flask if left to his own devices.

"So are you any good?" Tib asked. He did not seem hostile in his questioning, which was a great improvement over his previous behavior.

Argentia shrugged. "I'm still alive."

"Good answer," Griegvard said.

"You said it *was* tough. Are you retired?" Kest asked.

Argentia took another swallow of liquor. "I guess. I just sort of fell into the work to begin with. One thing led to another, and I ended up working for Relsthab—the former Archamagus—and everything was crazy for awhile." She paused reflectively. "What I want now is just to get Ikabod back and be done with this whole thing. After that, maybe I'll settle down."

I doubt it, Kest thought. *She has wild horses in her eyes...*

"How do you know the Crown so well?" Tib asked.

Argentia grinned. "I saved her life."

"You *what*? How? When?"

"That's a *really* long story, and I don't think one for tonight. We should rest. We've an early start. Maybe I'll tell some of it tomorrow." She capped the flask and stood, stretching.

"Ye'll be wantin' t' leave wit th' sun again, I'm fer guessin'," Griegvard grumbled.

Argentia arched her brow. "I definitely wouldn't say I *want* to, but that's the plan. Is that a problem?"

"Aye. Decent people're lettin' th' sun get a fair head start on th' day afore they're risin'."

"Griegvard..." She put her hands on her hips.

"Bah! All right, all right. Just kick me til' I'm wakin'. If I'm not wakin', I'm dead, and ye kin go on witout me."

While the rest of the camp prepared to turn in, Argentia approached Thorne, who was still standing apart. Though she moved with her usual quiet steps, he turned before she reached him. He looked at her and looked away again, out into the night, where the mountains of the Gelidian Spur rose in the distance like daggers of shadow.

"I'm sorry about your friend," Argentia said. "Truly."

"And what do you think that means to me?" Thorne said coldly. "Nothing. Less than nothing." He knew Argentia's involvement with Vloth was innocent, but he could not find it in him to forgive the fact that she had made an enemy of the guildmaster and Vendi had died for it.

"I just wanted—"

"I do not care," he interrupted. "Go. Take your drink and your silly tales and leave me be. I've no use for your foolishness."

"What the hell is wrong with you?" Argentia flared. "You think you're the only person who's ever lost someone?"

"I've lost more than you could imagine."

"I doubt that!"

Around the campfire, the others were pretending not to watch them. *God damn it, this was just what I wanted to avoid...* Argentia took a deep breath and got herself a little under control. "Look, Thorne, all I want to know is if we're going to have a problem here."

"The twins are my only concern. As long as you bring me to them, I do not care what you do."

"Fine," she said. "Keep it that way."

That was the last they spoke until they reached the East Gate.

35

"Thorne can't help the way he is," Augustus said to Argentia the next day.

"You mean he can't help that he's an arrogant jackass?"

"No." The wizard shook his head. "He's a good man. A tormented man, but still a good man."

"Whatever."

Augustus let the subject drop. It was just as useless to argue with the stubborn huntress as it was to argue with Thorne.

The company rode on.

Over the next days, the rift between Argentia and Thorne remained, but the camaraderie between the rest of the group grew. Even Griegvard, as gruff and dour a dwarf as Argentia had ever known, came around, telling tales of Stromness, including that of Argentia and her friends and their triumph at the Ancient's funeral games.

Augustus also provided entertainment with his talent for juggling—enhanced, Tib swore, by his magic. One evening Argentia started a spirited shooting contest with Carfax's handbow.

Griegvard praised the cyclopean weapon as "almost as good as dwarf craft," but he couldn't shoot it worth a damn. "Bah! Foes're fer bashin' wit hammers and axes, not fer shootin' wit toys," he grumbled. "But it's a good weapon fer a girl."

Crostian and Tib shot well, Augustus better, and Guntyr better still—especially since his hand all but enveloped the tiny bow—but Kest outmatched even Argentia, winning the duel when he shot down six stones that Augustus tossed simultaneously into the air.

Thorne did not shoot at all.

A week after departing Duralyn, the company passed into the Gelidian Spur and reached the East Gate of Stromness, called in dwarfish *ra-durin*.

The gate looked much as Argentia remembered it: unremarkable stone flanked by two tall jumbles of rock that looked like poorly constructed pillars. "Watch this," she said to Augustus as Griegvard went and pounded his palm against the stone.

"More games?" Thorne muttered scornfully.

"If you don't like the way we're going, walk *over* the mountains instead. Get to Nord in two months—or never," Argentia shot back. She was tired of Thorne's childish behavior. "I'm trying to help you, so quit acting like I'm an enemy."

"Believe me, were I to treat you as an enemy, you'd not be standing there now," Thorne said.

"Oh, I wouldn't be too sure of that." Though she knew he was just baiting her, Argentia's blue eyes flashed. "But we can find out any time you—"

"Aeton's bolts! Will you look at that!" Tib exclaimed.

The stone facade, its magic activated by Griegvard's touch, was all aglimmer, its illusion vanishing to reveal two huge, imposing iron doors. The twin pillars similarly sloughed off their rocky disguise, becoming giant iron statues of dwarves in full armor.

Statues that moved.

Grating and grinding, the twin giants bent forward at the waists, their bearded visages studying the company, the great axes leaning between their feet shifting, ready to lift and strike. The men from Argo fell back.

"Golems," Augustus gasped.

"What were ye expectin', a bunch o' silly ballista 'n archers?" Griegvard scoffed. "Dwarves're knowin' how t' defend what's theirs."

"Who goes?" one of the iron golems boomed.

"Griegvard Gynt, home on th' business o' King Durn. Now be openin' th' damn doors."

The golems straightened. One seized an iron ring anchored to the door beside it and drew the immense portal open. Beyond was a torch-lit corridor of worked stone and a quartet of armed, armored dwarves.

"Got word from th' King," the lead guard said to Griegvard, pointedly ignoring the humans and Augustus. "Yer ride's waitin'."

So began the company's journey on the Iron Way.

36

Five days down the rails, the company came out of the tunnels and into the holt of Stromness.

"Yer bein' treated t' a rare sight fer human eyes, no mistake," Griegvard announced as their cart ground to a stop. They disembarked, looking around at the intricate workings of the dwarven delve. Argentia had known what to expect, though a second sight of the dwarf city was impressive still. The Watchmen had not.

They were amazed.

Tunnels with arched entrances branched off in all directions. The floors were cut stone, perfectly patterned. Clusters of glowing crystals set on the walls provided the first substantial light they'd seen in days. The air was cool, but not uncomfortably so.

Dwarves were coming and going, some pushing carts of ore, some hauling sleds of metal, others simply marching past, bound for distant areas of the holt. The company could see the glow of the furnaces from the various chambers. The smells of fire and forge were thick in the air. The clanging din of smithing was everywhere, a timpani of hammer and anvil punctuated by the noise of dwarves at work: shouting, arguing, laughing, and singing in their guttural baritones.

"Yer hood," Griegvard said to Argentia.

Argentia nodded. Dwarves were the most misogynistic race she'd ever encountered. During her first trip to the holt, she'd learned that dwarf women did not speak in public. In fact, she realized as she drew her hood low to conceal her face, she'd never seen a female dwarf at all. They had to exist, of course, but where were they? *Maybe they keep them chained in some lower hall...*

The company moved away from the cart. Many dwarves who passed them cast suspicious glances at the humans. Finally, a group approached.

Their tunics and aprons were filthy with soot, their eyes dark and accusatory. They jostled about the company, close and hostile, hammers at the ready. "Who're these?" one demanded of Griegvard. "Pris'ners?"

"King's guests," Griegvard answered. "Takin' 'em north." Argentia hoped there would be no trouble; though they traveled with Durn's leave, the King was far away.

"Jest move 'em along," the other dwarf said. "Don't want 'em pollutin' Stromness more'n necessary." Several dwarves laughed at that.

"Hey—" Tib started to protest.

Argentia kicked his ankle hard to shut him up.

"Get 'em out o' here, Griegvard," the dwarf who had spoken first said. "Good journey 'n good riddance," he added. With more laughter, the group broke up and Griegvard hustled the company into a tunnel leading to the northbound rails.

"Sorry fer that," he said when they had left the central hub behind. "Dwarves're shy o' strangers, and not all th' holt's agreein' wit th' King's plan."

"Maybe time will change that," Argentia said.

"Aye, mayhap 'twill." Argentia caught a hopeful gleam in Griegvard's eye that showed her much of his fierce loyalty to his king. "Come on," he said gruffly. "Northbound cart's over there."

Two dark-bearded dwarves were waiting for them at the departure platform: twin brothers Argentia had met on her first trip down the dwarven rails. "They told us we'd be takin' humans. Should've known it'd have somethin' t' do wit ye," Doli said when Argentia dropped her hood.

"But goin' north this time, not east. Makin' harder work fer us, o' course," Noli added. "Where're yer other companions? This ain't th' same barbarian."

Argentia grinned. "New companions, new direction—I wouldn't want you two to get bored."

"Do you know *everyone*?" Tib asked. Argentia made a face at him. Turning back to Doli, she asked how long the journey north would take.

"Five days. Should be a week, but me and me brother can do it faster."

"How long to the tribe after that?"

"Two days, mayhap three."

That left ten days to reach the pyramid before Ikabod's moon was up, and they still didn't know how far Vloth's palace was from the barbarian settlement. *Cutting it close...*

"Let's not waste time." Argentia tossed her packs into the cart.

Heard a yelp.

"What?" She pulled the packs out again. One was her faithful old traveling bag, almost as worn and battered as her boots. The other was a new bag she'd packed in Aventar, full of clothes for Nord, where the turn of seasons from summer to autumn was likely to be colder than the coldest of Teranor's winter nights.

Argentia opened the spare pack.

"Mirk banged head," the meerkat hiding within complained.

"What in Aeton's name are you doing here!" Argentia exclaimed.

"Mirk wants to see ice triangle."

"Oh, Solsta is going to kill me," Argentia moaned, shaking her head in disbelief.

"What is that?" Kest asked as the meerkat squirmed free of the pack.

"This is Mirkholmes," Argentia said. "The Crown's meerkat."

"It talks?"

"Yes, Mirk talks," the meerkat sniffed. "Mirk has many talents."

"Like what?" Tib laughed.

"Like this." Mirk thrust his tiny paws forward, darting blue aether that stung the lieutenant in the chest and sent him hopping back.

"Where did you learn that?" Augustus blurted.

"I thought we were not wasting time," Thorne broke in tersely.

Argentia glanced darkly at him, but she couldn't argue. "He'll explain it on the way," she said, resigned to the meerkat's company: she certainly couldn't leave him with the dwarves or send him back on his own. "Let's get moving."

37

North.

Doli and Noli worked the hand pump, accelerating the cart to mad speeds that had even Argentia holding her breath. Miles flashed by in tunnels and over bridges. Their stops were few and brief. The brothers were almost tireless, and Griegvard and Guntyr were willing to spell them when they did need rest.

Three days out of Stromness.

"What are those?" Kest asked, pointing to the streaks of silver shot through the walls of a tunnel.

"'Tis mithryl yer seein'," Griegvard said reverently. "Dwarf silver. No finer weapons or armor than them made o' mithryl cast by Drim's children."

"I thought elven weapons were of superior craft," Guntyr said.

Argentia grinned as Griegvard launched into a predictable, expletive-rich tirade against elves and the idiot notions of humans. "Th' King best get this trade goin' just t' get them fool ideas from yer great block heads!"

Guntyr merely smiled.

"Are dwarven weapons really better?" Augustus asked. He'd spent most of the past days engaged with Mirk, whom he found endlessly fascinating. "I've never used a weapon—I don't know," he added defensively when Griegvard scowled at him.

"Aye, yer a strange one, fer true," the dwarf muttered. Like all his kind, he had little use for his beardless cousins, who could neither mine nor fight with any great skill, and he was particularly leery of a halfling who used magic.

"Well?" Augustus pressed, genuinely curious.

"Is th' damn sky blue?" Griegvard snorted.

And they rolled on.

38

The elk did not sense the barbarian.

The great animal sniffed the air, wide nostrils flaring delicately. Its fiercely antlered head swiveled slowly, wary of any hint of danger. Satisfied, the elk bent toward the narrow stream that forged its sluggish course through the snow-covered tundra of the northland.

As the elk drank, the barbarian continued to watch. He was nearly close enough to attack, but he was not there to kill the elk. In truth, even with his bow and harpoon he would have been hard pressed to bring down the massive deer.

But soon, Sturm willing, I will meet that test...

Exmoor's rite of manhood was in two moons. He would be sent off alone to survive for a week in the wilderness. He would have no supplies but what he could forage and no weapons but those the Council chose to give him.

That was trial enough, but to return alive was not sufficient to pass the test. To earn his name as a full tribesman—one able to join the hunting parties, sit on the Council, and take a wife—he had to return with a kill: a sign of strength proved in blood. He would eat the heart of that animal in a ceremony, and its spirit would follow him through his days of manhood.

Any animal would do, but Exmoor wanted to make a good kill. No foxes or hares for Kozar's son. He wanted something that would bring great honor to his family, atoning for some of the shame that had fallen on them when Brieki had been taken.

Exmoor wanted an elk.

A white bear would have seemed the more logical choice. They were the paragons of arctic strength: towering monstrosities often more than a dozen feet tall and capable of laying waste to whole settlements. But Exmoor, like all barbarians, knew that the elk was by far the most dangerous of Nord's creatures: wholly unpredictable when roused, and nigh impossible to kill.

I will. Sturm will watch over me, and I will not fail...

He had kept his intention private, even from his family. To boast of a thing and fail was worse than fleeing from danger, and there was no guarantee he would even encounter an elk during his rite.

But he had encountered one today; surely that was a sign of Sturm's favor.

Forgetting his duty as a sentry, Exmoor stalked the elk, letting his spirit come near the animal's spirit. When the time of their conflict came—

The elk snapped its head up, snorting in alarm.

Exmoor cursed silently. Had it scented him somehow? He was well concealed on the frozen ground, downwind from the animal. *It's startled—*

And that was when the barbarian finally heard the noise he should have heard many minutes earlier.

39

It was the company's third day in Nord.

After the tight dark of the dwarf tunnels, the open, windswept, rolling landscape seemed dizzyingly immense and unendingly bleak. *It's like Yth, only colder*, had been Argentia's first impression. She was more acclimated now, and understood the essential difference between the desert beyond the Black Crags of the Sudenlands and the tundra north of the Gelidian Spur was not in temperature, but temperament.

Yth was a true wasteland, devoid of all life beyond a handful of predators: a broken place, abandoned by men and gods. Nord was cold and harsh and it could kill cruelly, but it could also sustain.

And it did.

As the company followed the ruts left by the dwarven ore-sleds westward away from the mountains, the land leveled into frosted plains crowned with coniferous brush and stretches of forest. They saw herds of huge deer—elk and caribo, Guntyr named them—white foxes, spotted owls that flew by day, and blue geese by the gaggle. That night, the howls of wolves played a symphony beneath stars that looked like diamonds laid out on an eternity of black velvet.

Argentia was amazed that anything could survive the Nordic dark. When the sun set, the temperature plunged. Argentia had thought she'd prepared for this extremity. Her cloak, trapper's hat, and gloves were all of white rabbit. Despite her hatred of sleeves, beneath a rabbit vest and fleece scarf she wore a gray wool sweater with a rolled neck that reached up to her chin. But the Nordic cold had teeth and it bit fiercely. When the wind gusted, it slapped so sharply it took her breath. It was not until she spent many minutes crouched beside the fire that she believed she could feel all her face again.

The first night was horrible. Even with their fire, the travelers were bitterly cold.

The second night was worse. *We need something*, Argentia thought miserably, looking at the others huddled near to the ineffectual flames, hunched and shaking. She remembered the esp.

"What's that?" Kest asked as she set to work brewing the drink. "Caf?"

"Not quite. You'll see."

Though she seemed confident, Argentia had only made esp once before, and it had been a disaster. She was determined to do better this time.

As the water boiled and she ground the beans in a mortar, she became aware that Guntyr was watching her with great interest. "What?"

"Grind them more finely. It will brew better."

Argentia was surprised. "Have you had this before? It's very rare."

"I did not come from Nord to Argo directly, Lady. I have known an elf or two in my time. Here, let me see." He took the bowl from her and began to work the mortar. The firelight flashed silver off one of his fingers.

"Shiny ring," Mirk peeped from beside Augustus. The meerkat liked the halfling more than any of the others in the party except Argentia, with whom he camped and generously afforded space in what he had claimed as 'Mirk's blankets.'

"I've never seen you wear jewelry. Where'd you get that? From Bryget?" Augustus asked.

"Yes, from Bryget," Guntyr replied after an embarrassed hesitation. "For protection. Before we left."

"I thought Nordens didn't believe in nonsense like that," Tib laughed.

"A Southling conceit Bryget has adopted. I put no faith in it."

"Don't be too sure," Argentia said, touching her dragon's tooth.

Guntyr shrugged his huge shoulders. "Taking it made Bryget happy. Its purpose is served." He handed the mortar back to Argentia. "It is ready."

Argentia dumped the grounds into a sachet and lowered the sac into the boiling water. A few minutes later, the delicious aroma of roasted pecans and honey filled the night.

"That smells great," Tib said.

"Wait 'til you taste it." Argentia divvied up the esp. Closed her eyes and inhaled the steam from her own cup, thinking of Carfax. *To you*, she toasted. Drank. Whether it was Guntyr's grinding or her own better Fortune with her second try, the esp was as she remembered when Carfax had made it: strong and deliciously bitter, hot all the way down. She felt the sharpening of her vision and the clarity that accompanied the elven beverage.

The lieutenants were suitably impressed. "Trust the elves to create such a potent drink," Augustus said.

"Don't got nothin' on dwarf stout," Griegvard muttered. But he drained his cup.

"Thorne?" Argentia asked. He was sitting on the edge of the group and had not touched his cup.

He ignored her.

"Try it," Tib said to Thorne. "It's better than a pipe."

"No." Thorne rose and walked away.

"What the hell is his problem?" Tib got up.

"No, it's all right," Argentia said.

Tib went anyway. "Thorne," he called.

The renegade captain turned to face the lieutenant.

"Why do you hate her?" Tib asked. "You're wrong about her, you know," he continued when Thorne did not answer. "I was too. I thought for sure she was leagued with the twins. But I was wrong. If you can't see it, if you don't want to see it, if you want to keep alienating her—"

"I was not in the habit of explaining myself to you when I was your captain, Tiboren. I do not intend to begin doing so now."

"You're blind and you don't even know it."

"Your opinion does not interest me. I know my course—to avenge Vendimar."

"That's why we're *all* here!"

"Not all of us."

"Why don't you let her help? She would. She wants to."

"Wrong. She wants to rescue her butler."

"She should! He's still *alive*, remember? Who has more stake than her in seeing the twins dead? She's the one they were hunting. You don't think she'd rest easier knowing they were gone?" Tib waited for a response, hoping he had voiced reason enough to pierce Thorne's misperceptions.

Thorne turned on his heel and strode off.

Argentia, who had caught snatches of the conversation, felt a pang of disquiet. She didn't care what Thorne thought of her, but she didn't want a divided camp.

Tib returned to the fire, looking frustrated. Argentia poured him a small measure of esp and placed a hand on his arm. "Let it be. I appreciate what you tried to do, but I'm a big girl. I can take care of myself."

"That's no excuse. He's—"

"An arrogant jackass?"

"Exactly," Tib said.

Argentia turned and shot a triumphant grin at Augustus. The halfling spread his hands in defeat. "You win, you win," he said.

"Just know the rest of us are sorry for what happened in Argo," Tib added, finishing his esp and lighting up his pipe.

Argentia didn't think she'd ever met a group that dwelt more on the past. It was enough to make her crazy. "You were doing your duty, that's all. Keep doing it now. Don't turn your back on Thorne because of me. Whether he likes it or not, he's going to need help with those twins. A lot of help."

40

Despite Argentia's admonishment, the tension among the Argosians was still there with the dawn. There were no open hostilities, just a heightened sense of distance from Thorne and disappointment from Tib, Kest, and Augustus. Guntyr remained his mostly silent self. Griegvard shrugged it all off as more "human foolishness."

They went on until Kest spotted tendrils of smoke leaking up against the blue of the horizon. "Look," he said, pointing.

"Aye, that's it," Griegvard confirmed. "O'er that last ridge there."

Anticipating fire and warmth and an end to this stage of their journey, the company quickened their pace. Up ahead, a solitary elk lifted its head warily from a narrow stream, water dripping from its massive snout as it regarded the approaching strangers, assessing any danger.

Spooked it, Argentia thought, her boots crunching along. *Of course, we're making enough racket for Vloth to hear us at his pyramid, wherever the hell it is...*

The elk bounded effortlessly across the stream and turned to keep a suspicious eye on them. "Good eats, them things," Griegvard said. "But tough as hell t' kill. Takes three or four o' them barbarians t' bring one down."

"How many dwarves would it take?" Argentia teased.

"One, o' course. What're ye askin' such a stupid question fer?"

"Oh, just curious."

"Ye breakin' me stones, girl?"

"Me? Never."

"Bah!"

Grinning beneath her hood, Argentia walked on. The plumes of smoke grew closer. She caught a sharp tang on the wind, unmistakable in any clime. *The Sea of Sleet....* On its coast, Griegvard had told them, they would find the Walros settlement.

Argentia breathed deep of the salt air, which never failed to lift her spirits.

The barbarians seemed to materialize out of the very ground.

One moment there was nothing but tundra. The next the company was surrounded by a score of giant men.

A score of giant men with harpoons.

41

"Halt or die, Southling dogs!" the leader of the Nordens ordered. "You are intruders upon the lands of the Walros. Answer Kozar: what purpose have you here?"

The company had drawn their weapons and formed a ring within the ring of barbarians. The Nordens were huge, well armed, and alert. The travelers were outnumbered, cold, and surrounded.

Argentia had faced worse odds in her life—but not many. "What the hell is this?" she growled at Griegvard. "I thought you knew these people."

Griegvard pushed forward. "Get them damn sticks out o' me friends' faces, Kozar son o' Rendel—or by Drim's anvil ye can go back t' makin' yer weapons o' rocks instead o' dwarf metal. How'd yer bloody tribe like that?"

Kozar, a towering block of muscle in skins and hides with a fur cloak hanging behind his broad shoulders, threw back his chiseled, blonde-bearded head and roared laughter. "Forgive me, my good dwarven friend. I did not see you amid these others, nor did my son number you among those he spied approaching."

"Father, I have failed you," Exmoor said.

"You did well to alert the tribe with such speed," Kozar replied. "But to know friend from foe is the true purpose of the sentry. Had blood been spilt here and Griegvard Gynt slain, a grievous time we would have had explaining the accident to his kin and king."

"I will not forget, Father."

"We're needin' t' speak wit Gozal," Griegvard said.

Kozar stroked his thick beard. "A dwarf aiding Southlings who seek the men of Nord. A strange party indeed." He addressed the company. "Before I agree to bring you before my king, it is custom that you show your faces and state plain your purpose, that if you keep honor it may bind you to your words, and if you do not, the lie will tell in your eyes."

The company lowered their hoods. "One of our cousins," Kozar murmured, seeing Guntyr. "And what have we here?"

Kozar's surprise was not unique. There was much pointing and sudden conversing in Nordic, all of it directed at Argentia and the red tresses that fell beneath her white fur hat.

Finally Kozar raised a hand. "They want to know how you trapped the fire in your hair," he said. "They think you a sorceress. Are you?"

For Aeton's sake—this nonsense again? It was not the first time men of foreign lands had thought Argentia was a sorceress because of the color of her hair. "No. Just a redhead."

Kozar arched his brows, and then translated. The barbarians laughed and grinned at Argentia. "What?" she asked.

Griegvard looked up at her, shaking his head. "In their tongue, red's th' word fer a loose woman. Basically ye told 'em yer easy t' bed."

"Oh that's just great."

Kozar raised a hand again. "Your faces are fair enough, even that strange one there. Fey blood is in those veins, though child you seem."

Bowing, Augustus conjured several globes of light that danced between his hands and vanished up his sleeves.

The barbarians, who were almost as suspicious of spellcraft as dwarves, recoiled in surprise, whispering what sounded like "shaman."

"Wizard, enough." Thorne said. He knew the halfling was only trying to defuse some of the tension, but he wished Augustus would have acted with more discipline rather than tipping even a hint of his abilities. They might have need of his true magic at any moment. Now that element of surprise was gone.

"Who leads the Southlings?" Kozar asked, catching Thorne's commanding tone.

"I do," Argentia said, quickly and decisively. Thorne said nothing.

If Kozar was surprised, he did not show it. "And your purpose? Why have you sought the Walros?"

"We're looking for a pyramid built of ice. King Durn of Stromness said you could lead us—"

Argentia broke off as the harpoons were suddenly leveled at the company again and the Nordens stepped closer.

"Why do you seek that accursed place?" Kozar demanded. Argentia understood that only her answer stood between them and a fight for their very lives. The others tensed around her: they knew it, too.

"My friend is a prisoner there. I have to get him back." Argentia blew a strand of hair out of her eyes, held Kozar's wrathful gaze, and waited.

Finally Kozar motioned and the harpoons lifted away. "Impossible," he said flatly. "The pyramid is impregnable."

"But Father—" Exmoor protested.

"Silence!"

Exmoor flinched at the rebuke. Kozar ignored him. "Come," he said to the company. "You wished an audience with King Gozal. You shall have it. The tribe will be most interested to hear what you propose."

42

Led by their barbarian escort, the company crested a last rise in the tundra. Argentia had been pondering why the mention of the pyramid had elicited such a vehement reaction from the Nordens—knowing Vloth, there was surely some villainy involved—but the vista that opened before her wiped those thoughts from her mind.

The land sloped gently away to a sea such as Argentia had never seen before. The deep gray water thrashed as if in torment along a rocky shore, raising a veil of mist. Beyond the waves and the curtain of spray, where great seabirds wheeled, was the ice: jagged and majestic crags rising from the water like the peaks of mountains almost drowned in some cataclysmic flood. Struck just so by the white disc of the sun, they flashed the same cobalt blue of Argentia's eyes.

Along this rugged stretch of coast stood the settlement of the Tribe of the Walros: pine-and-stone huts of simple, sturdy craft with no pretensions beyond shelter from the bitter cold. Argentia remembered her friend Kodius explaining his fascination with Teranor's architecture by saying, "In Teranor, many things are built for beauty. In Nord, all things are built for survival."

Kozar ushered the company toward the council hall, a long, low building, larger than any four other dwellings combined, with several stone chimneys that were the source of the smoke they had seen earlier. In the center of the settlement, they passed a stone-ringed fire-pit. It was dormant now, but Argentia could easily imagine it blazing up in the dark, giving light and warmth against the frigid nights. She also saw they were attracting a goodly amount of attention, and took the opportunity to study the Nordens.

The men were all tall and strong. Their faces were weathered by the harsh elements of their lives, but their pale gazes were bright and undefeated.

Not since her encounter with the elves of Falcontyr's Forest had Argentia seen such similitude among a people. The Nordens were all various shades of blonde, with tanned skin, strong jaws and raw cheekbones above heavy beards. Handsome in a rugged way, but a bit too hirsute for her tastes.

The women were tall enough to make Argentia feel short. As tan and blonde as the men, they also favored buckskins and long-sleeved tunics, but wore their hair in thick plaits instead of loose manes.

Several of the women pointed at Argentia and whispered to each other, no doubt commenting on her pale skin and flaming hair. Griegvard and Augustus drew their share of whispers as well, while other women made eyes at Guntyr. Many of them seemed amused by Tib's stature. He was shorter than most of the Norden children who were standing silent and protective near their mothers and sisters, watching the strangers with wary gazes.

Kozar lifted a huge elk-bone horn hanging beside the entrance to the council hall and blew a note that rang heavy and clear across the arctic air. At its sound, the women and children dispersed, and the men tromped into the hall. Argentia counted three score at least.

"Wait," Kozar said. He followed the other men into the hall, leaving Exmoor and a half-dozen other young, beardless men to keep watch over the company.

"What's going on in there?" Tib asked.

"Palaver," Griegvard replied. "Tribe decides e'rythin' by vote."

"Will they help us?" Kest asked.

Mirk peeked out of Argentia's pack. "Time for food?" he asked, blinking sleepily.

"Shhhh!" Argentia hissed.

"But Mirk—"

"Quiet!" They were already in a tenuous situation. She didn't want a talking animal making matters worse—but from Exmoor's wide eyes, she saw the damage was done. Luckily, she was saved from any explanations by the swift return of Kozar.

"Come," he said.

Like the throne hall of Aventar, the council hall of the Walros was longer than it was wide. Fires burned in the hearths in each wall. It took a few moments for the warmth to sink into the company. Only then did they realize how truly cold it was outside.

Kozar led the company to the mouth of a U-shaped table where some sixty Nordens were seated and staring at them with hard eyes. Argentia noticed that most of the men appeared to be either younger than her or some twenty winters older.

At the far end of the hall, above the largest hearth, a giant skull was mounted on the wall. Its domed head had one vast eye socket and two sabre-like tusks protruded from its upper jaw. *A walros*, Argentia guessed. The thing must have been fearsome in life. It remained imposing even in death.

Seated on a throne of elk bone and antlers beneath this trophy was King Gozal. The hide of a white bear was flung over the table before him, its head staring at the company, its forepaws dangling toward the floor.

"Gozal One-Ear, here are the dwarf-friend Griegvard Gynt and his Southling companions," Kozar announced.

Placing his huge hands on the bearskin, Gozal rose. He was short for a Norden, but made up for his relative lack of height in breadth. Like a giant dwarf, he was almost as wide as he was tall, and all of that flesh was hard muscle. Half his face was a mass of scars, including one jagged slice that ran down his forehead, passed over his eye, and continued down his cheek.

"White bear gave me this," Gozal said. His voice was gravel. He swiveled his head, and Argentia saw where he had earned his name. His right ear was gone. The side of his head was just a mass of shiny white tissue leading down into the other scars on his face. "Now I eat off his hide. Who among you can boast such a feat?"

What is this horseshit? Argentia frowned.

"King o' th' Walros, we come t' ye fer—" Griegvard began.

"I know why you have come!" Gozal interrupted. "Answer me. Who among you can boast such a feat as Gozal's? Speak your deeds of strength! Prove yourselves worthy of the aid of the Walros!"

The company glanced at each other, uncertain what to do.

"Speak!" the King demanded. "Or have you weak Southlings no deeds to boast?" There was a ripple of scornful laughter around the table.

"This is ridiculous!" Argentia snapped.

Gozal glowered at her. "Ware, wench. You have a quick tongue."

"But a quicker hand." Argentia drew her handbow and fired twice. Silver crescents screamed across the hall, shattering the antlers to either side of Gozal's head.

"Insolent wench!" A Norden to her left leaped up. "You dare—"

Pivoting smoothly, Argentia fired a third time, blowing the hatchet out of the barbarian's grasp even as he cocked his arm to throw. "There's no time for games," Argentia said. "Either give your aid or be damned."

Around the hall, Nordens were rising, reaching for their weapons.

"Hold!" Gozal boomed. Then he chuckled, a noise that turned into a deep laugh as he brushed chips of bone off his shoulder. "By Sturm, you've *spirit*, wench!"

"Then honor it," Argentia said, holstering the handbow. "Help me."

"Let the Tribe speak," Gozal said. "Shall we aid these Southlings in finding the *obludra's* pyramid?"

Some swiftly, some slowly, the Nordens around the table began to stand. Not all rose, but many more did than remained seated.

Gozal nodded. "So says the Tribe."

43

"That was a foolish thing you did." Thorne stepped in front of Argentia. The company was waiting outside while the Tribe selected their guides. "If you missed—"

"I didn't miss." Argentia retorted. "And I got us the help we needed. Like I told you before—if you don't like the way I do things, find your own goddamned way to the pyramid."

Thorne started to reply, but abruptly turned away, burning the ground with his smoldering gaze.

"Bet that hurt," Tib whispered to Augustus, unable to contain a measure of satisfaction as Thorne was forced to choke on his pride to serve his vengeance.

Augustus nodded but didn't reply. Though he shared Tib's sentiment, he found it troubling. After Thorne's wife and child had been murdered, Thorne had devoted himself to the Watch. After Vendi had been murdered, he had devoted himself to revenge. *When that's gone, what will you have left, my friend?* the halfling wondered.

Kozar emerged from the hall. He was smiling. "Exmoor and I have been chosen to guide you to the pyramid," he said. "Unfert will go as well." He pointed to a very tall, almost slender Norden, who approached and introduced himself.

"How far a journey?" Argentia asked Kozar.

"Ten days."

We'll just make it...

While the sleds and supplies were readied, the Nordens set a feast in honor of their guests. The great bonfire was lit. Huge fish were spitted on long skewers and roasted over the flames.

"What are they?" Argentia asked. She'd never seen them in Argo or any other port of call.

"You have never had char?" Exmoor asked. He and his parents were sitting with the company. "You Southlings are strange indeed."

"Exmoor, treat our guests more politely," his mother, Elsina, chided.

"Yes, Mother." Turning back to Argentia, he said, "I am honored to be your guide, and to have the chance to—"

"Exmoor," Kozar interrupted. "You will have ten days to chatter their ears off. Let them eat in peace."

"Yes, Father," Exmoor said.

A shadow fell across the company. "You." The speaker pointing down at Guntyr was an unkempt Norden with angry, bloodshot eyes. A flagon of mead was clenched in his fist. "Get up."

Trouble, Argentia thought. She'd noticed this one sitting beside Gozal in the hearth hall. He had been the one of the last to stand in support of aiding them.

"Don't." Thorne put a restraining hand on Guntyr's shoulder.

Guntyr pulled away and rose to face his opponent. He was shorter by about half a head. "What do you want?" he asked.

"Kroth, let our guests be." Kozar also rose, with Exmoor quickly following.

"Gozal's impressed by tricks with weapons. I'm not," Kroth sneered. His voice was slurry with drink. "Let's see what strength you really have."

"I do not wish to kill you," Guntyr said quietly.

"Pretty words, coward. What tribe did you flee, coward? Or traitor? No man of Nord goes willingly to the soft lands beyond the mountains. What tribe have you disgraced? Tell me, that I may send your coward's corpse back to them."

"I am a citizen of Argo." Guntyr's voice was dangerously calm. "I have no tribe. That part of my life is behind me."

Kroth tossed the contents of his flagon into Guntyr's face.

"Kroth, stop this!" Kozar stepped forward. Kroth shoved him away. Guntyr still had not moved.

"Coward," Kroth goaded him. "You are too long among the Southling dogs. You have forgotten your honor. Forgotten the ways of Nord."

"Not all of them."

With a movement so sudden even Argentia could barely mark it, Guntyr's hands caught Kroth's head and twisted violently. There was a loud snap. Kroth fell at Guntyr's feet.

"Aeton's bolts!" Tib and the rest of the company scrambled up in disbelief. Around the fire-pit, all had gone ominously silent. Kozar, Exmoor, and Elsina drew back, leaving Guntyr standing above Kroth's body.

Not good... Argentia doubted the volatile Nordens would take well to the death of one of their Tribe, however much the lout had deserved it.

Kozar barked orders in Nordic. Barbarian warriors surrounded the company with the same speed they had used in surprising them on the tundra. Harpoons glinted sharply in the firelight.

"Ye damn fool," Griegvard spat at Guntyr. "Ye know what ye done?"

"He has spilled the blood of the Tribe of the Walros," Kozar answered before Guntyr could reply. Shaking his head, he turned to the ring of guards. "If any of them move, kill them. I will go tell King Gozal his son is dead."

44

The company was back in the council hall. This time their prospects appeared even grimmer than when they'd first stood before the Tribe.

Gozal rose and gestured to the vacant seat at his right hand. "Speak your defense," he said to Guntyr, his voice tight with emotion.

Guntyr said nothing.

Gozal nodded, as if that silence spoke volumes. "Kozar and the other tribesmen gave their voices for you. A matter of honor, they said." He paused, grimacing as he fought for self-control. "I know my son. I believe their words," he added sadly. "A man must have leave to defend his honor. That is the Code of Nord. I will impose no blood penalty for it, though the loss is nearer to my heart than even my own life."

The company did not have time to be relieved.

"Though I spare your life, there must be punishment for spilling the blood of the Tribe," Gozal continued. "Kroth was arrogant, but he was strong. He will be missed." He paused again. "The price of his life is thus. No help shall you have of the Walros. Go, all of you, and never return your death-bringing faces here, else the blood penalty will be claimed. So swears Gozal One-Ear."

Argentia felt her hope collapse. The pyramid was ten days distant—in what direction she had no idea. Without the help of the Nordens, they might wander for weeks without ever finding it. *Ikabod doesn't have weeks...*

"Right of Challenge," she said boldly, stepping forward.

There was much surprised muttering around the huge table, and some incredulous laughter. Gozal lifted his hand for silence.

"Right of Challenge is no light matter," he said. "How is it that a Southling, and a wench, comes to speak such words to the Tribe?"

"I am well traveled. The Code of Nord is not unknown to me." That was a bit of a boast, but Argentia figured it was in keeping with the local custom. In truth, what she knew of the Code she had learned from Kodius, and that was little. *I just hope it's enough to pull this off...*

"Then you know that only a blood penalty merits a Challenge," Gozal said. Since no Norden would so dishonor himself to speak in defense of his actions, a relative or friend was permitted to perform a Challenge on their behalf. If they succeeded, the condemned man would be spared. If they failed, death would come for both of them.

"If you don't help us, my friend in the pyramid will die. Only with your aid can we reach him in time to save him. A blood penalty merits a Challenge." Argentia let her echo of the King's words hang in the air.

"What do you propose?" Gozal growled. Argentia had argued him into a corner. He could not deny the Challenge now without disgracing the Code.

"Fair terms. We win, you give us the guides you promised. We lose, and we accept your banishment."

Gozal nodded slowly. "Let the Tribe speak."

One by one, the Nordens rose, this time to a man. All held the Code's sanctity above every other point of honor.

"So says the Tribe. One among you shall suffer the Challenge—"

"I will," Thorne said, cutting him off.

"The Tribe will decide," Gozal replied coldly.

Thorne cursed under his breath.

"That scrawny, dark haired little weasel!" a tribesman shouted, pointing at Tib.

"Hey!" Tib protested. Thorne glared at him and he shut up.

"What of the dwarf?" a second barbarian suggested.

"Not the dwarf. We dare not risk the enmity of his kin," another countered.

"The small one, then," said a fourth man, pointing to Augustus. "He is surely their weakest."

"Nay!" one of the men who had been in Kozar's party said. "The halfling is a shaman. He will cheat us with his magic."

The company could only look on helplessly as the Nordens argued back and forth, debating whom to select. Finally Gozal lifted his hands.

"Wench, you voiced the Challenge. *You* shall undertake it."

Your mistake, Argentia thought.

45

Argentia stood in the shallows of the Sea of Sleet.

Foaming surf splashed cold around her boots. The gray water was violent beneath persistent mist, the waves breaking hard in fast sets.

Gonna be a rough ride, Argentia thought, glancing at the small craft floating beside her: a one-man canoe that the Nordens called a *kyak*.

"Do you understand the Challenge?" Gozal asked. He was standing with the other tribesmen on the rocky beach. The women and children remained back by the huts.

Argentia nodded. She was to row out to a floe, steal an egg from the nest of one of the great seabirds, and deliver it unbroken to shore. "Sounds simple enough," she muttered, certain there were about a thousand dangers the barbarians had left unspoken. *Doesn't matter...* Ikabod needed her, so she needed the Nordens, so she was going.

Thorne caught her arm. Like Argentia, he was given to trust his own abilities over another's. It was difficult for him to stand and watch his chance to find the twins come to rest on the efforts of a woman he in part blamed for the very death he sought to avenge. "Do not fail," he said.

Argentia looked him in the eyes. "I won't."

She turned and pushed the kyak out into the Sea of Sleet. The freezing water numbed her legs. The waves thundered and roared, soaking and buffeting her as she tried to get out past the first line before mounting the kyak. She fought forward, her boots slipping on the shifty sand, and got slammed by the next foaming surge.

Staggering, she clung to the kyak to stay upright. Took another hit, the spray leaving her half blind. *This isn't working...*

A new wave gathering with a tidal rumble. While the withdrawing surf sloshed icily around her thighs, Argentia hauled herself into the kyak and started paddling. She'd practiced the back-and-forth motion in the shallows, and was a natural in most any type of watercraft, but the kyak required an incredible amount of balance and precision. The Sea of Sleet was not inclined to be kind to a novice.

The incoming wave broke just in front of Argentia, the surf-surge spinning the kyak backwards. Argentia fought for control, almost capsized to the left, jerked her weight to the right, almost capsized that way, somehow kept upright, and settled to a stop having lost most of the distance she'd gained on foot.

She felt the eyes on her from the beach but didn't turn. She imagined Thorne's disdainful glare. *Get it together, Gen. You can do this...*

She let another wave break and wash past the kyak. Started out again in the brief calm, watching the water before her rise into a slobbering hill.

Go go go... She propelled the kyak up the liquid slope and down the back.

Another wave was already rising.

On the shore, Griegvard, Thorne, and the lieutenants looked on nervously as Argentia fought her way into the sea. Guntyr stood a space apart, silently watching the Challenge his actions had forced.

The others knew that Kroth had provoked the incident, but they could not help feeling betrayed and angry at this foul turn of Fortune: a turn made worse by the fact that it was so unlike Guntyr to lose his composure. *I've never seen that,* Kest mused. *He just snapped. Maybe returning to Nord affected him more than we noticed...*

But it was too late for such lamenting.

"It's all on her now," Tib said. "If she doesn't make it back with that egg—"

"Do not say that," Thorne interrupted harshly. "Do not even think it."

Silently, they turned back to the Sea of Sleet, where the waves and mists had swallowed Argentia.

46

The kyak burst beyond the last of the waves. Suddenly everything was clear and bright and almost still.

Grateful for the respite, Argentia stopped rowing. Her body was immaculately conditioned, but the ocean was inexorable. Her arms and shoulders ached from battling the piled combers. She was drenched and freezing, her hat plastered to her head, her clothes to her body. As she floated on the open water, with mists blocking her view of the shore and nothing but sky above and a ceaseless sea of icy atolls ahead, she felt suddenly isolated and alone.

Shaking the feeling off, Argentia marked the iceberg with the albatross nest. The floe was bent like a wizard's hat. Its sides were rugged and steep, but the crest looked flat enough to walk on. Argentia could see the aerie, made of pine boughs from the inland woods. The albatross did not appear to be in residence.

Smiling at her fortune, she dipped her double-bladed oar resolutely into the water and—

What the hell is that?

The fin, huge and black, cut through the water off to her left, rising from the depths like some terrible, shadowy blade. It was a dorsal, and Argentia guessed it was taller than she was. *If that's a shark, I'm in serious trouble...*

She drew the oar slowly out of the water. The fin glided past, silent as a ghost. She could make out the shape of the thing beneath the surface: a huge fish of some sort. *Thirty feet easy...* She had little desire to get closer for a more accurate measurement.

When the fin disappeared into the misty veil, Argentia exhaled a breath she hadn't realized she'd been holding and started paddling again. She reached the iceberg without incident. Grounding the kyak, she started up the slope of the floe. The wind cut her like a thousand daggers. She tried not to think about how cold she was, or how she could already feel her clothes stiffening—

"Ca-runk!"

Argentia looked up sharply. At first she though she was hallucinating from the cold, for it seemed a lion was stalking towards her. Indeed, the thing had the mane, head, and forelegs of a lion, but the sleek, brown-furred body of a seal. Later she would learn it was a celeon; there and then she didn't give a damn what it was called.

The celeon uttered another barking "Ca-runk!" and charged. Its great paws propelled its heavy-tailed body across the ice with clumsy speed.

Why is nothing ever easy? Argentia drew her katana, shifted her boots to meet the charge, and slipped.

She lost her sword as she hit the ground. The celeon leaped for her. She rolled aside, feeling the ice shudder as the thing slammed down where she had been. Scrambling to her feet, she grabbed her blade, but now the celeon was between her and the top of the floe, and two more of the things were coming in from the left.

God damn it! Fighting three of these things on ice was not something she relished—not when she had an option.

A flick of her katana bayed the nearest celeon, and Argentia took off running to the right, angling towards the water to keep her balance. With some quick distance between her and the pursuing animals, she sheathed her sword, cut up the slope again, and lashed her whip around a jag of ice above her.

Using the whip as a towline, Argentia scrambled up the floe. When she reached the jag, she looked down.

The celeons were coming, but awkwardly: the slope was nearly too much for them. Argentia made certain of her footing and snapped her whip again, snaring another hold and climbing hard.

Almost there...

The celeons continued to grunt and bark below as Argentia lunged from her last whip-hold and pulled herself onto the crest. There was the nest.

And the albatross!

The giant seabird was the size of an eagle, with mottled grey feathers and a long yellow beak. It spread its wings, a span of nearly ten feet, fanning the air with its dirty avian scent as it screeched in warning.

Argentia hoped she wouldn't have to kill it—there was a faerie story about a mariner who had murdered an albatross and damned himself and his crew—but if she had to, she would. She needed the egg.

The huntress and the albatross moved at the same instant, surging forward to clash on the flat crest. Argentia dove low. The albatross swept just above her. She took advantage of the miss, scrambling to the aerie. There were three eggs, each the size of an oculyr. Argentia picked one up. It was not fragile, but solid and weighty, like a loupe melon from Sormoria.

The quick-circling albatross slammed into her back. Argentia lost the egg, twisting wildly as the bird's weight bore her down into the nest. She was engulfed in a stinking storm of feathers from the hurricane wings, followed by a lightning bolt of bright pain as the beak lanced into her shoulder.

Screaming, Argentia grabbed the greasy wings and flung the bird aside. It tumbled across the crest, flapping off the ground, spearing towards her as she rose.

With desperate inspiration, Argentia made a weapon of her scarf, flinging the sodden wrap like a bola, striking the albatross out of the air. The bird fell, tangled and thrashing. Argentia grabbed an egg and raced to the edge of the crest.

The celeons were waiting below.

Screw it... Argentia stepped off the edge and ran down the floe, letting her momentum take her faster and faster towards the bellowing celeons. She veered toward the smallest one of the trio. It reared up, thrusting its chest out in challenge, leonine jaws snapping eagerly.

Argentia vaulted it apace.

Her boots shot out from under her as she landed, and she gave up her body, slamming down on her back with no effort to break her fall. All her focus was on keeping the egg securely cradled between her arms and her fur vest.

The icy slope blasted the breath from her lungs. She went spinning down, the world starbursting behind her eyes as she dragged her heels, trying to stop her wild ride. The rough ice tore at her, sharp as gravel. She skidded to a halt not three feet from the edge of the floe and lay there, groaning and dazed.

"Ca-runk! Ca-runk!"

Cursing, Argentia twisted to her knees. The celeons were charging, chuffing and snorting out bursts of breath like smoke from dwarven war machines.

Argentia forced herself up and staggered to the kyak. Clambering in, she set the egg securely in her lap and shoved away from the floe. *Made—*

The celeons plunged into the water after her.

Argentia paddled like a woman possessed, hoping to avoid or outdistance the celeons. It was useless. As clumsy as they were on land, the celeons were fleet and deadly in the water. They pursued and caught the kyak, butting it from below, ramming and clawing at its sides, trying to capsize it.

Argentia used the oar to fend off the charging celeons. If she could just get to the break point, the waves would take her in, but she couldn't paddle and fight, and every hit might be the kyak's last.

Abruptly, the attacks stopped.

The celeons scattered through the slaten water. Argentia was alone amid the ice floes. A dreadful foreboding gathered upon her. She looked around. Saw nothing. In the queer stillness she could hear the roar of the waves—

The Sea of Sleet exploded before her as the orka breached.

47

The leviathan seemed to rise forever.

Its back was a dark tower, its belly white as the floes. Water poured off its bulk in cataracts as it hung for an instant, poised in all its terrifying glory, before slamming down.

The wave of its impact blasted over the kyak, almost swamping it. Argentia covered the albatross egg with her arms, bracing herself with her legs as the little craft rocked wildly. She risked lifting a hand to wipe away the water dripping into her eyes from her soaked hat, looking desperately around for the monstrous creature.

The orka had vanished.

At least it got rid of those other things... Her heart still pounding from the near disaster, Argentia put the paddle to the water again.

She was about halfway to the waves when she saw the fin. Moments later the bi-colored head of the orka appeared, its yawning mouth full of triangular teeth and big enough to swallow the huntress and her boat whole.

It was upon her almost before she could react. A desperate thrust of the paddle shoved the kyak hard to port. The orka plowed past. Its wake tossed the kyak sideways. As Argentia fought frantically for control, she saw the fin making a wide arc. *Oh shit—it's coming back...* She knew she'd been lucky the last time. *Have to get to shore...*

She went full bore for the waves, the kyak skimming the surface, leaping ahead. *Got a chance—*

The albatross fell upon Argentia, its beak knifing at her face. Shouting in surprise, she ducked away just in time. Her hat was stabbed off her head. Huge wings battered her. She got the paddle up, jabbing at the bird.

The kyak was flung backwards as the orka surged across its path. The albatross attack had checked Argentia's momentum, and the monster had overshot the boat.

The great bird was still hovering, squawking furiously. "Get away!" Argentia swung violently at it, forcing the albatross to retreat.

Out to the right, the orka was circling again.

The albatross dove, but this time Argentia let it attack. Tucking her head down and hunching her shoulders against its vicious flurry of pecks and buffets, she kept the paddle in the water, striking the kyak forward, racing towards the waves.

Come on, come on...

Argentia rowed up the back of a wave and down into the trough, picking up speed. The albatross was momentarily dislodged, but resumed its assault as soon as it reoriented. It took all Argentia's discipline not to stop rowing to thrash the hateful thing out of the air.

Another climb and slide, and another, and Argentia was almost to the breakline, the waves growing larger, towing her forward. The kyak mounted a final comber. Poised on the crest, Argentia dropped the oar, covering the egg as the boat dipped in the frothing crest and plunged down, riding the wave toward shore.

The albatross was knocked away. Mist and roaring foam were everywhere, obscuring the frantically waving figures on the shore. Argentia caught a snatch of voices screaming:

"—hind you!"

She twisted around.

The orka was there.

Undaunted by the powerful surf, it rushed upon the kyak. There was no way Argentia could dodge it this time.

As the orka slammed into the kyak, Argentia stood up. The impact drove the boat clear out of the water and launched Argentia into the air.

"Thorne!" Argentia flung the egg out with both hands: a high, arcing toss toward the shore.

Then she plunged into the water and the pounding surf sucked her down.

48

After what seemed an eternity of waiting helplessly with the others on shore, Thorne finally saw Argentia's kyak appear out of the mists. The little craft was no more than fifty yards from the beach. Like the parchment boats Thorne had been fond of running when the storms overflowed Argo's gutters in a long-ago and lost youth, it came shooting in amid the waves, rising and falling in the spray.

A giant bird hovered above it, harrying Argentia.

"Why in hell doesn't she kill that thing?" Tib asked as boat and bird disappeared for a moment in the booming foam.

"I don't think— It's gone!" Kest said as the kyak emerged from the spray alone, riding high in the breaking wave. "Aeton's bolts! Look at that!" He pointed to the monstrous black form driving upon the kyak.

"Orka!" Kozar cried. All along the beach the Nordens began shouting and waving wildly. The orka was the only sea creature formidable enough to kill the Tribe's avatar, and thus the sworn enemy of the Walros.

"Behind you!" Augustus shouted to Argentia.

"Damn girl's gonna die out there!" Griegvard growled. Though dwarves despised water, he ran into the sea. Kest had an arrow to his bow but no shot—and none of them could possibly be in time to help Argentia.

"Look out!" Tib shouted as Argentia stood up just before the orka crushed the kyak, blasting it out of the water.

Thorne heard Argentia cry out his name as she was launched clear of the broken kyak. Saw her fling something like an oculyr into the mists. *The egg...*

The throw was a good one: on line—but falling short.

No... Thorne ripped his cloak off, spreading it in his hands as he splashed into the water. The surf tried to cut his legs from under him. He lunged the last distance.

Caught the egg loosely in the basket of his cloak just before it disappeared into the sea.

A wave slapped him over. He scrambled back to his feet, clutching his cloak in one hand, raising it high as he stumbled to shore.

King Gozal approached. Thorne opened his dripping cloak. Gozal looked from the egg to Thorne. Said nothing. "She was tasked to deliver the egg to shore," Thorne said. "The manner of delivery was not specified."

For a moment Gozal continued to stare at Thorne. Then he nodded. "You say true. The Challenge is fairly won," the King declared.

"Have our sleds prepared," Thorne said.

"Where's Argentia?" Augustus said.

Thorne turned back to the water. The orka was a receding fin. The kyak was washing ashore piece by splintered piece.

Of Argentia there was no sign.

"The Sea of Sleet is cruel and jealous," Kozar said. "What her waves take, they do not always return."

Though they were resigned to nature's violence, the Nordens remained with the company, keeping hopeful watch. Waves crashed in. Rolled out. Long minutes passed.

Finally, they conceded Argentia lost.

"Such bravery is to be honored," Gozal said. "We will feast her memory ere we send you on your course. She died well."

"Not so." Guntyr pointed down the beach.

Several hundred yards away, on the very edge of vision, a form crawled out of the shallows and collapsed.

49

"She is coming."

"When did she leave?" Togril Vloth asked. He had expected this message. Lady Dasani could not hope to find his Frost Palace without the aid of the Nordens, and even among those wild people the guildmaster had his spies.

"Not yet, but soon," the barbarian said. "They have won sleds from the Tribe."

Vloth leaned back from the oculyr and folded his fat, ringed fingers together. Nearly three weeks had passed since his arrival at the Frost Palace. While he had calmed considerably since that first day, he was still anxious to be done with this and return to Telarban to make certain of his security.

The wizard Mouradian was constructing a new mirror, but it would not be finished for a fortnight. Dasani was ten days away. That gave the guildmaster at least four days to dispose of her before he left, or the option to simply keep her prisoner and make an end of her at his leisure after matters were settled in Telarban.

The possibilities were delicious. If he waited—

Vloth's piggish eyes narrowed. "They? She is not alone?"

"She travels with three Southling dogs, a dwarf, a halfling, and another Norden."

Vloth frowned. Save for the dwarf, that fit the description of the party that had invaded his guild—except for one problem.

One of those the barbarian had named was dead back in Telarban.

Thwack!

162

Salis Yip's toothy stripe lashed Ikabod again. The butler convulsed. He would have fallen, but for the chains binding him to the wall.

"Sa-so!" Again and again Yip struck. The punctures from the scorpion-barbed whip formed droplets of blood on Ikabod's bare back and shoulders. Venom from those stingers wracked the butler, sending him into convulsions.

Finally the Whipmaster stopped. His mottled chest was heaving. Sweat ran down his bandy shoulders. Transported by the pleasure of testing his various weapons on Ikabod, he had nearly forgotten that the butler was not to be killed until the Dasani woman had found him.

Had he gone too far?

Yip unlocked the manacles. Ikabod fell limply to the crystal floor. "Up! Worthless old fool. Up!" Yip kicked Ikabod savagely, but the butler was beyond rising.

Yip placed a calloused hand on the butler's narrow chest. Felt a fluttering heartbeat and shallow, rattled breathing. "Sa-so. Lives." Ugly relief lit Yip's slanted eyes. He took a curative potion from his satchel of dark tools. This was not the first prisoner he would bring back from the brink of death.

"Now drinks." Yip grabbed the old man's wispy hair. Ikabod gasped reflexively. Yip poured the contents of the bottle in the butler's mouth and roughly tilted Ikabod's head back.

Ikabod choked, spewing anti-venom all over. Cursing, Yip flung the bottle away and took another from his pouch. This one had a long, hollow needle through its cork. The butler, blue-faced and twitching, did not even feel Yip wrench his gaunt arm steady and jam the needle home.

Almost immediately Ikabod's spasms ceased and his lungs sucked in air.

As the Whipmaster knelt there, waiting to be certain the anti-venom took, he contemplated the effectiveness of his scorpion lash. It was a good tool, but he was working on something even better. Inspired by the landscape of Nord, he had conceived an ice whip capable of freezing whatever it struck. He hoped to complete it in time to test it on the butler.

"Yip!"

The Whipmaster jumped at Vloth's voice. The guildmaster did not usually come to the pyramid's dungeons. Glancing nervously at the bloodied, unconscious butler, Yip rose and bowed low, his palm-like coif flopping. "Sa-so, Guildmaster?"

"Find the twins. I have need of their skills."

In the secret space they had discovered, Puma and Pantra crouched close to the oculyr, watching eagerly as the smoke within the magical orb cleared.

"Hello, Father," they said in unison.

"Children," replied the wizard in the glass.

Though he had sold them to Vloth for the price of a magical diamond, Puma and Pantra remained Mouradian's most prized creations. When they had contacted him and begged his aid in their revenge, the Island Wizard had done his part, delaying the fashioning of a new gating mirror for Vloth, leaving the guildmaster stranded in the pyramid that the twins intended would become his tomb.

"Is all in readiness?" Mouradian asked.

"All is…"

"Most ready," the twins said.

"You are certain of your escape?"

"We know the way…"

"And we will come home."

"Beware Vloth's rings," Mouradian warned. "Their magic is powerful."

"Then we will bring you the fat one's fingers…"

"As gifts," the cat-women promised.

Puma and Pantra left the secret space beneath the storage room. They hid the stolen oculyr until they had need of it again, and were ascending the ramp leading to the upper levels when Salis Yip confronted them.

"Sa-so! Vloth wants," the Whipmaster said, glaring suspiciously at the twins. "What is bitches about?" he demanded. A whip snaked restlessly over the ground by his sandaled feet, its tip glowing like a poker.

"That is none…"

"Of your business."

We could kill him now, Pantra thought.

No. We wait, Puma replied. She wanted to slaughter the hated Salis Yip as much as her sister, but they had been patient thus far. They would hold to their plan, keeping Vloth and his wretched minion convinced of their loyalty right up to the moment they tore them apart.

Even so, they would cringe no more before this Nhapian worm. He had the advantage when they were in chains. In a fair fight they knew the outcome would be very different.

"Ware your speech…"

"With us, little man," they warned.

"Or we will rip your tongue out…"

"And eat it while you watch."

The twins stared at the Whipmaster with such predatory certainty that for a moment Yip was almost unnerved. He recovered, cutting the air with the whip, but with *mrrrrows* of disdain, the twins strode insolently past him and on to their audience with Togril Vloth.

Later, Vloth was limping to his harem when Yip hailed him.

"What is it?" the guildmaster asked crossly. "If you've killed the butler—"

"No, no," Yip said quickly. "Old man lives, Guildmaster. It is the two."

"The twins?" Puma and Pantra had gone gleefully to their task, so glad to be loosed from the Frost Palace that they had not even argued when Vloth insisted they return with their prey alive. "What of them?"

"Too subtle. Too subtle, sa-so, and too silent. Always sneaking. Always skulking. Heed Yip, Guildmaster. They are very dangerous to have about, sa-so."

Vloth ran a fat hand over his bald head. He had been considering this same problem for several weeks. The twins were marvels of magecraft and peerless killers, but they were also wild and unpredictable. Their appetite for destruction had caused the mess in Argo, forcing him to improvise his gauntlet against Dasani. True, they had been the models of subservience since their scourging, but the guildmaster had no doubt they would soon enough revert to their wayward habits.

"Very well," Vloth decided. "After Dasani is finished—and *only* after—they are yours to kill."

50

Argentia woke in warmth.

She felt weight atop her. Blinked her eyes open. Saw the light of the fire in a nearby hearth. She was in a low bed of fur blankets. Sighing, she let herself drift.

When she woke again, it was to Thorne's terse knock. He entered without waiting for an invitation. "So, you survived," he said.

"Try not to sound so pleased," Argentia said, coming fully conscious. She rolled to her back and propped herself on her elbows. They were in a small hut. "What happened? The egg?" She knew she'd taken a great risk with her throw. The egg might have broken or been lost to the sea. "You caught it?"

Thorne nodded. "That was the most foolish thing you've done yet."

"What else could I do? There was no way to beat that thing to shore!"

"Foolish," Thorne repeated. "But also brave. Very brave," he added grudgingly. "Were it not for your daring…" He left the rest unspoken.

"Hey, I just made the throw." Argentia shrugged, surprised by the change in Thorne's tone and manner. "If you hadn't caught it…"

"True."

"See?" Argentia smiled at him. "When we work together…"

Thorne said nothing. Argentia persisted. "Look, Thorne. I know you blame me for your friend's death because the twins came to Argo looking for me. I can't change what you feel, but I'm telling you straight—we're going to need each other to finish this."

Thorne frowned. The frustration plain on his scarred face made him look very old and tired. It was not easy for him to admit when he was wrong, even to himself, but he saw now that Tib had spoken true. He had let his bitterness and his consuming revenge blind him.

Though he would never give Argentia the satisfaction of an apology, he could not deny that whatever blame he laid on her for Vendi's death, her retrieval of the albatross egg had balanced that scale. Perhaps it was time for him to set his grudges aside and become again what he once had been: a leader instead of a solitary avenger.

"I know," he said finally, catching the firelight in his haunted eyes. "I know."

"Truce, then?"

"Truce."

They clasped forearms, and so began an uneasy accord between the huntress and the former Watch captain.

"How did I get here?" Argentia asked. She remembered throwing the egg and hitting the water. After that everything was a jumble of tumbling blackness, terrible cold, and roaring pressure. *The waves must have washed me in...*

"The current dragged you far down the beach. You crawled to shore. The Nordens carried you here and their shaman tended you."

"What time is it?"

"Past dawn," Thorne replied. "The others are waiting."

"Then let's go." Argentia tossed the furs aside, rose, and stretched her aching arms over her head. She was wearing only a silver brassiere and a turquoise thong.

"I would expect more modesty from a lady," Thorne said.

Argentia arched a brow. "I would expect a gentleman to turn around."

"You gave me no chance to."

"You should have been faster."

"I think I liked it better when we didn't speak," Thorne huffed as he turned away.

"Very funny. And they say you have no sense of humor."

"Do they? My loyal lieutenants."

Argentia grinned and dug her clothes out of a pile beside the bed. They were warm and dry, if stiff. She dressed quickly. "Where is everybody?" she asked when they stepped outside. After the warmth of the hut, the arctic air was inhumanly cold. Argentia winced and hugged her arms across her breasts, exhaling a frosty plume of breath. *How do they stand this every day?*

"They are returning the King's son to fire and the sea," Thorne said. "They have been there since dawn." He pointed to the beach. Argentia saw a crowd of Nordens and smoke rising from a pyre. A small boat waited to bear the remains into the ocean.

Wouldn't mind going that way myself...

It was a strange thought for Argentia. She rarely considered how she would die—pursuing some fool adventure or another, she was sure—much less what would happen to her afterwards. Now she hoped that when death finally struck her down, it would be in the company of someone who knew her well enough to ensure her remains were given to the sea.

Somehow I doubt I'll be so lucky....

Pushing aside her macabre thoughts, Argentia followed Thorne through the silent settlement. The others were waiting outside a long, low building, where Exmoor and Unfert were preparing the sleds and dogs.

God, they're like wolves, Argentia thought. The sled dogs were big and strong and handsome, with large padded paws and shaggy gray coats patched with black and white. Angular ears sat atop lupine heads, and tapered snouts held rows of fierce teeth.

As Argentia and Thorne approached, one of the dogs broke away and came to investigate them. It looked even more like a wolf than the others, with a coat of black threaded with shimmering pewter. It ignored Thorne entirely, stopping before Argentia and barking deeply.

"Hello there." She let the dog sniff her hand and crouched down, scratching the thick fur behind its jaws and stroking its silky, silver-sable neck. "Ready to run?"

The dog woofed, its startlingly gray eyes—the color of a storm-sky over the sea—looking alertly into her own. Argentia laughed, stood up, and gave the dog a pat. "Go on."

"Lady feels better?" Mirk asked, scampering over. "Mirk was worried," he added, peering earnestly up at Argentia, his whiskers twitching.

Argentia caught him up and kissed his fuzzy forehead. "I'm fine."

"Then put Mirk down." The meerkat squirmed free, wiping at his fur where she had kissed him.

The others surrounded her. "Have a nice swim?" Tib asked. He had his pipe clenched between his teeth.

"The water was a little chilly. You should try it, though."

"I'll pass, thanks."

Kozar emerged from a nearby hut. "I am glad to see you well," he said to Argentia. "Norden medicines are strong, but we feared your exposure had been too great. There are few who can boast they survived an orka's attack *and* the Sea of Sleet at full tide."

"Call it the luck of the damned," Argentia said.

"The luck of the damned?"

Argentia smiled. "Nothing. Just something a friend said to me once."

Kozar nodded. "Whatever luck it is, let us hope it lasts."

"I've done all right so far. Is everything set here?"

Kozar explained that the first part of their journey would be made on foot.

The sleds could not be used until they came to the Ice Reaches of Frijd, which were three days out from the settlement. On the tundra, whose frost was not so deep as it appeared, their sharp runners would sink beneath the weight of the riders.

"Better get moving, then," Argentia said.

"As soon as you are ready."

About an hour later, the company set forth at a hard pace. That night, they sat around a large fire sipping esp made by Argentia after loud demand from the others. She did not have enough to brew the beverage every night, but after the day's walk and her ordeal in the Sea of Sleet, she figured she could use some herself.

"You have made a friend," Exmoor said. The lanky young barbarian had spent most of the evening near Argentia. He was twenty, and a beautiful woman of any race was going to have all his attention.

"What do you mean?"

"Look there." Exmoor pointed. The gray-eyed dog was lying on Argentia's bedroll, head on its paws, watching her.

"Hey," Argentia called to the dog. "What are you, my shadow?"

The dog thumped its thick tail on the ground.

"Strange," Exmoor said. "That one almost never approaches people."

"What's his name?" Argentia asked.

"Name?" Exmoor laughed. "He is a dog. Why would he have a name?"

Argentia arched both brows. "Ah, right. Never mind."

"Perhaps you will consider a trade: the dog for the meekat?" Exmoor was fascinated by Mirkholmes.

"It's *meerkat*—and no. Mirk's not a pet. At least, he's not my pet. He belongs to the Crown of Teranor, our ruler."

"Yes." Exmoor nodded. "Such a creature is a fitting companion for a King."

Argentia didn't even bother correcting him on that count. Women were not subservient in Nord, as they were in some other lands she'd visited, but she sensed the idea of a female ruler would be impossibly foreign.

Draining the rest of her esp, Argentia rose and went to her bedroll. Hands on her hips, she looked sternly down at the dog. "All right—get off."

The dog yawned.

"Come on—off." Argentia dropped to her knees and threw her arms around the dog. Try as she might—and try she did, much to the amusement of the others—she could not fight him off her bedroll.

Finally she gave up and collapsed next to the dog, stroking his muscular side. "You have a name," she whispered. "Don't you..."

51

"Ha!" Argentia leaned into the icy wind and cracked the sled's reins.

At the lead of a five-dog line, Shadow's silver-dark body surged in response, and they went hurtling even faster, the sled skittering and skipping over the Ice Reaches that spread to the horizon like a vast frozen ocean.

This was their first day riding, but Argentia was a quick study. Moving out wide, she pulled past Kozar and Exmoor on one sled, then Tib, Guntyr, and Augustus on the next. Unfert, riding with a load of supplies, was already behind. Thorne and Kest were ahead.

"Damn ye, girl!" Griegvard roared, clinging to the rope tethers behind Argentia. "Ye get us tossed from this bloody contraption and I'll pound ye one!"

Laughing, Argentia urged the dogs on, rushing up alongside Thorne's sled. He glanced over, his eyes locked with Argentia's, and he cracked his own reins.

They raced, but Shadow proved the difference. As if attuned to Argentia's will, the wolf-dog gained momentum with each stride, his efforts spurring the four dogs behind him to run even harder until they had claimed the lead. Looking back, Argentia snapped Thorne a jaunty salute. He shook his head, and for once there was no malice or disgust in that gesture.

If I tried that a week ago, he probably would have ordered Kest to shoot me, Argentia thought, shaking her own head in amusement at Fortune's strange turn.

When they set camp that third night Kozar estimated that another full week's trek would be needed to reach the pyramid. "I had hoped to be faster," he said.

"How do you know the pyramid's location?" Argentia asked.

Kozar hesitated and looked at Unfert. "Tell them," the other Norden said.

"For five winters the pyramid has stood upon the Ice Reaches. Perhaps it has been there longer—but five winters at least, for it was five winters ago that the great shame was visited upon the Tribe," Kozar began. "Raiders came. A troop in armor. Food and supplies and what you would call treasures—ivory and pearls from the sea—were left untouched. Instead they took—"

"Women," Argentia said flatly.

Kozar looked relieved at not having to speak it himself. "How did you know?"

"I've seen Vloth's men do it before."

"Vloth?"

"Togril Vloth. The man who built the pyramid."

Kozar nodded slowly. "Seven women were taken by the raiders. Not one older than twenty winters, all the most beautiful of our Tribe."

"Did you not resist?" Thorne asked. He had an abiding hatred of thieves. It culminated with murderers—thieves of life—but a bare notch below were those who preyed on women and children: rapists and kidnappers—thieves of innocence.

"We are Nordens," Kozar said, his pale eyes gleaming. "Ten men, three women, and five children died fighting among the huts. After the enemy escaped with their prizes, King Gozal sent a score of warriors in pursuit. Ten days we gave chase, across the tundra, across the ice, until we came to the pyramid."

"And? What happened?" Tib asked.

"We were slaughtered," Kozar whispered, bowing his head. "In numbers the match was even, but they had armor our spears could not penetrate. When the fighting was done, only two others and I lived. We were taken before the lord of the pyramid—the fat *obludra* you name Vloth. He vowed that if we attempted to win our women back again, he would annihilate the Tribe. To prove his word, he executed the other men."

"And you were released," Kest said.

"To my shame, I was sent back to deliver the message to the Tribe."

"Surely you did not heed such threats," Thorne said.

"What could we do?" Kozar demanded, flushing angrily. "We are Nordens, and have no fear of death, but we are not fools. With nigh thirty warriors lost, it was doubtful whether the Tribe would survive even the next winter. Yet we did, and four more after that. Some who were children have grown into their beards in those winters, and we have not forgotten our shame. Dwarven steel we have now, from good Griegvard's holt." He lifted his spear. The silvery tip gleamed. "When we meet the enemy again, this and its brothers will pierce their armor and bring us victory."

"Tell them Kozar's stake in that victory," Unfert said.

A shadow crossed Kozar's face. "Brieki, my daughter, was one of those taken."

"Stinkin' bastards," Griegvard muttered. The others nodded. Though none of them had children, they were none of them strangers to loss. They could imagine Kozar's pain, even if they could not fathom it.

"Five years you have waited revenge," Thorne mused, thinking of his own rush to give Vendi's ghost peace. "How?"

"The good of the Tribe comes above all else," Kozar said.

"But Brieki's waiting is over," Exmoor blurted. "In a week she will be free!" There was silence around the campfire in the wake of the young Norden's words.

"Care to elaborate?" Argentia finally asked, though she was afraid she already knew. Kozar's glare at Exmoor told her what the answer would be.

"We still do not have the strength in the Tribe to muster a force of warriors," Kozar said. "But Sturm blessed us in your arrival. We will guide you to the pyramid, according to our bond. Once there, you will do as you must and we will free Brieki and the other women."

"So we're yer bloody distraction?" Griegvard said. "I'm surprised at ye, Kozar. Thought th' Nordens were better'n cheap deceivers."

"If it will save Brieki and the others—"

"I ain't questionin' yer motives, just yer tactics. We ain't th' enemy, remember?"

"You could have told us, instead of using us," Argentia agreed, fighting to keep the anger from her voice. Now it seemed they had three purposes in assailing the pyramid. *This is bound to be a disaster....*

"It is our shame," Kozar said. "We alone must be the ones to set it right."

Too frustrated to even argue, Argentia let the matter drop. But she went to her bedroll thinking that the only one besides Mirk she could truly trust on this venture was probably Shadow.

52

Argentia dreamed of the dragon again and woke in an ill temper.

The nightmare did not trouble her as much as the situation with the Nordens. Now more lives than just theirs and Ikabod's were at stake. There was a great chance many people would die if they failed.

It weighed on her. She decided to talk to Kozar. Working together, they stood a much better chance of freeing all Vloth's prisoners.

She started over to where the Nordens were packing the supply sled. "Wait, Red," Griegvard called.

"What?"

"I know what yer about. I'm tellin' ye, don't bother."

"Why not?"

"They will not be moved," Thorne said quietly, looking at Guntyr.

"It is the way of the North," the barbarian agreed solemnly. "The way of honor."

"Screw that," Argentia said. "Their honor's going to get people killed. I'm not going to stand by and let that happen."

Griegvard shook his head. "Stubborn as a dwarfess," he muttered. "Go on. See fer yerself, then."

"I will, thank you."

A few minutes later Argentia was standing red-faced before the men of the Tribe of the Walros while Kozar rebuked her offered assistance. "It must not be," he said. "I warn you, do not persist in this insult."

"Don't worry," Argentia spat. "I won't." She stalked back to her bedroll in a perfect fury over the barbarians' intractable idiocy. "Not one word," she growled as she passed the dwarf and the others.

Mirk, who was lounging in Argentia's blanket, scampered away before he could become a target for her ire. The meerkat was well acquainted with the female temperament and the savvy little animal had learned to seek quick shelter when he sensed such storms.

Shadow did not retreat, but he, too, kept clear of Argentia as she crouched and jammed her belongings into her pack.

"Lady?"

Argentia looked up at Exmoor. "What?" Her voice was colder than the ice beneath her boots.

"I have angered my father with my hasty words last night," he said. "Now he has angered you, so that fault also traces to me."

"Whatever."

"Please, listen."

Argentia stood up. The young barbarian towered above her, but there was such defiance in her posture—arms folded, full lips pursed in aggravation—that Exmoor backed up a pace. Argentia blew the perpetually hanging strand of hair out of her eyes. "What?" she repeated.

"You must understand, this is a matter of great honor to the Tribe, but especially to my father. The others who lost daughters died in the attack. He alone lives with the shame of his failure."

"That's no excuse for keeping secrets and refusing our aid."

Exmoor shook his head. "He will neither ask for nor accept aid."

"Then what did you come to tell me?"

"That I will—"

Whatever Exmoor was going to say was cut off by an outburst of commotion from across the camp.

"Get out of there, rat!" Unfert bellowed, kicking at Mirkholmes. The meerkat, who had been rooting about in the barbarian's pack, dodged adroitly and scampered back to Argentia.

"Mirk is not rat," he complained, whiskers trembling. "Mirk will savage giant man's nose!"

"Calm down," Argentia said.

Unfert stormed over. "Keep that vermin away from what's mine or I'll see it spitted and roasted for the night's meal."

"Leave him alone," Argentia replied, flipping her cloak wide to reveal her handbow. "He meant no harm. If you so much as touch him, I'll make sure you live to regret it."

"It will take more than that toy to back up such a boast."

"Care to find out?"

Unfert dropped a hand to his dagger.

Shadow growled in warning, his dark hackles rising.

"Break this up!" Thorne bawled. Stepping between them, he dragged Argentia aside while Kozar grabbed Unfert.

"Stop this!" Kozar said to Unfert. "We are bound by our honor to bring them safely to the pyramid, and we will see it done."

Unfert shrugged free. "You were warned," he said, casting a final glare at Mirkholmes as he walked away.

The meerkat managed a passable imitation of an obscene gesture in reply. "Mirk does not like him at all," he muttered.

I don't like any of this, Argentia thought. "Well, keep out of his things," she chided. "You know better than that."

"Mirk was curious."

"Don't be. We have enough trouble already. Understand?"

"Mirk understands."

The little animal looked so crestfallen that Argentia felt badly for snapping at him. "All right," she said. "Help me finish packing and I'll let you drive the sled."

"Can Mirk go fast?" the meerkat asked, brightening immediately.

"Fast as you want."

They broke camp without further incident. The ride was good for Argentia. The wind blowing in her face through the long day's run scoured away her anger. Her mind went back to Exmoor, who had been about to say something before Unfert's outburst. *I think he was going to ask for help, despite his father....*

Argentia was almost certain of it. She resolved that she would help the Nordens—whether they wanted her to or not.

53

There was no further talk among the company of what had happened in the camp, or what might happen when they finally reached the pyramid. They simply journeyed on, racing the moon across the Ice Reaches of Frijd.

Five nights out, they saw a curtain of colored lights dancing on the dark horizon.

"Pretty," Mirk said, pointing.

"What is that?" Argentia asked. The dogs, even Shadow, were skittish, but Argentia and the others were awed by the spectral display. They looked to the Nordens for an explanation, but it was Augustus who spoke first.

"Norden lights," he whispered. "I've heard of them—most magi have. I never thought they really existed, though."

"But what are they?" Argentia pressed.

"No one knows." Augustus shrugged. "It's said the lights are the caul of the world, cast aside by Aeton. Some even go so far as to say they are the source of all aether."

"Bah! Any dwarf'll tell ye what yer seein're demons o' th' upper airs," Griegvard chimed in.

"Demons?" Unfert sneered. "Those are the spirits of departed warriors riding through the night in search of new glories."

"So yer sayin'," the dwarf retorted.

"And so we believe in the Tribe of the Walros, but I have heard these other tales as well, and more besides," Kozar said, playing peacemaker.

Whatever the truth of the Norden Lights, they were undeniably splendid: sworling violets and pinks and flickers of green, like slow-bursting aethereal firesprays across the darkling sky. Places of great beauty always brought out the deeply hidden romantic in Argentia, and she lamented that she did not have someone to share this magnificent sight with. *Not someone. Carfax...*

She knew she would never truly get over losing him. Though she had made herself move on, part of her would always belong to Carfax. Their love had been all too brief, but it had burned true for the time that was theirs. She would not forget one moment of it, even if those memories haunted her for the rest of her days.

As she watched the cosmic aurora, she remembered that Carfax had been among the cyclopes of the Skystones and had wandered across many lands in his hunt for the demon. *Maybe he did see them....*

The dragon's tooth token at her throat glinted. Suddenly the ranger did not feel so far away at all.

In the deep of that prismatic night, Guntyr held the watch.

He stood on the edge of the camp, away from the firelight and the bedrolls, and listened for the approach of the intruders. They were out there. He could not see them, but he could hear them coming.

Barely....

Their stealth was superb. He wondered what their purpose was. Were they spies? Assassins? He also wondered how they had known to come, and to come downwind of the camp to avoid alerting the dogs.

It could only mean there was a traitor in the company. *It will not go well for him when he is discovered....*

But that did not matter to Guntyr.

What did matter had just materialized out of the darkness: two tall shadow-forms, wraithlike in their silence, emerald eyes glowing as they sprang for him.

54

Wild barking shattered Argentia's sleep.

She was on her feet with her katana drawn before she was fully awake. *What the hell?*

Mirk stood on her bedroll, his little sword at the ready. Shadow was beside him, muzzle peeled back. He was facing out of the camp, snarling at something unseen. The other dogs were straining at their tethers in a barking cacophony.

The strange lights still hovered in the sky. They had made the dogs edgy earlier in the evening, and Argentia wondered if they were somehow responsible for this outburst. *I don't think so...*

"Guntyr!" Thorne shouted over the canine chorus. He and the rest were up as well, weapons out, looking warily around the fire.

Seeing nothing but darkness.

"Guntyr!" Thorne shouted again.

Argentia had a very bad feeling. "Torches!" she shouted. "Quickly! And somebody shut those damned dogs up!"

She tossed a brand from the fire to Thorne. Grabbed a second for herself. Exmoor was trying to calm the dogs. Kozar did not move far from his son, but the rest of them fanned out, searching.

Guntyr was gone.

Argentia followed Shadow. Found the place where the Norden had been keeping watch. There was a confusion of footprints in the snow: Guntyr's big boots and many imprints from what might have been one person, had they not converged on the Norden from two different angles. Those prints were smaller. Feminine.

The twins... Argentia felt an angry shudder go through her. It was unnerving to think of how perfect the twins' stealth was, but what troubled Argentia the most was something she could not quite yet place.

"What'd ye find, girl?" Griegvard stomped up.

"Tracks. He's been taken by Vloth's twins."

"Alive?" Thorne joined them, the others lieutenants close behind.

"So far as I can tell. There's no blood on the snow, but there are also only two sets of tracks going away."

"They were carrying him?" Tib sounded incredulous. Then he remembered how strong the cat-women were. "Damn," he muttered.

"They can't have gone far. Harness the dogs," Thorne ordered.

"No." Kozar walked up with Exmoor and Unfert behind him. "The Ice Reaches are not traveled by night," the barbarian said firmly. "There are worse things than white bears that roam these plains. In the day, they · can be seen and, with Sturm's mercy, avoided. By night we would have no chance."

"Then I'll go alone," Thorne said. "I already lost Vendi. I will not lose Guntyr."

"Then wait for daylight," Tib said, stepping in front of Thorne. "Don't be a fool. You have no idea what might be out there, and night gives every advantage to the twins. *Think*, Thorne. If you want to help Guntyr, then wait."

For a moment, Tib stood there, hearing the echo of his words, wondering if Thorne was going listen to him or crack his head open with his baton.

The change in Thorne over the past few days had not escaped the attention of his lieutenants. Since they left the Walros settlement, he had been as stern and spare of speech as ever, but it was clear the hostilities between him and Argentia had subsided. There were even flashes of relaxation and human emotion—at least as much as Thorne was capable of—beneath his mask of excruciating focus.

This was the first test of whether those changes were genuine.

"Dawn is not far off," Kozar said. "They go afoot, and with a heavy burden. We go on sleds, and we have their track. We will overtake them before noon."

Thorne looked scornfully at the group. *Cowards who are afraid of the dark,* he thought. But he remembered what had happened on that ill-fated night when the bloodshot moon had lighted his way to East Wharf, and he and Vendi had rushed headlong into an encounter with the twins from which only he had emerged alive. Angry as he was at the decision to await the dawn, he understood that it was the safest course.

"If he dies, it is on your heads," Thorne said bitterly. Then he turned and walked back into the camp.

"Let him be," Argentia said. "I'll try to talk to him later."

"Yeah, that'll help," Tib scoffed.

"It might," Augustus ventured. When Tib looked at him, the halfling shrugged. "What? He listened to you, didn't he? He's not incapable of taking advice, you know. It just doesn't come easily to him."

Argentia could sympathize. She was much the same herself, and though she had remained silent, staying behind while the twins escaped did not sit well with her either. *But if we die in some ambush in the night...* They couldn't risk it. Not with the lives of Ikabod, the Walros women, and now Guntyr at stake.

They returned to the camp, but not to their bedrolls. They had lost one of their own to the dark, and could not but wonder whether there was danger lurking still, just beyond the light.

Two guards were posted. Thorne sat by himself again. The others huddled around the fire, sharpening weapons and talking uneasily. Argentia made esp. Deprived of sleep, they would need its potent properties to see them through the next day.

As she stirred the brew, she wrestled with the question that had escaped her earlier. Came up with an answer, but not one she liked.

When the esp was finished, Argentia took two cups and walked over to Thorne. "Here, drink this."

He ignored her.

"Quit being such a jackass and just drink it!" Argentia said.

Thorne looked at Argentia for a long moment, then took the cup and knocked back the esp at a single swallow. "Satisfied?"

"No. Yes—but there's something else."

Thorne waited for her to continue. The esp was pulsing through him: harsh in his mouth, warm in his belly. There was a tingle of acuity in his eyes. His senses were alert, sharp. His mind was calmer, and something told him he should listen to the huntress.

Argentia glanced around. Satisfied that they were isolated and out of earshot if they spoke softly enough, she sat beside Thorne. "How did they know we were coming?" she whispered.

Thorne's eyes narrowed as he reached the same conclusion Argentia had already come to. "One of the Nordens?"

"Unless it's one of yours."

"Impossible. As well suspect the dwarf."

Argentia agreed. "What should we do? If we confront them, we risk losing our guides. They won't stand quietly for accusations of treachery."

"We have the track. We don't need guides."

"We need the dogs," she reminded him. "And a track is only a path. It tells us nothing of the land. You heard what Kozar said."

"I have seen little danger besides the cold," Thorne replied.

"Trust me," Argentia said. "Would you walk through the Undercity at night without being wary?" Thorne shook his head. "The wilds are far, far worse, and I've never traveled land like this before, so I can't even begin to tell what to watch for."

Thorne considered this while Argentia sipped her esp. "Then we cannot confront them until we know who the traitor is," he said.

"Exactly. If it's only one of them, the others will likely turn against him as well. If it's two of them—or all of them—we could have trouble."

"Which is it, do you think?"

She hesitated. "I don't much like Unfert, but Kozar was Vloth's prisoner. There could be more to that story than he's telling."

"And the son?"

"Doubtful, but anything's possible."

Thorne nodded.

"You'll tell the others?"

"I will not have to." None of the lieutenants were fools. They would wonder sooner or later how the twins had found them.

"All right. Just make sure it gets kept quiet."

"We must learn the truth quickly," Thorne said.

"I know." *If we don't, we'll probably find out the hard way when we reach the pyramid...* Argentia finished her esp and rose. "Get some rest. We're going to need it."

As she walked back to her bedroll, where Shadow was waiting with Mirk curled against his side, she almost laughed at the ironies the night had brought. Thorne, who had been concerned only with revenge, now found himself on a rescue quest of his own, and she, who had spent so much effort trying to unite them all into a cohesive group, had been forced to drive a spike between them and the Nordens.

Just my luck, Argentia thought, and settled down to wait for dawn.

55

Noon came with no sign of the twins and Guntyr.

The company had the trail still: now no longer two sets of tracks, but three. It seemed the twins had tired of lugging the Norden along and were forcing him to run with them at a pace beyond what the sled dogs could match.

Argentia could not understand it. "How can he keep up?"

The lieutenants were equally perplexed. They knew Guntyr was strong as a field ox, but even his stamina would wear at the relentless pace set by the twins.

"If he must run for his life, then he will run," Kozar said. "Do not underestimate a Norden."

I won't, Argentia thought, glancing at Thorne. *Not any of them...*

The next afternoon, Kozar saw something he didn't like.

He tapped his son on the shoulder as they sledded along. "Look there." He pointed toward a mound in the snow. It was several feet tall and had a concave opening in its peak, like a small volcano.

"Frijdiformicans?" Exmoor said.

Kozar nodded grimly. Ice ants were the scourge of Nord: giant burrowing insects that had been known to ravage entire villages. "I had hoped to reach the pyramid without encountering them," he said.

"The signs are few and scattered, Father. Perhaps we still can."

"Doubtful, boy," Unfert shouted. He had pulled his sled up alongside. The mounds had not escaped his attention either. "We must be very wary now."

That evening—a full week out from the settlement beside the Sea of Sleet—brought the company's first sight of Vloth's pyramid. It appeared as a flash on the horizon: a giant piece of glass caught in the setting sun.

"Was that—"

"Aye," Griegvard said before Argentia could finish her question. "Hell else could it be? Out here in th' middle o' damn nowhere, flashin' like that."

At camp, Kozar confirmed that they had seen true. "Yes. We are close. Very close." His eyes fixed on the point in the darkness where the pyramid waited.

Argentia wondered if his thoughts were of rescue or treachery.

56

Two more days across the Ice Reaches.

The evidence of the ice ants had increased. Scores of mounds littered the landscape like miniature mountains. The twins and Guntyr remained invisibly ahead.

That no longer mattered so much. The pyramid, now a clearly defined geometry breaking the horizon, was less than a day distant. The company would find both friends and enemies there.

"Moon's end," Argentia said. "We just made it."

"So, now that we're here, what's the plan?" Tib asked, blowing pipe smoke into the dawn air.

They were discussing options while the Nordens prepared the sleds when Augustus noticed Griegvard crouched off to one side. The dwarf's hands were pressed into the snow. His eyes were closed, his face was crunched in concentration. "What is it?" the halfling asked.

Griegvard's eyes opened. He had the look of one awakening from a deep sleep. "Mayhap nothin'," he grunted, straightening and wiping his hands. "Earth's troubled. I can feel it. Somethin's—"

"Damn you, rat! Give me that!"

Everyone spun at Unfert's roar. Mirkholmes was racing away from the barbarian's pack. He had a glass orb clutched in his paws.

Unfert gave chase, but Mirk zigzagged madly, dodging the Norden's attempts to stomp him to death. He broke clear and reached the safety of the group, ducking behind Argentia's leg.

"Thieving rat!" Unfert shoved Thorne and Kest aside.

The tip of Argentia's katana brought him up short. "Not one more step," she warned.

"What in Sturm's name are you about?" Kozar demanded, rushing over. Exmoor was close behind him.

"Let your friend tell you," Argentia said, her blade never wavering, her eyes never leaving Unfert. "I want to know where that oculyr came from."

"Mirk found in bag," the meerkat added, peeking around from his hiding place.

"Unfert, answer," Kozar said. "What is this thing?"

Unfert glanced around. Saw steel in every Southlander's fist. Even Kozar and Exmoor had their hands on their weapons, though they had not yet drawn them.

"Talk!" Argentia ordered.

Unfert went stubbornly silent.

"Fine," Argentia said. "It can talk for you. Augustus—you're up."

The meerkat set the oculyr down on the snow and Augustus waved his wand above it to activate its magic. "*Vealle*," he said, commanding the oculyr to reveal its last image. Smoke began to coalesce in the orb, then cleared to show a crystalline room, a huge bed of silk pillows, and Norden women in the scanty apparel of a Brajenti harem.

Not exactly the image Argentia had expected, but damning enough.

"That's Brieki!" Exmoor shouted. "Brieki! Brieki!"

But if his sister could hear him, she made no reply.

"What is the meaning of this?" Kozar demanded.

"Is that how Vloth turned you?" Argentia said to Unfert. "Promised you the women when he was done with them? Promised you Kozar's daughter for your plaything?" She shook her head. "You're pathetic."

"Damn you all!" Unfert spat. With wild suddenness, he spun to flee.

Slammed into Griegvard.

The dwarf grunted at the impact but remained rooted in place, his sturdy legs and stony body absorbing the blow. The barbarian staggered back. Tib dove and tripped him and Thorne dropped hard onto his chest. "Traitor!" He pressed his baton across Unfert's throat.

The snow behind Argentia erupted.

She spun in time to see the giant albino insect looming up, four of its segmented legs snapping at her. She slashed her katana as the chitinous embrace enfolded her and then she was gone, sucked down into the snow.

"Watch out!" Kest cried as the ground burst open in a dozen places around them.

"Frijdiformicans!" Kozar shouted.

The ice ants were the size of ponies, white as snow, with wedge-shaped heads, huge, multifaceted eyes, and clashing mandibles. They fell upon the company with savage swiftness.

In the sudden chaos, Unfert flung Thorne off, stumbled to his feet, and ran. "Stop him!" Thorne shouted. Before he could scramble up, an ice ant pinned him from behind.

Augustus summoned the aether. He had a clear shot at the barbarian, but Thorne was in trouble.

Fire sprayed in streams from the halfling's fingers, boring holes into the ice ant's head and thorax. It toppled off of Thorne, twitching and smoking in the snow.

"I said stop the barbarian, damn it!" Thorne shouted, rising to his knees.

Unfert was speeding off in one of the sleds.

"He's out of range!" Augustus said.

"Not mine." Kest unshouldered his longbow. "Cover me."

The melee faded into background noise as Kest's focus honed on the fleeing Norden. He aimed, judging wind and speed, angle and trajectory, assimilating all those details with the uncanny speed of a natural marksman. He drew a breath. Exhaled.

Dimly he heard the twang of the bowstring's recoil. Watched the long flight as the arrow chased down the Norden. *True...*

He did not see the actual impact, but the sled veered suddenly, spilling Unfert's body into the snow, where it lay still.

"Help!"

Tib had lost his sword and was crawling frantically away from an ice ant. The monster pinned him. Tib screamed. Kest knocked another arrow, knowing he would be too late.

Kozar lopped the ice ant's head off with one great sweep of his hatchet.

"The dogs!" Exmoor shouted. A pair of ants had burst up near the sleds. The dogs were going mad, tangling themselves in their harnesses as they tried to run.

Exmoor's well-thrown spear ended one ant at a stroke. He raced over and jerked the weapon free. The other ant rounded on him with surprising speed. His spear was torn from his grasp and he was knocked onto his back. He kicked and shoved. Serrated jaws snapped. Fire bloomed in his shoulder. *Oh Sturm—is this how it ends?*

The ant convulsed atop him and went still: dead weight.

"Ye can come out now," Griegvard said, twisting his huge axe loose from the wreckage of the ice ant and stomping off to find another foe.

After the din of battle, the bloodied Ice Reaches of Frijd were very quiet.

Fifteen ice ants were dead. The rest had retreated into their holes, caving them in behind them to prevent pursuit.

Kest, Kozar, and Augustus had escaped unscathed. The others bore painful tears from serrated jaws and forelegs, but none of the wounds were life threatening. They looked around, dazed by the suddenness of the assault, the treachery of Unfert, the loss of Argentia.

Shadow was by the hole where Argentia had disappeared, growling and pawing at the snow-filled cavity.

"What do we do?" Augustus asked. They all looked at Thorne.

He pointed to where Unfert had fallen. "Make sure he's dead. If he's not, finish him and bring back the sled. Then get ready to ride."

"Ye can't just leave her!" Griegvard protested, wiping at blood trickling from a gash across his brow.

"She's gone," Thorne said harshly. "We have to go on." He hesitated a moment, and then added. "It's what she would want us to do."

"He is right," Kozar agreed. "No man has ever been taken into a frijdiformican hole and lived to tell the tale. Let it be said she died well, and let our deeds at the pyramid sing to her memory."

Shadow howled. The company lifted their gazes from the collapsed pit that had claimed Argentia Dasani.

On the horizon, the Frost Palace of Togril Vloth glinted in the Nordic sun, mocking them.

57

Kest's arrow was buried in Unfert's back.

A stain of red, mortally bright in the colorless landscape of Nord, spread over the snow beneath the barbarian. "May the Hells find out your spirit and Sturm's lightning wrack you forever, treacherous dog!" Exmoor said, spitting on Unfert's corpse.

"Aye, if his be th' last o' th' treachery," Griegvard said. He jabbed a finger at Kozar. "How're we knowin' th' rest o' ye ain't leagued just th' same?"

The barbarian flushed. "Kozar is no traitor! My *daughter* is imprisoned in that pyramid, you bearded stump. For the first time in five winters I have laid eyes on her. I will have her free!"

"Mayhap at th' price o' our lives," Griegvard countered. "E'er think o' that?" he asked the lieutenants and Thorne. "Mayhap fer deliverin' us t' Vloth this one'll get his daughter back. Mayhap t'were th' plan from th' beginnin'."

"Beware," Kozar warned.

"You will not speak so of my father!" Exmoor leveled his spear at the dwarf.

Griegvard swung his axe up. "Wouldn't be tryin' yer toothpick against this, boy."

"Stop it!" Augustus shouted. Spear and axe went flying in a pulse of aether. "All of you!" The halfling stepped between Griegvard, Exmoor, and Kozar—absurdly small but with a fierce determination on his cherubic face. "*Vloth* is the enemy, you fools!"

Kest and Tib exchanged a glance and did well to hide their smiles as the three who had nearly come to blows stared in astonishment at the halfling. People were always underestimating Augustus and his powers, usually to their regret.

"The wizard is right," Thorne said. The dwarf's suspicions were not far from ones he and Argentia had harbored when they first broached the possibility of treachery from the Nordens, but now her voice came to him from another conversation: *I'm telling you straight: we're going to need each other to finish this…*

"What of the insult to my honor?" Kozar retorted. "It cannot go unanswered."

"Answer it by proving true." Thorne speared his falcon's gaze at the barbarian. "Betray us, and you will end like that one." He pointed to Unfert's body. "But battle is coming. I would have your strength, for we have lost much of ours."

Kozar measured Thorne with his own gaze. Finally, he nodded. "Then you shall have it. And I swear on the life of my daughter, if I prove you false, let her pay the forfeit," the barbarian said, straightening proudly.

"So be it," Thorne said. He was taking a chance, but there was no choice. "Ready the sleds. We waste time."

They broke camp. It took all Kozar's coaxing to urge Shadow away from the pit where Argentia had fallen and get him harnessed to a sled. "Where is the meekat?" Exmoor asked suddenly.

They looked around. There was no sign of Mirkholmes. The last time anyone remembered seeing him was right before the ice ants attacked. "He had the oculyr," Kest said. "Next to Argentia."

"He must have gone down with her," Tib said. "That's three we've lost now."

"We will get Guntyr back," Thorne promised. "Guntyr, the butler, the women. We will get them all back."

The lieutenants looked at him in some surprise: not at the determination in his voice, or what he had said, but what he had not said.

"What about the twins?" Tib asked.

Thorne's scarred face became a thing of stone in the early light. "I have not forgotten."

58

By noon the pyramid was within striking distance.

The depleted company paused in the shelter of a last gentle rise; it was the best cover the bleak environs offered. *For now...* Thorne thought. "Wizard."

"Yes, sir." Augustus stepped before Thorne, falling into a pattern of command that they had performed time and again in Argo.

"We need a storm."

"A storm," the halfling echoed, more pensively than incredulously.

"A blizzard. The more snow the better."

"Um—have you gone mad?" Tib asked.

"There are many who would say I have been mad for years," Thorne replied. "But in this I am not mad. There is nothing but open ground between us and that pyramid. It may be that surprise is hopeless, but I would try what we may, and would not have us picked apart by archers or magi or whatever else Vloth has waiting in his defense as we attempt to find the door."

"Is there a door?" Kest asked. Now that they had arrived, it seemed they were woefully unprepared for this assault.

"On the side facing us," Kozar said. "And to bring cover is a wise tactic. Vloth's men met us on this field, and we did not reach the pyramid save as prisoners." He looked at the ground, and the others could tell he was reliving the harrows of that battle, the disgrace of being taken.

Exmoor placed a hand on his arm. "This time will be different, Father."

Kozar nodded. "Sturm has granted me a second chance. I will not fail again."

"What can you tell us of the pyramid?" Thorne asked.

"Nothing," Kozar answered. "Save for my audience with the *obludra,* I was made to wear a blindfold until I was released."

"Great," Tib muttered. "Like the guildhouse all over again."

"We survived that," Kest said, rubbing frost off the fletchings of his arrows.

"Right, so let's press our luck and try it again."

"Do you have a better idea?" Thorne asked.

"No," Tib admitted.

"Then cease your chattering and let the wizard work."

"Almost ready," Augustus said, channeling the aether. His fingertips were already glimmering blue, but he was hesitant. Controlling a single element was not difficult magic. Controlling the mixture of wind and temperature and precipitation necessary to create a storm was something else entirely.

"Count your minutes, *obludra*, for they grow short!" Exmoor said, shaking his spear.

"What's an *obludra*?" Tib asked. "You and your father are always saying it."

"It is the guildmaster. Vloth," Exmoor said.

"So it means 'guildmaster'?"

"It means 'dung pile,'" Kozar said. "How would you call an abductor of women?"

"That's about right." Tib laughed.

"Tiboren," Thorne warned.

"All right, all right."

Augustus folded his glowing hands together. "Here goes nothing."

59

"Who are you?" Togril Vloth demanded. "Answer me!"

Beside the guildmaster's chaise, Salis Yip flicked a whip in anticipation. Flanking the prisoner, Puma and Pantra did not stir, but their green eyes gleamed.

Standing between the twins, Guntyr smiled mockingly. His form began to glimmer and shift. Puma and Pantra hissed in surprise, backing away. Salis Yip stopped his incessant twitching as the Norden became a black-clad elf.

Vloth had expected some transformative magic was at work, yet Gideon-gil's appearance startled him badly. The assassin was one of the few on Acrevast who commanded the guildmaster's respect—with good reason.

But those first surprised instants passed, and Vloth's confidence returned. He had his rings, and Puma, Pantra, and Yip to defend him. If the elf had come to kill him, he'd lost the ripeness of the moment. "A subtle trick," Vloth said. "How?"

Gideon-gil merely stood there, black as shadow, pale as ice, unreadable as a starless night. Then, with an amused smirk, he raised his hand. A silver band flashed in the light. "You are not the only one with magic rings."

"A trinket," Vloth said, his scornful words masking his desire to add such a ring to his collection. "Why have you come?"

"I fear that my reasons are rather complicated," Gideon-gil admitted. "We should palaver—privately."

"Guildmaster, trust no back-knifing elf," Salis Yip urged, snapping his whip.

"Your guildmaster's life is in no danger from me, I assure you," Gideon-gil said quietly. He leveled his jade gaze on the Whipmaster, silently warning the Nhapian that his own life might be in great jeopardy if he spoke again.

Wisely, Yip held his tongue. The elf, known to him only by dark reputation, seemed disconnected from the world around him in some essential way: a detachment that made Gideon-gil not merely dangerous, but deadly.

Puma and Pantra, who had sensed the brief contest of wills, snickered just loudly enough for Yip to hear. He glared, but mastered his temper, reminding himself that the time was shortly coming when he would settle matters with the cat-women for good.

Gideon-gil turned back to Vloth. "It will be worth your while to hear me."

Vloth inhaled thoughtfully. What game was the assassin playing? There was only one way to find out. It was a risk, but the assassin had always dealt fairly with Vloth in the past. "Leave us," he ordered the others.

Puma and Pantra *mrrowed* in disappointment.

"But we brought him…"

"As you said…"

"And we did not kill him or hurt him…"

"Or play with him at all…"

"And we did not harm the others…"

"Or even their growling, nasty, barking dogs."

"We were very good," Puma added.

"Very obedient," Pantra purred.

"May we not stay?" they pleaded together.

The twins did not really care what the elf wanted with Vloth—so long as he did not deprive them of their own revenge by killing him—but they knew if they were permitted to stay it would gall Salis Yip even more.

"No," Vloth said.

The twins *mrrrowed* again, pouting.

Vloth was unmoved.

Puma and Pantra sniffed, tossed their manes, and sulked from the chamber. Yip sneered at their backs as he made his own departure through another door.

"Your minions do not like one another," Gideon-gil observed slyly.

"Have you come so far merely to comment on the state of my house?" Vloth replied tersely. He had realized that the assassin must have been present at the attack on his guild in Telarban—how else could he have come to wear the guise of a Norden who had been dead since that night?

"Did you kill Ravail as well, or was it some other guard of mine whose face you hid behind?" he asked.

The elf clapped his hands quietly three times. Vloth clenched his teeth. The assassin was all but laughing at the impunity with which he'd invaded the guildhouse. "Ravail was valuable to me," the guildmaster said.

"He can be replaced," Gideon-gil said. His own esteem of the lieutenant was much less; after all, he had killed him easily enough. "I am offering you something of infinitely more worth, Guildmaster."

"What?"

"A bargain."

60

For the first time since arriving at his Frost Palace, Togril Vloth was pleased. Gideon-gil's bargain was thus: he would watch the twins destroy Dasani, and then he would challenge them himself. If he killed them— and Vloth thought he would—the chameleon ring would be given as payment for the duel. The guildmaster would also receive a percentage of Gideon-gil's fee for allowing him to execute one of the men accompanying Dasani—apparently the contract that had gotten the elf involved in this game in the first place.

If the twins prevailed, Vloth could still execute them at his convenience, and he would take both the elf's ring and the right to say that he had devised the death of Teranor's most fabled killer—words that would only enhance his already mighty stature on the streets.

No matter the outcome, Vloth could not lose.

"To your bargain, elf," the guildmaster said, raising a grilled prawn in salute and biting the head off the giant crustacean.

Suddenly the room darkened, as if night had dropped over the land at noon. Vloth looked up. The whole of the pyramid was magically illuminated, but the chambers on the top level had transparent ceilings instead of the frosted blocks that composed the walls of the palace.

Overhead, dark clouds roiled and snow scourged the air.

What is this? There were blizzards in Nord, of course, but never in this season. Vloth was perplexed for a moment, his wide face shifting into a deep scowl. Then, slowly, he smiled. Limping over to an oculyr, he conjured an image of Salis Yip.

"Alert the men," he said.

In another chamber of the Frost Palace, Gideon-gil was also pleased.

He sat cross-legged on the crystal floor, deep in the strange trance-state that for elves was sleep. In short order he expected he would play his bout with the twins, and afterward complete his contract for Krung. Parting with a portion of that fee was nothing to him—not that he believed the Magistrate had any intention of paying, but that was another matter for another time. Even losing the chameleon ring meant little. In truth, he had grown bored with the dissembling device. He would have ransomed much more for this chance to prove his blades against the cat-women.

When the twins had come for him, Gideon-gil had offered no resistance. They struck swiftly and brutally, but he rolled with those attacks, shifting just enough to deflect the impact without seeming to, and collapsed into their arms, letting them race away with him across the snow and into the night even as he heard the dogs erupt into chaotic barking and the camp come awake.

Many minutes of sprinting later the twins flung him down. He surprised them by rolling easily to his feet and facing them in the dark.

"Who are you?" they demanded in unison, emerald eyes glowing. Their voices were laced with curiosity. They did not appear even slightly winded by their tremendous exertion, but paced close about him in a stalking circle. To Gideon-gil's exacting eye, their bodies appeared physically perfect. They exuded feral danger and an animal sexuality so strong it stirred even the cold elf to wonder how many men had fallen to their exotic charms—and then to their razor claws.

"Your form lies…" the blonde said.

"But your scent can not," the brunette said.

"You are not the Norden," they completed together.

"Take me to Togril Vloth," the elf replied, undaunted by this exposure. "That is what you came to do, is it not? I am not what I seem, true, but what I am will remain hidden until your master is present."

A strange look passed between the twins, as if they were communicating without speaking. They nodded simultaneously.

"Then we hope…"

"You like to run."

So they ran, day and night, with few pauses to rest. If the twins wondered that Gideon-gil could match their pace, they made no sign of it. Indeed, they barely spoke to him again for the entire journey, keeping a suspicious, but never a fearful, distance.

A noise roused the elf from his reverie. It was not even on the same level of the pyramid, but to his ears it sounded as if it was directly outside the door: the heavy-booted tread of armored men.

So it begins, he thought, not rising or even opening his almond eyes. The taking of Dasani and her friends was no concern of his. Only what happened after concerned him. Vloth had embraced Gideon-gil's bid to duel the twins, setting only the stipulation that the cat-women first be allowed to make an end of Argentia Dasani. Of course, that opened the possibility that the twins would fall to the huntress, but the brief taste he'd had of their skills had been enough for Gideon-gil to doubt such a thing would be.

It seemed that he had found his challenge at last.

61

Head bowed, Augustus summoned the storm.

The wind howled. The day grew eerily dim as clouds swept in from nowhere, building like the combers on the Sea of Sleet until they engulfed the sky between the company and the pyramid. They were not black thunderclouds, but a dead species of gray that was infinitely more sinister.

For a long moment the world was held beneath a threatening stillness. Then the wind began to blow again. *My God*, Kest thought. *I can smell the snow...*

"*A natyr fre!*" Augustus cried, clapping his hands together.

Sapphiric aetherlight flared between the halfling's palms—and the snows came.

Not a few flurries that gathered substance into a storm, but a downpour, a deluge of snow that was caught in the gale and blown like a white hurricane upon the crystal pyramid. In seconds, that triangular shape was gone in the distance, veiled behind curtains of snow.

Thorne waved for the company to move out. He took the lead, running the dogs hard towards the swirling white storm.

They entered the blizzard.

The wind was everywhere, driving cold, wet snow into their faces. The world whited out instantly. They couldn't see the pyramid. Couldn't see each other. Didn't even know if they were still running in the right direction.

The sudden and complete disorientation was terrifying even to men who thought themselves hardened to danger. An elemental beast had been unleashed, and they were utterly at its mercy—of which there was none.

Just keep going.... Thorne whipped the reins, forcing the equally confused dogs on. *Just keep—*

He squinted. *Aeton's bolts!* Not ten yards ahead, a shape rose up in the snow. Thorne yanked the reins, bringing the sled to a skidding halt. The blizzard had skewed distance and time. They had crossed the plain much faster than he had expected.

Thorne vaulted out, running for the wall. The others piled behind him. "Cut it off!" Thorne shouted to Augustus.

"I can't! It's out of control!" Augustus shouted back. The storm had passed beyond him, its power too primordial for him to master. It would burn itself out in time, but how much time the halfling could not guess. It seemed to be getting stronger with each passing minute. "We have to get inside!"

Tib cupped his hands to his mouth and shouted, "Where's the goddamn door?"

"It was here!" Kozar shouted back.

It did not seem to be there any longer.

The company stumbled along the base of the pyramid, heads bent to stave off some of the slapping snow, each holding to the person ahead. Already the drifts were up to Exmoor's knees, and Augustus' waist. Kozar swept the halfling up and carried him.

Thorne found the doorway. He had been scraping one shoulder along the pyramid to keep from losing all sense of reality in the maddening storm. Suddenly that support vanished, spilling him into a small recess. His fall yanked Tib in after him, and the others quickly filled the space. The snow-wind pounded at them from behind.

There was no door.

Griegvard stared at the flat crystal wall. He turned to Kozar. "Ye said—"

"It was here!" the barbarian raged. Stepping forward, he pounded his fists against the crystal.

There was a flash, and the wall slid upward.

"What did you do?" Tib shouted, stepping backwards in surprise.

"Never mind! Inside!" Thorne ordered.

The company ducked into the pyramid, snow and wind chasing them until the door slid down again, cutting off the elements.

"Thank Drim we're out o' that bloody mess," Griegvard muttered. Beneath his battered helm, his wild beard and bushy brows were crusted with ice.

"Yeah, but what *is* this place?" Tib asked, shaking snow from his hood.

They looked around in a silence that after the storm was both welcome and strange. Within, as without, the Frost Palace was crystal. A tremendous column rose to the apex of the pyramid, dominating the triangular space. Ramps crisscrossed the air between the pillar and the catwalks, linking level to level. Magic provided blue light and warmth. For the first time in days the company could not see their breath leaking before them.

"Where do you think Brieki is, Father?" Exmoor whispered. "In one of those?" Three cave-like doorways offered possibilities on the ground level, but Kozar had no idea which of them, if any, might hold his captive daughter, and there was the whole rest of the pyramid to consider.

"Where is *anybody*?" Kest muttered suspiciously. Thorne and Griegvard were already moving ahead. "I don't—"

Before he could complete his warning, armored guards rushed from all three chambers. "Trap!" Kest cried. The company rang their weapons free.

Roaring, Griegvard charged. "Come on, ye damn—"

A quarrel nailed him in the chest. Griegvard staggered but didn't fall. Crashing upon the astonished archer, he swept his great axe in an arc that slammed through insectile armor, flinging the broken guard aside. "Next!" the dwarf bellowed.

Three guards buried him in a pile of thrashing limbs and battering maces.

"Sturm! Sturm!" The barbarians rushed to join the fray.

"No!" Thorne grabbed Exmoor from behind, spinning him around. Kest and Tib blocked Kozar. "This round is theirs," Thorne said, staring grimly at the ring of crossbows and the score of armored opponents, with others no doubt waiting in reserve. There couldn't win against such odds. *If we must, we will try—but not yet....*

"You can't save Brieki this way," Kest said harshly as Kozar continued to struggle. Hearing his daughter's name seemed to break the barbarian's battle-haze. Kozar calmed, his barrel chest heaving as the guards closed in, surrounding them.

Griegvard, separated at last from his axe, was dragged over to the rest of the company. He sat up, his face battered and bloodied, a quarrel jutting from his mithryl chestplate. "Bah! Was just gettin' fun," he groaned.

"Welcome to my Frost Palace." Togril Vloth limped down the ramp to the ground level. "I trust you find the hospitality to your tastes?" The guildmaster was flanked by Puma and Pantra and trailed by a shirtless Nhapian whose flesh looked badly scalded.

At the sight of the twins, something snapped in Thorne. All his admonitions of patience were forgotten. With sudden speed, he jammed his elbow into the teeth of the nearest guard and broke past another, his face a contortion of fury as he charged the cat-women.

The twins were already gliding down to meet him.

Thorne swung his baton. Puma twisted sideways, her clawed hand flying out in a seemingly casual swat that tore Thorne's scarred cheek open at almost the same instant Pantra's spinning kick drove into his stomach, sending him to his knees.

Thorne gasped for air. Gathered himself for one last attack, refusing to fail Vendi while there was life in him.

He rose, striking.

Puma caught his wrist. Pantra plucked the baton from his hand and smashed it across his bloodied face, shattering his nose and dropping him in a heap.

Puma made a motion as if washing her hands of something distasteful. Pantra let the baton fall disdainfully beside Thorne. Side by side, the twins sauntered away from Thorne's broken form and resumed their positions next to Vloth.

"I hope the rest of you will forbear such foolishness," the guildmaster said. He surveyed the group. The triumphant smile left his bloat face. "Where is Dasani?"

"Dead," Tib said.

"What?" Vloth hissed.

"You heard me. She's dead. Killed by an ice ant on the plain this morning. Just before we shot your spy."

The second jab was meaningless, but the first hit harder than Tib had hoped.

"You *lie!*" Vloth spat. He turned to his guards, almost quivering with rage. "None of you saw her? The redheaded woman?"

"She was not with this group, Guildmaster," one of the guards said tentatively.

"You are certain?" Vloth asked.

"Yes, Guildmaster."

"You are *wrong!*"

The guard flinched—he'd seen Vloth kill men for less—but the guildmaster had already forgotten him.

"She is here," Vloth snarled. "She must be here!"

The guildmaster tattooed his walking stick on the floor in agitation. His entire bald head was flushed. His fleshy lips worked silently. He looked like a giant child about to pitch a tantrum. Under much different circumstances, Tib would have found it amusing. Now he viewed it as a sign that the prospects of their survival were dim indeed. *He's completely crazy....*

"Take them to the cells," Vloth commanded suddenly. A ring flared on one of his fat fingers. His voice boomed in the spacious pyramid—as if he were not speaking to the company so much as to someone he could not see. A red-haired huntress, perhaps.

"I will grant you until sunset," Vloth said. "If Dasani has not appeared by then, I will kill one of you each hour until she does—and before you die, you will suffer unimaginably."

The twins *mrrrowed* laughter and the strange-looking Nhapian cracked a whip in applause as the company was herded off. When they were gone, Vloth wiped a palm over his sweating face. He did not believe Dasani was dead: Fortune was no such whore as to deprive him of the pleasure of killing his hated enemy—not after all he had endured to bring her to this place.

No, she is here. Somewhere...

He considered the situation in silence a few moments more, and then began issuing orders.

62

Ikabod heard noises outside the opaque door of his crystal cell.

It sounded like a great procession of people. The butler, who was huddled on the floor, struggled slowly into a sitting position. He had clothes again: a threadbare peasant shirt and patched burlap trousers that were worth next to nothing against the frigid air and the colder floor. A straw mattress, even a pile of hay, would have been welcome relief, but even those meanest amenities were absent.

That was the least of his problems.

Ikabod coughed: a harsh, painful rasp. He hunched forward, gasping, until the fit subsided. Then he tried to stand. His back screamed. His legs buckled, knees cracking loudly as he collapsed back to the floor. He wondered if he would ever walk fully upright again.

During his internment in Vloth's guildhouse, Ikabod had tried to maintain a level of daily exercise by pacing his cell, keeping a hand to the wall to navigate in the dark. As the days wore to weeks and the weeks to months, his discipline and his old body failed him. Now he was feeble, half-blind, mostly crippled, and sick.

Very sick.

Torture, malnourishment, and exposure had taken their toll. Though he could not know it, he looked very like the skeleton Argentia had discovered wearing his uniform in far away Telarban.

It was to Argentia that Ikabod's groping mind went as he shivered miserably in his cell. She was alive, he knew, else he would not be alive himself. *Those sounds. Has she come?*

In the course of his long and brutal imprisonment, Ikabod had passed beyond hope. Now he was surprised to discover that a dull species of that virtue could still exist in that wasteland of the soul.

Argentia was coming. Ikabod hoped he might live to see her again, if only to tell her he was sorry and to say good-bye. He knew he was far gone; he could feel death in him. But if he could just hang on a little longer—

The crystal door to Ikabod's cell slid open.

The butler raised his head.

"Up!" Salis Yip barked.

The Whipmaster swaggered in without bothering to close the door behind him. "Guildmaster want. But first, this." He unfurled one of his many whips, snaking it along the glittering ground to flick at the butler. "Maybe last time, sa-so."

Ikabod's heart sank. Here was what he had heard without his cell—not Argentia at the head of some rescuing force of knights, but the sadistic, foreign dog of a torturer come yet again.

Yip clapped chains about Ikabod's emaciated wrists and tore the shirt off the butler's back. The torture-master had come daily to abuse Ikabod, sometimes for Togril Vloth's amusement, sometimes for his own perverse pleasure. Ikabod knew that several times he had almost died from Yip's beatings. Each time the Nhapian's healing potions—draughts whose the lingering effects were likely what had allowed Ikabod to survive his captivity for this long—had brought the butler back.

There had been a time, at the lowest point of his captivity, when despair owned him, that Ikabod had prayed for the mercy of death.

Now that no longer seemed best.

The serpentine coil in Yip's hand began to glow blue. "Sa-so!"

The icy lash descended, but the pain—even this cold-searing lick—meant nothing anymore. Ikabod would endure it, and he would wait, if he could, for Argentia.

And then...

The frost whip branded him again. Ikabod shuddered, clenching his teeth against a cry of pain. Tears leaking from his single eye, he silently began a new prayer.

Part IV
Crystal Fall

63

Mirkholmes blinked back into consciousness.

He rose, shaking snow vigorously from his fur. He remembered stealing the oculyr from the evil-smelling barbarian, and the start of the battle among the humans, then a heavy vibration in the earth, and something erupting around him, and falling into darkness.

And now, here he was.

"Mirk wonders where *here* is." He looked around, whiskers twitching. He was in a tunnel of ice. The cold air was full of alien smells—and one familiar scent.

He went cautiously toward it, passing the shattered remains of the oculyr. Found Argentia crumpled amid piles of snow and ice beside the body of a giant insect. He thought the monster was dead—there was a great deal of stinking ichor on the snow—but he wasn't certain.

"Lady?" Mirk poked Argentia, keeping one wary eye on the ant. She did not respond, but he could hear her breathing.

For several minutes the meerkat paced back and forth, waiting for Argentia to awaken. Finally he grew tired of his vigil. Summoning the aether, he sent a sharp jolt of magical energy at Argentia's ear.

"Ow! Damn—what?"

Mirk leaped back as Argentia shoved wildly away from the ice ant. She tumbled forward out of the drift. Banged her head against the wall. "Owwww…"

Mirk watched as Argentia sat up in the dark, rubbing her head and turning it slowly from side to side. He heard the vertebra in her neck pop. She sighed.

"Lady?"

Argentia looked instantly toward the meerkat's voice. "Mirk?"

"Mirk is here."

"Where? I can't see anything."

The meerkat concentrated. A moment later, a small globe of blue aether floated up in the air, suffusing the tunnel with a sapphire glow.

Argentia came to her knees. She looked at the carcass of the ice ant. When it had caught her and dragged her under, she'd thought she was finished, but the single slash she'd managed with her katana had killed it even as it pulled her down.

She remembered falling, then nothing. *Must have blacked out...* She touched her head gingerly. Her ear also hurt, as if she'd been stung by a wasp. "Where are we?" she asked, dusting off her rabbit-fur hat and snugging it back down on her head.

"Under ice."

"Obviously," Argentia said, rolling her eyes.

She wondered if the others had been attacked on the surface. If they had been, were they dead or alive? Were they looking for her? How much time had passed? She didn't think she'd been unconscious for that long, but she just didn't know.

And Unfert. Hope they killed him. If they didn't, I will...

First she had to get out of this tunnel. The ceiling was too low for her to stand so she crawled over and retrieved her katana from where it lay beside the ice ant. Even dead, the thing was revolting. "All right, let's get the hell—"

The sentence died unfinished. Looking up, Argentia could see the place where she and the ant had fallen. The hole that led to the surface was now packed with crumbled snow and ice.

Argentia maneuvered her way under the hole and reached up, trying to push through the blockage. *No good. It's solid...* She could not know that the ice ant tunnels were designed to collapse in on themselves, covering the monsters' retreat; she only knew that she was in a lot of trouble.

Cursing, she sank back down to her knees and bowed her head.

"We not go?" Mirk asked.

"Quiet. I need to think."

She was cold, shivering beneath her cloak. *Come on, focus, Gen. There has to be a way out. Think...* She looked at the ice ant. She had bested it with a lucky strike, but wouldn't want to try her odds against a horde of them in a tunnel where she couldn't even stand to fight.

I have to do something... She thought about it some more. Found a glimmer of hope. Like their miniature cousins, the ice ants lived underground, but they surfaced to forage or hunt. If she went through the tunnels and managed to remain undetected, she might find another tunnel to the surface that wasn't blocked.

"Mirk, how long can you keep that light up?"

"Mirk can keep light for long time. This was in easy pages of book."

Argentia smiled despite her situation. She always found it amusing that the clever meerkat had managed to steal his magical knowledge from the tomes of the Archamagus. "All right, but you tell me if you need to rest."

"Mirk will. We are going now?" He sensed the change in Argentia: from defeated to determined.

"Yes." She reached out and patted his head.

"Which way?" the meerkat asked.

Argentia considered. "Northeast," she muttered. "We were heading northeast toward the pyramid." But how could she know which way they were facing now?

She looked up at the blocked passage to the surface. The ant had come from behind her. *But I turned before I fell...and woke up facing this way...* It was hopeless. She might have turned about dozens of times in her fall. "Mirk, can you find northeast?"

"That way." Mirk pointed at the wall in front of them.

Figures... "You're sure?"

"Mirk is sure."

"All right. Try to keep us headed in that direction."

"North and east," Mirk confirmed.

Following the meerkat and his blue light, Argentia crawled off into the tunnels of the ice ants.

64

While she crawled, Argentia wondered again about the others. She hoped they were still going on and that they would be able to rescue Ikabod and the Norden women when they arrived at the pyramid.

She still hoped to get there herself, but she was beginning to face the possibility that she might end her life lost in these frozen tunnels, which had innumerable side-branches and ancillary passages, some of which led only to dead ends. They took erroneous turns down several of these and were forced to back up—a hellish process—but so far the plan to go northeast was working.

For Argentia, the tunnels were worse than the labyrinth in the Temple of Avis-fe, which she had conquered during her adventure in the Sudenlands. At least in the labyrinth she'd been able to walk and had signs to give her a sense of progress. Here she crawled over rough ice until she was sure her knees were bloodied messes, and her back and shoulders ached from the contorted posture as they went from one cramped passage to the next to the next without end.

Mirk complained that he was hungry. They had no supplies—Argentia's pack was with the sleds and dogs at a camp that seemed very distant to her now. Starving was the least of her worries. If they didn't find a way out before nightfall, freezing to death below the arctic surface was a frighteningly real possibility.

Outside, noon had passed, the white circle of the sun invisible behind a sudden blizzard, and afternoon was wearing away.

In the tunnels of the ice ants, all was claustrophobic, blue-lit monotony—until they found the hole.

It led down into a sort of chute, and it was wide enough to make it awkward for Argentia to cross. She couldn't quite reach the other side by leaning forward, and she wasn't sure she trusted her legs enough to fling herself across: she had been crawling for a long time.

Have to get past it one way or another.... Down was the one direction she was sure she did not want to go.

Mirk had already leaped across, and Argentia was trying to get a good hold with her boots on the slippery surface for a long lunge when she heard the noise. It was the sound of something scuttling over ice—and it was coming from the chute.

Coming fast.

Oh shit... "Mirk!" she hissed. "Get back! Get—"

The ice ant poked its head and forelegs out of the hole. Its long antennae twitched. Its mandibles scissored. It made a quizzical clicking noise—part surprise, part curiosity—as it focused its gaze on the meerkat.

Mirk squealed and scrambled backwards.

"Hey!"

At Argentia's shout, the ant's angular head whipped around.

Argentia plunged her dagger hilt-deep in its multifaceted eye.

The ant tumbled back down the chute in a flail of limbs, almost taking Argentia with it. She released her dagger and threw herself across the gap.

"Lady almost crushed Mirk," the meerkat chided. "Where is Lady going?"

Argentia was already up and crawling. She didn't know where that chute led, but she was willing to wager that where there was one of those ants, there were others.

Speed would be their only hope now.

And luck...

65

Turn after turn, Argentia and Mirk went on. There was neither sign nor sound of pursuit, but Argentia refused to slacken the pace until exhaustion sank its claws into her and she had no choice but to stop. She was starting to see spots of light that were not Mirk's fading blue globe.

She forced herself a last distance and slumped against the wall alongside an opening to another tunnel. If worse came to worst and she was found there, at least she had an option for an escape. The decision was borne of instinct. By this point she was barely conscious of her movements, much less the reasons behind them.

"Just a few minutes, Mirk," she husked. She was flexing her fingers in her rimed gloves, trying to loosen the cramped, frozen digits, when sleep took her without a fight.

Mirk waited more than a few minutes. He knew it was dangerous to linger in these tunnels—he could smell the strange scents of the giant insects, which meant they were not so far off down one or another of the many passages—but he also understood that the Lady needed this rest.

"Mirk is still hungry," he grumbled, pacing back and forth. Finally, victim of his insatiable curiosity and determined to take his mind off the food he would not be having, he wandered off.

Argentia snapped awake.

For a horrible instant she was completely dazed, as if someone had hit her hard enough to rattle her mind. She remembered stopping to rest, and then nothing.

She realized what must have happened. Cursed her weakness and stupidity. *Those ants could have come and killed us...*

All that was in the split second before she opened her eyes to utter darkness.

"Mirk?" she croaked. Her heart raced in blind panic. She couldn't believe the meerkat would have deserted her. *Something must have happened to him...*

She shoved away from the wall, every stiff and frozen joint cracking in protest. The darkness in the tunnel was absolute. "Mirk!" she repeated as loudly as she dared. "Mirk!"

No answer—but there were other noises: the scratching and chittering Argentia had known inevitably she would hear ever since she'd first awakened in these benighted tunnels.

The sounds of ice ants on the march.

Argentia closed her eyes again, listening. The sounds were getting louder.

Her luck had run out.

Almost.

She remembered the tunnel she'd stopped beside. Reaching out a hand in the black, she pawed at the wall until she found empty air: the mouth of the tunnel. She scrambled in and started crawling, dragging her left hand along the wall to hold her position. It slowed her down, but she couldn't risk going fast with no idea what lay ahead.

The sound of her sharp breathing filled the narrow passage. The dark played tricks with her mind. Every jut of ice that scrapped against her boot seemed to be the foreleg of an ant lunging to snare her.

Instead, those harrowing minutes in the dark ended when a faint and familiar glimmer of blue materialized up ahead.

Mirk... Argentia didn't know whether to be thankful or to throttle the meerkat. Able to see a little better, she crawled faster. "Mirk—get over here!"

The meerkat appeared. "Good," he said. "Now Mirk does not have to wake the Lady. Guess what Mirk found?"

Before Argentia could answer, the tunnel behind her was filled with a horrendous clatter. "Go! GO!" Argentia shouted.

With Mirk and his sapphire globe racing ahead, Argentia crawled for her life. Fear and adrenaline gave her desperate speed, but the furiously chittering ants were gaining.

Suddenly Mirk's blue light disappeared. Before Argentia could react, the floor of the tunnel sloped sharply down. With a wild cry she went sprawling, skidding and tumbling down the slide, spilling out into an open space lit by a wash of diffuse light.

She rolled hard, came up fast, galvanized by the danger. A trio of ants burst out of the tunnel after her, but Argentia had room to fight now.

She ripped her katana from its scabbard, steel flashing in the pale light, the pain in her half-frozen hands forgotten. Her blue eyes gleamed.

The ants came and died.

Without the element of surprise, their attacks were clumsy and predictable. Argentia took them apart, hacking limbs away, breaking them down.

In moments, she stood over the last ant and plunged her blade squarely into its back, cutting short its death keen. Its final shivering spasm ran all the way up her arms before she yanked her blade free. Glancing into the tunnel to make certain no other ants were coming, Argentia wiped her blade on her cloak and looked around.

"My God, Mirk. Where are we?"

66

They were in an ice cavern like nothing Argentia had ever seen.

The light came from giant, magically illumed icicles clustered on the high ceiling above a ragged gorge stretching some hundred yards across to a sheer wall. An ice bridge spanned the chasm, arcing up to a cave high on the wall.

"Mirk found way out," the meerkat said, eagerly leading Argentia to the mouth of another tunnel.

"Did you go up?"

"No, but Mirk can smell air from outside. And Mirk does not think bugs make steps."

"Neither do I," Argentia agreed. Her gaze went from the ice-carved stairwell Mirk had found back to the bridge and the lofty cave at its far end. Despite her initial confusion, she had a strong suspicion she knew what this place was after all.

She pointed across the gorge. "Northeast?"

"North and east," Mirk nodded.

That's got to be it... "Come on." She started toward the bridge.

"Lady is going the wrong way," Mirk said.

"No, I'm not. Now come on."

The bridge was wide enough for at least four to go abreast. Though it appeared to be ice, it was made of smooth crystal: magically generated or at least magically reinforced, Argentia guessed. Crystal posts and handrails ran the length of the span, offering a little sense of security against the dizzying prospect of falling into the chasm, whose bottom—if it had one—was far beyond sight.

Once they trusted the crystal, which looked fragile as glass but felt hard as steel, it did not take them long to cross the gorge. What Argentia had mistaken for a small cave on the far side was really the mouth of a low-ceilinged tunnel. Unlike the bridge, it actually was ice—something she discovered when she slipped and nearly fell.

Moving more carefully, they went on, their way lighted now by glowing crystals lining the walls at periodic intervals. Not far beyond a disturbing pile of small skulls, they came to the end of the tunnel. A series of rungs cut into the wall formed a ladder to a trapdoor in the ceiling.

Argentia climbed up and braced her hand against the trapdoor. *Probably locked anyway...*

It was.

"Let Mirk see?" the meerkat said.

Why not? Argentia thought. When she nodded, Mirk scampered up the ladder and climbed onto Argentia's shoulder so he could reach the trapdoor. He ran his tiny paws along the seam, feeling for something. "*Ikbar!*" he peeped. A fork of blue-white aether shot from his paws. A moment later Mirk poked Argentia's hat. "Lady can open door now."

Argentia pushed on the trap and it lifted a little. The meerkat's magic had melted the simple locking mechanism in the floor above. "Mirk, you're amazing!" Argentia planted a kiss on Mirk's head.

"Lady is slobbering on Mirk."

"Am not!" Argentia laughed and then held up a finger to make sure she had the meerkat's attention. "All right. You go first. Carefully. See what's there. If there are people—guards—you have to tell me where they are. And be careful," she repeated.

"Mirk is always careful."

"Hey, that's my line."

If an animal could smile, Mirk did. Then he slipped off Argentia's shoulder and up through the crack she raised in the trapdoor. The last she saw of him was his tail as he scurried silently off.

Several minutes passed. Argentia waited anxiously, one hand on the hilt of her katana, the other holding the trapdoor slightly open. She was just beginning to truly worry when Mirk's fuzzy face suddenly reappeared above her. "Safe," he said.

Relieved, Argentia pushed the trapdoor all the way open, climbed out, and carefully lowered the door again. It fit perfectly into a crystal floor in a crystal storage room, confirming her suspicion that the tunnel, bridge, and steps were a secret escape from Vloth's pyramid.

Crunch!

Argentia spun, heart pounding.

Mirk looked up guiltily. His mouth was crammed with walnuts. Beside him, a burlap sack sported a hole from his tiny sword.

"Mirk!"

"But Mirk is hungry," the meerkat managed between swallows.

"Just come on," Argentia snapped, moving forward, not wanting to think about how hungry and thirsty she was herself.

"Cruel Lady," Mirk muttered, but he followed.

The soft blue light emanating from the roughhewn crystal walls was gloriously warm. Argentia felt parts of her that she hadn't even known were frozen begin to thaw out. *I've had enough of being cold for at least the rest of my life…*

The cave-like chamber widened as they moved out from its depths. It was full of crates and sacks and barrels. There were enough supplies to feed a battalion, which Argentia crabbily admitted was not something that boded well for someone who intended to sneak in and out.

Or it could all just be to feed Vloth… Argentia snickered.

"What is funny?" Mirk asked.

"Nothing." The meerkat's confused expression made Argentia want to laugh all the more. Biting her lip, she drew her katana and edged to the doorway, peering out into the triangular space of Vloth's pyramid.

"Now where, Lady?" Mirk asked, his amber eyes alive with curiosity.

"I don't know."

The Frost Palace, dominated by the massive central column and the webwork scaffolding of the ascending and descending ramps, was a stark and strange contrast to the opulent halls of the guildhouse in Telarban.

It was also huge.

Argentia counted ten levels. Though each appeared to have only three chambers—one in each corner of the pyramid—who knew how many interior rooms were beyond those initial doors? *It could take forever to find Ikabod in here. And where the hell is everyone, anyway? This place must have dozens of servants, never mind the guards…* Argentia knew she should have seen someone by now, yet the pyramid remained eerily silent and deserted.

The Frost Palace was another of Togril Vloth's traps.

Once again, there was nothing Argentia could do but walk into it.

67

Mirk followed in Argentia's shadow.

The meerkat was much enamored of shiny things, and the interior of the pyramid sparkled and glimmered like diamonds. He wanted to explore—and to see if he could pry a crystal or two loose for himself—but Argentia was moving with a purpose past the platform-ringed pillar toward the far side of the pyramid.

Quick searches of the other two chambers on this level revealed one to be a second storage room, much the same as the one they had come from, and the other possibly a guard house, though it was as abandoned as the rest of the pyramid seemed to be.

Argentia wondered if Thorne and the others, who surely had arrived before her if they had survived the ice ants—and she couldn't imagine that they had all fallen in that ambush—had already won the day. *Doubt it....* Even if he had been defeated, Vloth would never have yielded without a fight, and Argentia saw no bodies or bloodstains or other obvious remnants of battle. In fact, the crystal floor gleamed as if it had just been polished.

Maybe it's another hoax... Perhaps Ikabod was gone, if he had ever truly been here at all. Perhaps everyone was gone, and she was meant to discover nothing but another mocking message from Vloth, leading her on to the next stage in his twisted gauntlet.

Only one way to find out...

Argentia was moving to the first ramp when she realized Mirk had vanished.

I don't believe this! Argentia looked about again. There was no sign of the meerkat. She stamped her boot angrily, hoping the noise would catch Mirk's attention. She couldn't shout for him, and she couldn't wait.

"God damn it all," she muttered. Trusting the meerkat to find his own way back to her, Argentia headed swiftly and quietly up the first ramp, made a half-circle around the central pillar on the narrow platform, and ascended the ramp to the second level, all the while waiting for the guards to burst from their cover.

None did.

She reached the catwalk of the second level. Picked one of the three cave-chambers at random. She paused outside the entrance. Heard nothing. Went in.

The room opened out to her left. The crystal floor was covered with a shaggy fur carpet. Several long couches and ottomans were artfully positioned around a circular bed. Huge and low, it was draped in deep red satin and laden with large black pillows.

Flung down amid these like a broken puppet was Ikabod.

Argentia caught her breath. Heart suddenly pounding, she rushed to the bed. "Ikabod—"

Her voice had no strength. A memory of the scene in the dungeon of Vloth's guild stabbed up so sharply that she almost did not dare to touch the butler, fearing he was an illusion or—worse—that for all her efforts she had come too late, and he was truly dead this time.

When she marked the shallow drafting of Ikabod's frail chest, iron chains unwound from her spirit and a weight of stone fell from her heart. *Thank God…*

Argentia touched Ikabod's haggard face, scruffed with the white bristles of an old man's beard. She saw the eye patch, the cuts and bruises, the marks of many lashings visible through the rips in the cheap peasant garb. *Oh Ikabod, what have they done to you?* Bitterness welled in Argentia, crying in its lion's voice to avenge these hurts.

No, just get him out…

"Ikabod."

He stirred, coughing. Argentia winced at that noise. It was the rattle of dirt in a grave. She marked how pale his skin was: waxy and almost blue. Though the temperature in the pyramid was warm in this chamber and in the hall below, she guessed that not all the rooms were so accommodating. In addition to whatever tortures Vloth had devised for Ikabod, it appeared he had kept him half-frozen as well. *You bastard. If he dies, you die too…*

Argentia glanced toward the doorway to make certain no one was sneaking in on her. "Ikabod."

Ikabod groaned and woke. "Easy," Argentia said. Ikabod shrank from her, raising a weak arm in a warding flinch. "Easy," Argentia repeated. "It's me."

Ikabod stared, his eye focusing, recognition dawning. Tears welled and leaked down the seamed plain of his cheek. "My...Lady," he croaked, squeezing her hand as he fought off another bout of coughing. "You should not...have come. Danger here. I'm sorry—"

"Shhhh." Argentia hugged Ikabod close, fighting her own tears. "I'm fine. We're getting out of here," she said.

And that was when she heard the laughter.

68

"How touching," Togril Vloth said.

A section of the crystal wall to the left of the bed had gone transparent. Behind this partition, the guildmaster sat on a chaise, his immensity flanked by the cat-woman twins. A black-clad elf leaned against the wall behind the couch, his arms folded across his chest.

What the hell is he *doing here?* Argentia had last seen Gideon-gil escaping the Crown's camp at Hidden Vale, after his arrows had saved Solsta from a rival assassin. His presence in Vloth's pyramid was a complete surprise— and not one Argentia relished.

The noise of boots took her attention from the tableaux behind the glass. The entrance to the chamber was filled by Vloth's armored guards, led by a short, bandy-legged Nhapian with a whip. He was shirtless, and his hairless flesh was mottled with splotches of red.

"Welcome to my Frost Palace, Lady Dasani," Vloth said. "Your punctuality is impressive. I was just about to issue the order for the first of your friends to be executed."

Well, I guess I know what happened to the others... "Let them go," Argentia said.

"No, but I will let them live until my business with you is finally ended," Vloth said. The twins *mrrowed* laughter.

"If your business is with me, then let them go," Argentia insisted.

"No." Vloth shook his head. "They killed my men in Telarban. I am not in the habit of letting such offenses go unpunished. Nor am I in the habit of letting my enemies run free when I have them in my power."

"Then let Ikabod go. He's just an old man. He's suffered enough."

"He is dear to you. He could *never* suffer enough," Vloth spat.

Argentia realized then the true depths of the guildmaster's hatred for her. It was frightening. "What do you want?" she asked, stalling, trying to figure a way out.

"Your death."

"Sorry, not interested."

Vloth smiled. "Amusing. Nonetheless, you will die tonight. Puma and Pantra will see to that." The twins emerald eyes flashed and they licked their ruby lips in anticipation. "Yip, bring the old fool to me. We'll let him watch her die before we kill him, too."

"Sa-so, Guildmaster." The Nhapian flicked his whip. The guards moved forward, surrounding Argentia and Ikabod.

"Get away. Save yourself," the butler said as he was hauled roughly to his feet. "Go!" He pushed feebly at a guard, trying to create a distraction. The guard's armored fist rose to strike him.

Argentia caught the guard's wrist, spun him to his knees, pulled a knife from her belt and pressed it beneath his chin. "Don't touch him. Any of you."

A whip cracked. Sudden pain flared in Argentia's hand. The knife dropped from her numb fingers.

Salis Yip stepped forward, his lash trembling like a serpent, his smile wide and evil. "Silly girl. What you do now? Nothing, sa-so." The whip leaped up to sting Ikabod's groin. The butler collapsed on the bed, convulsing.

Argentia rushed to Ikabod's side. The guards moved in, separating them. The Nhapian took Ikabod himself, his hard fingers digging into the old man's flesh until the butler gasped in pain.

"Silence—sa-so!" Yip cracked his whip again.

From Ikabod's cringe Argentia understood that the Nhapian was responsible for most of his injuries. She glared at the torturer. *I'll remember you...*

Yip giggled and motioned the guards to take her away.

Argentia managed to meet Ikabod's eye. "Don't worry, I'll get us out of this," she said. *Somehow...*

69

From a shadowy nook outside the chamber, Mirkholmes watched as Argentia and Ikabod were led away. His whiskers quivered, his ears stood sharply from his head, his amber eyes glowed, and his breath came in short hisses as the men in armor—more knights, he presumed, though they did not look like the Sentinels of Aventar, and they had cruel, evil scents (though none so cruel or evil as the one man without armor)—and his friends vanished from sight.

Mirk's fierce posture drooped into confusion. He did not know what to do. He had wandered away from Argentia in his search for shiny stones—she was certain to be furious about that—and when he found her again, she was surrounded by these many strange, unfriendly men.

"Lady needs help," Mirk realized. His demeanor brightened. "Mirk will help," he vowed, scurrying off.

Argentia was left alone in a cell-like room. The locked door was opaque crystal with a barred window. She wondered if it was the same cell where they'd kept Ikabod.

Worry about more important things, she chastised herself. *Like how you're going to get out of this mess...*

Argentia paced a frustrated circle. She imagined she'd been in worse situations before, but she couldn't think of one. Even if she beat the twins, there was Vloth and all his men to contend with. If it were only her, she was sure she could at least escape, but Ikabod was at their mercy, and she wasn't leaving without him.

The others, too. And the Norden women... "And why not throw in the servants and a few pieces of treasure while I'm at it? God—there's no damned way!"

Hush... Carfax's voice.

Argentia let out a long breath, calming. She could only deal with one matter at a time. *First the twins, After that, I'll make things up as I go...*

Calmer, Argentia looked at the small sack by her boots. Inside was a phial of potion that would heal her, left by Salis Yip on the order of Togril Vloth, who apparently wanted a fair—or at least an amusing—combat between Argentia and the twins. Argentia doubted Vloth believed her a match for Puma and Pantra even if she was uninjured, but it was just like the guildmaster to want the satisfaction of prolonging her destruction by letting her fight at her best.

She meant to make his mistake a costly one.

She uncorked the phial. *Could be poison,* the skeptical voice in the back of her mind warned.

I don't think so. He wants to see me torn apart...

Not all poisons kill. This might be something to slow you or sicken you...

Does it really matter? I'm exhausted already.... Argentia swallowed the draught. It went down hot and quick, like the liquor she favored. Almost immediately she noticed the pain in her hand subsiding, the feeling returning to her fingers. *Working...* She felt warmer, more alert, as she did just after drinking esp. She wondered if the potion was also some elvish derivative. *Whatever, as long as it—*

"Mirk is here!"

Argentia spun around. The meerkat was standing on the small ledge where the window bars met the crystal of the door. "Mirk can unlock," he offered.

Argentia started to nod, then changed her mind. "No, wait. There's something else you have to do," she said to the meerkat. "Listen."

70

Mirk was long gone when Salis Yip and the guards arrived to collect Argentia.

She had spent the rest of her time in preparation.

The potion coursing through her had wiped away the last of the weariness—she did not even want to think about how many miles she might have crawled through the ice ants' tunnels—and the myriad minor injuries she'd accrued. She doffed her hat and cloak, stripped her rabbit vest and heavy sweater. Dropping down, she did quick, hard push-ups until her breath came in steady pulses and the veins and muscles in her bare arms stood out. Then she swiveled smoothly into a crouch, rose, and drew her katana, spinning it through a sequence of cuts and counters, limbering the last creaks of cold from her body.

She felt good. Fluid. Ready.

Sheathing her sword with a snap, she arranged herself cross-legged on the crystal floor and waited.

A quarter-hour later, Yip and the guards brought Argentia up the ramps to a level high in the pyramid. They entered a triangular chamber that boasted only two furnishings: a font on a marble pedestal and an upright mirror, its ovular frame burnished gold, its feet carved in the likeness of an eagle's talons. A second door on the far side of the chamber led back to the catwalk.

There was no sign of the twins, but Vloth was waiting by the mirror, and Gideon-gil lounged against the wall. Ikabod was there as well, kneeling, his hands chained, his head bowed. He did not look up when Argentia entered.

Yip lashed the stone beside the butler with his whip. Ikabod flinched. It took all Argentia's self-mastery not to draw her handbow and blow the sadistic grin right off the vile Nhapian's face. *Just wait…*

"Welcome again," Vloth said. He wore an intricately patterned black and gold silk robe over voluminous pants, in the style of Nhapia and parts of the Sudenlands. A golden diadem sat on his bald brow, and he was propped on his walking stick.

"How's your knee?" Argentia asked. By the paroxysm of rage that shifted across Vloth's face, she guessed the damage had been extensive.

"When you are dead, it will pain me no more," Vloth said. From the way his eyes were crawling over her tight halter and leather pants, Argentia thought that her death was not foremost on his mind.

She stared back hard, loathing his gaze but refusing to flinch.

Vloth slurped lewdly and then returned to business. "I see you have come prepared to fight. Too prepared, perhaps." He gestured at Argentia's arsenal. "You may choose one of your weapons only. The rest will be removed."

Two guards came toward Argentia.

"Don't." She froze them with her voice. "I'll do it myself." She unhasped her weapons-belt, put it on the ground, and raised her hands, palms towards Vloth.

"The knife in your boot, Lady," Gideon-gil said. The enigmatic elf had not altered his lounging position; he merely regarded her with those depthless jade eyes and inclined his head a bare fraction.

Frowning, Argentia pulled the secreted blade from the back of her boot and dropped it with the rest of her things.

"Is that all?" Vloth asked, not bothering the hide his exasperation.

The elf nodded.

"Good." Vloth pointed one of his many rings at the mirror. The glass flared to life, becoming starry aether. "Through there. The twins are waiting."

It was a good tactic, Argentia reflected. Now she would have to waste precious seconds adjusting to a new environment: one the twins would already know.

"Watch this for me," she said to one of the guards, tapping her weapons-belt with her boot. "I'll be back for it."

Vloth smiled. "I very much doubt that."

"We'll see, pig."

The smile fell off Vloth's face. His eyes narrowed. "That will be your last insult. Remember it well," he said coldly. "Good-bye, Lady Dasani."

Without bothering to reply, Argentia moved forward.

Ikabod raised his head. "My Lady," he said.

Argentia snapped him a salute and stepped into the magic mirror.

71

She comes! Puma and Pantra thought.

The mirror in the room where they waited pulsed brightly. The twins growled in anticipation. They had hungered for this since Argentia had escaped them on the docks of Argo. They planned to take their time with her. To savor this kill nearly as much as they would savor killing Vloth.

At first, Argentia thought the blackness was an aftereffect of the aethereal mirror-passage. When it didn't clear after a sickeningly vertiginous moment, she knew she was in trouble.

The chamber was pitch dark.

She felt a rush of air. Pain tore across her right arm, then across the left side of her back as the twins slashed past, striking and vanishing into the dark again.

Steeling off the hurt, Argentia drew her katana. Somewhere in the black, the night-seeing twins purred laughter.

The noise was many feet away, Argentia judged. The echo led her to guess the room was quite large.

Not good…

Argentia took a cautious step forward, blade extended. Turned against a sudden sense of motion.

Too slow.

Claws raked her left thigh and the right side of her back. She hissed in pain, stumbling, lashing wildly, hitting nothing.

She got her balance and closed her eyes, removing the disorientation of staring into the dark. She felt/heard the twins come again. Spun to her left. Thrust her katana into empty air. Got torn open across her right side and her left shoulder.

Teeth clenched, Argentia flourished with all her speed, hoping to catch one of the twins as they passed. Her strikes found only the void of their wake.

From across the lightless chamber, more laughter.

"*Mrrrow*—she is sweet," Puma said, making licking noises.

"Yes," Pantra agreed. "Let us take another taste."

Togril Vloth, Gideon-gil, Salis Yip, and Ikabod watched the combat between Argentia and the twins in the waters of the font. The guildmaster found magic endlessly fascinating. Magic was power, and power of any sort was always of the greatest interest to Togril Vloth.

The darkness in the mirror chamber was magical as well, affecting only those who entered the room. The onlookers could view the battle quite nicely. They saw Argentia rock back on her heels, blade flailing, trying to guess and intercept the twins as they sprang in upon her, striking as they passed.

Argentia staggered under the latest barrage. Puma and Pantra circled her, licking their bloodied claws, then made another attack.

"See how they toy with her," Vloth gloated.

Salis Yip chuckled fiendishly.

Ikabod grimaced but said nothing. He could not help Argentia in what he imagined were her last moments of life, but he could at least honor her by keeping this vigil.

Gideon-gil was silent as well. The elf was busy studying the cat-women's tactics. Already he had seen a weakness. He wondered if Argentia would figure it out, or if she would simply be cut to pieces.

72

In another part of the pyramid, Mirkholmes was faced with a problem of his own: how to free seven people from a dungeon cell with a guard at the door.

The guard might not chase him if he tried to lure him away, and Mirk didn't think he could defeat him in a fight—not with all the armor the guard boasted, which left only his ugly, bristly face visible. Mirk might have tried to use magic on the guard, but he had expended a great deal of it already today, and his powers were too weak for a spell he could be sure would do the job.

Still, Mirk understood that he could not fail at this mission. The Lady was counting on him to free the others they had traveled with. Though he could be frivolous and easily distracted, when given a task the meerkat took his responsibilities very seriously. Besides, the Lady had not even yelled at him for disappearing in search of shiny stones, and he appreciated that.

He crept closer, hoping he might see something that would help him decide what to do.

He did.

The prisoners were held in a cell behind a door of crystal bars that were thick as spears, hard as steel.

Thorne, his nose smashed, the swollen flesh beneath his eyes a blasted purple, blood dried in streams on his mouth and chin, crouched with his head bowed into his hands. He did not move. He did not speak, not even to tell Tib to stop his incessant jabbering. There was a sense about him of something waiting to erupt.

Griegvard slept on the crystal floor, snoring like a bellows.

The barbarians paced. For men whose ways were of the open tundra and battle unto death, the imprisonment was particularly hard to bear.

"Wonder where Guntyr is," Tib said.

Kest had borne the brunt of Tib's ramblings for these many hours. It was beginning to get on his nerves. He started to make a sharp retort, then stopped. *Where* is *Guntyr?* There were three other cells in this chamber. None of them were occupied.

"There must be other cells."

"I hope so."

"Why take the trouble of bringing him here just to kill him?" Kest asked.

"Maybe he tried to escape, or wouldn't tell them what they wanted to know. Or both. Who the hell knows? Not me."

"Then why ask where he is?" Kest snapped.

"Hey, I was just wondering—"

"Quiet!" Augustus hissed.

The others looked at him in surprise. Since they had been taken, the halfling, whose hands had been bound behind him to prevent him casting any spells, had remained withdrawn. The thought of death did not disturb him—it was merely a return to the aether—as much as the idea that they all seemed to be resigned to it.

He wanted to rally them, to give them hope, but he couldn't think of a single thing to say that wouldn't sound foolish. So instead he listened to Tib chatter and Griegvard snore. Watched the barbarians pace. Wondered if Thorne would ever lift his head; he was clinging to some vague notion that the Captain would somehow find a way out of this for them.

When all that became too much, he would simply stare out of the cell at the soothing blue crystal walls—which was what he was doing when he saw the key ring floating across the chamber.

He blinked several times, thinking he was losing his mind, perhaps from starvation; he had missed at least two meals today, and it felt more like three.

The key ring was still floating through the air.

73

Though his ability to cast spells was impaired, there was nothing wrong with Augustus' ability to tune to the aether. He sensed it flowing like a small stream from somewhere outside the chamber, propelling the keys towards them.

He also sensed that the magic was weakening quickly—and the keys were still a good ten feet away.

"Look!" he said when the others stopped talking, keeping his voice hushed so as not to alert the guard. Something in his tone must have reached Thorne in his faraway mental hell, for he raised his head. When he saw the keys, his eyes gleamed.

Tib looked at the halfling in astonishment. "I thought you said you couldn't cast without your hands."

"It's not me," Augustus said.

"What shamanism is this?" Kozar asked.

"I know not, Father, but if it gets us those keys…" Exmoor said excitedly.

"They're sinking," Kest said.

They watched as the key ring, now five feet away, dipped precariously in the air.

"The magic's failing," Augustus said.

"It'll make it," Tib said. "It has to make it."

Save Griegvard, who was still asleep, and Thorne, who remained crouched, they were all pressed against the bars, watching the keys come within three feet…two feet…

Clank! They fell to the floor a foot short of the bars.

The guard turned. "Hey—what?" He slapped stupidly at his belt, where the key ring had been hanging beside his sword, and rushed forward.

Thorne lunged, stretched his arm through the bars, and snared the key ring. Scrambling up, he shoved Tib aside and jammed one of the keys into the lock.

"Hey! Give those back!" The guard grabbed Thorne's arm. "Give—"

Kozar's hand shot out of the cell, clamped against the back of the guard's helmet, and jerked him face-first into one of the crystal bars. The crash of the impact shook the entire door.

The guard struggled, but Kozar was relentless. They had their chance to escape now, to rescue Brieki. His massive forearm bulged as he continued to force the guard's head against the bar.

The magical crystal would not yield.

The barbarian would not yield.

The guard gave a cry that was cut off by a terrible crunching noise. Blood suddenly dribbled down his forehead. His eyes glazed. His body went slack.

Kozar let go. The guard toppled backwards, a dent in his helmet several inches deep, as if it had been cloven by an axe.

Thorne tried another key. The lock tumbled. He threw the door open.

"Griegvard!" Augustus kicked the dwarf.

Griegvard woke with a grunt. "'Bout friggin' time somebody figured a way out o' this bloody cage," he grumbled, following the others into an alcove where all their weapons were piled on a table.

As they hastily rearmed, Mirk came in. The meerkat was exhausted, all his magic spent, but he was satisfied. The prisoners were free. He had not failed the Lady. He thought Solsta would be proud of him.

"The meekat! You're alive!" Exmoor exclaimed.

"*Meer*kat," Mirk muttered peevishly. "Mirk and Lady both. Lady sent Mirk to get you out. Mirk tried. Mirk is sorry he could not bring the keys all the way."

"You brought them close enough," Augustus said. They had freed him of his bindings and he was rubbing his chafed wrists. "A well-turned spell."

Mirk's amber eyes gleamed happily. "Mirk is very hungry. You do not have food?" he asked hopefully.

"I do," Exmoor said. He dug into his back for some dried berries. While the meerkat ate, fastidiously licking his tiny paws after each berry, the others tried to set their course.

"We'll be findin' Argentia," Griegvard said in a tone that brooked no argument.

"She will be where Vloth and the twins are, do not doubt it," Thorne replied.

"But will Brieki and the others be there as well?" Kozar asked.

"And what about Guntyr?" Kest added, picking up the thread of conversation he and Tib had abandoned. "We have to find him, too."

"Can you lead us?" Thorne asked Mirk. But the meerkat had curled up in Exmoor's pack and was fast asleep.

"We must find Brieki," Kozar said firmly. Beside him, Exmoor nodded.

"How?" Tib asked. "Those girls could be anywhere."

"We will find them." Without waiting for an answer, Kozar rushed out. Exmoor grabbed his pack and ran after his father.

"Follow those fools," Thorne growled. "Before they bring every guard in this place on our heads."

Instead of guards the barbarians found a servant bearing a stack of trays. The terrified man tried to flee, but Exmoor tripped him up—the trays fell with a loud crash—and Kozar hoisted him off the ground, shaking him until his teeth rattled.

"The women!" the Norden demanded. "Where are the women?"

"Below!" the man gasped. "Second level!"

"And the guildmaster?" Thorne said. "Where are Vloth and his twins?"

"Up!" the man gasped. "Please don't kill me!" Urine dribbled down his leg, staining his white uniform.

Snorting in disgust, Kozar slammed the servant to the ground. "Move and I will gut you like a char," he warned. Then he turned to Exmoor. "Down," he said.

"And we go up," Thorne ordered his lieutenants.

"I don't think—" Kest began.

"There is no time to argue." Thorne snapped. His face was a ruin, but his voice and manner could still command. "Wizard, go with the Nordens. Get the women and get out. Be swift. Fortune follow you."

"Sturm guide your hand to your vengeance," Kozar said.

The group split up.

They would not all meet again.

74

Fighting for her life in the dark, Argentia faced the terrible truth: she was losing badly.

She'd ducked or dodged a few attacks, but she'd been cut more times than she could count—her limbs and torso were wet and sticky with her blood—and kicked and punched besides. Despite her conditioning and Yip's potion, she could feel herself flagging under the twins' relentless assault.

Now they were out there, invisible and silent, stalking her, and she wasn't sure how much more she could stand—or how she could even defend herself, much less hope to win this bout. All her training against the Crown's pards was for naught. The darkness simply gave the twins too much of an advantage.

They proved it again in another attack. One blow raked Argentia's abdomen, and as she struck vainly in the direction of that fast-fleeing cat-woman, the other twin clawed her from behind.

Spinning, Argentia stabbed out with her katana. Screamed in frustration when the blade missed its mark. Safely distant, the twins laughed at her.

Something about that laughter spurred a memory
(*Oh Pantra, I don't think...*
She wants to play anymore...)
from their first battle.

A fist slammed her ear. Argentia turned with the blow, stumbling directly into a kick coming from the opposite side. Her ribs buckled. The breath smashed from her lungs. She doubled over but kept her feet.

Straightening slowly, Argentia sheathed her sword at her hip.

The twins knew she could not see them coming, so they made their angles of attack away from where her weapon was, confident she was too slow to catch them no matter how swiftly she reacted.

And that was true—because all along she'd been attacking the wrong twin.

Argentia kept her hand on the hilt of her covered blade. She had stolen part of the twins' edge now—they couldn't account for a weapon they couldn't see—but what she was planning was madly dangerous. As good as she was with her blade, she was tired and battered. If she missed, or if the twins changed their tactics, it was over.

"What is she about?" Vloth said. "Is she giving up?"

In the watery image of the font, Argentia was a torn and bloodied mess. She could barely stand, and she had sheathed her sword.

No, Argentia. Do not yield, Ikabod thought.

"Sa-so. She is beaten," Yip declared. Though he hated the cat-women, he did admire the callous way they had tortured the woman into submission.

Gideon-gil—who had determined somewhat to his disappointment that the twins would not be so much of a challenge after all—watched this turn of events with interest, sensing that Lady Dasani had some last trick to play. The elf did not doubt that this one would be subtler than a dagger hidden in her boot.

Puma and Pantra stalked Argentia with their customary silent, measured paces. They were in no hurry to attack: apparently the game was ended. Without her sword, Argentia could not hope to beat them.

But they remembered the docks as well, when Argentia had sheathed her sword only to surprise them with her whip and fend them off long enough to escape.

A trick?

A trap? the twins wondered at each other. It seemed likely, but they knew they had hurt Argentia badly. It could be that she was simply yielding, hoping for mercy.

There would be none.

But the twins were crafty killers. Though the scent of Argentia's blood goaded them, the calculating, human parts of their minds tempered their bestial instincts. If this was a trap, they would not rush straight into it.

Another pass, Puma thought.

Yes, Pantra agreed. *As before.*

And then…

She dies.

There was no point to toying with prey that did not want to play.

With a flick of a nod at her sister, Puma led the attack from the right. Pantra, on the left, pounced forward a moment later for the second strike.

Argentia's hand was tight on the hilt of her katana. Waiting in the dark to be attacked, knowing she was not going to defend herself, was wracking her nerves. The urge to draw her weapon again was frighteningly strong, but she resisted.

She listened hard, focusing as she had focused against the pards. She would have only a split second to react—

Claws lacerated her arm. She turned hard and fast with the blow, her katana flying from its sheath, sweeping out as she continued spinning…

Pantra saw Puma's hit turn Argentia about. She sprang—

And suddenly the katana was there, slashing at her stomach…

The sheath-strike was perfect.

Argentia whipped her katana across, intercepting the second twin instead of chasing the first. Her blade was hip-high and rising when it connected at last with solid flesh. Argentia pulled the stroke through with an exultant growl.

The twin fell away, wauling, and the other cat-woman screamed in concert, as if she felt her sister's pain.

Argentia marked her and flashed across the space, striking back and forth, hoping for another hit. A hiss told her she was close. She feinted a jab. Swept a wide arc out to the left and back to the right.

She felt the blade bite for an instant, then clawed hands fastened on her and flung her down with horrible strength. She hit hard. Slammed her head. Lost her katana. Scrambled wildly.

There was a pulse of light as the mirror flared to life, sucking the twins away.

Before the aethereal afterglow went out, Argentia crawled quickly to her katana. She rose, meaning to follow and finish the battle, but the desperate energy that had infused her last moments deserted her. The dark world wobbled. She was suddenly back on her knees, consciousness fast fading, gone before she hit the crystal floor.

75

"Get back in there!" Vloth roared as Puma and Pantra came falling out of the mirror. The guildmaster was crimson with rage.

"Yaaaaooo…"

"Oowwww!" the cat-women wailed. They were clinging to each other on the floor at the base of the mirror.

Pantra had twisted aside just quickly enough to avoid being disemboweled, but she was bleeding from a vicious slash across her stomach; Puma had been cut on her upper arm. If they heard Vloth amid their anguished writhing, they made no effort to heed him.

Salis Yip, who knew how intolerant the sadistic twins were of their own pain, laughed. "Don't like hurts, sa-so."

"Well *done*, Lady," Ikabod murmured.

"Shut up, you old fool!" Vloth shouted. He rounded on the twins again. "I told you to get back in there and kill her!"

The twins shook their heads, mewling pitifully.

"Worthless bitches! You dare defy me?" Vloth swung his walking stick at the twins.

Puma caught it.

With a noise of outrage that was almost more female than feline, she flung the stick aside, rose, and slapped Vloth across the face, drawing four furrows of blood from his cheek. "*Mrrrrow!* No more! Our time as slaves…"

"Is ended," Pantra completed. She stood. One hand clutched her wounded stomach, but the light in her emerald eyes was more of hatred than pain. Snake-quick, she cracked Vloth across his other cheek, matching her sister's cuts.

Vloth staggered backwards. Touching his torn face, he stared at the crimson on his fat fingertips in astonishment. "You—"

The twins hissed savagely, stepping forward—

Terrified cries erupted outside the chamber—

The guards stationed in the doorway suddenly toppled into the room, followed by a wild-looking dwarf swinging an incredibly large axe.

76

"Dyin' time!" Griegvard Gynt shouted.

Behind him came Thorne, Kest, and Tib, weapons drawn. They had met no resistance as they followed the ramps up to the penultimate level of the pyramid. Before the guards there could do more than raise a cry, Griegvard was upon them like a boulder bounding down ahead of an avalanche, his huge axe hacking, knocking them back into the chamber.

The twins wheeled and saw the new attackers. With *mrrrows* of surprise, they fled out the chamber's other doorway. Thorne gave a cry and raced after them.

Vloth was reeling at the twins' betrayal—he had never trusted them completely, but such open-faced treachery had still caught him by surprise—and this even more unexpected assault by his escaped prisoners, who were making short work of his sentries. "Stop them!" he shouted to Gideon-gil.

"Stop them yourself," the assassin laughed, withdrawing into an alcove at the rear of the chamber.

"More treachery!" Vloth pointed at the charging dwarf and blasted him down with a bolt of lightning from one of his many rings.

Guards from the lower levels of the pyramid burst in, drawn to the cries and clash of combat, but Vloth had decided it was against his interests to await the outcome of the battle. "Come on!" he snapped at Salis Yip, who was scourging the stunned dwarf with an icy whip.

Yip whirled and followed the guildmaster into the mirror.

Darkness surrounded them.

Vloth touched one of his rings. The chamber came to light. They stood before a mirror identical to the one they had just passed through, this one hanging on a wall. The room was just a wide, empty space. The crystal floor was spattered with blood from the combat between the twins and Argentia.

The huntress lay where she had fallen. "Vile whore! Bring me her head for my trophy room," Vloth ordered. Then, eager to place as much distance as possible between himself and his enemies, he limped from the chamber, cursing the treacherous twins with every hobbled stride.

"Just'ee and Yip now, beauty, sa-so." The Whipmaster crouched above Argentia, rolled her onto her back, and squeezed her breasts roughly. It was likely the cat-women would escape, denying Yip his chance to kill them, but he could make up for that somewhat with Argentia. His eyes roved over her. He tugged at her navel ring. He would claim it as a trophy and wear it in his ear.

He could not linger too long, he knew, but there was time to torture Argentia at least a little before he took her head. It was only a question of how to begin: He could freeze her nipples with his ice whip and snap them off. *Sa-so. Then hair...* It was the color of flame already, and begged to be set afire.

Engrossed in the possibilities, the Whipmaster did not notice the flash behind him.

Ikabod staggered across the chamber and looped his shackled hands over the torturer's head.

"Saaaa—" Yip's cry of surprise was cut off as the chain bit into his throat. Ikabod, his love for Argentia and hatred of Salis Yip giving him inspired strength, choked the Nhapian, forcing him down.

Yip surged forward, trying to flip his assailant off him. The trick nearly worked, but at the last instant Ikabod jammed his bony knee between Yip's shoulders and reared back, digging the chain deeper into the Whipmaster's throat.

Yip's eyes bulged from his purpling face. His whole body jerked like a marionette possessed by some demonic puppeteer. The torturer's last, strangled gasps were music to Ikabod's old ears, but even more so was the fatal snap—and the sudden silence.

Wha...

Argentia came back to consciousness. She sat up slowly. Her whole body hurt from what felt like a thousand cuts and bruises. She touched her head gingerly where it had banged against the floor. Felt blood. *Great...*

"Lady."

Argentia turned just as Ikabod slumped beside Salis Yip's corpse, his hands still chained around the Nhapian's throat.

"Ikabod!" Once again Argentia did not know how long she'd blacked out, or what had transpired in the interval to lead her butler and Vloth's torturer to this chamber.

She crawled over and shoved Yip's body away. *Got what you deserved, bastard*, she thought as she took the butler in her arms. "Ikabod, are you all right?"

Ikabod raised his head weakly. A spasm of coughing wracked him.

"Don't you die on me," Argentia said. "Don't you dare."

The butler gasped in a long breath. "I…am fine…now."

Argentia closed her eyes. *Thank you…*

You're not out of this yet, that relentless voice within her warned. Argentia knew it spoke true. "Where are Vloth and the twins?"

"Vloth is gone." Ikabod pointed to the door. "The twins—I do not know. There are others fighting."

Mirk must have got them out…

Ikabod coughed wretchedly and started to swoon again, but Argentia steadied him. She spotted a ring of keys on Yip's belt. Found the one that released Ikabod's hands. "Can you walk?" Ikabod nodded. Grabbing her katana, Argentia helped the butler slowly to his feet. "Come on."

The mirror blazed, spilling Argentia and Ikabod into the font chamber.

"Sure, be showin' up *after* th' fightin's done," Griegvard said, dislodging his great axe from the chest of the last guard. Nine others lay strewn about the chamber. The dwarf's face and blonde beard were splashed with blood, and his mithryl armor was blackened by the lightning from Vloth's ring, but if he was injured, it didn't show.

"Did you need my help with this rabble?" Argentia was fighting dizziness that might not have been entirely due to the brief aetherwalk, but she felt herself getting her wind back, bringing with it the strength to carry on. *No choice. I've got to get Ikabod out of here…*

"Bah! Take a lookit yerself, then be tellin' me who was needin' help."

"Hey, I had it all under control," Argentia said. Then she saw Kest kneeling beside Tib. "What happened?" she asked, her survivor's levity vanishing.

"He's hurt," Kest said. He had unlaced Tib's leather vest. There was a dark stain spreading on the lieutenant's shirt. One of Vloth's men had caught him with a lucky stab beneath the arm while Tib was battling another guard.

Looks bad, Argentia thought grimly. She had seen more than her share of mortal wounds.

"It's bad," Kest said, confirming Argentia's fear.

"You're…overreacting," Tib managed weakly. His pale, drawn face told another story.

"Where are the others?" Argentia asked suddenly.

"Th' barbarians and th' halfling went after th' women," Griegvard said.

"And Thorne?"

"After them damn cat-twins."

Oh God… Argentia quickly strapped on her weapons-belt. "Where? How long?"

"Minutes. That way," Kest said.

Argentia rushed out the door. *Up or down?* She leaned over the rail.

Far below, the twins were racing toward the same storage chamber that Argentia had used to enter the pyramid. Thorne was one level above them, closing fast.

Argentia ran back into the font chamber. "Get Tib and Ikabod out."

"I don't think we can move Tib. He may die," Kest said.

"If you don't move him, he *will* die. If you can get him out, there's medicine with the sleds. You still have the sleds?"

Kest nodded.

"So get them out." Argentia looked at Griegvard. "Swear to me you'll get them out."

"On me life. But what're ye about, girl?"

"I'm going after Thorne."

"Why?"

"Because." She kissed Ikabod's cheek. "Stay with them. They'll get you out."

"Be careful, Lady," Ikabod said. He was looking at a woman who appeared too torn and bloodied to even move, but from the fire in Argentia's eyes, he knew it was useless to argue.

Argentia grinned. "Always am."

Then she was running.

77

Down.

Argentia pushed herself past pain, past exhaustion in an effort to save a man who for the most part of their acquaintance had scorned and mistrusted, if not outright hated her. She could have let him go. There was Ikabod to think about, and Tib, who was badly injured, and if she was going to pursue anyone through this madhouse of a pyramid, shouldn't it be Togril Vloth?

So she could well have let Thorne go. Let him die seeking the vengeance he craved—for the twins wounded were apt to be the twins at their most lethal—but that simply was not in her. The compass of her heart had pointed this as the right course, and it was not her nature to disobey its line.

Then go faster, for Aeton's sake... Already the twins had vanished into the storeroom, and Thorne was not far behind, while she was still several levels above them.

Faster...

Argentia ran on, scarcely seeing the bodies of guards fallen on the catwalks and ramps, not hearing the cries of battle as she circled the second level, arcing down to the first and finally to the ground, where she broke into an all-out sprint, her red braid flying behind her, her battered ribs throbbing, her myriad cuts burning, her breath coming in short gasps, her boots threatening to stumble if she gave them the chance.

Faster...

In the tunnel beneath the Frost Palace, Puma and Pantra paused to survey their work one final time. They were pursued, they knew, and they would deal with that pursuit momentarily.

Once they had finished here.

The piled skulls had come with the cat-women from Argo, prizes taken from Orik Totenkampf after they had killed him. The cunning devices were enchanted with incendiary dweomers. The twins had used two to destroy the warehouse at Argo's Watch garrison, and left another in Argentia's Westing House suite. The rest they had brought to the Frost Palace, not really with any intention of using them; they had simply become a part of their belongings.

A part Togril Vloth knew nothing of.

He will learn, Puma thought.

Yes, he will learn soon, Pantra replied. She had her hand pressed to the wound in her stomach, which was leaking bright blood at an alarming pace. She had run hard, and felt very weak and queasy: sensations utterly unknown to her until now.

Puma sensed it. She made a querulous purring noise. Pantra whimpered in reply. *I am so hurt, sister*, she moaned in their strange, silent speech.

Puma crouched, moved Pantra's hand aside, bent her head to her sister's belly and began to lick at the wound. But her ministrations could not staunch the flow. She actually felt the cut pulsing blood against her mouth.

Mrrooooooow... Pantra had tears in her green eyes.

Be strong, Puma urged, rising. *We will go swift to safety. We will find a healer...* But she had no idea where they would find a healer in this forsaken, frozen wilderness. *Perhaps Vloth...*

No! We are done with him. We will not go back, Pantra insisted.

Slowly Puma nodded. Their course was set. *Then let us*— She looked up sharply, sniffing the chill air.

They had lingered almost too long.

Moving simultaneously, the twins activated the skulls. Their original plan had been to dispatch Vloth and then, purely for spite, destroy this pyramid that had been their miserable prison. Though the guildmaster might have escaped them, the pyramid would not. The skulls, cleverly set directly beneath the pyramid's great central column, would unleash enough of a blast to shatter that support and bring the whole palace crashing down.

Quickly!

Hurry!

The man-scent was even nearer. The twins could hear him clearly now, and this tunnel was no place for battle. Puma put her bloodied arm around her injured sister, leading her out of the tunnel, their steps perfectly balanced even on the ice.

Behind them, the glowing orange light in the skulls' eye-sockets grew brighter.

78

Thorne dropped down the ladder from the trap door in the storeroom into the tunnel.

He was gasping already, and when he hit the ice of the tunnel and his legs shot out from under him, what little air he had was slammed from his lungs. He lay in a heap, feeling as if he'd been pierced by a spear.

Get up! He struggled for footing, found it for a moment, but slipped back to his knees. Growling, he forced his way up again, staggering ahead, one hand braced on the frozen wall, the other clenching his baton. There would be work for that stick shortly.

He saw a throbbing orange light, coming from a pile of skulls. A vague sense of danger raised the hairs on his neck when as he passed by the gruesome, glowing array—then the skulls were gone from sight and mind. Only the pursuit mattered.

It came to an end moments later.

Thorne emerged from the tunnel into an ice cavern. A chasm opened before him, falling away forever. Upon the bridge spanning this abyss were the twins.

"Stop!" Thorne ran towards them, his eyes ablaze in his ruined face. The twins turned, waiting. The brunette stepped in front of the blonde. That was fine. It made no difference to Thorne which one died first.

But Pantra spread her hands in a gesture of surrender that brought him up short. "Mercy!" she cried, swaying weakly. Her upraised palms were covered in blood. "We are hurt. Please…"

"Let us live," the other whined from behind her.

"Let us go," they begged together.

"You showed no mercy to Vendi," Thorne said. "Nor to the others you killed. The vagrants. The child. Mercy? No, let there be no mercy for such as you. Not while I live."

"Then..."

"Die."

Pantra ducked as Puma sprang over her, crashing into Thorne. He staggered, one arm lifting to protect his eyes from Puma's claws, trying to strike with his baton.

Puma batted the weapon aside and rode Thorne to the ground. Pantra pounced, her slashing hand ripping across Thorne's forehead.

Screaming in pain, Thorne twisted and thrashed beneath their onslaught, but there was no quarter from the twins. This was not play, it was survival.

Puma caught Thorne by the face, mashing his head against the bridge. Stars blazed behind Thorne's eyes, and his whole world seemed to shake...

The first thing Argentia noticed when she entered the tunnel again was the cold. She had no cloak or winter garb this time. After the warmth of the Frost Palace, the icy enclosure was impossibly frigid.

The second thing she noticed was the orange light flaring from the pile of skulls.

Aeton's bolts! Unlike Thorne, Argentia knew without doubt there was danger here. *I saw them on the way in. Why didn't I recognize them? I should have known...*

She cursed her stupidity, but the skulls had been inert when she first saw them, and it had been easy enough to dismiss them as some ghastly monument or even the larder of some subterranean creature that had made the tunnel its home. Now their pulsating glow revealed them unmistakably for what they were.

Argentia guessed that the twins had set them. Whether their intent was to cover their escape or to destroy the pyramid—or both—she did not know, but from the number of skulls, this explosion would likely make the one that had destroyed her suite in the Westing House seem like a wizard's firework.

The others. Oh my God...

The realization of the danger Ikabod and the rest were in almost stopped Argentia in her tracks. But there was nothing she could do. She had no idea how to disarm the skulls, or even if the skulls could be disarmed, and no time to figure it out. The one in the Westing House had exploded only seconds after she'd tripped its magic.

Trusting Fortune to get Ikabod and the others out alive, Argentia raced recklessly over the ice. All her fabulous balance was put to the test to keep her on her feet, and she burst from the tunnel onto the bridge so fast that she actually slammed into the railing to break her momentum.

Wincing at the jarring impact to her ribs, which she feared were once again broken, she looked up and saw the twins killing Thorne.

Argentia drew on the run, aiming the handbow as she bore down upon the twins. They didn't see her. She had a clear shot.

Gotcha... Argentia pulled the trigger—

—and was blasted clear off her feet.

79

In the harem chamber of the Frost Palace, Brieki and the other girls of the Tribe of the Walros heard but did not understand the strange sounds echoing through the pyramid.

For five long years, this crystal prison had defined their existence. In the beginning, they had railed against their internment and tried to escape. Vloth had ordered one of the girls executed. Meaning to set an example by her death, he made the remaining girls watch.

They tried to escape again the next day.

Recognizing that Norden women held the same ideas of honor as the men, Vloth substituted subtlety for force. He poisoned their drink with a drug that rendered the girls submissive to his whims.

Months passed into winters. The whetstone of time ground down resistance. The girls came to accept the Fortune that made them captives in this crystal palace, prisoners of a luxury and largess wholly foreign to their rearing.

It was not so horrible a fate.

The soft beds, the warm chambers that only looked like caves of ice, even the revealing silken garments became things of custom and habit and even enjoyment. Their eunuch captor was watchful only when Vloth was present, and that was a thankfully infrequent occurrence.

When the guildmaster was there, he made his demands and the girls serviced him accordingly. At those times, they took wine mixed with the drug. While those draughts did not make them forget, they dulled their senses and made them not care.

The rest of the time, they passed long and lazy days and nights in the glittering rooms of the Frost Palace and grew from beautiful, hard girls into beautiful, soft possessions.

Reclining atop the pillow-laden bed, Brieki ran an elk-bristle brush through corn-silk tresses that flooded past her waist. Her pale blue eyes were glazed and listless. The guildmaster would be calling for her and the other girls before long, so they had all shared the special wine with their meal.

Now she was lost in a pleasant fog that made everything seem slow and speculative. She felt she could quite happily go on grooming her hair until Vloth sent for them, or until morning, or until—

A voice pierced the stuporous veil like an eagle's clarion ripping through a cloud. It was instantly recognizable even after five winters of its absence.

Brieki vaulted from the bed, heart pounding. The brush clattered from her suddenly trembling hands. She didn't hear it. She had ears only for that voice bellowing her name over and over again.

The other girls, all riding the waves of the potion, barely glanced at her, but the eunuch in the doorway grunted, "Sit down," and raised a huge hand in warning.

Brieki defied him. Cupping her hands to her mouth, she shouted as she'd not shouted since that fateful day when men in black armor had come and taken her.

"Father! I'm here, Father! Hurry!"

80

Kozar, Exmoor, and Augustus fought a running battle to the harem. When Kozar's bellows were finally answered by Brieki's cry, the Nordens were infused with a kind of berserker force unlike anything the halfling had ever seen—and against which nothing could stand.

Guards were cut down by harpoons, hatchets, and hunting knives. The dwarf-craft of these arms was more than a match for the guards' armor, but so enraged were the barbarians that Augustus thought they would have made dried sticks serve as lethal weapons.

The halfling tagged along in their destructive wake. This was his type of battle. He was virtually unnoticed, and barely needed his magic until they reached the harem.

There Ophar the eunuch blocked the way. He was a Makharanian giant, black of skin, black of dreadlocks, massive and imposing enough to give even the Nordens a moment's pause.

"Stop!" Ophar ordered. He wore a purple vest that hung open over his monumental slab of stomach, flowing green silk pants, and sandals on his splayed feet. In his hand was a length of heavy iron chain.

"Father!" Brieki screamed from somewhere in the room behind the eunuch.

That was all the spurring Kozar needed. With a cry to Sturm, the Norden flung his harpoon at the eunuch's torso: an impossible target to miss. Ophar twirled the chain, his reflexes deft for so huge a man, and swatted the spear aside.

Undaunted, Kozar charged. He was giving up perhaps three inches in height and two hundred pounds in flesh to this monster, but he came like a storm, slamming the eunuch's jaw with a punch that would have staggered a white bear.

Ophar's head snapped back.

That was all.

The eunuch smiled down at Kozar—blood and quite a few teeth spilled out of his mouth as he did—and delivered a clubbing strike of his own, smashing the Norden aside as if he were a toy.

"Sturm!" Exmoor cried, charging.

Ophar stepped to meet him.

Augustus, engaged in holding a half-dozen guards at bay with bursts of aether, heard Exmoor's cry of pain. Whirling, the halfling saw the barbarian was down, and the giant's chain was lifting to crush him.

Brieki got there first.

With a banshee shriek, she sprang at Ophar, smashing her brush into his ear. The firm bristles lit Ophar's head with the pain of a hundred stinging asps. He dropped his chain, clutching his ear.

"Get down!" Augustus shouted. Brieki dropped to the floor an instant before the halfling's magic blew Ophar back into the harem, where all six of the Norden girls fell upon him.

More of Vloth's guards charged up the ramp. Most went after the two barbarians, but one veered to attack Augustus just as the halfling flung his magic at Ophar. He saw the man coming at the last moment, in time to duck but not quite fast enough to dodge completely. A mace grazed his head, knocking him sprawling. The guard raised his mace to finish the job.

Mirk leaped up, clamping his jaws on the man's vulnerable nose.

The guard jerked backwards, stumbling in tear-blind agony—one step too close to the ramp.

Mirk jumped clear as the guard lost his balance and tumbled down to land in a broken tangle of limbs on the catwalk below.

"Foul tasting, filthy—pah!" Mirk spat, wiping at his violated mouth.

"Thanks," Augustus managed, rubbing his bloodied head as he sat up. He was quickly on his feet again, throwing more magic at the harem doorway, where the barbarians were battling Vloth's guards.

Within the harem, Brieki and the other women were vainly trying to subdue Ophar. The battle had awakened them to the suddenly real possibility of escape—a dream that had smoldered like a deep ember for these past winters: dim and weak and cool, but never dead. The hold of the sedating potion evaporated in the surge of blood and energy and hope.

But Ophar was too much for them.

The girls had no weapons but their nails and brushes, and though they used these fiercely, the giant had absorbed all their blows and managed to get to his knees, flinging three of the six away. He clapped two of the remaining girls violently together. Their heads struck awkwardly. Ophar heard a neck break, but one dead harem girl was better than facing Vloth after allowing the lot to be taken. He dropped the girls and rose from the bed.

"Woman killer!" Kozar slammed an elbow into the side of a guard's head, smashing him out of the way. Snatching his harpoon from the floor, he plunged it into Ophar's chest.

"Gah—" The eunuch took a ponderous step back. Looked down at the spear. Frowning, he grabbed the haft and ripped it free. Blood spurted. Ophar seemed not to notice. He flung the harpoon down, steadied himself, and grabbed for Kozar.

The barbarian sidestepped. Ophar swiped again, backing Kozar into a corner, and then flung his bulk forward.

With nowhere to dodge, Kozar was pulverized between the eunuch and the wall. A man of less strength and stature would have been crushed like a fly. Kozar, borne beyond pain by five winters' fury, merely bellowed and drove his forehead into the giant's nose.

Ophar howled and slammed Kozar against the wall again.

"Father!" Exmoor leaped at Ophar from behind and buried a hatchet in the eunuch's back. As Ophar staggered, Kozar bulled the giant away from the wall. Together, the barbarians hauled the roaring behemoth down, pummeling him.

Ophar heaved them off. Forcing himself to his knees, he swayed like a tree about to topple, groping for Exmoor's hatchet, which was stuck in his back.

Kozar came up with his harpoon and smashed the shaft across Ophar's already broken nose, stunning the eunuch. Rising to his full height, the barbarian raised the spear two-fisted above his head. "Sturm!" he roared, driving the weapon into giant's skull as if he were punching an awl through the ice to make a fishing hole.

Ophar crashed down, a broken monolith of flesh.

"Oh father!" Brieki flew to Kozar and was crushed in his arms. Exmoor joined them, and all the other girls rallied around their saviors. Augustus went to the girl that Ophar had killed and gently closed her eyes, shaking his head sadly.

"Out," Kozar said after a moment in which joyful tears ran unnoticed from his eyes as he came to believe that this was not some dream. His daughter truly was alive and with him again. "Out now."

In minutes, Kozar's party reached the ground level of the pyramid.

They were halfway to the door when the explosion hit.

It rammed through the base of the Frost Palace like a great, whelming fist of flame and heat. The blast bloomed, opening its fingers, scourging the pyramid as it rose, then seemed to clench in upon itself with a bass and deadly THOOOOM, liquefying the bottom of the pillar even as a series of secondary explosions shot tendrils of fire up the column's length.

Groaning like some mortal thing stricken unto death, the Frost Palace shuddered under this infernal discharge, and began to fall.

81

Ikabod, Griegvard, Kest, and Tib were still three levels up in the palace when they saw the barbarians appear in the open space below.

They had fought only one battle (to the dwarf's disappointment) but had been slowed by the butler and Tib, who was unconscious and had to be carried by Kest.

"Drim be damned—they got th' girls!" Griegvard said.

And the world heaved like a ship in a storm.

The walkway buckled, flinging them down. Kest lost his hold on Tib, who skidded helplessly toward the drop beneath the railing.

Griegvard dove, pinning Tib on the bouncing, shuddering crystal, feeling the heat from the roaring explosion go searing past like a belch from his forge in Stromness. This was followed almost instantly by smaller blasts that shook the pyramid again and again.

Then, a moment of calm.

Kest and Ikabod were clinging to the railing. Fresh blood ran down the butler's forehead. Both men were badly dazed. Kest couldn't tell if he was still shaking, or if the whole structure was. Above, where the crystal peak had been ripped open, he could see the night. Below all was flame and smoke. "What—"

Griegvard shifted off of Tib and pressed his cheek to the crystal. With his innate attunement to all things of the earth, he could feel the pyramid's dangerous instability. *Bloody Hell...* "Hold on!" he warned.

The collapse began.

The shock wave knocked the barbarians senseless like a hot slap from Lyoki, God of Flame. Stunned for several moments, they forced themselves to their feet and regrouped. The air was clouded with acrid smoke. The stench of burning crystal clawed at their nostrils and throats. Fire was everywhere.

High above, the pyramid was falling. Great chunks of crystal dislodged, plummeting through the smoke like gargantuan hailstones. The central pillar, its foundations obliterated, sundered. Cracks raced up it like lightning—then all at once it split and crumbled, taking ringed footpaths, ramps, and walkways with it.

"Kest! Tib!" Augustus watched helplessly as the catwalk his friends were trapped on broke away from the wall and toppled into fire and smoke. "No!" The halfling ran forward. A wave of flame repelled him. The others were lost in the thickening pall. The pyramid was falling about him in smashing thunder and glassy shrapnel.

"Cover! Cover!" Kozar cried.

One of the Norden girls, mad as a mare in a barn fire and heedless of Kozar's voice, ran towards the door and got pulverized by a chunk of crystal.

A section of walkway toppled and crushed two guards and a servant as they tried to escape.

We're all going to die... Bravely, Augustus tried to raise an aethereal shield. "Here!" he shouted over the avalanche noise, casting a glittering webwork of blue magic up against the falling debris.

The ground bucked beneath his feet. He fell and struck his head and knew no more.

82

Argentia's shot went barely wide.

Even with her aim jarred by the tremendous detonation behind her, the silver streak still blasted a hole in the crystal just past Pantra's head, making the cat-woman *yaow* in alarm.

Argentia saw none of this. She was bludgeoned by a tidal wave of heat and hit the ground before she was fully aware she'd been thrown forward.

As she lay there, stunned and gasping, her dragon's tooth token glared sharply, perhaps catching a reflection off the crystal. Its bright gleam brought her back to her senses. She raised her head.

The twins were stalking toward her: one last bit of unfinished business in this nasty, cold place. One last morsel of revenge.

Argentia shoved up. Her handbow was still on the bridge, but out of reach. She uncoiled her whip. The twins paused, their green eyes narrowing. Behind them, Argentia saw Thorne's torn body lying at the edge of a wide gap where part of the bridge had collapsed in the explosion's shock wave. She didn't know if he was dead or alive.

"Come on, you bitches," she challenged. "Let's end this."

The twins charged.

Argentia lashed her whip sidearm and low.

The twins stopped short with impossible swiftness.

The whip coiled around the base of a post. Before Argentia could flick it loose, Pantra yanked it from her grasp and flung it aside with a disdainful hiss. It dangled off the bridge like some hangman's hemp.

Argentia went for her katana.

Puma was faster. Ducking in, she blocked Argentia's draw, clawed the huntress across the abdomen, and slung her towards Pantra. "A gift…"

"…for me? How sweet." Pantra swept Argentia's legs from under her and kicked her over the side.

259

Grabbing desperately, Argentia caught the crystal edge of the bridge. She struggled for purchase, trying to pull herself up. *No good…*

This time, she was finished.

The twins knew it. With identical smiles, they crouched above the huntress. Puma teased a nail across Argentia's knuckles. "Shall we pry her fingers one by one…"

"Or bite them— *Mrrrrow!*"

Thorne barreled into Pantra, hauling her up in a terrific clench. She wauled in anguish, blood gushing from her wounded stomach.

Shrieking, Puma sprang upon Thorne, ripping at his face and throat.

Thorne staggered forward, pitching over the railing above Argentia, meaning to take the twins to their death with him.

With one last burst of feline agility, Pantra lashed out. Her ten claws pierced Argentia's hips to the bone.

Argentia screamed. Lost her hold on the bridge.

Fell.

Something serpentine flashed in the periphery of her vision. She flailed at it.

Caught her whip.

She was jerked down with terrible force as the line snapped taut. The quartet dangled above the abyss, twisting and swaying in space: Argentia clinging to the whip, Pantra clawing to her hips, Thorne's arms cinched about Pantra's waist, and Puma, who had been dislodged from Thorne's back, wrapped about his leg.

For a moment they simply hung there.

Then Argentia's grip began to fail.

Dragged by the weight of three, her arms almost wrenched from their sockets, there was no way she could hold on. No way at all.

The whip slithered inch by inch through her weakening hands. *No…*

Her hands slipped. For a terrifying instant they were falling, but Argentia caught hold again, just above the whip's handle. The whole group jounced violently on the line. Argentia screamed as the pain tore through her shoulders, but clenched her grip.

She felt a struggle of movement beneath her. Dared to look down.

Thorne had one arm clasped about Pantra. The other groped at his belt.

Came up with a dagger.

"No!" the twins screamed as one.

"Thorne don't!" Argentia shouted.

Thorne's eyes met Argentia's. His face was a carnage—not even the scar on his cheek recognizable—and his throat gushed crimson, but his gaze was clear and lucid.

"Please! Do not!" the twins begged.

Thorne's lips parted in a falcon's merciless smile. "For Vendi."

He plunged the dagger into Pantra's side.

The scream came from both twins as Pantra spasmed in agony, her claws ripping free of Argentia's hips.

All the weight was suddenly gone.

"THORNE!"

Argentia's cry mingled with the twins' echoing wail as the trio fell away from her, tumbling together, locked still in their fatal embrace as the darkness of the ice chasm swallowed them down to the darker black of death: Puma, Pantra, and Tierciel Thorne...

83

A shadow fell over Argentia.

"Well," Gideon-gil said. The assassin had slipped unseen from the alcove in the font chamber while Ikabod, Kest, and Griegvard were tending Tib and had followed Argentia, Thorne, and the twins. He watched their battle after the explosion—a touch from the cat-women even he had not anticipated—curious to see who would live and prepared to make certain that particular participants did not.

"You have a curious knack for survival, Lady Dasani, though your situation remains precarious." Gideon-gil smiled. "Will you not ask me to draw you up?"

The elf's appearance was the last thing Argentia had expected, but she would accept no aid from a killer like Gideon-gil. Gritting her teeth, she held on tighter to the whip.

A black dagger appeared in the elf's hand. "One cut, Lady, and you can learn if your friends are still falling."

Still Argentia only glared at him. If the assassin was going to send her to her death, she wanted to stare him in the eyes as he did so.

"Defiant to the last, eh? Good. You, at least, do not disappoint." The blade vanished. The elf looked down at Argentia. He was beginning to wonder if he had chosen the wrong party in that dark room to measure as a potential challenge.

"If you will not take my aid, will you at least take my advice?" Gideon-gil accepted Argentia's silence as assent. "If he lives, Vloth will never stop hunting you."

More silence.

The elf raised his hand. "Do you see my ring, Lady? A useful device. Mark." Gideon-gil's form glimmered and was replaced by another.

"Guntyr!" Argentia gasped.

"Alas, no," The barbarian's body glimmered again and Gideon-gil reassumed his true shape. "I fear the good Guntyr has been dead since Telarban. I met him in Vloth's guild. He was slow, but I found his skin a convenient way to travel."

"Why?" Argentia managed, trying not to feel the pain in her arms, the chafing fire in her clenched hands.

"To keep close to my quarry, though he escaped me in the end—after a fashion." Gideon-gil gestured at the abyss.

Thorne... "You—"

"I shouldn't tax myself with speech, Lady, were I in your position. If you have questions, ask them of Magistrate Krung in Argo—should you find him before I do."

The elf slipped off his ring and set the silver circlet on the bridge. "If you can reach this, it is yours. I trust you will know what work to put it toward." He stared silently at Argentia for a moment. "We are not so different, you and I," he added musingly.

"We are nothing alike, assassin!" Argentia spat.

Gideon-gil spread his hands in mock apology. "As you will. And so, farewell, Lady Dasani. Perhaps we shall cross paths—and blades—in the future, when you are strong enough again to give me some true sport."

"Go to Hell!"

Gideon-gil bowed and spun away. Argentia saw him reappear moments later, leaping the broken space in the bridge, racing down the far side and into the tunnel of the secret steps without a backwards glance.

Bastard... Anger spurred Argentia. She pulled herself up the whip, but flagged after gaining little more than a foot. She was exhausted and hurting and she knew she could not make this climb. She was not even sure how much longer she could hang on.

Still, for long moments she did hang on, the only sound her frosty breathing, the only sensation the freezing cold. It would be the cold that killed her, numbing her until she could not feel her hands any longer. Then she would fall, and likely not even realize she'd lost her grip until it was far too late.

She wondered if it wasn't better to just let go.

No—I will not...

The spark of anger struck by Gideon-gil's words flared again, this time at her own weakness. If her Fortune was to die today, so be it, but she would resist until her last breath. Until her hands could hold her no more, and then a few seconds longer. Death could come for her, but it would have to work to take her.

She started to climb again.

Went hand over hand until she had drawn herself up enough to use her thighs to help, and then her feet. Went without pause, for fear that if she paused she would falter entirely. Went and went until, minutes later—she would never know how many, really, only that they seemed like many more than they were—she dragged herself onto the bridge and collapsed.

I don't think I can move my arms... For some reason this made Argentia laugh. She lay upon a bridge of crystal, laughing until those laughs—not quite sane with relief—became gasps. "Oh...oh God." Her stomach hurt, her lungs ached. "No more," she whispered. "No more—I'll die."

With an effort, Argentia got to her hands and knees, but a wave of vertigo washed over her and she slumped down again, lost to time and place.

84

The shaking stopped.

Kozar rolled off of Brieki, whom he had covered when the collapse threatened them. "Are you all right?" he shouted. His ears were ringing so badly as he sat up that he could not hear his daughter's reply, but she knelt up and seemed to be frightened but unharmed. *Thank Sturm...*

Exmoor was helping two of the girls to their feet. Kozar did not see the other two. Augustus' magic shield had shunted much of the crystal debris away, but there were bodies all around: guards, servants—and there were the missing girls, crushed by chunks of the walkways. *Why did they not heed me?*

Shaking his head, he sought Augustus. Spotted him behind Brieki, crumpled like a small child. Crawling over, he placed a broad hand on the halfling's back. Felt the rise and fall of breathing—

Brieki screamed.

Kozar whirled. Though the fire was not spreading, they could feel the hot pant of its breath, and the smoke was thickening.

Through this pall came a red-eyed apparition.

Kozar threw himself between the thing and Brieki. He drew his dagger only to have it slapped from his rising hand.

"I'm on yer side, ye damn fool!" Griegvard was covered with ash and whitish powder. His helm had a massive dent and blood trickled freely down the side of his face.

"Your eyes!" Kozar exclaimed. The dwarf's eyes were glowing as red as the flames behind him.

"Fer seein' in th' dark. Dwarf trick—no time t' explain. I'm needin' help."

"Get your sister and the others out," Kozar said to Exmoor. "And do not forget the halfling. Go quickly."

Exmoor started to protest.

"Do as I say, boy!"

"Father, what—" Brieki began.

Kozar hugged Brieki close and kissed her forehead. "Go with Exmoor. Go, now. I'll be right behind you."

Kozar watched Exmoor take the halfling over his shoulder and make for the exit from the pyramid with his sister and the other women in tow. *Sturm, see them out*, he prayed. Already it was becoming hard to breath, but more than the smoke and fire, Kozar feared they had not seen the last of the collapse. He had witnessed glaciers in the Sea of Sleet split and fall in upon themselves, and knew that the initial crash was usually followed by one or two others that completed the catastrophe.

Ducking low, the barbarian followed Griegvard deeper into the pyramid. It was much hotter here, the smoke stinking and black. He covered his mouth and nose. Squinted through burning eyes, stumbling over and around barricades of fallen debris until the dwarf led him to the others. Two were kneeling. One was lying very still.

The dwarf grabbed the body. "Help them two." Kozar managed to get the others up. They came slowly, weakly, more staggering and leaning on him than walking, but somehow they made it to the doorway, with Griegvard coming behind them.

A piece of walkway had collapsed before the door. In the small space on the far side, Brieki and the other girls were huddled around the unconscious halfling while Exmoor slammed himself repeatedly against the door. The surrounding wall had buckled and warped, and the portal would not open.

Kozar helped his charges to climb over the collapse. He caught Exmoor before the boy could fling himself against the stubborn door again.

"With me," Kozar said. He sat with his back pressed to the fallen walkway, boots spread wide against the door. Exmoor mimicked his position. "Together," Kozar growled. He wished he could catch a decent breath, but the air was acrid, foul, and poisonous. Only opening this door would change that.

Father and son pistoned their legs with all their might. There was a grating of crystal on crystal.

The door did not budge.

Gasping, their lungs burning, the barbarians dropped their feet.

"Bah! Yer lettin' a bit o' stupid rock stop ye?" Griegvard lay the body he'd been towing down beside Augustus and set his shoulder to the door.

As he drove forward, the barbarians pushed again with their legs. The door moved slightly. "Harder!" the dwarf exhorted.

Kozar and Exmoor heaved, pitting tundra-born strength against mage-formed crystal. They grimaced at the terrible strain in their backs and thighs but they did not stop pushing until they felt the crystal door begin to yield and open.

Cold air poured in, sucking at the smoke, invigorating the escapees. They lacked the leverage to force the door farther, but the crack they had opened looked to be enough. "Out!" Kozar grunted.

One by one they went sideways through the door, the girls first, followed by the Argosians. The barbarians passed the halfling through, then the other body. Exmoor slipped out with only slightly more difficulty than his sister, and Kozar scraped his burly chest and back raw, but managed to squeeze past.

Griegvard could not.

"Bloody Hell!" Out came the dwarf's huge axe, hacking away at the crystal, widening the door.

"Mooooooove!"

The dwarf spun. A guard was clambering over the collapsed walkway. Without hesitation, Griegvard reversed his axe and cut him down. The man had likely been trying to escape, but the dwarf was taking no chances, and he had scant mercy for those who served such ilk as Togril Vloth.

He turned back to the door, carving a passage. He was nearly done when he felt the ground shiver. "Get clear!" he shouted to Kozar.

Tossing his axe ahead of him, Griegvard forged into the space. He stuck at the end, where he hadn't been able to finish his work.

Kozar grabbed him by the arm and wrenched him free.

"What're ye, daft? I said get clear!" Griegvard shouted.

"Dwarves have strange ways of showing thanks."

Griegvard grabbed his axe. "This ain't th' time fer a bloody etiquette debate. Just run, ye damn fool!"

They ran, churning through powdery snow. The others were already at the sleds. Kozar waved for them to retreat farther. "Move—"

With a tremendous roar, the remains of the Frost Palace collapsed, shaking the frozen earth and hurling a huge gout of smoke at the moon.

When the cloud cleared, the heap of rubble that remained could in no way be identified as a pyramid.

85

Gen…

Carfax? She knows she must be dreaming.

Gen—get up.

I don't want to. It's cold.

Get up. Now, Gen…

And it seems that in the dream—for an instant—she can see him again. He is wrapped in silver and blue: ghostly, aethereal, but still her Carfax, still her love, true down to the brands on his cheeks, the glimmer in his storm-gray eyes.

Reaching for him

Argentia snapped awake.

Her scrambling hand set something silver skittering across the bridge. It was the ring Gideon-gil had left for her. She watched helplessly as it slid toward the edge.

Stopped with inches to spare.

Grabbing the rail, Argentia pulled herself to her feet. She held on tightly, waiting for the dizziness to pass. Her arms were made of lead, her torn hips an agony like nothing she'd known. Bright bloodstains dripped down her leather pants. The tips of her fingers were an ugly looking shade of blue, and she couldn't feel her nose or lips very well.

But I'm alive. Now if I can just get the hell out of here…

Argentia started to turn, then stopped and looked back at the ring. She had an urge to kick it into the chasm. Instead, she bent and, reaching very carefully with her uncertain fingers, lifted it up and deposited it in her belt pouch.

Collecting her whip with equal care, she went back toward the tunnel. As she paused to recover her handbow, she noticed the debris that had been spewed in front of the tunnel opening. Her heart sank. *Please, no...*

A few feet inside the mouth of the tunnel Argentia found the disaster she'd dreaded. The explosion had caved the passage in, leaving a pile of ice chunks and slabs that she could not hope to dig her way through.

Argentia sagged against the wall. She was trapped. Gideon-gil might have been fleet enough to leap the twenty-foot gap in the bridge, but that was a feat beyond Argentia even at her best. *What do I do now?*

Frustrated, she kicked at a chunk of ice. It skidded into the wall and ricocheted back to her. She stopped it with her boot. Stared at it. Her mind flashed up a memory that seemed from a lifetime ago: in the hallway of the Westing House, sliding between the Watchman's legs. "You're mad," she muttered.

But was she?

She kicked the chunk out onto the bridge. Walked after it as it slid all the way to the end and shot out into the void before dropping out of sight.

She tried to gauge the chance. The break had happened just after the midpoint of the arch. The far side of the split was lower than the side where she stood. With enough of a running start and the elevation of the arch to help, she thought it just might work.

Nothing to lose...

A few minutes later she was ready to try. If she failed, she would plummet to her death, but at least she would do so under her own control. She could accept that.

Bright Lady—watch over...

Argentia took a deep breath. Her hands, already raw and torn and frostbitten, were almost frozen to the slab of ice she held before her. She scuffed her boots a few times, kicking off as much rime as she could. Rolled her neck back and forth. Stared at the gap and the spot she'd picked to dive.

She felt the rush of energy building in her: a final burst. The last burst of her life? *Go—NOW!*

Argentia exploded forward, willing herself once more past pain and exhaustion, sprinting harder than even she'd run in her escape from the crypt of the Revenant King. She hurtled out onto the bridge. Threw herself down.

The edge rushed towards her. Was suddenly beneath her. She was airborne, soaring over the void on a sled of ice, cutting through the frozen air—

Slamming down on the far side, clearing the lip by half a body-length.

She spun sideways, tumbling off the ice, sliding out of control toward the side of the bridge—

A shattering blow stopped her, but it was a long second before she realized she was no longer moving—and that she felt nothing beneath her boots again.

She had crashed into one of the posts. Her legs were dangling off the bridge.

Terror jolted through her and she scrabbled backwards, kicking and scrambling her way to the middle of the span. She sprawled there with her heart pounding, gasping for breath that would barely come.

Oh, my ribs… Argentia didn't know how many were broken—it felt like all of them—but she knew she'd done some serious damage even before she coughed up scarlet blood. *Not good….*

Slowly, Argentia forced herself to her feet. The ice sled was gone, fallen into the chasm. She gave it a weary salute and staggered away, clutching her side as she went.

At the mouth of the secret steps she rested. As she leaned against the wall, she felt the ground tremble beneath her: a thrumming vibration, like the quiver of a bowstring. *What now?* She was too tired to even care, but she raised her head as a grinding noise issued from across the chasm.

The far side of the bridge fragmented, huge pieces plunging silently into the abyss.

Argentia shuddered. A few minutes earlier she had been on that part of the bridge. *If I didn't wake up when I did…*

She pushed the thought aside, but as she turned to follow the path Gideon-gil had taken to the surface, she closed her frozen fist tightly about the dragon's tooth token.

Climbing the steps was impossibly painful. Every breath was a dagger-thrust. When she stumbled and fell, unable to catch herself, she coughed up more blood and lay still for many minutes before going on again. She did not try to rise, but crawled doggedly, sometimes dragging herself up a step at a time, until—at last—she emerged once more to see the stars in the black vault of the Nordic night.

Argentia wept as she struggled from the exit, which was disguised as an ice-ant mound. She lost her balance again and tumbled down into a bed of fresh snow.

Gasping at the shocking wetness, Argentia sat up and looked around. In the moonlight, Vloth's pyramid was a formless, shattered hulk. The ice-ant mounds stood like shadowy sentinels around the corpse of some great felled beast. Ground snow flurried in the gnawing wind.

Ikabod... Hardly knowing what she was about, Argentia wobbled to her feet and began walking toward the wreck of the pyramid. She collapsed once more after the first few steps, toppling into the snow.

Argentia tried to rise again, but there was a darkness coming for her that she could not fight any longer. She felt herself drifting away in blissful cold. One by one, the moon and stars dimmed and went out.

Distant in that black, a dog began to bark.

86

The survivors regrouped.

Kest knelt beside Augustus, trying to wake him. The lieutenant had come through the disaster with only minor injuries, and was facing the hard prospect that he might be the sole member of the group returning to Argo. Tib's neck had been broken in the walkway's collapse. There was no sign of Thorne or Guntyr, and little hope they lived. If Augustus died, Fortune would have spared only Kest.

But after a few minutes, Augustus stirred and roused. Overjoyed, Kest hugged the halfling. "The others?" Augustus asked when he'd recovered enough to sit up without feeling like his aching head would burst.

Kest looked away. Augustus' dark eyes went wide. "Oh. Oh no. No." He saw Tib's body, which Exmoor had arranged peacefully near a sled. "Oh, Tib. Was it—"

"The fall," Kest said. "I don't...I don't think he suffered."

Augustus put his hands to his face, weeping for the man who had often teased him mercilessly yet who had been a true and good companion for many years. *I can't believe it...*

Tears trickling bright in the moonlight, he asked, "Thorne? Guntyr? Argentia?"

"Trapped inside, somewhere," Kest said, his voice choking. "Gone."

Nearby, Kozar took fur cloaks and heavy sealskin wraps from the supply sled and draped them about the girls. He had brought boots as well. No pair fit correctly, but all of them were warmer than the satin slippers the girls had worn to freedom.

"What's yer plan?" Griegvard asked the barbarian. "Can't be stayin' here."

"For tonight, we've no choice. The Ice Reaches are not traveled by night," Kozar reminded the dwarf. "We must stay until dawn. Let us rest and tend our wounds. That is the best course now. But first we must have a fire or the women will freeze."

They rounded up the dogs and the sleds and moved away, finding a spot distant from as many ice-ant mounds as they could. Kest went to Ikabod. The butler stood apart, a wrap that Kozar had given him hanging about his bony frame, his monocular gaze fixed on the dark shape of the shattered pyramid, now a cairn for so many.

"We'll have a fire soon," Kest said. He knew what the butler was seeking, and knew it was a futile watch. "Come take some warmth." When Ikabod did not move, Kest placed his hand on the butler's shoulder. "If they were in there, they're gone. No one could have lived," he said quietly, as much to himself as to Ikabod.

At that moment, Mirkholmes scampered over the drifts of snow and into the camp.

Forgotten in the chaos, he had escaped the second collapse by sheer nerve, wriggling and slipping through narrow holes and slim spaces until at last he found his way free.

"Thank you very much for waiting for Mirk," he cheeped irritably.

"Aeton's bolts!" Kest's hope lifted on sudden wings. He crouched down in the snow before the meerkat. "Did you see anyone else?"

Mirk blinked his amber eyes, and then lowered his head sadly. "Mirk saw none alive."

Kest shuddered and sighed. Straightening slowly, he walked away.

Ikabod flinched, but did not alter his vigil. Amazingly, the fall that had killed Tib, injured Kest, and knocked a goodly dent in Griegvard Gynt's helm, had left the butler unscathed. He wore dried blood on his head and face from striking the rail as the collapse began, but he had been thrown clear upon impact.

If his old bones could survive such a doom, how could he not hope that Argentia might have also survived?

There was a tug on his leg. "Mirk is cold," the meerkat complained.

Stooping stiffly, the butler lifted the little animal into his arms. He glanced at the camp. The barbarians had struck a fire. Though he knew he could not change Argentia's fate even if he stared at the broken pyramid until his other eye went out, part of him thought to ignore the beckoning warmth, to keep this watch until cold and exhaustion felled him.

But he knew that would not be what Argentia wanted.

If his worst fear had come to pass, and Argentia had given her life to save him and these others, it would do no honor to her memory if he died tonight from heartbroken stubbornness. *No, you must live, old man. You must, else her death was for naught...*

Still, Ikabod would not give up on Argentia so easily. He had tended her home and waited with a parent's patience while she rode through unknown dangers in distant lands and she had always returned. He would never truly believe she was dead until he saw her body.

Tomorrow, in the light, he would search—with the others, or alone, if he had to. If he could not find her, he would return to Duralyn and enlist the help of the Crown and the Archamagus.

He would not abandon Argentia—alive or dead—to this forsaken place.

Mirk shivered against him. "We will go in a moment," Ikabod said.

And Shadow began to bark.

87

All the camp looked to the dog.

Shadow had been lying docilely at the head of his sled. Now he was standing with his hackles raised, barking and pawing at the snow.

Hands went to weapons, the company fearing another attack by the ice ants or some other of Nord's nocturnal menaces. But there was nothing to be seen charging out of the dark in any direction.

Shadow would not quiet. Instead, he grew more agitated, his barking more insistent. The other dogs on his team were up now as well, adding their voices.

"Shut them mongrels up," Griegvard snapped. "Me damn head's sore enough."

"Soft, soft," Exmoor said, going over to the sled. Shadow looked at him hopefully. "Good. Quiet. Good." Exmoor patted Shadow on the head and turned away.

With a growl that sounded like disgust, Shadow suddenly vaulted forward, bursting his harness and tearing off into the night.

"Bloody Hell's th' matter wit 'im?" Griegvard wondered.

Cursing, Kozar pulled a brand from the fire and mounted a sled. "Exmoor, come. We need that dog."

Exmoor swung up behind his father. They went chasing after Shadow.

Found Argentia.

88

Shadow had caught Argentia's scent on the wind when she emerged from the subterranean steps. When the barbarians pulled up beside him, he was standing over the fallen huntress, licking her face.

Argentia made a weak and futile effort to rise. Her fluttering eyes focused for an instant on Kozar and Exmoor. "Thorne…fell," she whispered.

Then she collapsed back and did not come again to even a semblance of waking. The barbarians brought her quickly to the camp. The others rushed to her side. "My God, what happened to her?" Augustus blurted.

Argentia's entire body was lacerated from the twins' claws, to say nothing of the deeper punctures they found on her hips. Her breathing was harsh and labored. The flesh above her damaged ribs was viciously swollen and already bruising.

Ikabod touched a trembling hand to Argentia's face. "Lives," he breathed. "We must help her!"

There were some medicines from the Walros shaman in the company's supplies. They parsed them out, bestowing the most on Argentia. The chief danger was the cold, especially for Argentia, Ikabod, and the girls, who wore little beneath their cloaks and blankets. They kept those five as close to the fire as possible.

The others waited out the watches of the night nearby, brooding on what had passed and what might yet come. "Father?" Exmoor asked. "What if the frijdiformicans attack?"

"They do not like fire," Kozar said quietly, glancing to make sure Brieki had not heard. He wanted her and the other girls to rest, not to keep awake in fear. "If they come, they come." He tightened his grip on a harpoon. "We will be ready."

Whether for fear of the fire or because the whelming that had shaken the earth earlier that night had sent them scurrying to deeper tunnels, the ice ants did not come.

At dawn the survivors started for the Walros settlement. They ran hard to dark that day and the next, but by noon of the third day it became clear that they were too slow.

Argentia was deathly pale and wracked with fever. There was blood on her lips at every breath. The shaman's medicines had healed the lesser wounds from the beating the twins had given her, but whatever was broken within her was beyond the powders and potions.

"She ain't gonna make it," Griegvard said during a pause in their run. "We gotta go faster."

"We cannot go any faster," Kozar said. "Already we are pushing the dogs too hard. There is nothing more we can do."

"Let me take her," Augustus said.

"Take her?" Kozar asked, uncertain what the halfling meant.

"With magic," Augustus clarified. "I can bring her swiftly to your village."

"Then bring us all."

Augustus shook his head. "We're too many. I don't have that strength, and even if I did, the dead cannot go by the aether. I won't leave Tib."

Kozar considered. "How many?" he asked.

"I've never brought more than five with me."

"Bring all the women."

"No. I'm staying, Father," Brieki said.

"You will go with the others."

Brieki tossed her golden tresses. "Let the old one go in my stead. He is not well."

"Nonsense. I am fine," Ikabod said. "You go, child." But even as he spoke he raised a hand to stifle a cough that, bad to begin with, had been growing steadily worse.

"I'm staying, Father," Brieki insisted.

Finally Kozar nodded. To the two girls—Elki and Gisel—he instructed, "Bring news to expect us in seven dawns. See that Shaman Ulkar uses his powers well on those two. I would find them alive on my return."

Kest drew Augustus apart. "Can you do this? Over this distance, to a place you've only seen once?"

The halfling spread his little hands. "I'm not sure."

89

He could.

The teleport landed them square in the middle of King Gozal's hall. The flash of aether sent several barbarians sprawling from their seats and others diving for their weapons.

Fortunately, it took only a moment for them to recognize the halfling, Argentia's red hair, and Elki and Gisel, both of whom were sisters of men seated with the king. Finding even two alive was more than the barbarians had dared to hope. The announcement of the fall of the *obludra* Vloth and the return of the girls turned the village of normally stoic Walros into a riot of celebration.

Amid the rejoicing, Kozar's instructions were not forgotten. Argentia and Ikabod were given over to the care of the shaman.

Ulkar was ancient and gnarled as a piece of driftwood, shorter than many a child of the tribe, and cloaked in albatross feathers. His magic restored Ikabod and brought Argentia back from the brink of death, but it did not wake her.

"Her spirit sleeps," the shaman said.

And it slept still a week later, when the others sledded in.

90

When Argentia finally did awaken, it was to find Ikabod sitting beside her.

"How do you feel, Lady?" the butler asked.

Argentia yawned deeply. She felt weak, but it was a warm and comfortable weakness, as if she was awakening from the longest night's sleep of her life.

In truth it had been ten nights, but she did not know that yet.

"Good," she said, stifling a second yawn with the back of her hand. "Tired." She looked at the butler. Suddenly her eyes widened. "Ikabod! You're alive! Oh thank God!" She shoved free of fur coverings and threw her arms around him.

"Go easy, Lady," the butler said. "All is well."

At the foot of the bed, Shadow raised his head from his paws and barked. The sound echoed loudly in the fire-lit hut. "Where are we?" Argentia asked.

"Among friends."

The voice came from behind her. She turned quickly—a movement accomplished with no pain whatsoever—and saw Kozar, Exmoor, a girl who could only be Brieki, Kest, Augustus, Mirk, and Griegvard.

"'Bout friggin' time ye woke up," the dwarf grumbled. "Thought ye were gonna sleep straight through t' th' damn thaw."

Confusion filtered across Argentia's face. "How long— Where's Tib? What happened?"

They told Argentia of the escape from the Frost Palace, Shadow's discovery of her in the snow (she had only the vaguest recollection of this), Augustus' teleport, and their own arrival back at the settlement of the Walros, where wounds were tended, another feast was set and celebrated, and Brieki was reunited with her mother.

At the next dawn, a ceremony had been held to commemorate the four girls who had not returned from the pyramid, and Tiboren Gyre was given to the sea with all the honors that the Nordens bestowed on fallen heroes.

"I'm so sorry," Argentia said when Kest concluded the tale, which had passed from one to another of the group in the telling. She was sitting up, sipping strong tea. "And thank you. Thank you all for getting Ikabod out, and for coming for me."

"Thank th' damn dog fer that. We figured ye fer dead, girl," Griegvard said.

Argentia grinned, knowing the dwarf—like all dwarves she'd ever met—was hiding his feelings behind his gruffness. "Then thank *you*, Shadow."

The dog looked up briefly, thumped his tail, and settled his head back onto his paws again, looking supremely satisfied.

"Ye heard our tale—now what in th' bloody Hell happened t' ye?" Griegvard asked. "How'd ye get t' th' damn pyramid after them ants took ye? And how'd ye get out after it fell?"

"And what of Thorne?" Augustus added. Kozar had told them Argentia's words, but they felt they owed it to their Captain to hear what the huntress could tell of Thorne's last minutes.

"Let her rest," Ikabod chided, sensing the heaviness in Argentia as the questions forced her to face all that had happened in and beneath the Frost Palace. "She does not wish to speak on it so soon."

"No. It's all right." Argentia looked around her: at Ikabod, wrapped in a heavy fur and healthy once more—though she still was not used to seeing him with the patch on his eye. At Kozar and Exmoor sitting close on either side of the pale and beautiful Brieki. At loyal Griegvard. At Mirk, who once again had saved them all. And finally at Kest and Augustus, the remnants of the group that had followed her from Argo.

She had much to tell that would greatly impact those two. She wondered for a moment if it was not better, kinder, to keep the things she knew silent. *No. Thorne would have wanted them to know...*

Argentia took another sip of tea and decided to cut to the heart of the matter. It was not her escape in the ice ant tunnels—Mirk could tell that tale if he wished—or her battle in the dark that were important. Only what had happened afterwards, on the bridge.

"The twins are dead," she said flatly. "Thorne killed them. Died killing them. I went to save him, and he saved me instead." She paused, feeling the weight of Fortune's irony. "But that's not all."

She told them of her encounter with Gideon-gil. Showed them the ring of the chameleon as a proof when they met idea that the elf had masqueraded as Guntyr with open disbelief.

"That's the ring," Augustus agreed quietly. He remembered asking if Bryget had gifted the jewelry to the Norden. "Aeton's bolts—the guise was perfect."

"No," Kest said. "In form, maybe, but not in person. This explains why he attacked King Gozal's son." That act had rung false with the Guntyr they knew, but in the press and rush of events, they had given it too little thought.

"And why he knew how to prepare the esp," Argentia added. It was frightening to think that there had been a dagger in their midst, so close and so completely hidden for so long.

Augustus sighed. "Then Guntyr is dead."

"Since Telarban," Argentia confirmed. "Gideon-gil killed him in Vloth's guildhouse."

"When we were separated," the halfling whispered, folding his hands together. "Ah, God, what will we tell Bryget?"

"The truth," Kest said. "That her husband died a warrior." He looked at Argentia. "You're certain Gideon-gil named Magistrate Krung?"

"Krung. That's what he said. 'If you have questions, ask them of Magistrate Krung in Argo—should you find him before I do.'"

"That goddamned traitor!" Kest turned to Augustus. In the look that passed between them, Argentia saw that the reap of Thorne's vengeful harvest had not yet ended.

That evening, Argentia wrapped herself in a sealskin blanket and went down to the shore to watch the sun fall into the Sea of Sleet.

She wondered what had befallen the boat that had borne Tib's body away. Perhaps it had already been staved. Perhaps it still sailed on toward the fiery horizon. Though they had been at odds in the beginning, she had liked the lieutenant well enough by the end, and was sorry he was gone.

I'm so tired of all of this... Death, vengeance—all because she had defied the will of a madman.

And I'm not even sure if it's over, she thought bleakly. Ikabod was safe, but was Vloth dead? No one knew, and Argentia had seen too many of Vloth's magic tricks to believe the destruction of the Frost Palace had also claimed the guildmaster's life.

I'm not that lucky...

A wave crashed high on the rocky beach, splashing against her boots. Argentia watched it recede. Another rolled up in its place, the sea relentless, inexorable. She heard the echo of Gideon-gil's voice: *If he lives, Vloth will never stop hunting you...*

Argentia knew that. From the beginning—when the twins revealed who had sent them—she had recognized that Vloth would have to be dealt with if she truly meant for this to end.

Until now, she had run the guildmaster's gauntlet to save Ikabod. That was done. The closing moves would be played for different stakes.

Staring out over the harsh waters of the Sea of Sleet, Argentia made a plan.

Part V

End Game

91

Argo.

Winter night held the city in its dead grasp. The wind howled off the White Sea. Though there was no snow, it was a bitter blow that shook and rattled at the windows of the Watch garrison.

Magistrate Krung walked into his office, locked the door behind him, and threw his cloak on a chair. Seated at his desk, he pulled open the bottom drawer, found his flask, and took a long swallow of liquor to warm himself against the chill.

Choked on it when the figure slipped out of the drapes.

"You!" Krung gasped.

"Your powers of observation remain canny, Magistrate," Gideon-gil said.

"Is it done?" Krung demanded. His mind was whirling in panic, but he somehow found a facade of composure.

"Thorne is dead. He never knew your precious little secret to begin with. All that remains between us is the matter of my fee."

"Proof?" Krung asked, stalling. If what Gideon-gil said was true, the elf was the last person alive who could link him to Vloth's twins and Thorne's murder. He couldn't allow anyone, even Gideon-gil, to walk free with that knowledge. He had never intended to, but he had believed he would have had some advance notice from the elf, and a chance to arrange a trap.

"I do not lie about my work, Magistrate," Gideon-gil said coldly. "Your proof is that I am here and Thorne is not."

Krung felt sweat break out on his scalp, making his head itch fiercely, but he made no move to scratch it. If he was going to take Gideon-gil by surprise—and he knew his only chance was to take him by surprise—a sweaty hand might prove his undoing. "I...I wasn't expecting you tonight.

I have some of the money, though. Here, in this drawer. The rest is at my home, but I'll get it."

"Let us begin with what is in the desk."

Krung nodded, trying to keep the feral gleam from his eyes as he bent his head, ducking as if looking for something in the back of the drawer. "Ah—there it is." He reached in.

Came up with the crossbow.

Before Gideon-gil had time to even unfold his arms in defense, Krung squeezed the weapon's trigger.

The bowstring snapped forward on an empty stock. Its twanging reverberation was very loud in the chamber.

"Missing this?" Gideon-gil asked, holding up a small dart. A flick of his hand sent the tiny missile at Krung's face. The Magistrate swatted it away as if swiping at a fly.

Only when he felt the prick against his palm did he realize his mistake.

"No," Krung whispered. The crossbow fell back into the drawer as he looked at his hand, where a single drop of blood marked the dart wound.

"I warned you that venom would speed you to your grave," Gideon-gil said.

"Hel—" Krung tried to cry for aid, but the poison was swift. His swimming vision saw three of Gideon-gil coming forward.

Five of him.

A dozen.

Then all the room, all Krung's world, was as black-clad as the elf.

92

Two mornings later, Kest Eregrin and Augustus Falkyn returned to Argo and were arrested at the city gates.

After a great feast in celebration of their triumph over the *obludra* Vloth (in which they were all made honorary members of the Tribe of the Walros) the company had left Nord by the dwarven rails, going first to Stromness, where they parted ways with Griegvard—the dwarf made a great show of pretending to be glad to be rid of them—and then to Duralyn, where they left Argentia, Ikabod, and Mirk. Argentia had wanted to speak in their and Thorne's defense if they were arrested, but the Watchmen insisted that they face the consequences of their deeds on their own.

The journey had been good for Kest and Augustus. It had given them time to think, to see the events that had passed in a clearer light, and their initial instinct to avenge blood with blood had waned. "If we kill Krung then we've murdered a Magistrate," Kest said. "A corrupt worm, but still a Magistrate. And we can't even say we acted as Watchmen, because we've probably already been expelled from service."

"What do we do, then? We can't let Krung go free."

"Hardly," Kest agreed. "We'll have the Magistrates decide his fate."

"Risky," Augustus said. "We might not even get a chance to tell our story. And who's to say we'll be believed if we do? Krung's powerful. His word might stand against two Watchmen who deserted the city."

"All true. But I don't know what else to do. I'm not like Thorne. I can't live on principle and duty alone—or on revenge. Besides, it's up to us now to secure Thorne's legacy. We need to make the truth known about why he did what he did. We owe him that much, at least."

Augustus considered, and then nodded. He knew his friend was right, and he reminded himself of this when they were taken under guard to the dungeons to await trial for desertion and dereliction of duty. They had served the machinery of justice for many winters. Now they would have to trust it to serve them.

The Court of the Magistrates was imposing by design. The accused entered under armed guard, passing through windowless doors onto the floor of what was essentially a semicircular pit. There was a wooden table whereon sat the Oathstone, but there were no chairs or amenities of even the meanest sort. The wall of the pit was dark granite, gray veined with green. It rose some fifteen feet above the bare stone floor. Arrayed in an arc atop this barrier were the seats of the Magistrates.

Krung's seat, Kest and Augustus noted, was empty. They were not certain whether that boded well or ill. For the moment, they had other concerns.

"You are here to answer for your actions," Head Magistrate Gringoir said. He was a small, slim man of some sixty winters, his white hair clipped short, his moustache drooping long past a trim goatee, his eyes a keen blue-gray. He had risen through the ranks of the Watch and was widely regarded as a canny and fair judge. What little hope Kest and Augustus felt they had lay in the fact that Gringoir had always been able to discern between the letter and the spirit of the law. "How do you plead?"

"With respect to the desertion of our assignment, guilty as charged," Kest said. "Regarding any dereliction of duty, however, we maintain to the contrary that we have in fact done our duty to the city and the Watch."

Gringoir did not look surprised. "Explain yourselves."

"The root of our actions begins in this very chamber," Kest replied, causing a ripple of murmurs among the Magistrates. "For our part, it was the discovery of Mikael Greystone's body that set us on our course."

Again, that ripple. Greystone's body had been found the day after Thorne's lieutenants had disappeared. The Watch knew Gideon-gil had done the killing, but not why, or what Greystone's death had meant for the pursuit of Thorne.

"Continue," Magistrate Optelian bid, a thoughtful scowl on her pinched face.

So Kest, with periodic interjections from Augustus, told what they had learned of the treachery of Magistrate Krung and the plot to assassinate Thorne.

"Then it's true beyond doubt!" Magistrate Celorn burst out, igniting a clamor in the Court.

"Order!" Gringoir rapped a heavy gavel.

"Pardon, sir?" Kest said. "What is true?"

"Magistrate Krung is dead," Gringoir replied. "The circumstances left the question of his loyalties somewhat suspect."

Kest and Augustus exchanged glances. "How?" the wizard askéd.

"He was murdered," Optelian said. "Two nights ago—by Gideon-gil." She did not sound overly dismayed. "There was a note pinned to his desk by a black dagger. It said 'Forfeit for failure to pay his debts.' There was also a diamond earring."

"A diamond earring?" Augustus said. "Let me guess. An echo?" Using magic akin to that of an auralith, echoes captured sound and could respeak their contents upon command.

"Yes," Optelian said. "One that contained an interesting conversation between Magistrate Krung and Gideon-gil concerning Krung's designs on Captain Thorne."

"Then you knew the truth already," Kest said angrily.

Magistrate Barako stood and pointed down at Kest. He was newly appointed to the Court and a disciple of Magistrate Krung. "We knew what we heard from the echo. A man might confess to anything if Gideon-gil had a knife to his throat. Any of us here would lie to save our lives. And I remind the Court that we are not here to try Magistrate Krung, Aeton rest his spirit. We are here to try these two deserters."

"Those trials may not be as mutually exclusive as you seem to believe," Gringoir said mildly. "There is more to your tale," he prompted Kest and Augustus. "You left to save Thorne—did you?"

"No, sir," Kest said. "Gideon-gil killed Sir Reth and the knights on the road. We arrived too late to save them, but Thorne was still alive."

"So Gideon-gil leaves his quarry alive now?" Barako scoffed.

"I do not pretend to know Gideon-gil's mind," Kest said with a shrug. "We found Thorne and we joined him to hunt down Vendimar Stelglim's real killers."

"That case was closed!" Barako shouted. "The killers were found dead in the Undercity."

"No," Kest said. "They weren't. But they're dead now—though it cost Thorne, Guntyr, and Tib their lives to see it done."

"Dead too!" old Magistrate Tanerive exclaimed. "Fell day indeed that we should learn of the loss of so many of the Watch."

"Yet you were spared," Barako said to Kest and Augustus. "Why? So you could come back and spin this wild tale to justify the actions of a murderer and a traitor?"

"Thorne was no murderer and no traitor," Augustus retorted. "He did what was right as he saw it. And so did we."

"I wonder you're not in league with Gideon-gil yourselves," Barako said. "Perhaps you hired him to kill Magistrate Krung because he knew the truth about you and Thorne. It's all just a little too convenient if you ask me."

"Fortunately we did not ask you, Barako," Gringoir said. "And it is my turn to remind you that this remains my Court and I will not tolerate accusations, surmises, or charges brought without evidence."

"What of defenses brought with no evidence?" Barako retorted. "These men disappear for months and return with claims that a fugitive from justice has been killed, but they have no body—nor any bodies of the knights or their comrades to show. They could be lying—"

"The Oathstone does not think so," Optelian noted. The crystal on the table beside Kest and Augustus had remained dark throughout their account.

"Fine! Even if they are telling the truth, that does not exonerate them from their crimes."

Gringoir tugged his long moustache and then nodded slowly. "Is there aught else?" he asked Kest and Augustus.

"That is all," Kest said. "Judge as you will."

93

The lieutenants were escorted to a holding room, where they suffered in uncertainty: Kest sitting quietly, Augustus juggling balls of aether to battle his nervousness.

They knew the process: the Magistrates would recess so each could consider the case in private, reconvene to vote, and then deliver their verdict. They had given up trying to guess the outcome. They felt Gringoir was at least sympathetic to them, and his voice carried great weight, but Barako and some of the others hadn't seemed swayed. Many of them had disliked Thorne, and Kest wouldn't put it past them to cast guilty ballots just to spite the Captain.

"We did the right thing, didn't we?" Augustus asked Kest when the bailiff collected them to escort them back for sentencing.

"We did," Kest said, patting his friend on the back. "Come what may, we did."

In the Court, the Magistrates filed into their seats. Gringoir remained standing to cast the judgment. "Lieutenant Eregrin, Magus Falkyn, you are charged with the desertion of your posts and willful dereliction of your duty as Watchmen of Argo."

Kest and Augustus stood stern and straight, awaiting their doom.

"Whatever your intentions, noble though they may have been, these crimes remain. The Court has found you guilty. The sentence is expulsion from the Watch and banishment from the city."

Lyrissa—I'm sorry, Kest thought. Augustus stared at the ground.

"However," Gringoir said. "It has come to my attention during our recess that perhaps not all the pertinent information regarding this case was divulged at the hearing. I feel it is my duty to bring this new information to the Court."

Kest and Augustus glanced at each other as Gringoir held up a scroll. Neither knew what the parchment might be.

Gringoir cleared his throat. "I have here a letter from the Crown. It appears the defendants neglected to mention that in the course of their... adventures they were requisitioned by Her Majesty to serve the Throne on a diplomatic mission in Nord."

"Preposterous!" Barako exclaimed. "Gringoir, what is the meaning of this?"

"The meaning?" Gringoir echoed. "Perhaps if you would permit me to finish reading the meaning would be less obscure. The letter continues:

'With consideration for their valor and losses suffered in service to the greater good of the realm, we urge that all charges against them be dropped and every provision be made for their untrammeled return to their duties in the Watch of our great city of Argo. Know that they have our thanks on behalf of the Crowndom.'

"It is signed 'Solsta Ly'Ancoeur, Crown of Teranor,'" Gringoir concluded.

"And you're certain it's no forgery," Magistrate Manski—another of Krung's lackeys—asked. "We are dealing with a wizard among the accused."

"I am quite certain Magus Falkyn had nothing to do with this letter," Gringoir said. "Let us say the method of its delivery precludes that."

"So there is truth to this?" Magistrate Optelian asked Kest and Augustus. "You were in Nord?"

"That is true," Kest said.

"On a diplomatic mission for the Crown?"

Steel diplomacy, maybe, Kest thought. But he could work with this. "Yes. Vendi's killers sought asylum there with a hostage. As we were already in pursuit, we were asked to join Lady Argentia Dasani's mission to negotiate the prisoner's release. There was an emissary from Stromness with us also."

"A dwarf, now! Extraordinary," Old Tanerive said. "A fine tale."

"Yes, a fine tale indeed," Barako said scornfully. "Which does nothing as I see it to exculpate these men. Their crimes were against Argo, and were committed before they came into the service of the Crown—if they ever truly did."

"The Court is aware of that," Gringoir said. "However, since the Crown has requested clemency, I am of the strong opinion that clemency be granted. Are there any objections?"

There were, but not in sufficient number to carry the vote.

"The Court finds for the dismissal of all charges. Go home, both of you," Gringoir said. "You are expected back in three days to resume your duties."

Kest and Augustus stared at each other, speechless with disbelief as Gringoir's gavel slammed the case closed.

In the corridor outside the court, still stunned by the sudden turn of events, Kest and Augustus moved through a crowd of Watchmen on their way here and there in the garrison. From the corner of his eye, Augustus saw a robed figure leaning on the wall. The man nodded as Augustus and Kest passed—and winked.

By the time Augustus realized who it was he'd seen and spun to look again, Ralak the Red had vanished.

94

Telarban.

Winter wind off Crescent Lake. The snow-crusted streets, silver beneath the moon, were nearly as cold as Nord.

Togril Vloth had escaped the fall of his Frost Palace. With the aid of his magic rings, the guildmaster made his hard course out of Nord and back to Telarban. His absence had shaken his guild. Factions within his house and the remnants of opposition once crushed and broken had risen up, thinking Vloth dead and his leavings ripe to be plundered.

Vloth returned just ahead of this storm. After a few violent weeks during which the gutters of Telarban ran with blood, he restored his place and power. There were still questions to be answered, to be sure—the fates of the treacherous twins and a certain bounty huntress were chief among them—but for the moment the guildmaster had enough to occupy him just setting his house back in order.

When the oculyr on the table beside his chaise flashed, Vloth turned a frowning face to the crystal ball. "What?" he demanded.

"A woman's here, Guildmaster," the guard said.

"What woman?" Vloth was instantly suspicious.

"Dimytri brought her in, Guildmaster. Way he tells it, she's been asking all over the city for you."

"Show me."

The girl appeared in the swirling crystal. She was tall and wrapped in a heavy cloak. When she lowered her hood, Vloth rocked back on his couch. "Bring her before us."

Vloth would not have been surprised to see the twins—even one of them—nor would he have been surprised to see Argentia Dasani.

He was, however, surprised to see Brieki.

"You are far from home," the guildmaster said, his piggish eyes narrowing with a hard, almost angry focus that belied his broad, welcoming smile. He motioned the barbarian girl to approach.

She came obediently, dropping her cloak behind her as she passed the huge bed that dominated the chamber. Cold moonlight streamed through the window. A fire crackled in a hearth. Lamps glowed golden on tables and in sconces.

In all this light, Togril Vloth scrutinized Brieki. His guards would not have let her past if she was holding any weapons or wearing any jewelry—especially any rings (Vloth had Gideon-gil to thank for alerting him to that particular danger)—but Vloth was taking no chances.

An opal on his beckoning hand possessed the power to detect invisible objects. Had it flashed, Vloth would have killed the girl without so much as a question. But the stone remained dull. "Well," Vloth mused, satisfied that the small purse tied to Brieki's sash was her only accessory. "Shouldn't you be casting nets into the Sea of Sleet with the rest of your barbaric kin?"

"My Guildmaster." Brieki bowed her head. "Not all of us desired to be rescued."

"Oh, indeed?" Vloth eyed her skeptically. Brieki's appearance had brought a dark thought. If the women of his harem had escaped, that increased the chances that some other, more dangerous women had also escaped.

"You took us from harshness," Brieki said. "Showed us beauty. Leisure. I found they were not things I could easily change for the life I knew as a child—so I ran."

"You made the journey here alone?"

Brieki raised her head proudly. "I am still a Norden."

Vloth smiled, letting his gaze rove over Brieki's body: the tall frame, strong but not muscular; the heavy bust in the beaded brassiere, the wispy harem pants that rode low on her hips and clung to her long, lean legs, blousing above her slippered feet. The hair that poured like sunlight down her back. "So you are. What do you wish of me?"

She bent and whispered humidly in his ear. "A place with you. There will not come one night when you regret it."

Vloth felt molten lust stir in him. He wanted Brieki in a way he had never wanted her in the Frost Palace. There, among the sisters of her tribe, he had taken her beauty for granted. Here in Telarban she was as exotic as an ice orchid; a potent reminder of why he had first been so inflamed by the barbarian women.

"You shall have your place." Vloth had not had a proper harem mistress for several years. *This one will do quite well,* he thought, reaching to pull her down to him.

Brieki placed her palm on Vloth's chest. "Wait," she bid. "I brought you something." She raised her small purse.

"Hurry up with it." Vloth did not really care what trinket she might have brought to please him. Her body was the only treasure he was interested in. His massive hands clamped her buttocks, feeling their heat through the diaphanous silk. "I hunger."

Brieki unfastened her purse. It opened with a spill of blue light.

Her hand blurred into that eldritch glow. "Eat this," she said.

Vloth had time to think that it was impossible that a weapon—even one so small—could come out of that tiny purse. Then Brieki rammed the silver handbow into his mouth.

Vloth gagged, his eyes bulging with terror. Brieki's entire form glimmered, and suddenly it was not the silk-clad Norden girl, but Argentia Dasani in her halter, buckskins, and battered boots standing before him.

"This is your only warning," Argentia said. "If you send one more person after me or anyone close to me—an assassin, a wizard, a street thug, anyone at all—I'll come back and kill you." Her blue eyes were floes on the Sea of Sleet: cold promises of death. "I got to you tonight, I can get to you again. You'll never know I'm coming. You'll never be safe. Believe it—and don't test me."

Argentia yanked her handbow out of Vloth's mouth and slammed her knee up into his jaw. Spittle arced across the room as Vloth's head snapped back and he toppled with a heavy thud from the couch to the floor.

Argentia glanced at the door, expecting the guard to come barging in. There was no danger of that. The man who watched Vloth's door had heard many strange noises from these chambers. He knew better than to interrupt when Vloth was with a woman.

After a moment, Argentia judged she was safe enough, but she had no intention of wasting time. Reaching once more into Ralak's magic purse, she drew forth a long coil of rope and anchored it to the nearest foot of the bed.

She raised her handbow. Paused. Looked at Vloth: a crumbled colossus, helpless on the floor. *You're really going to let a madman like him live? After all he did?* She pointed the handbow at Vloth's bald head. *End it...*

Her finger hovered over the trigger. One shot was all it would take to rid her world of Togril Vloth. One little shot.

No... With a sharp shake of her head, Argentia turned and fired at the window. The aethereal crescent from her handbow blew the glass apart.

That got the guard's attention.

"Guildmaster?" Pounding at the door.

Time to go...

"Guildmaster?" The shout from the hall came again, followed by more pounding.

Out went the rope, and out went Argentia.

95

A Watchman paid by Bendrake Ironclaw let Argentia discreetly out of Telarban through a little-used door beside the city's south gate. She left the road. Walked down a long slope of snow-frosted grass to the moon-spackled expanse of Crescent Lake. It was colder by the water and she shivered. Her halter and buckskins were little improvement over the harem silks of her magical masquerade.

She wasn't going to linger, but there was one last thing to be done.

By the time the company had arrived in Duralyn after leaving Nord, Argentia felt almost back to her old self again. Physically she was fine, but a shadow lay on her mind.

She knew only her patience would see it lifted.

Solsta welcomed them warmly. The Crown was particularly glad to see Ikabod alive, and she was so overjoyed to have Mirk back that it was doubtful she would have punished him even before she learned of his pivotal role in the outcome of the quest. After hearing that tale, there was no way she could even chide the meerkat, though she did make him promise before all their witness that he would never again run off without telling her.

Argentia remained in the castle for several weeks, her future course once again in the hands of Amethyst Pyth. She passed her days and nights in ease, keeping time with Solsta when the Crown was free; walking in the winter gardens, the warm air fragrant behind glass walls; losing herself in the library; and cleaning and organizing the chambers she had shared with Carfax.

Really she was waiting.

Finally Amethyst brought her the information she needed. The answer was what Argentia had expected, if not necessarily what she wanted.

Togril Vloth had returned to Telarban.

Argentia doubted that her actions tonight had finally freed her of the guildmaster, but she was comfortable with that. The alternative—murdering him in cold blood—was repugnant. She had killed many times, but only in defense of her own life or to avenge the death of someone dear to her.

Still, she thought about the feel of her handbow in Vloth's mouth. One twitch of her finger would have blown apart his head like a hammerstroke to a melon, putting an end to any threat—but that would have reduced her irredeemably, bringing her closer to a soulless killer like Gideon-gil, whose only answers for his enemies were cut from implacable black steel.

Even so, there were limits to her mercy. If Vloth forced her hand and she had to return and kill him, she would.

"It's your play, fat man," she said, glancing back at the city. "As far as I'm concerned, this game is over."

Propping her left foot on a nearby rock, Argentia pulled off her boot and slipped the chameleon ring from her toe, where Vloth's guards had never thought to search for it. The ring had proved useful, but Argentia hated it in some primal way she did not fully understand. She toyed with the idea of giving it to Ralak as payment for the aethereal purse she'd borrowed, but she didn't know when she would be returning to Duralyn, and she didn't like the idea of holding the ring for that long. It made her feel dirty.

Besides, knowing Ralak, he's already contrived some way for me to repay him... In Argentia's experience, wizards always did.

She looked at the ring in her hand for a moment longer, then closed a fist around it and flung it as far out as she could over Crescent Lake. It twinkled against the night, dropping silently into the silver-black waters with hardly a splash.

Watching it, Argentia thought of Carfax, fallen. Of Thorne and Tib and Guntyr and dozens of others—all gone, yet she carried on. She was a survivor. At times she did not know if that was as much a gift as a curse, but it was truth.

Maybe that's enough...

With a sigh, Argentia turned from Crescent Lake, pulled her boot back on, and walked up the slope from the shoreline to the road, where a carriage had just rolled to a stop.

"My Lady." Ikabod greeted her from the driver's board.

"Punctual as ever," Argentia said with a grin. She climbed onto the board and slipped her legs beneath the lap blanket.

Shadow canted his lupine head at her, nacreous eyes gleaming. Argentia hugged an arm around his strong neck, pressing her forehead to his. The wolf-dog had followed her from the Walros settlement. He refused to be left behind, and finally Argentia had given up trying.

"Lady, take this," Ikabod said. He had clambered down and gone into the carriage to find a cloak for Argentia.

"Thank you." She pulled the white fur around her.

"And this as well," the butler added, drawing Argentia's dragon's tooth token from a pocket. The magic of the elven craft could not be altered or hidden by the power of the chameleon ring. Not wanting to be betrayed by the familiar token, Argentia had left it with Ikabod for safe keeping when she went after Vloth.

Shadow barked, eager to be underway.

Argentia refastened the dragon's tooth token about her neck and ruffed Shadow's head. "Ready?" she asked Ikabod.

"Ready, Lady," the butler replied. He did not ask her what had happened in the guild. That Argentia had made the meeting with the carriage was all that mattered to him.

Argentia took the reins and snapped the horses into motion. "Then let's go home."